THE WORLD'S CLASS

TRELAWN
AND

ARTHUR WING PINERO was
of Portuguese Jewish descen
with only a minimal schoolin
of ten in his father's office. S
from the law and became an
Irving's Lyceum company, where his ability to write for the stage soon
proved itself a better resource than his ~~~~~~~~~~ 1883 he married
another performer, Myra H ~~~~~~~~~~~~~~~~ write full-time. He
had a run of outstanding successes, ~~~~~~~~~~~~ ively English form
of farce, at the Court Theatre 1884–7, and climbed rapidly to be the leading
dramatist of his day. His pre-eminence was confirmed by his epoch-making
The Second Mrs Tanqueray, a departure in serious social drama that was much
more highly regarded than the importation of Ibsen's work into England. He
spent much time and energy working to improve conditions for theatrical
professionals, serving on campaigns and committees, coming to be regarded
as the father of the British stage; in 1909 he was knighted. In his writing he
continued to develop, to refine and tirelessly to experiment in theatrical form.
His dominance, although often attacked by other aspirants with less purchase
on theatrical success, continued until the First World War. His astringent,
and increasingly cynical insight into the human condition went out of fashion,
but he never stopped writing and developing, up to his death in 1934.

JACKY BRATTON is Professor of Theatre and Cultural History at Royal
Holloway, University of London. Her publication and research ranges over
many aspects of nineteenth-century British culture. She has written on many
kinds of performance; her last book concentrated on the relation between the
stage and the British Empire.

MICHAEL CORDNER is a Senior Lecturer in the Department of English and
Related Literature at the University of York. He has edited editions of
George Farquhar's *The Beaux' Stratagem*, the *Complete Plays* of Sir George
Etherege, *Four Comedies* of Sir John Vanbrugh and, for the World's Classics
series, *Four Restoration Marriage Comedies*. He has also co-edited *English
Comedy* (Cambridge University Press, 1994) and is completing a book on *The
Comedy of Marriage 1660–1737*.

PETER HOLLAND is Judith E. Wilson Lecturer in Drama in the Faculty of
English at the University of Cambridge.

MARTIN WIGGINS is a Fellow of the Shakespeare Institute and Lecturer in
English at the University of Birmingham.

DRAMA IN WORLD'S CLASSICS

Christopher Marlowe
Doctor Faustus and Other Plays

Arthur Wing Pinero
Trelawny of the 'Wells' and Other Plays

Oscar Wilde
The Importance of Being Earnest and Other Plays

Chapman, Kyd, Middleton, Tourneur
Four Revenge Tragedies

THE WORLD'S CLASSICS

═══

ARTHUR WING PINERO

The Magistrate
The Schoolmistress
The Second Mrs Tanqueray
Trelawny of the 'Wells'

═══

Edited with an Introduction by
J. S. BRATTON

General Editor
MICHAEL CORDNER
Associate General Editors
PETER HOLLAND   MARTIN WIGGINS

Oxford   New York
OXFORD UNIVERSITY PRESS
1995

Oxford University Press, Walton Street, Oxford OX2 6DP

Oxford New York
Athens Auckland Bangkok Bombay
Calcutta Cape Town Dar es Salaam Delhi
Florence Hong Kong Istanbul Karachi
Kuala Lumpur Madras Madrid Melbourne
Mexico City Nairobi Paris Singapore
Taipei Tokyo Toronto
and associated companies in
Berlin Ibadan

Oxford is a trade mark of Oxford University Press

British Library Cataloguing in Publication Data
Data available

Library of Congress Cataloging in Publication Data
Pinero, Arthur Wing, Sir, 1885–1934.
Trelawny of the 'Wells' / Arthur Wing Pinero; edited with an
introduction by J. S. Bratton.
p. cm.—(The World's Classics)
I. Bratton, J. S. (Jacqueline S.) II. Title. III. Series.
PR5182.T8 1995 822'.8—dc20 94–12320
ISBN 0–19–282568–2

1 3 5 7 9 10 8 6 4 2

Typeset by Pure Tech Corporation, Pondicherry, India
Printed in Great Britain by
Biddles Ltd,
Guildford & King's Lynn

CONTENTS

ACKNOWLEDGEMENTS

I WOULD like to thank the Series Editors and Christine Webb for their meticulous commentary upon text and notes; George Rowell for his characteristically friendly advice, as well as for his scholarship in his edition of four of Pinero's plays; John Mackenzie for information about Anglo-Indian history; and Peter Bailey for the serious discussion of bottled beer.

INTRODUCTION

SIR ARTHUR WING PINERO (1855–1934) was the leading British
dramatist of the late Victorian period, regarded in the late 1880s and
the 1890s as the major playwright working in English. His plays were
eagerly anticipated by audiences and seized upon by managements
confident of their earning power. He was in a position to dictate his
own terms, both financial and artistic, to the leading theatres of
London and New York. His second social-problem drama, *The Second
Mrs Tanqueray*, was greeted with a chorus of extravagant praise and
awed admiration from the critics that inevitably provoked its own
backlash—the aspiring but unproduced young dramatist George
Bernard Shaw sneered that they had all been taken in by the
'substitution of dead machinery and lay figures for vital action and
real characters'.[1] The onrush of Modernism in the theatre quickly left
Pinero behind, and his tenacity to the supreme status accorded him
so early became first an annoyance and then an embarrassment in a
changing theatrical world. It took until the 1980s, a hundred years
from the date of his earliest successes, for directors and readers to
revisit his drama unencumbered by an attitude to its place in the
cultural politics of Modernism, and to discover a body of work full of
interest, including several plays of great vitality and stage potential.

   The position of a dramatist whose work touches precisely the right
note to please a large, loyal audience which gives him support and
acclaim, winning middlebrow critical approval but provoking an
avant-garde to scorn and condemnation, is not peculiar to Pinero nor
to the late Victorian period. We might liken his situation to that of
Alan Ayckbourn in Britain in the 1970s and 1980s, and the two
dramatists have much in common. Pinero was essentially a theatrical
artist, his development led by experimentation in stage forms; he took
personal charge of the staging of his plays, as well as their subsequent
presentation to the reader. His work shows both a reliance on
theatrical tradition and a movement away from the overtly theatrical
comic genres—farce, comedy of manners—towards plays perceived as
'serious', 'realistic', and 'psychological'. This perception, however,
was that of the middle-class audience whose lives were his familiar

---

   [1] 'An Old Play and a New One', repr. in *Our Theatre in the Nineties*, rev. edn.,
3 vols. (1932), i. 41–8 (46).

subject-matter and whose values he personally shared; it is their sense of (stage) reality that his work satisfied, rather than any abstract or theorized Realism. He was well aware of this, and counted it as his proper task, in converting an innate dramatic talent into a talent for the theatre, to discover and develop 'the style of drama really adapted to the dramatist's one great end—that of showing the age and body of the time his form and pressure'. He acknowledged cheerfully that this bound him to his own period:

the instinct by which the public feels that one form of drama, and not another, is what best satisfies its intellectual and spiritual needs at this period or that is a natural and justified instinct. Fifty years hence the formula of today will doubtless be as antiquated and ineffective as the formula of fifty years ago; but it is imposed by a natural fitness upon the dramatist of today, just as, if he wants to travel long distances, he must be content to take the railway train and cannot either ride in a stagecoach or fly in an airship.[2]

Pinero's steam-train formulae have not become as ineffective as he expected: his willingness to attend both to the demands of the stage and to the nuances of his contemporaries' sensibility contributes to the continued life of his plays today. The best of them are beautifully made, often of considerable interest for their form, and they project a very precise picture of the late Victorian middle-class world as it wished to see itself.

As a writer for the stage, Pinero was by no means automatically accorded the upper middle-class status that he valued so greatly. He was uneasily aware all his life that theatre people, however wealthy and famous, were still liable to exclusion from respectable society, and indeed might be seen as its enemies. His consciousness of this is perceptible both in his plays and in the way in which he conducted his relationship with the theatre. He was born into a downwardly-mobile middle-class family, the son of John Daniel Pinero, whose father, a Portuguese Sephardic Jew, had Anglicized himself by a change of spelling and achieved considerable success as a London solicitor. John Daniel was given a good start in his father's profession, but he seems to have been very casual in exercising it, and his son Arthur was educated at a charity school and set to work in his father's office at the age of 10. He was stage-struck, a regular member of the audience of clerks and tradesmen at Sadler's Wells Theatre, near his family home; but his theatrical aspirations included, even at that early date, a sense of the importance of status and social success. He used

[2] 'Robert Louis Stevenson: The Dramatist' (1903), 27–8.

to go out of his way to stand and watch the doors of the Garrick Club (whose membership included the leading men of the stage and the learned professions), and regarded his eventual admission to membership there as the realization of 'the goal of his life'. He recorded this decades later, in a speech at a Club dinner held in his honour. In that speech he joked that, in his boyish ignorance, he no doubt failed to recognize the members he saw, and 'frequently mistook an eminent barrister for a popular comedian'.[3] The jocularity of the comparison does not conceal the importance, in Pinero's eyes, of the fact that some stage entertainers shared their leisure hours with pillars of the establishment.

He went on the stage in 1874, after his father's death. He did not achieve eminence as an actor, however, rising only to a very modest success in Irving's company. He found his *métier* when he began to write, providing short comic pieces suitable to fill out Lyceum bills and then, in 1881, seeing his first full-length play, prophetically called *The Money-Spinner*, staged at the St James's Theatre. His rise to fame as a writer was rapid, and also remarkable in another way: in a theatre dominated by actor-managers, where the writer did not necessarily even find his name among the credits, his work became a draw. He set about establishing dramatic authorship as a calling of importance and authority. He gave up acting in 1884, and in 1885 his first great success, *The Magistrate*, was staged at the Court Theatre. A run of similarly successful farces followed briskly, and Pinero began to assert himself. By the 1890s he alone made all the important decisions about the staging of his plays. Working from a ground-plan as well as from his plot and cast of characters, he created a final text, to be printed, with detailed stage directions, before the first rehearsal. He informed his first biographer:

All that we call 'business' is in the printed matter which I carry into the theatre. Why should it be altered when it has all been carefully and even laboriously thought out, every detail of it, during the process of construction? . . . Expression is multiform and simultaneous; to alter one phrase is to weaken all . . . Rehearsal is not—or certainly should not be—a time for experiment.[4]

From 1891, after a successful campaign by Pinero and other dramatic authors for legal protection for their copyrights in America, each of

[3] Wilbur Dwight Dunkel, *Sir Arthur Pinero: A Critical Biography with Letters* (Chicago, 1941), 11, 32.
[4] H. Hamilton Fyfe, *Sir Arthur Pinero's Plays and Players* (1930), 259.

his plays was published after the first staging. This version differed from the rehearsal copies not because changes were made in production, but because Pinero was careful to present his plays as literature in their own right, providing a clear, readable description of the blocking and stage business as he had conceived and carried it out.

His aggressively authoritarian way of working as a director was necessary to a degree, to redress the balance of power which had rested so exclusively with the actor-managers, and they were indeed disagreeably surprised by his refusal to cut his cloth to suit them. His plays, however, were so brilliantly successful when they were cut to Pinero's precise pattern that George Alexander, John Hare, and Augustin Daly found themselves yielding control of their own stages to this new force. It was a style that he had learnt in part from Irving (and it is significant that he never wrote a play for his master once he was established as a dramatist), but in the hands of a writer it was made to serve the preconceived text in a way that was new to the stage; it contributed, perhaps rather more than did the plays themselves, to the transformation of British theatre around the turn of the twentieth century, its appropriation by an intellectual élite. From his own point of view, financial success, the exercise of power, and recognized artistic autonomy all contributed to the establishment persona which he coveted; it was acknowledged when, in 1909, he was awarded a knighthood for his services to the theatre.

After *The Magistrate* came two more, equally successful, farces at the Court, first *The Schoolmistress* in March 1886, and then *Dandy Dick* in January 1887. He was entering a very prolific period, and he was not satisfied with simply repeating the farce formula that he had evolved; *Sweet Lavender*, a hit at Terry's Theatre in 1888, is a sentimental comedy, and *The Profligate*, staged at the Garrick in 1889, is a completely new departure, a 'realistic' serious drama about the sexual double standard. Pinero intended it to end with a suicide, but John Hare refused to stage it unless he provided a conventional ending, with the wronged wife forgiving and saving her profligate husband from himself. Pinero had a more accurate sense of his audience than the manager did, and for his next play, *The Second Mrs Tanqueray*, he demanded, and was granted, the freedom to follow his own instinct as to what they were ready for. It was hailed as 'a great play' and established him in the position of power and respect, both in the theatre and in London society, for which he had been working. He maintained it for a decade, producing many kinds of plays with success—social dramas, comedies, and, in 1898, *Trelawny of the*

'*Wells*', a 'comedietta' which framed his serious personal and social concerns in the form of an apparently conventional backstage comedy. But as his chosen subjects went out of date and his dictatorial writing and rehearsal style tended to alienate him from the centre of the theatrical life which gave meaning to his success, his plays were less well received, by the profession and by audiences, and even his unabated stylistic boldness and experimentation lost touch with the avant-garde directions of the new century. He continued to write until his death in 1934, an intransigent and increasingly isolated figure. This selection therefore spans his best period of work, from *The Magistrate* in 1885 to *Trelawny* in 1898.

Court Farces: *The Magistrate* and *The Schoolmistress*

In March 1885 *The Magistrate* opened at the Court Theatre, and was an instant success. In a theatrical culture generally hostile to innovation—in the same month *Nora*, translated by Frances Lord from Ibsen's *A Doll's House*, was greeted in the theatrical trade paper the *Era* as 'a silly play by silly players'—Pinero's play was heartily welcomed for its novelty. His capacity for being one step ahead of his time, enough to excite but not to frighten or alienate his contemporaries, had made its first great impression.

The West End theatre was more than ready for a new brand of comedy. It had already begun a revolution on the musical stage, where the vulgarities of cross-dressing and innuendo which characterized the old extravaganzas were being supplanted by the Gilbert and Sullivan operettas: in March 1885 the first night of *The Mikado* was eagerly awaited. Sentimental domesticity, as pioneered at the Prince of Wales's under the Bancroft management in the 1860s, could still hold the stage in comedy, but it was getting out of date. Tom Robertson's pretty details of simple home life and gentle humour were a little unsophisticated for the 1880s audiences, and already, in 1876, W. S. Gilbert had produced a wickedly hard-edged parody of mid-Victorian sentiment in his play *Engaged*. The idealization of hearth and home was by no means over, but it required an additional sharpness, an added brilliance of some kind, to revitalize it on stage. Pinero, characteristically making progress by an innovation in form, looked to the stylistic qualities of farce to provide this additional tang. He said that 'farce must gradually become the modern equivalent of comedy, since the present being an age of sentiment rather than of manners, the comic playwright must of necessity seek his humour in the exaggeration of sentiment'.[5] The patterning of farce is rigid and clearly defined: it removes the action to a stage world which operates by strict internal laws, bringing about predictable formal combinations—misunderstandings, disguisings, mistakes, coincidences—so that the plot and the action accelerate to the point of a climactic collision, when the wrong people meet in the wrong places, an explosion occurs, everything is thrown into the air, and falls back, miraculously, into order, and the play ends. In 1885 there were two versions of this basic pattern available to the dramatist, the English and the French.

The native farce tradition was firmly rooted in the popular theatre of the previous forty years. It was domestic, like sentimental comedy, but at a lower social level, portraying chiefly tradesmen and servants and set in the petty-bourgeois households, single men's lodgings, kitchens, inns, and streets of London. Taking the trade tools and domestic clutter of these ordinary people as props for its slapstick physical humour, the farce worked out a simple, mechanical, but completely fantastic plot which transformed them into the creatures of the world of dreams. It was untroubled by the unreality, the unnaturalness of its own proceedings, and often made comic capital out of its own staginess, dubbing its characters 'Marmaduke Snooks' and 'Jemima Faxdoodle', and making them break the frame of the illusion repeatedly to insert stage business, comic asides, or direct addresses to the audience or to burlesque other popular forms with melodramatic mannerisms or comic songs. As much as the vulgarity of their lower-class milieu, it was this stylistic freedom, characteristic of the popular dramatic tradition but increasingly problematic for the picture-frame stages of the West End, with their objective of a perfect illusion of modern life, which relegated such plays to the second-class theatres by the 1880s. Pinero, however, was too good a theatre craftsman to surrender that freedom entirely. In *The Magistrate* and *The Schoolmistress* he has servant figures, Popham and Tyler, with self-dramatizing dispositions, who gloomily revel in absurd melodramatic language and behaviour, and so admit the game of theatrical burlesque into a more rigidly realistic frame. More importantly, he still uses asides and direct address to the audience, including monologues like the one for Posket in the second act of *The Magistrate* and those for Rankling and Queckett in the third act of *The Schoolmistress*

[5] Quoted by Malcolm C. Salaman, in his introduction to the Heinemann edn. of *The Cabinet Minister* (1892).

which cry out to be treated as direct address, almost stand-up comedy. So skilfully does Pinero manage these devices, however, that contemporary critics praised his strict avoidance of the unfashionable mannerisms of old comedy, his perfectly preserved stage illusion. He achieved this effect by abstracting the method from the characters and settings with which it was associated, and using a class level that reflected his audience's personal experience, thereby convincing them of the play's realism. The burlesque figures of Popham and Tyler are admissible as servants only; the protagonists have to be drawn from the upper middle classes and reflect their concerns. 'Farce should treat of probable people placed in possible circumstances', as he put it—and their probability depended on audience recognition.[6] For a model for his plot and characters, therefore, Pinero turned to the imported French farce.

Throughout the century British dramatists had appropriated French plays, and among the rest Parisian bourgeois farces were being made over for the London stage. Charles Wyndham had founded his success at the Criterion on Palais-Royal farce, which had a reputation for clever immorality. He had the plays watered down just sufficiently in the course of translation to give Londoners the illusion of sophistication while preserving a safe degree of propriety. His adaptors had to reproduce the racy excitement of the concealments, chases, and guilty dénouements of the originals while eliminating the inevitable adultery on which they hinged. The most successful of all was the one which sailed closest to the wind, *The Pink Dominos*, translated by James Albery from the French of Hennequin and Delacour. Albery transplants its quasi-adulterous couples to Cremorne Gardens, an English site for dissipation which gives him the opportunity for low comic byplay between thieving waiters over expensive and execrable food. He sustains the illusion that respectable people are indulging in drunken sexual adventures by employing the device of a servant girl who, unknown to audience and characters alike, has dressed up in an old pink domino (that is, carnival disguise) of her mistress's and gone to the masked ball at the Gardens on her own account. It is she, rather than, as we have been led to think, either of the lady wives, who is pawed, kissed, and at one point burnt with a cigar by the would-be erring husbands. The men's behaviour was not, it would seem, unacceptable: as long as no lady had been compromised, all was well.

[6] Ibid.

The play did arouse scandal, but that only helped it to a record run of 777 performances.

The Magistrate made a conspicuous claim to be 'original' on its bills and programme, to distance it from the dubious moral atmosphere surrounding these translations; but the sophistication of the French formula is nevertheless one of its ingredients, along with the English preoccupation with hearth and home and a sentimental regard for middle-class morality. The domestic scene is moved decisively up-market, to the comfortable living-room of a leader of society, while the middle act is set in a 'French' location, a slightly dubious hotel, where to physical humour over food and drink—English slapstick carried to a superlative level—is added not flirtation and sexual confusion, but the confounding of completely well-meaning innocence.

The appeal of this successful blending of the two traditions of farce was powerful; it put the formal strength of the genre behind writing directed precisely at its particular audience. The mechanistic fantasy world of farce is a good vehicle for the ludic or carnival function of theatre, and it was this that Pinero was able to deliver to his audiences, the 'few thousand middle-class English people' for whom he was working.[7] His farces take dominant figures in the social hierarchy—magistrates, army officers, an admiral, a clergyman (in *Dandy Dick*)—and temporarily strip them of their power, which is then invested in a figure from the bottom of their ladder—a school-boy, a poor pupil teacher. Youth triumphs over experience, and an interval of play is enjoyed by the spectators; and then the 'natural' order is reasserted and all is put 'right' in the end. The experience is liberating, but safe, because the hierarchy is not threatened or challenged by the ritual inversion, but rather reinforced; its righting at the end makes it seem natural and inevitable, representing the real life that is the only alternative to anarchy. Cis, the boy in *The Magistrate*, is built up from a position of weakness in the opening scene—strewn with clues about his ambiguous potency which tease the audience with a pleasurable confusion of categories—to a domin-ance that reaches mythic proportions as he demonstrates a breezy *savoir-faire* beyond his stepfather's grasp, and eventually performs superhuman feats in the magistrate's defence—he is supposed to have run all the way from central London to the outlying district of

---

[7] Letter to Clement Scott, 16 Dec. 1887, complaining that this situation was bad for 'dramatic art': *The Collected Letters of Sir Arthur Pinero*, ed. J. P. Wearing (Minneapolis, 1974), 98–9.

Hendon. He represents the potent disrupting force of young masculinity; it is notable that Pinero refused to allow the casting of a woman, a common procedure for such roles, when the famous Ada Rehan volunteered to play it in the New York production. When the young man's proper hierarchical niche is finally established, he has already demonstrated that he is fit to move a step up the ladder, and Posket gives him a thousand pounds and permission to marry. He accepts happily; and, entering into the hierarchy, he reassures all his elders in the audience that the threat of their successors can be held in check and channelled by the power of money and law which is still in their own hands. Similarly, in *The Schoolmistress*, the unmanageable sexual aggression of young Reginald Paulover causes him to confront his wife's father in mad jealousy in the first act, accusing the girl of flirting with her papa, but he eventually accepts that he must wait his turn to mount the hierarchical ladder, and then his close resemblance to his father-in-law is happily noted, as they quarrel violently in undertones at the back of the scene.

The confusion of ranks during the action produces a *frisson* that must have been much more exciting to an English audience in the 1880s than the stale French-farce obsession with the frustrations of the bourgeois marriage. Colonel Lukyn (an army officer and therefore fair game to the traditionally anti-militarist British) is outraged at the indignity that he has suffered in being not merely arrested and gaoled, but de-classed, levelled with the unrespectable masses, by a potent physical symbol—he has been 'washed by the authorities'. The schoolmistress's idle and bankrupt aristocratic husband (again a traditional target for the scorn of a class that regarded itself as having earned its own pre-eminence) is presented as a plaything, his wife's little personal weakness; he is entirely her property. Throughout the play Pinero creates comedy from his weak, feminized behaviour. *The Schoolmistress* is in some ways the most interesting of the farces, offering the greatest promise for a revival today; it certainly embodies the most potentially subversive view of Victorian social structures. It offers a broader caricature of the patriarchal hierarchy than *The Magistrate*, with an array of masculine types ranging from the old bull Rankling down to little Mr Saunders, the treble-voiced midshipman. There is a moment in the third act when Paulover and the dashing young officer John Mallory quietly pick up the couch on which Rankling is asleep and carry him off into a darkened room; with the father disposed of, all the young people fall into each other's arms and scatter in search of private places.

Although rank and Rankling are restored to power at the end of the play, we are not returned to the status quo. Pinero seems to have been fascinated with the complexities of the position of women on the stage. That interest, in the shape of the title role, subverts the bourgeois fantasy and renders its message ambiguous. Caroline Dyott, the successful girls' school proprietor turned queen of the burlesque stage (originally played by a real and very successful female theatre entrepreneur, Matilda Vining, Mrs John Wood), is shown embarking upon her outrageous change of persona under the influence of Dionysus—she goes on the stage to finance a newly conceived passion for a kept man. She is mocked for her desires, but in the end she is not made to repent or reverse her transformation from an instrument of female subjugation to a Bacchic disruptive force; neither does she become a passive female, a mere wife. In mid-play she rides triumphantly up Piccadilly in her burlesque queen's costume on a fire appliance (a wonderful comic symbol of phallic power) and climbs on to the stage to collar her prey like a cat after a straying kitten. The earthy female power of the stage queen invades not simply the bourgeois home, but its very seed-bed and nursery, the school for young ladies. Pinero seems almost to be cocking a snook at the upright theatrical reformers of the previous generation and the earnest votaries of the intellectual drama in his own day, who strove to demonstrate that theatre was respectable, educational, and refined. The schoolmistress who takes to the stage offers a quite different transformation. When she finally discovers that her husband is not worth his upkeep, she makes that disappointment a stepping-stone to a freedom not even dreamt of previously—she becomes not a wife, but a husband. She announces that she will lock her spouse up at home on starvation allowance, while she enjoys the freedom and the fruits of her earning power as ' 'Rine, 'Rine, Honorine! | Mighty, whether wife or queen, | Firmer ruler never seen . . .'.

This extraordinary comic validation of female independence and earning power was one of many plays in which Pinero contributed to 'the woman question', an issue with which he obviously felt deep personal involvement. He was a supporter of the campaign for women's suffrage, sending a telegram of encouragement to the first meeting of the Actresses' Franchise League; in his plays he often focused upon the dilemmas of female characters, and in *The Profligate*, his first 'serious' drama, he attempted to shake the complacency of his audience by transposing the idea of the 'fallen woman' into masculine terms. His interest went deeper than merely contributing to a current debate, and was to persist long after theatre audiences had tired of plays on this theme; but in 1893 *The Second Mrs Tanqueray* chimed precisely with an urgent modern concern.

The Second Mrs Tanqueray

Pinero was not able to represent Paula Tanqueray's life choices, as he did Caroline Dyott's, as being professional, an assertion of female independence within the patriarchal structure. It was left to Shaw's Mrs Warren to fight that particular battle in the gender war. For Pinero as well as for his audience (this time at the St James's, under the young George Alexander, where Wilde's *Lady Windermere's Fan* had just been running), the transformation of the role of a wife into a commercial transaction, or rather a series of commercial transactions, by the kept woman, remained inescapably a question of corruption. It was shocking, an evil act that struck at the heart of the domestic ideology. The well-meaning Tanqueray and the supposed innocents Ellean and Hugh Ardale are damaged by Paula's cohabitation with a succession of men, just as she is herself: she can have no possible justification for what she has been and done. The belief that the fall of the 'fallen woman' was a transformation of good by the choice of evil, and as such was irrevocable, was central to the construction of that stereotype and the story which accompanied it. The society melodramas and well-made plays, as well as the many novels and stories on this theme which preceded *The Second Mrs Tanqueray*, are all shaped by this moral imperative, the need to reiterate and reinforce this topos and the view of female sexuality and subordination which it upholds. The neurotic frequency with which dramatists and other writers returned to it during the 1880s and 1890s shows how deeply the anxiety about the questions it raised struck into late Victorian culture. Pinero's contribution was greeted with such a disproportionate response—both furious rejection and wild enthusiasm, later followed by an embarrassed reaction—because he embodied that anxiety with such precision and laid it to rest with such accomplished art.

From a standpoint beyond that particular phase of the gender war, it is possible to say that it is still an excellent play, given the constraints upon it, and to agree with the contemporaries who hailed it as a turning-point in British writing, the moment when the mainstream London stage finally entered into the revolution brewing in the theatres of Europe. Contemporary critics were overwhelmed by the realism that Pinero achieved in handling the theme. They were right to be impressed. As an example, they singled out the little exchange between Paula and Ardale in Act III, a piece of dialogue whose realism helped to carry off the only stagy coincidence of the play, the reappearance of one of Paula's lovers as her stepdaughter's fiancé. In an emotionally strained exchange, they avoid confronting the catastrophic present by talking briefly about the pretty flat which they had once shared. All previous stage *femmes fatales* had been far too monstrous to give a single thought to furniture; Paula's humanity struck the contemporary audience with a force that horrified them. Today we are more likely to be moved by a larger verisimilitude, Pinero's capacity as an observer and recorder of mental suffering, in the precision with which he sketches Paula's self-destructive behaviour when she finds herself trapped, a victim of the final cruel deception: now she is really married at last, there is no possible world for her to inhabit, no acceptable way for her to behave. Interestingly, the only contemporary critic to read the second act in this way was a woman, voicing 'a girl's point of view'.[8] Pinero's analysis of the situation is inevitably bound by his acceptance of the morality that it embodies, but his observation and evocation of the psychic damage done to the woman who has internalized that morality, and been enslaved and destroyed by it, transcends his own limitations. That is why the role of Paula catapulted Mrs Patrick Campbell to stardom, and why it has remained a wonderful acting part ever since. Its enduring power after a hundred years is a sufficient answer to Shaw's sneering insistence that Paula is 'a work of prejudiced observation instead of comprehension';[9] his own strangely warped perception of women produced nothing so theatrically powerful.

Trelawny of the 'Wells'

Trelawny of the 'Wells' takes the theme of women's work and its challenge to the domestic and patriarchal ideology back into the world in which Pinero identified with that problem personally—the world of the theatre. It could be argued that the question was an emblem of his own ambiguous position, which he felt at some level to be feminized and marginalized, and that he wrote about it most interest-

---

[8] In a review in the *Theatre*, 1 Sept. 1893, entitled 'From a Girl's Point of View', quoted in John Dawick, 'The "First" Mrs Tanqueray', *Theatre Quarterly*, 9 35 (1979), 77–93 (86).
[9] 'An Old Play and a New One', 47.

ingly when he was able to use his own life experience to invest it with that submerged complex of feeling. The Bible that the notorious Mrs Ebbsmith (the fallen heroine of his next serious play after *Mrs Tanqueray*) flings into the fire and then burns herself to retrieve is a fake and fustian symbol of little power by comparison with the impact of Avonia's tights in her third-act entrance in *Trelawny*. The 1898 audience was puzzled by the play, perceiving it as a rather hackneyed backstage comedy, demanding broad acting styles which the modern cast could not encompass, and offering nothing new except what it perceived as a gratuitous emphasis on the dress style of the 1860s. Many column inches were expended by critics in commiserating with the ladies required to disfigure themselves by wearing crinolines. If we understand these clothes as those of Pinero's adolescence, when he was forming his fantasy of the conquest of the world through theatrical success, we can begin to see why he insists upon their accuracy. His identification with Tom Wrench, the figure in the play who was based on the dramatist Tom Robertson, has often been noted. Robertson was the writer of the 'cup and saucer' comedies with which, in the 1860s, the Bancroft management at the Prince of Wales's Theatre inaugurated a new realism, suited to the tastes of the fashionable audiences that they strove to attract. He certainly seemed to Pinero to be the founding father of a respectable theatre showing real people in rational situations. Pinero saw himself as inheriting that tradition. But one might equally say that in *Trelawny of the 'Wells'* Pinero projects his ambition to rise as a writer into the highest circles, and be recognized there for his superior sensibility and natural gentility, on to Rose Trelawny the actress. It is Rose who is both essentially respectable, a natural lady, and of the theatre, born and bred there (as Pinero was not), and she derives her moral and artistic power from that source, through her mother's advice and the quasi-mystical contact, via her, with Edmund Kean. Rose is distinct from all the others in her purity, emphasized by her exemption from the physical ridiculousness from which every other character suffers. Tom is perceptive and gentle throughout, but he is also shabby and a poor actor, condemned to play the back end of the pantomime dragon. The representatives of polite society, the Gowers, their heavy swell son-in-law and their timid daughter, even the lovesick Arthur, are as grotesque and ridiculous as the theatricals—Rose easily excels them in natural refinement and good manners. Superficially, the play says that her dilemma, the incompatibility of good breeding with a stage career which earns its bread by unladylike self-exposure in immodest clothes and the utterance of immoderate sentiments, will be solved by the elimination of the bad old theatrical ways and the appearance of the new, refined drama, like those written by Robertson and then Pinero. These new playwrights will address ladies and gentlemen, their equals, educating and refining them by means of an image of gentility carried by artists of a superior breeding; the barriers will be breached, and gentlemen will woo the ladies of the profession on their common ground, the stage. This fantasy was actualized in the first production by the employment of a young sprig of the aristocracy, Lord Rosslyn, to play the hero Arthur, whom Rose carries off into her own world. The fascination of the play, however, lies in the complication, perhaps the negation, of this rational modern ideal in a kind of subtext, which is created, appropriately, by the use of reference to, and evocation of, the old, unregenerate theatre—the theatre of Pinero's boyhood and before.

Rational improvement, the new realism, in the shape of Wrench's play, cannot take on board the irrational, playful, fantastic elements of theatre which are evoked in the first act, before Rose develops a consciousness of her superior gentility and loses contact with her art. The new drama comes to her rescue; but it is itself out of touch with its heritage and roots. It can only employ the old actor Telfer as a caricature of himself, and it has no place at all for the rest of the company from the Wells. It is Avonia, the suburban soubrette in the principal boy's tights, who stands up to Sir William Gower and bravely demands that the respectable world recognize the hypocrisy by which they enjoy women on the stage and despise them for being there; but she cannot be part of the offered solution, the translation of the stage to respectability, and she simply does not appear in the final act. Pinero must have had some consciousness of the inadequacy of Robertson's plays as the ultimate reconciliation between the theatre and respectable society: Sir William is converted to Rose's side not by the new play—which the old man sees is not a real play at all, but a pale reflection of real life, and 'Shakespeare knew better than that'—but by the evocation of the ghost of Edmund Kean, the 'splendid gypsy'. This moment of vision follows abruptly, and apparently rather oddly, on Avonia's plea; a chance mention of Kean sets off in Gower the Dionysian spirit of theatre, theatre as magic. He is touched by the memory of a transfiguring experience, its magic transforming him momentarily into an actor himself: he walks about the stage copying Kean's walk as Richard III, while Rose watches him, 'seriously'. On the plane of realism, this is perfectly preposterous. It carries the submerged meaning of the play.

Pinero was never to resolve this struggle with his sense of the dark, female power of the theatre, and its connection with irrational levels of the psyche which are completely unconnected with gentlemen's clubs and knighthoods for services to drama. The women who represent its embodiment include Caroline Dyott and Rose Trelawny, but Avonia Bunn is a more powerful, multidimensional instance; and the dramatist can find no place for her in his dénouement. From Avonia, the path leads down into the *demi-monde*, where Pinero seems to fear lurking sexuality and corruption, vulgarity as the heart of darkness. In *The Second Mrs Tanqueray* Lady Orreyed, née Mabel Hervey, is 'a lady who could have been . . . described in the reports of the police . . . as an actress', and she figures in scenes of appalling bitter humour which demonstrate the gulf between her essential vulgarity and Paula's suffering sensibility. *The 'Mind the Paint' Girl*, Pinero's favourite play and his final major attempt to articulate this complex of ideas and feelings, could be said to be about another Mabel Hervey. It concerns a chorus girl, empty-headed if good-hearted, who has unthinkingly drawn under her spell an array of men ranging from *demi-mondaines* and shady city types to an innocent and adoring young gentleman, Lord Farncombe. The theatre world that we are shown this time is bang up to date, with no nostalgia for a childhood magic and no emphasis on the theatre as a place for work. The ambience is of sleazy money and ugly slang, elderly men infatuated with desperately bright young girls, stupidity, lust, and avarice cynically usurping the excuses of art. The song that has made the heroine famous concerns the wet paint in her brand-new flat, all from Maples, and on her face, which is her excuse for not paying out to the purchaser of her furniture and favours. The climactic action, a series of revelations, accusations, and reversals which seems to be a nightmare combination of *Trelawny* with Shaw's *Mrs Warren's Profession*, is entirely without the charm, the magical atmosphere of the earlier play, and suggests Pinero's disillusion with the theatre: it is no longer a golden pathway to reconciliation, but a trap, a delusion, from which there is no retreat into the real world. Inevitably, given both his feminized image of the theatre and the moral climate in which he was conditioned, he finds out at this point that women are to blame, and both the chorus girl and her obtuse and irredeemably vulgar mother are made to suffer for it. It is a sad, bitter aftermath of

Pinero's lifelong immersion in the theatre and his concern with the social injustices of his day.

He was to produce yet one more play on the same theme, *The Freaks*, written in 1918, and although this was no more successful than *The 'Mind the Paint' Girl*, it is a more heartening place to end a survey of Pinero's life's-work, since, while it continues to stress the incompatibility of theatre people with the rest of society, it repudiates the disgust and self-hatred of that play. In *The Freaks* he demands that the audience acknowledge that the respectable characters—a selfish city knight, his snobbish wife, and his dull, timid suburban family—are less human, less mature, less loving, less generous, and less heroic than the collection of fairground freaks who this time represent the theatre at its lowest and most vulgar. To ensure that the audience is forced to absorb this denunciation of the theatrical consumer's complacency, Pinero uses not only conventional means of plot and characterization, culminating in an impassioned descriptive speech about the view of an audience from the platform of a sideshow, but also a vivid non-naturalistic device. Intruding upon the illusion created by the drawing-room box set, he lowers a painted drop showing an expressionistically violent caricature of the rich audience gaping at the poor, exposed performers. Finally defiantly loyal to his own, the experimental theatre artist in Pinero lived on to the end, despite every disillusion and rebuff. His contribution to European theatre has yet to be fully recognized and measured.

NOTE ON THE TEXTS

PINERO was actively involved in the battle for the international copyright protection of printed plays, and, as soon as it was established, he began, in 1891, to publish his own texts at the time of their first production. For this purpose, he edited the printed version used in rehearsals, changing little except the stage directions, which he amended to enable the reader to envisage his direction of the plays, cutting technical terms, especially in his instructions for stage movements, and expanding some descriptions of settings. These texts, published in a uniform series by Heinemann, form the basis of the present edition. *The Magistrate* and *The Schoolmistress*, produced in 1885 and 1886, were not printed until 1892 and 1894 respectively; *The Second Mrs Tanqueray* and *Trelawny of the 'Wells'* in 1895 and 1899. The texts printed here have been collated with the prompt and/or rehearsal copies, with the copies deposited in the Lord Chamberlain's collection after submission to his office for licensing, and with relevant modern editions. These are, in particular, George Rowell, *Plays by A. W. Pinero* (Cambridge, 1986), and Michael Booth's edition of *The Magistrate* in volume 4 of *English Plays of the Nineteenth Century* (Oxford, 1973).

Additional stage directions enclosed in square brackets are taken from the other early texts consulted. Those in *The Magistrate* and *The Schoolmistress* are derived from the licensing copies deposited with the Lord Chamberlain, now in the British Library; in the case of *The Second Mrs Tanqueray*, additions were derived both from the Lord Chamberlain's copy and from the prompt copy, which is also in the British Library. *Trelawny of the 'Wells'* was revised by Pinero himself for a revival at the Old Vic in 1925, at which point he dropped the disguising of Sadler's Wells Theatre, and made quite extensive alterations to the play-within-a-play in the final act. This version was published by French's in 1936 and included some corrections to the earlier text. These have been incorporated here, but the changes for the 1925 performance are only indicated in the notes to the present edition. The Heinemann text of the earlier version has been used as the copy text, since it represents the finished state of the play when it was first produced.

SELECT BIBLIOGRAPHY

Place of publication is London unless otherwise stated.

Pinero's own opinions about dramatic writing were not systematically recorded, but he had very definite feelings about the state of theatrical art and his own part in the end-of-the-century mission to rescue the stage from a morass of cheap vulgarity. His vision of the state of affairs at the time he began to write is contained in a chapter on 'The Theatre in the Seventies', in *The Eighteen-Seventies* (Cambridge, 1929), and he wrote about his own work in the foreword to *Two Plays* (1930). Other scattered remarks on playwriting in general are recorded in the preface to W. L. Courtney's *The Idea of Tragedy* (1900), and in occasional pieces about his contemporaries, such as a lecture on 'Robert Louis Stevenson: The Dramatist', delivered to the Philosophical Institution of Edinburgh in 1903, and another on 'Browning as a Dramatist', reproduced in *Transactions of the Royal Society of Literature*, 31 (1912), 255–68.

Pinero's plays found early and perhaps excessive critical favour, and have subsequently suffered from neglect and misprision. The contemporary estimate is most easily accessible in the work of William Archer, especially his *English Dramatists of Today* (1882), *The Theatrical World* (1893–7), and *The Old Drama and the New* (1923), and in the reviews of the journalist A. B. Walkley, whose judgements are collected in, for example, his *Playhouse Impressions* (1892), and *Drama and Life* (1908). The first eleven volumes of the Heinemann editions of the plays, which include *The Magistrate* and *The Schoolmistress*, have interesting introductions by Malcolm C. Salaman, obviously written either in collaboration with Pinero or with his blessing. The first book-length studies of Pinero, H. Hamilton Fyfe's *Arthur Wing Pinero, Playwright* (1902) and *Sir Arthur Pinero's Plays and Players* (1930) were largely biographical, and in 1941 (Chicago; London, 1943) W. D. Dunkel published *Sir Arthur Pinero: A Critical Biography with Letters*, in which he claims that Pinero was annoyed by Fyfe's journalistic inaccuracies, and so was eager to co-operate with Dunkel's own work. An earlier attempt to reclaim the dramatist from both excessive admiration and detraction was made by Clayton Hamilton, who published *The Social Plays of Sir Arthur Wing Pinero* in four volumes in New York in 1917–22, selecting only his most 'serious' plays for inclusion and claiming that they demonstrated his mastery of dramatic craftsmanship—a claim that has become the conventional way of damning all his work with faint praise. Modern scholarship has acknowledged Pinero's stature more readily than modern critical writing, and J. P. Wearing's *The Collected Letters of Sir Arthur Pinero* (Minneapolis, 1974) contains a world of information waiting to be explored and analysed. The best critical assessment to date is George Rowell's succinct and masterly introduction to his edition of (four) *Plays by A. W. Pinero* (Cambridge, 1986); see also his discussion of 'The Drama of Wilde and Pinero', in Boris Ford (ed.), *The Later Victorian Age* (Cambridge, 1989), 145–61. Stephen Wyatt's comments in *Arthur Wing Pinero: Three Plays* (1985) are also interesting. A renewed interest in questions of sexual politics on the stage has produced new writing on *The Second Mrs Tanqueray* in particular: see Catherine Wiley, 'The Matter with Manners: The New Woman and the Problem Play', in James Redmond (ed.), *Women in Theatre* (Cambridge, 1989), 109–21, and Judith Fisher, 'The "Law of the Father": Sexual Politics in the Plays of Henry Arthur Jones and Arthur Wing Pinero' (*Essays in Literature* (1989), 203–23). Penny Griffiths has contributed an introductory survey of Pinero's work to the Macmillan Modern Dramatists series (*Arthur Wing Pinero and Henry Arthur Jones* (1991)), stating very clearly Pinero's claim to be the founding father of modern British comedy, and a unique and authoritative dramatic voice. It would seem that the estimation of Pinero's work is at last beginning to shake off the influence of his reputation, and a steady trickle of stage revivals suggests that we are on the brink of a rediscovery of his plays.

A CHRONOLOGY OF ARTHUR WING PINERO

1855   Arthur Wing Pinero born, second child of a solicitor, John Daniel Pinero, and his young second wife, Lucy Daines; they live in Islington, near Sadler's Wells Theatre, during Pinero's childhood.

1860–5 Attends a charity school in Exmouth Street, Clerkenwell.

1865–70 Works in his father's office.

1870–4 Works as a solicitor's clerk.

1874   Becomes an actor; first engagement at the Theatre Royal, Edinburgh.

1876   Becomes a member of Henry Irving's company.

1877   First play, a curtain-raiser called *£200 a Year*, is performed at the Globe Theatre.

1879   *Daisy's Escape*, written for Irving, is successfully staged at the Lyceum.

1881   *The Money-Spinner* is a success at the St James's Theatre; joins the Bancrofts' company at the Theatre Royal, Haymarket.

1883   Marries Myra Emily Hamilton (stage name, Myra Holme), who worked to support her two children and dying first husband.

1884   Gives up acting and concentrates on writing.

1885   *The Magistrate* is staged at the Court Theatre.

1886   *The Schoolmistress* is staged at the Court Theatre.

1887   *Dandy Dick*, the third successful farce, is staged at the Court; Pinero is elected to membership of the Garrick Club.

1888   *Sweet Lavender*, a sentimental comedy, is a hit at Terry's Theatre.

1889   *The Profligate*, Pinero's first serious 'social-problem' drama, is staged by the actor-manager John Hare at the Garrick Theatre, with a softened ending demanded by Hare. After its success, Pinero determines to take full control of his own work.

1893   *The Second Mrs Tanqueray*, with the new discovery Mrs Patrick Campbell in the leading role, is a sensational success at the St James's, under the management of George Alexander.

1895   *The Notorious Mrs Ebbsmith*, Pinero's second serious play about the 'fallen woman' question, is performed at the Garrick.

1898   *Trelawny of the 'Wells'*, at the Court, receives faint praise from the critics. The succession of plays continues for another thirty years, but Pinero's peak of acclaim is past.

1909   Knighted for his services to drama; becomes the first President of the Dramatists' Club.

1912   *The 'Mind the Paint' Girl* at the Duke of York's Theatre, in Pinero's opinion his best play, is received coldly.

1918 *The Freaks* is performed at the New Theatre.

1919 Death of Myra, Pinero's wife.

1932 His last performed play, *A Cold June*, is staged at the Duchess Theatre.

1934 Dies in Marylebone, London.

THE MAGISTRATE

A Farce in Three Acts

The play was first staged at the Court Theatre, London, on 21 March 1885, with the following cast:

Mr Posket (magistrate of Mulberry Street Police Court)	*Mr Arthur Cecil*
Mr Bullamy (magistrate of Mulberry Street Police Court)	*Mr Fred Cape*
Colonel Lukyn (from Bengal, retired)	*Mr John Clayton*
Captain Horace Vale (Shropshire Fusiliers)	*Mr F. Kerr*
Cis Farringdon (Mrs Posket's son by her first marriage)	*Mr H. Eversfield*
Achille Blond (proprietor of the Hôtel des Princes)	*Mr Chevalier*
Isidore (a waiter)	*Mr Deane*
Mr Wormington (chief clerk at Mulberry Street)	*Mr Gilbert Trent*
Inspector Messiter	*Mr Albert Sims*
Sergeant Lugg (Metropolitan Police)	*Mr Lugg*
Constable Harris	*Mr Burnley*
Wyke (a servant at Mr Posket's)	*Mr Fayre*
Agatha Poskett (late Farringdon, née Verrinder)	*Mrs John Wood*
Charlotte (her sister)	*Miss Marion Terry*
Beatie Tomlinson (a young lady reduced to teaching music)	*Miss Norreys*
Popham (a servant at Mr Posket's)	*Miss La Coste*

2

Act One

THE FAMILY SKELETON

Scene One

The scene represents a well-furnished drawing-room in the house of Mr Posket in Bloomsbury.° Beatie Tomlinson, a pretty, simply dressed little girl of about sixteen, is playing the piano, as Cis Farringdon, a manly youth wearing an Eton jacket,° enters the room

CIS Beatie!

BEATIE Cis dear! Dinner isn't over, surely?

CIS Not quite. I had one of my convenient headaches and cleared out. (*Taking an apple and some cob-nuts from his pocket and giving them to Beatie*) These are for you, dear, with my love. [*He puts his arm round her waist and kisses her*] I sneaked 'em off the sideboard as I came out.

BEATIE Oh, I mustn't take them!

CIS Yes, you may—it's my share of dessert. Besides, it's a horrid shame you don't grub with us.°

BEATIE What, a poor little music mistress!

CIS Yes. They're only going to give you four guineas° a quarter. Fancy getting a girl like you for four guineas a quarter—why, an eighth of you is worth more than that! Now peg away at your apple.

Produces a cigarette

BEATIE (*munching her apple*) There's company at dinner, isn't there?

CIS Well, hardly. Aunt Charlotte hasn't arrived yet, so there's only old Bullamy.

BEATIE Isn't old Bullamy anybody?

CIS Old Bullamy—well, he's only like the guv'nor,° a police magistrate at the Mulberry Street Police Court.

BEATIE Oh, does each police court have two magistrates?

CIS (*proudly*) All the best have two.

BEATIE Don't they quarrel over getting the interesting cases? I should.

CIS I don't know how they manage—perhaps they toss up who's to hear the big sensations. There's a Mrs Beldam, who is rather a bore sometimes; I know the Guv always lets old Bullamy attend to her. [*Striking a lucifer*] But, as a rule, I fancy they go half and half, in a friendly way. (*Lighting cigarette*) For instance, if the guv'nor 30 wants to go to the Derby he lets old Bullamy have the Oaks°—and so on, see?

> *He sits on the floor, comfortably reclining against Beatie, and puffing his cigarette*

BEATIE Oh, I say, Cis, won't your mamma be angry when she finds I haven't gone home?

CIS Oh, put it on to your pupil. [*Drawing her face to his and kissing* 35 *her*] Say I'm very backward.

BEATIE I think you are extremely forward—in some ways. (*Biting the apple and speaking with her mouth full*) I do wish I could get you to concentrate your attention on your music lessons. But I wouldn't get you into a scrape! 40

CIS No fear of that. [*Blowing smoke into the air*] Ma is too proud of me.

BEATIE But there's your stepfather.

CIS The dear old guv'nor! Why, he's too good-natured to say 'Boo!' to a goose. You know, Beatie, I was at a school at Brighton when 45 ma got married—when she got married the second time, I mean—and the guv'nor and I didn't make each other's acquaintance till after the honeymoon.

BEATIE Oh, fancy your stepfather blindly accepting such a responsibility. 50

> *Gives him a cob-nut to crack for her*

CIS Yes, wasn't the guv'nor soft! I might have been a very indifferent sort of young fellow for all he knew.

> *Having cracked the nut with his teeth, he returns it to her*

BEATIE Thank you, dear.

CIS Well, when I heard the new dad was a police magistrate, I *was* scared. Said I to myself, 'If I don't mind my p's and q's,° the 55 guv'nor—from force of habit—will fine me all my pocket money.' But it's quite the reverse—he's the mildest, meekest—(*The door opens suddenly*) Look out! Someone coming!

> *They both jump up, Beatie scattering the nuts that are in her lap all over the floor. Cis throws his cigarette into the fireplace and sits at the piano, playing a simple exercise very badly. Beatie stands behind him, counting*

BEATIE One—and two—and one—and two.

> *Wyke, the butler, appears at the door, and mysteriously closes it after him*

WYKE [*in a whisper*] Ssss! Master Cis! Master Cis!   60

CIS Hallo—what is it, Wyke?

WYKE [*producing a decanter from under his coat*] The port wine what you asked for, sir. I couldn't get it away before—the old gentlemen do hug port wine so.

CIS Got a glass?   65

WYKE Yes, sir. (*Producing wineglass from his pocket, and pouring out wine*) What ain't missed ain't mourned, eh, Master Cis?

CIS (*offering wine*) Here you are, Beatie dear.

BEATIE The idea of such a thing! I couldn't!

CIS Why not?   70

BEATIE If I merely sipped it I shouldn't be able to give you your music lesson properly. Drink it yourself, you dear, thoughtful boy.

CIS I shan't—it's for you.

BEATIE I can't drink it!

CIS You must.   75

BEATIE I won't!

CIS You're disagreeable!

BEATIE Not half so disagreeable as you are.

> *They wrangle*

WYKE (*to himself,° watching them*) What a young gentleman it is! And only fourteen! Fourteen—he behaves like forty! Why, even Cook   80
has made a 'ash of everything, since he's been in the house, and as for Popham—! (*Seeing someone approaching*) Look out, Master Cis!

> Cis [*who is drinking the wine himself, chokes—then hastily hides the wineglass and*] *returns to the piano. Beatie is counting as before. Wyke pretends to arrange the window curtains, concealing the decanter behind him*

BEATIE One and two—and one and two—and one, *etc.*

> *Enter Popham, a smart-looking maidservant*

POPHAM Wyke, where's the port?   85

WYKE (*vacantly*) Port?

POPHAM Port wine. Missus is furious.

WYKE Port?

POPHAM (*pointing to the decanter*) Why! There! You're carrying it about with you!   90

WYKE Why, so I am! Carrying it about with me! Shows what a sharp eye I keep on the guv'nor's wines. Carrying it about with me! Missus will be amused.

> *Goes out*

POPHAM ([*to herself,*] *eyeing Cis and Beatie*) There's that boy with *her* again! Minx! Her two hours was up long ago. Why doesn't she   95
go home? [*Aloud*] Master Cis, I've got a message for you.

CIS (*rising from the piano*) For me, Popham?

POPHAM   Yes, sir. (*Quietly to him*) The message is from a young lady who up to last Wednesday was all in all to you. Her name is Emma Popham.   100

CIS (*trying to get away*) Oh, go along, Popham!

POPHAM (*holding his sleeve*) Ah, it wasn't 'Go along, Popham' till that music girl came into the house. I will go along, but—cast your eye over this before you sleep tonight. (*She takes out of her pocket handkerchief a piece of printed paper which she hands him between her*   105
finger and thumb) Part of a story in *Bow Bells*,° called 'Jilted; or, Could Blood Atone?' Wrap it in your handkerchief—it came round the butter.

> *She goes out; Cis throws the paper into the grate*

CIS   Bother the girl! Beatie, she's jealous of you!

BEATIE   A parlour-maid jealous of *me*—and with a bit of a child of   110
fourteen!

CIS [*coming to her*] I may be only fourteen, but I feel like a grown-up man! You're only sixteen—there's not much difference—and if you will only wait for me, I'll soon catch you up and be as much a man as you are a woman. [*Lovingly*] Will you wait   115
for me, Beatie?

BEATIE   I can't—I'm getting older every minute!

CIS   Oh, I wish I could borrow five or six years from somebody!

BEATIE   Many a person would be glad to lend them. (*Lovingly*) And oh, I wish you could!   120

CIS (*putting his arm round her*) You do! Why?

BEATIE   Because I—because—

CIS (*listening*) Look out! Here's the mater!

> *They run to the piano, he resumes playing, and she counting as*
> *before*

BEATIE   One and two—and one—and two, *etc.*

> *Enter Agatha, a handsome, showy woman, of about thirty-six,*
> *looking perhaps younger*

AGATHA   Why, Cis child, at your music again?   125

CIS   Yes, ma, always at it. You'll spoil my taste by forcing it if you're not careful.

AGATHA   We have no right to keep Miss Tomlinson so late.

BEATIE   Oh, thank you, it doesn't matter. I—I am afraid we're not making—very—great—progress.   130

CIS (*winking at Beatie*) Well, if I play that again, will you kiss me?

BEATIE (*demurely*) I don't know, I'm sure. (*To Agatha*) May I promise that, m'am?

> *Sits in the window recess. Cis, joining her, puts his arm round her waist.*

AGATHA No, certainly not. (*To herself, watching them*) If I could only persuade Aeneas to dismiss this *protégée* of his, and to engage a music master, it would ease my conscience a little. If this girl knew the truth, how indignant she would be! And then there is the injustice to the boy himself, and to my husband's friends who are always petting and fondling and caressing what they call 'a fine little man of fourteen'! Fourteen! Oh, what an idiot I have been to conceal my child's real age! (*Looking at the clock*) Charlotte is late; I wish she would come. It will be a relief to worry her with my troubles.

POSKET (*talking outside*) We smoke all over the house, Bullamy, all over the house.

AGATHA [*to herself*] I will speak to Aeneas about this little girl, at any rate.

> *Enter Posket, a mild gentleman of about fifty [wearing a pince-nez and smoking a cigar], followed by Bullamy, a fat, red-faced man with a bronchial cough and general huskiness*

POSKET Smoke anywhere, Bullamy—smoke anywhere.

BULLAMY Not with my bronchitis, thank ye.

POSKET (*beaming at Agatha*) Ah, my darling!

BULLAMY (*producing a small box from his waistcoat pocket*) All I take after dinner is a jujube°—sometimes two. (*Offering the box*) May I tempt Mrs Posket?

AGATHA No, thank you. (*Treading on one of the nuts which have been scattered over the room*) How provoking—who brings nuts into the drawing-room?

POSKET Miss Tomlinson still here? (*To Beatie*) Don't go, don't go. Glad to see Cis so fond of his music. Your sister Charlotte is behind her time, my darling.

AGATHA Her train is delayed, I suppose.

POSKET You must stay and see my sister-in-law, Bullamy.

BULLAMY Pleasure—pleasure!

POSKET *I* have never met her yet, we will share first impressions. In the interim, will Miss Tomlinson delight us with a little music?

BULLAMY (*bustling up to the piano*) If this young lady is going to sing she might like one of my jujubes.

Beatie sits at the piano with Cis and Bullamy on each side of her. Posket treads on a nut as he walks over to his wife

POSKET Dear me—how come nuts into the drawing-room? (*To Agatha*) Of what is my darling thinking so deeply? (*Treads on another nut*) Another! My pet, there are nuts on the drawing-room carpet!   170

AGATHA [*rousing herself*] Yes, I want to speak to you, Aeneas.

POSKET About the nuts?

AGATHA No—about Miss Tomlinson—your little *protégée*.
     [*Beatie plays anair softly on the piano*]

POSKET Ah, nice little thing.

AGATHA Very. But not old enough to exert any decided influence over   175
the boy's musical future. [*Looking up*] Why not engage a master?

POSKET What, for a mere child?

AGATHA [*looking away*] A mere child—oh!

POSKET A boy of fourteen!

AGATHA (*to herself*) Fourteen!   180

POSKET A boy of fourteen, not yet out of Czerny's exercises.°

AGATHA (*to herself*) If we were alone now, I might have the desperation to tell him all!

POSKET Besides, my darling, you know the interest I take in Miss Tomlinson; she is one of the brightest little spots on my hobby-   185
horse. Like all our servants, like everybody in my employ, she has been brought to my notice through the unhappy medium of the Police Court over which it is my destiny to preside. Our servant, Wyke, a man with a beautiful nature, is the son of a person I committed for trial for marrying three wives. To this day, Wyke   190
is ignorant as to which of those three wives he is the son of! Cook was once a notorious dipsomaniac, and has even now not entirely freed herself from early influences. Popham is the unclaimed charge of a convicted baby-farmer.° Even our milkman came before me as a man who had refused to submit specimens to the   195
analytic inspector.° And this poor child, what is she?

AGATHA Yes, I know.

POSKET The daughter of a superannuated General, who abstracted four silk umbrellas from the Army and Navy Stores—and on a fine day too!   200
     Beatie ceases playing

BULLAMY Very good—very good!

POSKET Thank you—thank you!
     [*Bullamy and Posket join each other by the fire*]

BULLAMY ([*aside to*] *Posket, coughing and laughing and popping a jujube into his mouth*) My dear Posket, I really must congratulate

8

you on that boy of yours—your stepson. A most wonderful lad. So   205
confoundedly advanced too.

POSKET [*rubbing his hands, delighted*] Yes, isn't he? Eh!

BULLAMY (*confidentially*) While the piano was going on just now, he
told me one of the most humorous stories I've ever heard.
(*Laughing heartily and panting, then taking another jujube*) Ha, ha,   210
bless me, I don't know when I have taken so many jujubes!

POSKET [*aside to Bullamy*] My dear Bullamy, my entire marriage is
the greatest possible success. A little romantic, too. (*Pointing to
Agatha*) Beautiful woman!

BULLAMY Very, very. I never committed° a more stylish, elegant   215
creature.

> [*Wyke enters with tea, which he hands first to Agatha*]

POSKET Thank you, Bullamy—we met abroad, at Spa, when I was
on my holiday.

BULLAMY [*facetiously*] I shall go there next year.

POSKET She lost her first husband about twelve months ago in India.   220
He was an army contractor.

> [*Wyke crosses to them with tea. Bullamy declines it, Posket
> takes a cup*]

BEATIE (*to Cis at the piano*) I must go now—there's no excuse for
staying any longer.

CIS (*to her disconsolately*) What the deuce shall *I* do?

POSKET (*pouring out milk*) Dear me, this milk seems very poor.   225
When he died, she came to England, placed her boy at a school in
Brighton, and then moved about quietly from place to place,
drinking—

> *Sips tea*

BULLAMY [*with concern*] Drinking?

POSKET [*putting his cup upon the mantelpiece*] The waters—she's a   230
little dyspeptic.

> *Wyke goes out*

We encountered each other at the Tours des Fontaines°—by
accident I trod upon her dress—

BEATIE Good-night, Cis dear.

CIS Oh!   235

POSKET [*Advancing to Agatha*] I apologised. We talked about the
weather, we drank out of the same glass, discovered that we both
suffered from the same ailment, and the result is complete
happiness.

> *He bends over Agatha gallantly.* [*She looks up*]

AGATHA Aeneas!   240

9

He kisses her; then Cis kisses Beatie, loudly; Posket and Bullamy both listen puzzled

POSKET Echo?

BULLAMY Suppose so!

He kisses the back of his hand experimentally; Beatie kisses Cis

Yes.

POSKET Curious. (*To Bullamy*) Romantic story, isn't it?

[*They stand chatting, Beatie comes quietly down to Agatha*]

BEATIE Good-night, Mrs Posket! I shall be here early tomorrow   245
morning.

AGATHA I am afraid you are neglecting your other pupils.

BEATIE Oh, they're not so interesting as Cis—(*Correcting herself*)
Master Farringdon. Good-night.

AGATHA Good-night, dear.   250

Beatie goes out quietly; Agatha joins Cis

POSKET (*to Bullamy*) We were married abroad without consulting
friends or relations on either side. That's how it is I have never
seen my sister-in-law, Miss Verrinder, who is coming from
Shropshire to stay with us—she ought to—

Wyke enters

WYKE Miss Verrinder has come, ma'am.   255

POSKET Here she is.

AGATHA Charlotte?

*Charlotte, a fine handsome girl [under thirty, elegantly dressed],
enters, followed by popham with hand-luggage*

AGATHA (*kissing her*) My dear Charley.

Wyke goes out

CHARLOTTE Aggy darling, aren't I late! There's a fog on the
line—you could cut it with a knife. (*Seeing Cis*) Is that your boy?   260

AGATHA Yes.

CHARLOTTE Good gracious! What is he doing in an Eton jacket at
his age?

AGATHA [*aside to her, hurriedly*] Hush! don't say a word about my
boy's age yet awhile.   265

CHARLOTTE Oh!

AGATHA (*about to introduce Posket*) There is my husband.

CHARLOTTE ([*to herself,*] *mistaking Bullamy for him*) Oh! How could
she! (*To Bullamy, turning her cheek to him*) I congratulate you—I
suppose you ought to kiss me.   270

AGATHA No, no!

POSKET [*advancing*] Welcome to my house, Miss Verrinder.

CHARLOTTE Oh, I beg your pardon. How do you do?

BULLAMY (*to himself*) Mrs Posket's an interfering woman.

POSKET (*pointing to Bullamy*) Mr Bullamy.   275
        Bullamy, aggrieved, bows stiffly

AGATHA (*to Charlotte*) Come upstairs, dear; will you have some tea?

CHARLOTTE No thank you, pet, but I should like a glass of soda
    water.

AGATHA Soda water!

CHARLOTTE Well dear, you can put what you like at the bottom of it.   280
        Agatha and Charlotte go out, Popham following

POPHAM (*to Cis*) Give me back my *Bow Bells*, when you have read
    it, you imp.
        Goes out

CIS By Jove, Guv, isn't Aunt Charlotte a stunner?

POSKET Seems a charming woman.

BULLAMY [*to himself, rubbing his hands and chuckling*] Posket's got   285
    the wrong one! That comes of marrying without first seeing the
    lady's relations.

CIS Come along, Guv—let's have a gamble—Mr Bullamy will join us.
        Opens the card-table, arranges chairs and candles

BULLAMY A gamble?

POSKET Yes—the boy has taught me a new game called 'Fireworks';   290
    his mother isn't aware that we play for money, of course, but we
    do.

BULLAMY Ha, ha, ha! Who wins?

POSKET He does now—but he says I shall win when I know the game
    better.
                                                                  295

BULLAMY What a boy he is!

POSKET (*rubbing his hands, delighted,* [*chuckling*]) Isn't he a wonderful
    lad? And only fourteen, too. I'll tell you something else—perhaps
    you had better not mention it to his mother.

BULLAMY No, no, certainly not.   300

POSKET [*in Bullamy's ear*] He's invested a little money for me.

BULLAMY What in?

POSKET Not *in*—*on* on Sillikin for the Lincolnshire Handicap.°
    Sillikin to win and Butterscotch one, two, three.°

BULLAMY Good Lord!   305

POSKET Yes, the dear boy said, 'Guv, it isn't fair you should give me
    all the tips,° I'll give you some'—and he did—he gave me Sillikin
    and Butterscotch. He'll manage it for you, if you like. 'Plank it
    down', he calls it.

BULLAMY (*chuckling and choking*) Ha! ha! Ho! ho! (*Taking a jujube*)   310
This boy will ruin me in jujubes.

CIS   All ready! Look sharp! Guv, lend me a sov° to start with?

POSKET   A sov to start with?

They sit at the table. Agatha and Charlotte come into the room
We didn't think you would return so soon, my darling.

AGATHA   Go on amusing yourselves, I insist; only don't teach my Cis   315
to play cards.

BULLAMY   Ho! ho!

POSKET   (*to Bullamy*) Hush! Hush!

AGATHA   (*to Charlotte*) I'm glad of this—we can tell each other our
miseries undisturbed. Will you begin?   320

CHARLOTTE   Well, at last I am engaged to Captain Horace Vale.

AGATHA   Oh! Charley, I'm so glad!

CHARLOTTE   Yes—so is he—he says. He proposed to me at the Hunt
Ball—in the passage—Tuesday week.

AGATHA   What did he say?   325

CHARLOTTE   He said, 'By Jove, I love you awfully.'

AGATHA   Well—and what did you say?

CHARLOTTE   Oh, I said, 'Well, if you're going to be as eloquent as
all that, by Jove, I can't stand out.' So we settled it, in the passage.
He bars flirting till after we're married. That's my misery. What's   330
yours, Aggy?

AGATHA   [*with hand to her head*] Something awful!
[*She walks distractedly across to the sofa and throws herself upon
it; Charlotte follows*]

CHARLOTTE   Cheer up, Aggy! What is it?

AGATHA   Well, Charley, you know I lost my poor dear first husband
at a very delicate age.   335

CHARLOTTE   Well, you were five-and-thirty, dear.

AGATHA   Yes, that's what I mean. Five-and-thirty is a very delicate
age to find yourself single. You're neither one thing nor the
other. You're not exactly a two-year-old, and you don't care to
pull a hansom.° However, I soon met Mr Posket at Spa—bless   340
him!

CHARLOTTE   And you nominated yourself for the Matrimonial
Stakes. Mr Farringdon's The Widow, by Bereavement, out of
Mourning, ten pounds extra.

AGATHA   Yes, Charley, and in less than a month I went triumphantly   345
over the course. But, Charley dear, I didn't carry the fair weight
for age—and that's my trouble.

CHARLOTTE Oh, dear!

AGATHA Undervaluing Aeneas' love, in a moment of, I hope, not unjustifiable vanity, I took five years from my total, which made me thirty-one on my wedding morning. 350

CHARLOTTE Well, dear, many a misguided woman has done that before you.

AGATHA Yes, Charley, but don't you see the consequences? It has thrown everything out. As I am now thirty-one, instead of thirty-six as I ought to be, it stands to reason that I couldn't have been married twenty years ago, which I was. So I have had to fib in proportion. 355

CHARLOTTE I see—making your first marriage occur only fifteen years ago. 360

AGATHA Exactly.

CHARLOTTE Well then, dear, why worry yourself further?

AGATHA Why, dear, don't you see? If I am only thirty-one now, my boy couldn't have been born nineteen years ago, and if he could, he oughtn't to have been, because, on my own showing, I wasn't married till four years later. Now you see the result! 365

CHARLOTTE Which is, that that fine strapping young gentleman over there is only fourteen.

AGATHA Precisely. Isn't it awkward! And his moustache is becoming more and more obvious every day. 370

CHARLOTTE What does the boy himself believe?

AGATHA He believes his mother, of course, as a boy should. As a prudent woman, I always kept him in ignorance of his age—in case of necessity. But it is terribly hard on the poor child, because his aims, instincts, and ambitions are all so horribly in advance of his condition. His food, his books, his amusements are out of keeping with his palate, his brain, and his disposition; and with all this suffering—his wretched mother has the remorseful consciousness of having shortened her offspring's life. 375

CHARLOTTE Oh, come, you haven't quite done that. 380

AGATHA Yes, I have—because, if he lives to be a hundred, he must be buried at ninety-five.

CHARLOTTE That's true.

AGATHA Then, there's another aspect. He's a great favourite with all our friends—women friends especially. Even his little music mistress and the girl servants hug and kiss him because he's such an engaging boy, and I can't stop it. But it's very awful to see these innocent women fondling a young man of nineteen. 385

CHARLOTTE The women don't know it.

AGATHA But they'd like to know it. I mean they ought to know it!   390
The other day I found my poor boy sitting on Lady Jenkins's
lap, and in the presence of Sir George. I have no right to
compromise Lady Jenkins in that way. And now, Charley, you see
the whirlpool in which I am struggling—if you can throw me a
rope, pray do.   395

CHARLOTTE What sort of a man is Mr Posket, Aggy?

AGATHA The best creature in the world. He's a practical philanthropist.

CHARLOTTE Um—he's a police magistrate, too, isn't he?

AGATHA Yes, but he pays out of his own pocket half the fines he
inflicts. [*Whispering*] That's why he has had a reprimand from the   400
Home Office for inflicting such light penalties. All our servants
have graduated at Mulberry Street. [*Quite crying*] Most of the
pictures in the dining-room are genuine Constables.

CHARLOTTE Take my advice—tell him the whole story.

AGATHA I dare not!   405

CHARLOTTE Why?

AGATHA I should have to take such a back seat for the rest of my
married life. Aeneas is immaculate—in these days of the equality
of the sexes it would make our positions too cruelly uneven.°

    The party at the card-table breaks up

BULLAMY (*grumpily*) No, thank ye, not another minute. (*To Posket*)   410
What is the use of talking about revenge, my dear Posket, when I
haven't a penny piece left to play with?

POSKET I'm in the same predicament! Cis will lend us some money,
won't you, Cis?

CIS Rather!   415

BULLAMY No, thank ye, that boy is one too many for me. I've never
met such a child. Good-night, Mrs Posket. (*Treads on a nut* [*and
winces. To himself*]) Confound the nuts!

AGATHA Going so early?

CIS (*to Posket*) I hate a bad loser, don't you, Guv?   420

AGATHA Show Mr Bullamy downstairs, Cis.

BULLAMY Good-night, Posket. Oh! I haven't a shilling left for my
cabman.

CIS I'll pay the cab.

BULLAMY No, thank you! I'll walk. (*Opening jujube box*) Bah! Not   425
even a jujube left and on a foggy night, too! Ugh!

    [*He goes out, passing Wyke, who enters with four letters on a
salver*]

CIS (*to Wyke*) Any for me?

WYKE One, sir.

CIS (*to himself*) From Achille Blond; lucky the mater didn't see it.
[*He goes out after Bullamy.*] *Wyke hands letters to Agatha, who takes two, then to Posket, who takes one* [*and sits by the table and wipes his glasses*]

AGATHA This is for you, Charley—already.   430
Wyke goes out

CHARLOTTE Spare my blushes, dear—it's from Horace, Captain Vale. The dear wretch knew I was coming to you. Heigho! Will you excuse me?

POSKET Certainly.

AGATHA Excuse me, please?   435

CHARLOTTE Certainly, my dear.

POSKET [*adjusting spectacles*] Certainly, my darling. Excuse me, won't you?

CHARLOTTE Oh, certainly.

AGATHA Certainly, Aeneas.   440
Simultaneously they all open their letters, and lean back and read
(*Reading*) Lady Jenkins is not feeling very well.

CHARLOTTE [*reading*] If Captain Horace Vale stood before me at this moment, I'd slap his face!

AGATHA Charlotte!

CHARLOTTE [*reading*] 'Dear Miss Verrinder, Your desperate flirta-   445
tion with Major Bristow at the Meet on Tuesday last, three days after our engagement, has just come to my knowledge. Your letters and gifts, including the gold-headed hairpin given me at the Hunt Ball, shall be returned tomorrow. By Jove, all is over! Horace Vale.'
[*Putting her hand to her eyes*] Oh, dear!   450

AGATHA Oh, Charley, I'm so sorry! However, you can deny it.

CHARLOTTE (*weeping*) That's the worst of it, I can't.

POSKET (*to Agatha*) My darling, you will be delighted. A note from Colonel Lukyn.

AGATHA Lukyn—Lukyn? I seem to know the name.   455

POSKET An old schoolfellow of mine who went to India many years ago. He has just come home. I met him at the club last night and asked him to name an evening to dine with us. He accepts for tomorrow.

AGATHA Lukyn, Lukyn?

POSKET Listen. (*Reading*) 'It will be especially delightful to me, as I   460
believe I am an old friend of your wife and of her first husband.

15

You may recall me to her recollection by reminding her that I am
the Captain Lukyn who stood sponsor to her boy when he was
christened at Baroda.'°

AGATHA (*giving a loud scream*) Oh!   465

POSKET My dear!

AGATHA I—I've twisted my foot.

POSKET [*looking down*] How *do* nuts come into the drawing-room?

CHARLOTTE (*quietly to Agatha*) Aggy?

AGATHA (*to Charlotte*) The boy's godfather.   470

CHARLOTTE When was the child christened?

AGATHA A month after he was born. They always are.

POSKET (*reading the letter again*) This is *very* pleasant.

AGATHA (*to Posket*) Let—let me see the letter, I—I may recognise
the handwriting.   475

POSKET (*handing her the letter*) Certainly, my pet. (*To himself*)
Awakened memories of Number One. [*Sighing*] That's the worst
of marrying a widow; somebody is always proving her previous
convictions.

AGATHA (*to Charlotte*) 'No. 19A, Cork Street!' Charley, put on your   480
things and come with me.

CHARLOTTE Agatha, you're mad!

AGATHA I'm going to shut this man's mouth before he comes into
this house tomorrow.

CHARLOTTE Wait *till* he comes.   485

AGATHA Yes, till he stalks in here with his 'How d'ye do, Posket?
Haven't seen your wife since the year '66, by Gad, sir!' Not I! Aeneas!

POSKET My dear.

AGATHA Lady Jenkins—Adelaide—is very ill; she can't put her foot
to the ground with neuralgia.   490

    Takes the letter from her pocket, and gives it to him

POSKET Bless me!

AGATHA We have known each other for six long years.

POSKET Only six weeks, my love.

AGATHA Weeks *are* years in close friendship. My place is by her
side.   495

POSKET (*reading the letter*) 'Slightly indisposed, caught trifling cold
at the Dog Show. Where do you buy your handkerchiefs?' There's
nothing about neuralgia or putting her foot to the ground here, my
darling.

AGATHA No, but can't you read between the lines, Aeneas? That is   500
the letter of a woman who is not at all well.

POSKET All right, my darling, if you are bent upon going I will accompany you.

AGATHA Certainly not, Aeneas—Charlotte insists on being my companion; we can keep each other warm in a closed cab.°   505

POSKET But can't I make a third?

AGATHA Don't be so forgetful, Aeneas—don't you know that in a four-wheeled cab, the fewer knees there are the better.

   Agatha and Charlotte go out. Cis comes in hurriedly

CIS What's the matter, Guv?

POSKET Your mother and Miss Verrinder are going out.   510

CIS Out of their minds? It's a horrid night.

POSKET Yes, but Lady Jenkins is ill.

CIS Oh! Is ma mentioned in the will?

POSKET [*shocked*] Good gracious, what a boy! No, Cis, your mother is merely going to sit by Lady Jenkins' bedside, to hold her   515 hand, and to tell her where one goes to—to buy pocket handkerchiefs.

CIS [*slapping his thigh*] By Jove! [*Struck with an idea*] The mater can't be home again till half-past twelve or one o'clock.

POSKET Much later if Lady Jenkins' condition is alarming.   520

CIS Hurray! (*He takes the watch out of Posket's pocket*) Just half-past ten. Greenwich mean,° eh, Guv?

   He puts the watch to his ear, pulling Posket towards him by the chain

POSKET What an extraordinary lad!

CIS (*returning watch*) Thanks. They have to get from here to Campden Hill and back again. I'll tell Wyke to get them the worst horse   525 on the rank.

POSKET My dear child!

CIS Three-quarters of an hour's journey from here at least. Twice three-quarters, one hour and a half. An hour with Lady Jenkins— when women get together, you know, Guv, they do talk—that's   530 two hours and a half. Good. [*Struck with another idea*] Guv, will you come with me?

POSKET [*horrified*] Go with you! Where?

CIS Hôtel des Princes, Meek Street.° A sharp hansom does it in ten minutes.   535

POSKET Meek Street, Hôtel des Princes! Child, do you know what you're talking about?

CIS Rather. Look here, Guv, honour bright—no blab if I show you a letter.

POSKET I won't promise anything.   540

CIS You won't! (*Seriously*) Do you know, Guv, you are doing a very
unwise thing to check the confidence of a lad like me?

POSKET Cis, my boy!

CIS Can you calculate the inestimable benefit it is to a youngster to
have someone always at his elbow, someone older, wiser, and better   545
off than himself?

POSKET Of course, Cis, of course, I *want* you to make a companion
of me.

CIS Then how the deuce can I do that if you won't come with me to
Meek Street?   550

POSKET Yes, but deceiving your mother!

CIS *Deceiving* the mater would be to tell her a crammer°—a thing, I
hope, we're both of us much above.

POSKET Good boy, good boy.

CIS *Concealing* the fact that we're going to have a bit of supper at the 555
Hôtel des Princes is doing my mother a great kindness, because it
would upset her considerably to know of the circumstances.
You've been wrong, Guv, but we won't say anything more about
that. Read the letter.

   Gives Posket the letter

POSKET (*reading in a dazed sort of a way*) 'Hôtel des Princes, Meek   560
Street, W.° Dear Sir, Unless you drop in and settle your arrears,
I really cannot keep your room for you any longer. Yours
obediently, Achille Blond. Cecil Farringdon, Esq.' Good heavens!
You have a room at the Hôtel des Princes!

CIS A room! It's little better than a coop.   565

POSKET You don't occupy it?

CIS But my friends do. When I was at Brighton I was in with the best
set—hope I always shall be. I left Brighton—nice hole I was in. You
see, Guv, I didn't want my friends to make free with your house.

POSKET [*weakly*] Oh, didn't you?   570

CIS So I took a room at the Hôtel des Princes—when I want to put
a man up he goes there. You see, Guv, it's *you* I've been
considering more than myself.

POSKET [*beside himself*] But you are a mere child.

CIS [*taking letter*] A fellow is just as old as he feels. I feel no end of 575
a man. Hush, they're coming down! I'm off to tell Wyke about the
rickety four-wheeler.

POSKET Cis, Cis! Your mother will discover I have been out.

CIS Oh, I forgot, you're married, aren't you?

18

POSKET Married!   580
CIS Say you are going to the club.
POSKET [*energetically*] But that's not the truth, sir!
CIS Yes it is. We'll pop in at the club on our way, and you can give
    me a bitters.
        Goes out
POSKET Good gracious, what a boy! Hôtel des Princes, Meek Street!   585
    What shall I do? Tell his mother? Why, it would turn her hair
    grey. If I could only get a quiet word with this Mr Achille Blond,
    I could put a stop to everything. That is my best course, not to
    lose a moment in rescuing the child from his boyish indiscretion.
    Yes, I must go with Cis to Meek Street.   590
        Enter Agatha and Charlotte, elegantly dressed [*for out of doors*]
AGATHA Have you sent for a cab, Aeneas?
POSKET Cis is looking after that.
AGATHA Poor Cis! How late we keep him up.
        Cis comes in
CIS Wyke has gone for a cab, ma dear.
AGATHA Thank you, Cis darling.   595
CIS If you'll excuse me, I'll go to my room. I've another bad headache
    coming on.
AGATHA (*kissing him*) Run along, my boy.
CIS Good-night, ma. Good-night, Aunt Charlotte.
CHARLOTTE Good-night, Cis.   600
AGATHA (*to herself*) I wish the cab would come.
        Agatha and Charlotte look out of the window
CIS (*at the door*) Ahem! Good-night, Guv.
POSKET [*crossing to Cis*] You've told a story—two, sir! You said you
    were going up to your room.
CIS So I am—to dress.   605
POSKET You said you had a bad headache coming on.
CIS So I have, Guv. I always get a bad headache at the Hôtel des
    Princes.
        Goes out
POSKET [*to himself, weakly*] Oh, what a boy!
AGATHA (*to herself*) When will that cab come?   610
POSKET Ahem! My pet, the idea has struck me that, as you are going
    out, it would not be a bad notion for me to pop into my club.
AGATHA The club! You were there last night.
POSKET I know, my darling. Many men look in at their clubs every
    night.   615

AGATHA A nice example for Cis, truly! I particularly desire that you
  should remain at home tonight, Aeneas.

POSKET (*to himself*) Oh, dear me!

CHARLOTTE (*to Agatha*) Why not let him go to the club, Agatha?

AGATHA He might meet Colonel Lukyn there.   620

CHARLOTTE If Colonel Lukyn is there we shan't find him in Cork
  Street!

AGATHA Then we follow him to the club.

CHARLOTTE Ladies never call at a club.

AGATHA Such things have been known.   625

> *Wyke enters*

WYKE (*grinning behind his hand*) The cab is coming, ma'am.

AGATHA Coming? Why didn't you bring it with you?

WYKE I walk quicker than the cab, ma'am. It's a good horse, slow,
  but very certain.

AGATHA We will come down.   630

WYKE (*to himself*) Just what the horse has done. (*To Agatha*) Yes,
  ma'am.

> *Wyke goes out.*

AGATHA Good-night, Aeneas.

POSKET ([*rising*] *nervously*) I wish you would allow me to go to the
  club, my pet.   635

AGATHA Aeneas, I am surprised at your obstinacy. It is so very
  different from my first husband.

POSKET Really, Agatha, I am shocked. I presume the late Mr
  Farringdon occasionally used his clubs?

AGATHA Indian clubs. Indian clubs are good for the liver, London   640
  clubs° are not. Good-night!

POSKET I'll see you to your cab, Agatha.

AGATHA No, thank you.

POSKET Upon my word!

CHARLOTTE (*to Agatha*) Why not?   645

AGATHA He would want to give the direction to the cabman!

CHARLOTTE [*to herself*] The first tiff. (*To Posket*) Good-night, Mr
  Posket.

POSKET [*shortly*] Good-night, Miss Verrinder.

AGATHA (*to Posket*) Have you any message for Lady Jenkins?   650

POSKET Confound Lady Jenkins.

AGATHA I will deliver your message in the presence of Sir George,
  who, I may remind you, is the permanent Secretary at the Home
  Office.

Agatha and Charlotte go out; Posket paces up and down excitedly

POSKET Gurrh! I'm not to go to the club! I set a bad example to Cis! 655
Ha! ha! I am different from her first husband. Yes, I am—I'm alive
for one thing. I—I—I—I—I'm dashed if I don't go out with the
boy.

CIS (*putting his head in at the door*) Coast clear, Guv? All right.
*Enter Cis, in fashionable evening dress, carrying Posket's over-
coat and hat*

CIS Here are your hat and overcoat. 660

POSKET [*recoiling*] Where on earth did you get that dress suit?

CIS Mum's the word, Guv. Brighton tailor—six months' credit. He
promised to send in the bill to you, so the mater won't know.
(*Putting Posket's hat on his head*) By Jove, Guv, don't my togs°
show you up? 665

POSKET I won't go, I won't go. I've never met such a boy before.

CIS (*proceeds to help him with his overcoat*) Mind your arm, Guv.
You've got your hand in a pocket. No, no—that's a tear in the
lining. That's it.

POSKET I forbid you to go out! 670

CIS Yes, Guv. And I forbid you to eat any of those devilled oysters
we shall get at the Hôtel des Princes. [*Pats him on the back*] Now
you're right!

POSKET I am not right!

CIS Oh, I forgot! (*He pulls out a handful of loose money*) I found this 675
money in your desk, Guv. You had better take it out with you;
you may want it. Here you are—gold, silver, and coppers. (*He
empties the money into Posket's overcoat pocket*) One last precaution,
and then we're off.
Goes to the writing-table, and writes on a half-sheet of notepaper

POSKET I shall take a turn round the Square, and then come home 680
again! I will not be influenced by a mere child! A man of my
responsible position—a magistrate—supping slyly at the Hôtel des
Princes, in Meek Street—it's horrible.

CIS Now, then—we'll creep downstairs quietly so as not to bring
Wyke from his pantry. (*Giving Posket the paper*) You stick that up 685
prominently, while I blow out the candles.
Cis blows out the candles on the piano

POSKET (*reading*) 'Your master and Mr Cecil Farringdon are going
to bed. Don't disturb them.' I will not be a partner to any written
document. This is untrue.

CIS No, it isn't—we are going to bed when we come home. Make   690
    haste, Guv.

POSKET (*pinning the paper on to the curtain*) Oh, what a boy.

CIS (*turning down the lamp, and watching Posket*) Hallo, Guv! hallo!
    You're an old hand at this sort of game, are you?

POSKET How dare you!   695

CIS (*taking Posket's arm*) Now, then, don't breathe.

POSKET (*quite demoralised*) Cis! Cis! Wait a minute—wait a minute!

CIS Hold up, Guv.
       Wyke enters
    [*To himself*] Oh, bother!

WYKE (*to Posket*) Going out, sir?   700

POSKET (*struggling to be articulate*) No—yes—that is—partially—half
    round the Square, and possibly—er—um—back again. (*To Cis*)
    Oh, you bad boy!

WYKE (*coolly going up to the paper on curtains*) Shall I take this down
    now, sir?   705

POSKET (*quietly to Cis*) I'm in an awful position! What am I to do?

CIS Do as I do—tip him.

POSKET What!

CIS Tip him.

POSKET Oh, yes—yes. Where's my money?   710
       Cis takes two coins out of Posket's pocket and gives them to him
       without looking at them

CIS (*to Posket*) Give him that.

POSKET Yes.

CIS And say—'Wyke, you want a new umbrella—buy a very good
    one. Your mistress has a latchkey, so go to bed.'

POSKET Wyke!   715

WYKE Yes, sir.

POSKET (*giving him money*) Go to bed—buy a very good one. Your
    mistress has a latchkey—so—so you want a new umbrella!

WYKE [*knowingly*] All right, sir. You can depend on me. Are you well
    muffled up, sir? Mind you take care of him, Master Cis.   720

CIS (*supporting Posket; Posket groaning softly*) [*Wyke laughing slyly*]
    Capital, Guv, capital. Are you hungry?

POSKET Hungry! You're a wicked boy. I've told a falsehood.

CIS No, you haven't, Guv—he really does want a new umbrella.

POSKET Does he, Cis? Does he? Thank heaven!   725
       They go out

WYKE (*looking at money*) Here! What, twopence! (*Throws the coins down in disgust*) I'll tell the missus.

CURTAIN

Act Two

IT LEAVES ITS CUPBOARD

Scene One

The scene is a supper-room° at the Hôtel des Princes, Meek Street, with two doors—the one leading into an adjoining room, the other into a passage—and a window opening on to a balcony. The room is rather gaudy, with plenty of white and gold etc., decorated in light colours, with mirrors in handsome frames on the right wall. At the back, on the left, is a door with a high-backed sofa covered in crimson velvet drawn across it. Down stage right is a table laid for supper, with two lighted candles.

Isidore, a French waiter, is showing in Cis and Posket, [the latter still very nervous and reluctant]

CIS Come on, Guv—come on. How are you, Isidore?

ISIDORE I beg your pardon—I am quite well, and so are you, zank you.

CIS I want a pretty little light supper for myself and my friend, Mr Skinner.

ISIDORE Mr Skinner.   5

POSKET ([*aside*] *to Cis*) Skinner! Is someone else coming?

CIS No, no. You're Skinner.

POSKET [*resigned*] Oh!

Wanders round the room

CIS Mr Skinner, of the Stock Exchange. What have you ready?

ISIDORE (*in an undertone to Cis*) I beg your pardon—very good—but   10
Monsieur Blond he say to me, 'Isidore, listen now; if Mr Farringdon he come here, you say, I beg your pardon, you are a nice gentleman, but will you pay your little account when it is quite convenient, before you leave the house at once.'

CIS Quite so, there's no difficulty about that. What's the bill?   15

ISIDORE (*gives the bill*) I beg your pardon. Eight pounds four shillings.

CIS Phew! Here go my winnings from old Bullamy and the Guv. (*Counting out money*) Two pounds short. (*Turning to Posket, who is carefully examining the scratches on the mirrors*) Skinner! [*No answer*] Skinner!   20

POSKET° Visitors evidently scratch their names on the mirrors. Dear me! Surely this is a spurious title—'Lottie, Duchess of Fulham'! How very curious!

CIS Skinner, got any money with you?

POSKET [*coming to Cis*] Yes, Cis, my boy.

    Feels for his money

CIS [*pointing*] You always keep it in that pocket, Skinner.

POSKET (*taking out money*) Oh, yes.

    Cis takes two sovereigns from Posket and gives the amount of his
    bill to Isidore, who goes to the sideboard to count out change

CIS No putting the change to bed, Isidore.

POSKET What's that?

CIS Putting the change to bed! Isidore will show you. (*To Isidore, who
comes to them with the change and the bill on a plate*) Isidore, show
Mr Skinner how you put silver to bed.

ISIDORE Oh, Mr Farringdon, I beg your pardon—no, no!

POSKET It would be most instructive.

ISIDORE [*shrugging his shoulders*] Very good. (*Goes to the table, upon
which he puts plate*) Say I have to give you change sixteen shillings.

POSKET Certainly.

ISIDORE Very good. Before I bring it to you I slip a little half-crown°
under the bill—so. [*Posket interested, with his glasses on*] Then I put
what is left on the top of the bill, and I say, 'I beg your pardon,
your change.' You take it, you give me two shillings for myself,
and all is right.

POSKET (*counting the silver on the bill with the end of his glasses*) Yes,
but suppose I count the silver, it is half a crown short!

ISIDORE Then I say, 'I beg your pardon, how dare you say that?'
Then I do so. (*He pulls the bill from the plate*) Then I say, 'The bill
is eight pounds four shillings. (*Handing the plate*) Count again.'

POSKET [*knowingly*] Ah, of course, it's all right now.

ISIDORE Very good, then you give me five shillings for doubting me.
Do it, do it.

POSKET (*in a daze, giving him the five shillings*) Like this?

ISIDORE Yes, like that. (*Slipping the money into his pocket*) I beg your
pardon—thank you. (*Handing Cis the rest of the change*) Your
change, Mr Farringdon.

CIS Oh, I say, Isidore!

    Blond, a fat, middle-aged French hotel-keeper, enters with a
    letter in his hand

ISIDORE Monsieur Blond.

BLOND [*speaking with a slight French accent*] Good evening,
Mr Farringdon.

ISIDORE (*quietly to Blond*) Ze bill is all right.

CIS Good evening. (*Introducing Posket*) My friend, Mr Harvey   60
Skinner, of the Stock Exchange.

BLOND Very pleased to see you. (*To Cis*) Are you going to enjoy
yourselves?

CIS Rather.

[*Proceeds to take off his overcoat, assisted by Isidore*]

BLOND You usually eat in this room, but you don't mind giving it   65
up for tonight—now, do you?

CIS Oh, Achille!

BLOND Come, come, to please me. A cab has just brought a letter
from an old customer of mine, a gentleman I haven't seen for over
twenty years, who wants to sup with a friend in this room tonight.   70
It's quite true.

Gives Cis a letter, [*then assists Posket to get rid of his overcoat*]

CIS (*reading to himself*) '19A, Cork Street. Dear Blond, Fresh, or
rather, stale from India—want to sup with my friend, Captain
Vale, tonight, at my old table in my old room. Must do this for
Auld Lang Syne.° Yours, Alexander Lukyn.' (*To Blond*) Oh, let   75
him have it. [*Returns letter*] Where will you put us?

BLOND You shall have the best room in the house, the one next to
this. This room—pah! Come with me. (*To Posket*) Have you
known Mr Farringdon for a long time?

POSKET No, no. Not very long.   80

BLOND Ah, he is a fine fellow—Mr Farringdon. Now, if you please.
You can go through this door.

Wheels sofa away [*from before door and unlocks it*]

CIS (*to Posket*) You'll look better after a glass or two of Pommery,
Guv.

POSKET No, no, Cis—now, no champagne.   85

CIS No champagne, not for my friend, Harvey Skinner! Come,
Guv—dig me in the ribs—like this. (*Digging him in the ribs*) Chuck!

POSKET (*shrinking*) Oh, don't!

CIS And say, 'Hey!' [*Gives a boisterous cry, then shakes Posket*] Go on,
Guv.   90

POSKET I can't—I can't. I don't know what it may mean.

CIS (*digging him in the ribs again*) Go on—ch-uck!

POSKET What, like this? (*Returning the dig*) Ch-uck.

CIS [*delighted*] That's it, that's it. Ha, ha! You are going it, Guv.

POSKET [*getting excited*] Am I, Cis? Am I? (*Waving his arm*) Hey!   95

CIS and POSKET Hey!

CIS Ha, ha! Come on! Serve the supper, Achille.

BLOND Ah! he is a grand fellow, Mr Farringdon.
        Cis and Posket go into the other room
   (*To Isidore*) Replace the *canapé.*°
        *There is a sharp knock at the other door. Blond follows Cis and
        Posket into the other room, then locks the door on the inside*
ISIDORE Come in, please.   100
        *Colonel Lukyn and Captain Vale enter the room. Lukyn is
        [about fifty-five] a portly, grey-haired, good-looking military
        man; Vale is [not more than thirty] pale-faced and heavy-eyed,
        while his manner is languid and dejected*
LUKYN This is the room. Come in, Vale. This is my old supper-
   room—I haven't set foot here for over twenty years. By George, I
   hope to sup here for another twenty.
VALE (*dejectedly*) Do you? In less than that, unless I am lucky enough
   to fall in some foreign set-to, I shall be in Kensal Green.°   105
LUKYN (*looking round the room sentimentally*) Twenty years ago!
   Confound 'em, they've painted it.
VALE My people have eight shelves in the catacombs at Kensal
   Green.
LUKYN Nonsense, man, nonsense. You're a little low. Waiter, take   110
   our coats.
        [*Isidore removes Lukyn's coat*]
VALE Don't check me, Lukyn. My shelf is four from the bottom.
LUKYN You'll forget the number of your shelf before you're halfway
   through your oysters.
VALE (*shaking his head*) An oyster merely reminds me of my own   115
   particular shell.
        [*Isidore begins to remove Vale's coat*]
LUKYN Ha, ha! Ha, ha!
VALE Don't, Lukyn, don't. (*In an undertone to Lukyn*) It's very good
   of you, but, by Jove, my heart is broken. (*To Isidore*) Mind my
   flower, waiter, confound you.   120
        He adjusts flower in his buttonhole. [*Isidore hangs coat and hats
        on pegs, up stage right*]
ISIDORE You have ordered supper, sir?
LUKYN Yes, on the back of my note to Mr Blond. Serve it at once.
ISIDORE I beg your pardon, sir, at once.
        He goes out. [*Vale sits by the table and leans his head upon his
        hand*]
LUKYN [*produces cigarette case*] So, you've been badly treated by a
   woman, eh, Vale?   125

VALE Shockingly. Between man and man, a Miss Verrinder—Charlotte. (*Turning away*) Excuse me, Lukyn.

> *Produces a folded silk handkerchief, shakes it out, and gently blows his nose*

LUKYN (*lighting a cigarette* [*from a candle on the table*]) Certainly—certainly—does you great credit. Pretty woman?

VALE Oh, lovely! A most magnificent set of teeth. All real, as far as   130
I can ascertain.

LUKYN No!

VALE Fact.

LUKYN Great loss—have a cigarette.

VALE (*taking case from Lukyn*) Parascho's?°   135

LUKYN Yes. Was she—full grown?

VALE (*lighting his cigarette*) Just perfection. She rides eight stone fifteen, and I have lost her, Lukyn. Beautiful tobacco.

LUKYN What finished it?

VALE She gave a man a pair of worked slippers three days after our   140
engagement.

LUKYN No!

VALE Fact. You remember Bristow—Gordon Bristow?

LUKYN Perfectly. Best fellow in the world.

VALE He wears them.   145

LUKYN Villain! Will you begin with a light wine, or go right on to the champagne?

VALE By Jove, it's broken my heart, old fellow. I'll go right on to the champagne, please. Lukyn, I shall make you my executor.

LUKYN [*sitting at the head of the table*] Pooh! You'll outlive me! Why   150
don't they bring the supper? My heart has been broken like yours.
It was broken first in Ireland in '55. It was broken again in London
in '61, but in 1870 it was smashed in Calcutta, by a married lady
that time.

VALE A married lady?   155

LUKYN Yes, my late wife. Talk about broken hearts, my boy, when you've won your lady, not when you've lost her.

> [*Enter Isidore with a large tray on which are two covered dishes, plates, a dish of lemons, bottles of champagne etc., which he places on the sideboard*]

[*Heartily*] The supper. (*To Vale*) Hungry?

VALE (*mournfully*) Very.

> *Enter Blond, with an envelope*

BLOND Colonel Lukyn.   160

LUKYN Ah, Blond, how are you? Not a day older. What have you
    got there?

BLOND (*quietly to Lukyn in an undertone*) Two ladies, Colonel,
    downstairs in a cab, must see you for a few minutes alone.

LUKYN Good gracious! Excuse me, Vale. (*Takes the envelope from*   165
    Blond, and opens it: reading the enclosed card [through a single glass])
    Mrs Posket—Mrs Posket! 'Mrs Posket entreats Colonel Lukyn to
    see her for five minutes upon a matter of urgent necessity, and free
    from observation.' By George! Posket must be ill in bed—I
    thought he looked seedy last night. (*To Blond*) Of course—of   170
    course. Say I'll come down.

BLOND It is raining outside. I had better ask them up.

LUKYN Do—do. I'll get Captain Vale to step into another room. Be
    quick. Say I am quite alone.

BLOND Yes, Colonel.   175
    Hurries out

CIS (*in the next room, rattling glasses and calling*) Waiter! Waiter!
    Waiter—r—r! Where the deuce are you?

ISIDORE Coming, sir, coming. I beg your pardon.
    Bustles out

LUKYN My dear Vale, I am dreadfully sorry to bother you. Two
    ladies, one the wife of a very old friend of mine, have followed me   180
    here and want half a dozen words with me alone. I am in your
    hands—how can I manage it?

VALE [*rising*] My dear fellow, don't mention it. Let me go into
    another room.

LUKYN Thank you, very much. You're so hungry too. Where's the   185
    waiter? Confound him, he's gone!

VALE All right. I'll pop in here.
    He passes behind sofa and tries the door leading into the other
    room

CIS (*within*) What do you want? Who's there?

VALE Occupied—never mind—I'll find my way somewhere.
    There is a knock; Vale draws back

BLOND (*without*) Colonel, are you alone? The ladies.   190

LUKYN One moment. [*In an undertone*] Deuce take it, Vale! The
    ladies don't want to be seen. By George—I remember. There's a
    little balcony to that window, step out for a few moments—keep
    quiet—I shan't detain you—it's nothing important—husband must
    have had a fit or something.   195

VALE Oh, certainly!

LUKYN Good fellow—here's your hat.
>   *In his haste he fetches his own hat [from pegs]*
BLOND (*outside, knocking*) Colonel, Colonel!
LUKYN One moment. (*Giving his hat to Vale*) Awfully sorry. You're
so hungry too. (*Vale puts on the hat, which, being too large for him,*   200
falls over his face) Ah, that's my hat.
VALE (*opening the window and going out*) My dear Lukyn—don't
mention it.
LUKYN (*drawing the curtain over the recess*) Just room for him to stand
like a man in a sentry-box. Come in, Blond.   205
>   *Blond shows in Agatha and Charlotte, both wearing veils*
AGATHA (*agitated*) Oh, Colonel Lukyn!
LUKYN Pray compose yourself, pray compose yourself!
AGATHA What will you think?
LUKYN [*holding out his hand, gallantly*] That I am perfectly en-
chanted.   210
AGATHA [*taking his hand*] Thank you. (*Pointing to Charlotte*) My
sister.
>   *Lukyn and Charlotte bow*
LUKYN Be seated. Blond? (*Softly to him*) Keep the waiter out till I
ring—that's all.
>   *The loud pattering of rain is heard*
BLOND Yes, Colonel.   215
LUKYN Good gracious, Blond! What's that?
BLOND The rain outside. It is cats and dogs.
LUKYN (*horrified*) By George, is it? (*To himself, looking towards
window*) Poor devil! (*To Blond*) There isn't any method of getting
off that balcony, is there?   220
BLOND No—unless by getting on to it.
LUKYN What do you mean?
BLOND It is not at all safe. Don't use it.
>   *Lukyn stands horror-stricken; Blond goes out. Heavy rain is*
>   *heard*
LUKYN (*after some nervous glances at the window, wiping perspiration*
from his forehead) I am honoured, Mrs Posket, by this visit—   225
though for the moment I can't imagine—
AGATHA [*coming to him and raising her veil*] Colonel Lukyn, we drove
to Cork Street to your lodgings, and there your servant told us you
were supping at the Hôtel des Princes, with a friend. No one will
be shown into this room while we are here?   230
LUKYN [*breathing heavily*] No—we—ah—shall not be disturbed. (*To*
himself) Good heavens, suppose I never see him alive again!

[*He arranges a chair for her beside the table. She sits*]

AGATHA (*sighing wearily*) Ah!

LUKYN I'm afraid you've come to tell me Posket is ill.

AGATHA [*surprised*] I—no—my husband is at home.   235

  A sharp gust of wind is heard with the rain

LUKYN [*starts*] Lord forgive me! I've killed him.

AGATHA (*with horror*) Colonel Lukyn!

LUKYN [*confused*] Madam!

AGATHA Indeed Mr Posket is at home.

LUKYN (*glancing at the window*) Is he? I wish we all were.   240

AGATHA (*to herself*) Sunstroke evidently. Poor fellow! (*To Lukyn* [*sweetly*]), I assure you my husband is at home, quite well, and by this time sleeping soundly.

  Cis and Posket are heard laughing in the next room

ISIDORE (*within*) You are two funny gentlemen, I beg your pardon.

AGATHA (*startled*) What is that?   245

LUKYN In the next room. (*Raps at the door*) Hush—hush, hush!

CHARLOTTE Get it over, Aggy, and let us go home. I am so awfully hungry.

LUKYN (*peering through the curtains*) It is still bearing him. What's his weight? Surely he can't scale over ten stone. Lord, how wet he   250 is!

AGATHA Colonel Lukyn!

LUKYN (*leaving the window sharply*) Madam, command me!

  [*He sits by Agatha*]

AGATHA Colonel Lukyn, we knew each other at Baroda twenty years ago.   255

LUKYN When I look at you, impossible.

AGATHA Ah, then you mustn't look at me.

LUKYN [*with natural gallantry*] Equally impossible.

CHARLOTTE (*to herself*) Oh, I feel quite out of this.

AGATHA You were at my little boy's christening?   260

LUKYN (*absently*) Yes—yes—certainly.

AGATHA You remember what a fine little fellow he was.

LUKYN (*thoughtfully*) Not a pound over ten stone.

AGATHA Colonel Lukyn!

LUKYN I beg your pardon, yes—I was at the christening of your boy.   265

AGATHA (*to herself*) One of the worst cases of sunstroke I have ever known.

LUKYN I remember the child very well. Has he still got that absurd mug?°

AGATHA Colonel Lukyn!   270

LUKYN Madam!

AGATHA My child is, and always was—perfect.

LUKYN You misunderstand me! I was his godfather; I gave him a
silver cup.

AGATHA Oh, do excuse me. [*Wiping her eyes*] How did I become   275
acquainted with such a vulgar expression? I don't know where I
pick up my slang. It must be through loitering at shop windows.
Oh, oh, oh!

LUKYN Pray compose yourself. I'll leave you for a moment.
          Goes to the window

AGATHA (*to Charlotte*) How shall I begin, Charley?   280

CHARLOTTE Make a bold plunge, do! The odour of cooking here, to
a hungry woman, is maddening.
          [*She rises and goes to the mirrors on the right, and at the same
          time*] *Vale softly opens the window and comes into the recess, but
          remains concealed by the curtain*

VALE (*to himself*) This is too bad of Lukyn! I'm wet to the skin and
frightfully hungry! Who the deuce are these women?

AGATHA Colonel Lukyn!   285

LUKYN Madam. (*Listening*) No crash yet.

AGATHA (*impulsively laying her hand upon his arm*) Friend of twenty
years! I will be quite candid with you. You are going to dine with
us, tomorrow?

LUKYN Madam, I will repay your candour as it deserves. I am.   290

AGATHA My husband knows of your acquaintance with the circumstances of my first marriage. I know what men are. When the
women leave the dinner table, men become retrospective. Now,
tomorrow night, over dessert, I beg you not to give my husband
dates.   295

LUKYN [*astounded*] Eh?

AGATHA Keep anything like dates from him.

LUKYN [*puzzled*] Mustn't eat stone fruit?

AGATHA No, I mean years, months, days—dates connected with my
marriage with Mr Farringdon.   300

LUKYN Dear me, sore subject!

AGATHA I will be more than candid with you. My present husband,
having a very short vacation in the discharge of his public duties,
wooed me but for three weeks; you, who have in your time courted
and married, know the material of which that happy period is made   305
up. The future is all-engrossing to the man; the presents—I mean

32

the present, a joyous dream to the woman. But in dealing with my past I met with more than ordinary difficulties.

LUKYN Don't see why—late husband died a natural death—wasn't stood on a balcony or anything.

AGATHA Colonel Lukyn, you know I was six-and-thirty at the time of my recent marriage!

LUKYN You surprise me!

AGATHA You know it! Be frank, Lukyn! Am I not six-and-thirty?

LUKYN [*bowing quickly*] You are.

AGATHA Very well, then. In a three weeks' engagement how was it possible for me to deal with the various episodes of six-and-thirty years? The past may be pleasant, golden, beautiful—but one may have too much of a good thing.

LUKYN (*to himself*) I am in that position now.

AGATHA The man who was courting me was seeking relaxation from the discharge of multifarious responsibilities. How could I tax an already wearied attention with the recital of the events of thirty-six years?

LUKYN What did you do?

AGATHA Out of consideration for the man I loved, I sacrificed five years of happy girlhood—told him I was but one-and-thirty—that I had been married only fifteen years previously—that my boy was but fourteen!

LUKYN By George, madam, and am I to subscribe to all this?

AGATHA I only ask you to avoid the question of dates.

LUKYN But, at a man's dinner table—

AGATHA You need not spoil a man's dinner. Not only a man's—but a woman's! Lukyn, Lukyn! Promise!

LUKYN Give me a second to think.

> Lukyn, turning away, discovers Charlotte [*who has wandered round the scene to the sideboard*] *in the act of lifting the covers from the dishes and inspecting the contents*

Ah, devilled oysters!

CHARLOTTE Oh!

> Drops dish-cover with a crash, and runs over to the table and speaks to Agatha

LUKYN Don't go—pray look at 'em again—wish I could persuade you to taste them. [*To himself*] What am I to do? Shall I promise? Poor Posket! If I don't promise she'll cry and won't go home. The oysters are nearly cold—cold! What must *he* be! (*Drawing aside the curtain, and not seeing Vale, he staggers back*) Gone—and without a cry—brave fellow, brave fellow!

AGATHA Colonel Lukyn.

LUKYN [*to himself*] Decay of stamina in the army—pah! The young   345
'uns are worthy of our best days.

AGATHA Colonel Lukyn, will you promise?

LUKYN Promise? Anything, my dear madam, anything.

AGATHA Ah, thank you! May I ask you to see us to our cab?

LUKYN Certainly! [*To himself*] Thank heaven, they're going!   350

AGATHA (*to Charlotte*) It's all right; come along!

CHARLOTTE (*to Agatha*) Oh, those oysters look so nice.

LUKYN (*to himself*) Stop! In my trouble, I am forgetting even the commonest courtesies to these ladies. (*To Agatha*) You have a long journey before you. I am sure your husband would not forgive me   355
for letting you face such weather unprepared. Let me recommend an oyster or two and a thimbleful of champagne.

AGATHA No, thank you, Colonel Lukyn.

CHARLOTTE (*to Agatha*) Say yes. I'm starving.

LUKYN As you please. (*To himself*) I knew they'd refuse. I've done   360
my duty.

CHARLOTTE (*To Agatha*) I was in the train till seven o'clock. Wait till you're a bona fide traveller°—accept.

AGATHA Ahem! Colonel, the fact is my poor sister has been travelling all day and is a little exhausted.   365

LUKYN (*horrified*) You don't mean to say you're going to give me the inestimable pleasure. (*Charlotte looks across at him, nodding and smiling*) I am delighted.

> *Charlotte sits hungrily at table; Lukyn fetches a bottle of champagne from the sideboard*

AGATHA (*to Charlotte*) Charlotte, I am surprised.

CHARLOTTE (*to Agatha*) Nonsense, the best people come here. Some   370
of them have left their names on the mirrors.

VALE (*behind the curtain*) This is much too bad of Lukyn. What are they doing now? (*Lukyn draws the cork*) Confound it, they're having my supper!

> *Lukyn passes round champagne*

CHARLOTTE Why doesn't he give me something to eat?   375

> *There is a clatter of knives and forks heard from the other room, then a burst of laughter from Cis [and a few words of song]*

AGATHA (*starting*) Charley, hark! How strange!

CHARLOTTE Very. This bread is beautiful.

> *Cis is heard singing the chorus of a comic song boisterously*

AGATHA Don't you recognise that voice?

CHARLOTTE (*munching*) The only voice I recognise is the voice of hunger.   380

AGATHA I am overwrought, I suppose.

> *Lukyn, with his head drooping, fetches the dish of oysters from the sideboard*

VALE (*behind the curtains*) He has taken the oysters. I've seen him do it.

LUKYN The oysters.

> *Lukyn sinks into his chair at the table and leans his head upon his hand; the two women look at each other*

CHARLOTTE (*to Agatha*) Anything wrong?   385

AGATHA Sunstroke—bad case!

CHARLOTTE Oh—poor fellow. (*She gently lifts the corner of the dish, sniffs, then replaces cover*) No plates.

AGATHA Ask for them.

CHARLOTTE You ask.   390

AGATHA You're hungry.

CHARLOTTE You're married. Comes better from you.

VALE (*behind curtains*) This silence is terrible.

AGATHA (*to Lukyn*) Ahem! Ahem!

LUKYN (*looking up suddenly*) Eh?   395

AGATHA There are no plates.

LUKYN No plates? No plates? It's my fault. Pardon me. Where are the plates?

> *Vale, still invisible, stretches out his hand through the curtain, takes up the plates and presents them to Lukyn, who recoils*

VALE (*in a whisper*) Here are the plates. Look sharp, Lukyn.

LUKYN Vale! Safe and sound! (*He takes the plates, then grasps Vale's extended hand*) Bless you, old fellow. I'm myself again. (*Going gaily to the table with the plates*) My dear ladies, I blush—I positively blush—I am the worst host in the world.   400

VALE (*to himself*) By Jove, that's true.

AGATHA Not at all—not at all.   405

LUKYN (*helping the ladies*) I'll make amends, by George! You may have noticed I've been confoundedly out of sorts. That's my temperament—now up, now down. I've just taken a turn, ha, ha! (*Handing plate to Agatha*) Oysters.

AGATHA Thank you.   410

35

LUKYN Ah! I've passed many a happy hour in this room. The present is not the least happy.

CHARLOTTE (*trying to attract his attention*) Ahem! Ahem!

LUKYN (*gazing up at the ceiling*) My first visit to the Hôtel des Princes was in the year—the year—let me think.   415

CHARLOTTE (*whispering to Agatha*) Isn't he going to help me?

LUKYN Was it in '55?

AGATHA (*quickly passing her plate over to Charlotte*) I'm not hungry.

CHARLOTTE You're a dear.

LUKYN (*emphatically*) It *was* in '55. I'm forgetful again—pardon me.   420
(*He hands plate of oysters to Charlotte, and is surprised to find her eating vigorously*) Why, I thought I—(*To Agatha*) My dear madam, a thousand apologies. (*He helps her and then himself*) Pah! they're cold—icy—you could skate on 'em. There's a dish of something else over there.   425

>   He goes to the sideboard; Vale's hand is again stretched forth
>   with the other covered dish

VALE I say, Lukyn.

LUKYN (*taking the dish*) Thanks, old fellow. (*He returns to the table and lifts the cover*) Soles—they look tempting. If there are only some lemons! Surely they are not so brutal as to have forgotten the lemons. Where are they? (*He returns to the sideboard*) Where are   430
they? (*In an undertone to Vale*) Have you seen any lemons?

AGATHA Pray, think less of us, Colonel Lukyn. Let me take care of you.

LUKYN You're very kind. I wish you would let me ring for some lemons.   435

>   Vale's hand comes as before from behind the curtain to the
>   sideboard, finds the dish of lemons, and holds it out at arm's
>   length

VALE (*in a whisper*) Lemons.

>   Agatha is helping Lukyn, when suddenly Charlotte, with her
>   fork in the air, leans back open-mouthed, staring wildly at Vale's
>   arm extended with the dish

CHARLOTTE (*in terror*) Agatha! Agatha!

AGATHA Charlotte! What's the matter, Charley?

CHARLOTTE Agatha!

AGATHA You're ill, Charlotte! Surely you are not choking?   440

CHARLOTTE (*pointing to the curtains*) Look, look!

>   They both scream

LUKYN Don't be alarmed—I—

CHARLOTTE What's that? ⎱
AGATHA Who's that? ⎰ (*Together*)

LUKYN I can explain. Don't condemn till you've heard. I—I—Damn   445
it, sir, put those lemons down!

CHARLOTTE He calls him 'Sir'—it must be a man.

LUKYN It is a man. I am not in a position to deny that.

AGATHA Really, Colonel Lukyn!

LUKYN It is my friend. He—he—he's merely waiting for his supper.   450

AGATHA Your friend. (*To Charlotte*) Come home, dear.

LUKYN Do, do hear me! To avoid the embarrassment of your
encountering a stranger, he retreated to the balcony.

AGATHA To the balcony? You have shamefully compromised two
trusting women, Colonel Lukyn.   455

LUKYN I would have laid down my life rather than have done so. I
did lay down my friend's life.

AGATHA He has overheard every confidential word I have spoken to
you.

LUKYN Hear his explanation. [*To the curtain*] Why the devil don't   460
you corroborate me, sir?

VALE (*from behind the curtain*) Certainly, I assure you I heard next to
nothing.

CHARLOTTE (*grasping Agatha's arm*) Oh, Agatha!

VALE I didn't come in till I was exceedingly wet.   465

LUKYN (*to Agatha*) You hear that?

VALE And when I did come in—

CHARLOTTE (*hysterically*) Horace!

VALE I beg your pardon.

CHARLOTTE It's Horace, Captain Vale.   470

VALE (*coming from behind the curtain, looking terribly wet*) Charlotte—
Miss Verrinder.

CHARLOTTE What are you doing here? What a fright you look.

VALE What am I doing here, Miss Verrinder? Really, Lukyn, your
conduct calls for some little explanation.   475

LUKYN My conduct, sir?

VALE You make some paltry excuse to turn me out in the rain while
you entertain a lady who you know has very recently broken my
heart.

LUKYN I didn't know anything of the kind.   480

VALE I told you, Colonel Lukyn—this isn't the conduct of an officer
and a gentleman.

LUKYN Whose isn't, yours or mine?

VALE Mine. I mean yours.

LUKYN You are in the presence of ladies, sir; take off my hat.   485

VALE I beg your pardon. I didn't know I had it on.

   He throws the hat away, and the two men exchange angry words

CHARLOTTE He's a very good-looking fellow; you don't see a man at
   his best when he's wet through.

AGATHA (*to Lukyn*) Colonel Lukyn, do you ever intend to send for
   a cab?   490

LUKYN Certainly, madam.

VALE One moment. I have some personal explanation to exchange
   with Miss Verrinder.

CHARLOTTE (*to Agatha*) The slippers. (*To Vale*) I am quite ready,
   Captain Vale.   495

VALE Thank you. Colonel Lukyn, will you oblige me by stepping out
   on to that balcony?

LUKYN Certainly not, sir.

VALE You're afraid of the wet, Colonel Lukyn; you are no soldier.

LUKYN You know better, sir. As a matter of fact, that balcony can't   500
   bear a man like me.

VALE Which shows that inanimate objects have a great deal of
   common sense, sir.

LUKYN You don't prove it in your own instance, Captain Vale.

VALE That's a verbal quibble, sir.   505

   They talk angrily.

AGATHA (*to Charlotte*) It's frightfully late. Tell him to write to you.

CHARLOTTE I must speak to him tonight; life is too short for letters.

AGATHA Then he can telegraph.

CHARLOTTE Halfpenny a word and he has nothing but his pay.

AGATHA Very well, then, Lady Jenkins has a telephone. I'll take you   510
   there to tea tomorrow. If he loves you, tell him to ring up 1338091.

CHARLOTTE You thoughtful angel!

LUKYN Mrs Posket—Miss Verrinder—ahem—we—

VALE Colonel Lukyn and myself—

LUKYN Captain Vale and I fear that we have been betrayed, in a   515
   moment of—

VALE Natural irritation.

LUKYN Natural irritation, into the atrocious impropriety of
   differing—

VALE Before ladies.   520

LUKYN Charming ladies—

VALE We beg your pardon—Lukyn!

38

LUKYN Vale. (*They grasp hands*) Mrs Posket, I am now going out to
  hail a cab.

AGATHA Pray do.   525

LUKYN Miss Verrinder, the process will occupy five minutes.

VALE (*giving his hat to Lukyn*) Lukyn, I return your kindness—
  my hat.

LUKYN Thank you, my boy.
        Lukyn puts on Vale's hat, which is much too small for him. As
        he is going out, there is a knock at the door; he opens it: Blond
        is outside

BLOND Colonel, it is ten minutes past the time of closing, may I ask 530
  you to dismiss your party?

LUKYN Pooh! Isn't this a free country?
        He goes out

BLOND (*following him out*) Yes, you are free to go home, Colonel. I
  shall get into trouble.

CHARLOTTE (*to Agatha*) I'll have the first word. Really, Captain 535
  Vale, I'm surprised at you.

VALE There was a happy time, Miss Verrinder, when I might have
  been surprised at you.

CHARLOTTE A few hours ago it was—'By Jove, all is over.' Now I
  find you with a bosom friend enjoying devilled oysters.   540

VALE I beg your pardon, I find you enjoying devilled oysters.

CHARLOTTE Horace Vale, you forget you have forfeited the right to
  exercise any control over my diet.

VALE One would think I had broken off our engagement.

CHARLOTTE If you have not, who has? I have your letter saying all 545
  is over between us. (*Putting her handkerchief to her eyes*) That letter
  will be stamped tomorrow at Somerset House.° I know how to
  protect myself.

VALE Charlotte, can you explain your conduct with Gordon
  Bristow?   550

CHARLOTTE I could if I chose; a young lady can explain anything.

VALE But he is showing your gift to our fellows all over the place.

CHARLOTTE It was a debt of honour.° He laid me a box of gloves to
  a pair of slippers about Forked Lightning for the Regimental
  Cup, and Forked Lightning went tender at the heel. I couldn't   555
  come to you with debts hanging over me. (*Crying*) I'm too
  conscientious.

VALE By Jove, I've been a brute.

CHARLOTTE Y—y—yes.

VALE Can you forget I ever wrote that letter?   560

CHARLOTTE That must be a question of time. (*She lays her head on his shoulder and then removes it*) How damp you are.
> *She puts her handkerchief upon his shoulder, and replaces her head. She moves his arm gradually up and arranges it round her shoulder*

If you went on anyhow every time I discharged an obligation, we should be most unhappy.

VALE I promise you I won't mention Bristow's slippers again. By   565
Jove, I won't—there.

CHARLOTTE Very well, then, if you do that I'll give you my word I won't pay any more debts before our marriage.

VALE My darling!

CHARLOTTE (*about to embrace him, but remembering that he is wet*)   570
No—no—you are too damp.

ISIDORE (*outside*) I beg your pardon, it is a quarter of an hour over our time.
> *Agatha has been sitting on the sofa; suddenly she starts, listening intently*

POSKET (*outside*) I know—I know. I'm going directly I can get the boy away.   575

AGATHA (*to herself*) Aeneas!

CIS (*outside*) All right, Guv, you finish your bottle.

AGATHA My boy.

ISIDORE (*outside*) Gentlemen, come—come.

AGATHA (*to herself*) Miserable deceiver! This, then, is the club, and   580
the wretched man conspires to drag my boy down to his own awful level. What shall I do? I daren't make myself known here. I know; I'll hurry home, and if I reach there before Aeneas, which I shall do, I'll sit up for him.
> *Lukyn returns*

AGATHA Is the cab at the door?   585

LUKYN It is.

AGATHA (*drawing her veil down*) Charlotte! Charlotte!

CHARLOTTE I'm ready, dear. (*To Vale*) Married sisters are always a little thoughtless.

VALE (*offering his arm*) Permit me.   590

LUKYN (*offering his arm to Agatha*) My dear madam.
> *They are all four about to leave when Blond enters hurriedly*

BLOND (*holding up his hand for silence*) Hush! Hush!

LUKYN What's the matter?

BLOND The police!

ALL (*in a whisper*) The police!   595

BLOND (*quietly*) The police are downstairs at the door. I told you so.

CHARLOTTE (*clinging to Vale*) Oh, dear! Oh, dear!

AGATHA Gracious powers!

BLOND Keep quiet, please. They may be satisfied with Madame
Blond's assurances. I must put you in darkness; they can see the   600
light here if they go round to the back.

> *Blows out candles, and turns down the other lights*

AGATHA and CHARLOTTE Oh!

BLOND Keep quiet, please! My licence is once marked already.
Colonel Lukyn, thank you for this.

> *He goes out*

AGATHA (*whimpering*) Miserable men! What have you done? Are you   605
criminals?

CHARLOTTE You haven't deserted or anything on my account, have
you, Horace?

LUKYN Hush! Don't be alarmed. Our time has passed so agreeably
that we have overstepped the prescribed hour for closing the hotel.   610
That's all.

AGATHA What can they do to us?

LUKYN At the worst, take our names and addresses, and summon us
for being here during prohibited hours.

AGATHA Oh!   615

CHARLOTTE (*to Vale*) Horace, can't you speak?

VALE By Jove, I very much regret this.

> *Isidore enters*

LUKYN Well, well?

ISIDORE I beg your pardon, the police have come in.

LUKYN The devil! (*To Agatha*) My dear lady, don't faint at such a 620
moment.

> *Blond enters quickly, carrying a rug [and blanket]*

BLOND They are going over the house! Hide!

AGATHA and CHARLOTTE Oh!

> *There is a general commotion*

BLOND They have put a man at the back. Keep away from the
window.   625

> *They are all bustling, and everybody is talking in whispers;*
> *Lukyn places Agatha under the table, where she is concealed by*
> *the cover; he gets behind the overcoats hanging from the pegs;*
> *Vale and Charlotte crouch down behind sofa*

41

Thank you very much. I am going to put Isidore to bed on the
sofa. That will explain the light which has just gone out.

> *Isidore quietly places himself upon the sofa; Blond covering him
> with the rug*

Thank you very much.

> *He goes out*

AGATHA (*in a stifled voice*) Charley! Charley!

CHARLOTTE Yes.   630

AGATHA Where are you?

CHARLOTTE Here.

AGATHA Oh, where is Captain Vale?

CHARLOTTE I think he's near me.

VALE By Jove, Charlotte, I am!   635

AGATHA Colonel Lukyn!

LUKYN (*from behind the coats*) Here, madam!

AGATHA Don't leave us.

LUKYN Madam, I am a soldier.

CHARLOTTE (*to Vale*) Oh, Horace, at such a moment what a comfort   640
we must be to each other.

VALE My dear Charlotte, it's incalculable.

> *Isidore gently raises himself and looks over the back of sofa*

CHARLOTTE (*in terror*) What's that?

ISIDORE (*softly*) I beg your pardon.

> [*He sinks back.*] *Blond enters quietly, followed by Cis and
> Posket on tiptoe, Posket holding on to Cis*

BLOND This way; be quick. Excuse me, the police are just entering 645
the room in which these gentlemen were having supper. One
of them is anxious not to be asked any questions. Please to
hide him and his friend somewhere. They are both very nice
gentlemen.

> *He goes out, leaving Cis and Posket*

POSKET Cis, Cis. Advise me, my boy, advise me.   650

CIS It's all right, Guv, it's all right. Get behind something.

AGATHA (*peeping from under the tablecloth*) Aeneas, and my child!

> *Posket and Cis wander about, looking for hiding-places*

VALE (*to Cis*) Go away.

CIS Oh!

LUKYN (*to Posket, who is fumbling at the coats*) No, no.   655

BLOND (*popping his head in*) The police—coming.

> *Cis disappears behind the window-curtain. Posket dives under the
> table*

AGATHA Oh!

POSKET (*to Agatha in a whisper*) I beg your pardon. I think I am addressing a lady. I am entirely the victim of circumstances. Accept my apologies for this apparent intrusion. (*No answer*) 660
Madam, I applaud your reticence, though any statement made under the present circumstances would not be used against you. Where is that boy? Oh! Madam, it may be acute nervousness on your part, but you are certainly pinching my arm.

> *There is the sound of heavy feet outside, then Messiter, a gruff, matter-of-fact Inspector of Police, enters, followed by Harris, a constable, and Blond*

BLOND You need not trouble yourself—take my word for it. 665

MESSITER No trouble, Mr Blond, thank you. (*Sniffing*) Candles—blown out—lately. This is where the light was.

BLOND Perhaps. My servant, Isidore, sleeps here; he has only just gone to bed.

MESSITER Oh! (*Taking a bull's-eye lantern from Harris and throwing 670
the light on Isidore, who is apparently sleeping soundly*) Dead tired, I suppose?

BLOND I suppose so.

MESSITER (*slightly turning down the covering*) He sleeps in his clothes?

BLOND Oh yes. 675

MESSITER Always?

BLOND Always—it is a rule of the hotel.

MESSITER Oh! Why's that?

BLOND To be ready for the morning.

MESSITER All right—all right. (*Throwing the rug and blanket aside*) 680
Isidore, go downstairs and give your full name and particulars to Sergeant Jarvis.

ISIDORE (*rising instantly*) Yes, sir—very good.

BLOND (*to Isidore*) Why do you wake up so soon? Devil take you!

ISIDORE I beg your pardon. 685

> *He goes out*

MESSITER What is underneath that window, Mr Blond?

BLOND The skylight over the kitchen—devil take it!

MESSITER Thank you—*you* can go down to the sergeant now, Mr Blond.

BLOND With pleasure—devil take me! 690

> *He goes out*

MESSITER Now then, Harris.

HARRIS Yes, sir.

MESSITER Keep perfectly still and hold your breath as long as you can.

HARRIS Hold my breath, sir?   695

MESSITER Yes—I want to hear how many people are breathing in this room. Are you ready?

HARRIS Yes, sir.

MESSITER Go!

> *Harris stands still, tightly compressing his lips; Messiter quickly examines his face by the light of the lantern, then walks round the room, listening, and nodding his head with satisfaction as he passes the various hiding-places. Harris writhes in agony; in the end he gives it up and breathes heavily*

Harris!   700

HARRIS (*exhausted*) Yes, sir!

MESSITER You're breathing

HARRIS Oh lor', yes, sir!

MESSITER You'll report yourself tonight!

HARRIS I held on till I nearly went off, sir.   705

MESSITER (*giving him the bull's-eye*) Don't argue, but light up. There are half a dozen people concealed in this room.

> *There is a cry from the women. Charlotte and Vale rise; Lukyn steps from behind the coats*

I thought so.

> *As Messiter turns, Agatha and Posket rise, Cis comes quickly, catches hold of Posket, and drags him across to the window*

CIS (*to Posket*) Come on, Guv. Come on!

> *They disappear through the curtain as Harris turns up the lights. Then there is a cry and the sound of a crash*

AGATHA They're killed!   710

MESSITER (*looking through the window*) No, they're not; they've gone into the kitchen and the balcony with them. Look sharp, Harris.

> *Harris goes out quickly*

LUKYN (*to Messiter*) I shall report you for this, sir.

MESSITER (*taking out his notebook*) Very sorry, sir; it's my duty.   715

LUKYN Duty, sir! Coming your confounded detective tricks on ladies and gentlemen! How dare you make ladies and gentlemen suspend their breathing till they nearly have apoplexy? Do you know I'm a short-necked man, sir?

MESSITER I didn't want you to leave off breathing, sir. I wanted you   720
to breathe louder. Your name and address, sir.

LUKYN Gur-r-r-h!

MESSITER Army gentleman, sir?

LUKYN How do you know that?

MESSITER Short style of speaking, sir. Army gentlemen run a bit   725
brusquish when on in years.

LUKYN Oh! Alexander Lukyn—Colonel—Her Majesty's Cheshire
Light Infantry, late 41st Foot, 3rd Battalion—Bengal—Retired.

MESSITER (*writing*) Hotel or club, Colonel?

LUKYN Neither. 19A, Cork Street—lodgings.   730

MESSITER (*writing*) Very nice part, Colonel.° Thank you.

LUKYN Bah!

MESSITER Other gentleman?

VALE (*with languid hauteur*) Horace Edmund Cholmeley Clive Napier
Vale, Captain—Shropshire Fusiliers—Stark's Hotel, Conduit   735
Street.

MESSITER (*writing*) Retired, sir?

VALE No, confound you—active!

MESSITER Thank you, Captain. Ahem! Beg pardon. The—the ladies.
Charlotte clings to Vale, Agatha to Lukyn

CHARLOTTE and AGATHA No—no! No—no!   740

LUKYN (*to Agatha*) All right—all right—trust to me! (*To Messiter*)
Well, sir?

MESSITER Names and addresses, please.

LUKYN Officer—my good fellow—tell me now—er—um—at the
present moment—[*Putting his hand in his pocket*] What are you   745
most in want of?

MESSITER These two ladies' names and addresses, please. Be quick,
Colonel. (*Pointing to Agatha*) That lady first.

LUKYN Christian names—er—ah—er—Alice Emmeline.

MESSITER (*writing*) Alice Emmeline. Surname?   750

LUKYN Er—um—Fitzgerald—101, Wilton Street, Piccadilly.

MESSITER Single lady?

LUKYN Quite.

MESSITER Very good, sir.

AGATHA (*to Lukyn, tearfully*) Oh, thank you, such a nice address too.   755

MESSITER (*to Vale*) Now, Captain, please—that lady.

VALE (*who has been reassuring Charlotte*) Haw! ha! This lady is—ah—
um—the other lady's sister.

MESSITER Single lady, sir?

VALE Certainly.   760

MESSITER (*writing*) Christian name, Captain?

VALE Ah—um—Harriett.

MESSITER (*writing*) Surname.

VALE Er—Macnamara.

MESSITER (*with a grim smile*) Quite so. Lives with her sister, of   765
course, sir?

VALE Of course.

MESSITER Where at, sir?

VALE Albert Mansions, Victoria Street.

CHARLOTTE (*to Vale*) Oh, thank you, I always fancied that spot.   770

MESSITER Very much obliged, gentlemen.

LUKYN (*who has listened to Vale's answers in helpless horror*) By
George, well out of it!
> [*The two ladies give a cry of relief.*] *Charlotte totters across to
> Agatha, who embraces her. Lukyn takes down the overcoats and
> throws one to Vale*

Vale, your coat.
> *Harris enters*

HARRIS (*to Messiter*) Very sorry, sir; the two other gentlemen got   775
clean off, through the back scullery door—old hands, to all
appearance.
> *Messiter stamps his foot, with an exclamation*

AGATHA (*to herself*) My boy—saved!

LUKYN (*to Harris, who stands before the door*) Constable, get out of
the way.   780

MESSITER (*sharply*) Harris!

HARRIS (*without moving*) Yes, sir.

MESSITER You will leave the hotel with these ladies, and not lose
sight of them till you've ascertained what their names *are*, and
where they *do* live.   785

LUKYN and VALE What!

AGATHA and CHARLOTTE Oh!

MESSITER Your own fault, gentlemen; it's my duty.

LUKYN And it is *my* duty to save these helpless women from the
protecting laws of my confounded country! Vale!   790

VALE (*putting his coat on the sofa*) Active!

LUKYN (*to Harris*) Let these ladies pass!
> *He takes Harris by the collar and flings him over to Vale, who
> throws him over towards the ladies, who push him away.
> Messiter puts a whistle to his mouth and blows; there is an
> immediate answer from without*

More of your fellows outside?

MESSITER Yes, sir, at your service. Very sorry, gentlemen, but you
    and your party are in my custody.   795
LUKYN and VALE What?
AGATHA and CHARLOTTE Oh!
MESSITER For assaulting this man in the execution of his duty.
LUKYN You'll dare to lock us up all night?
MESSITER It's one o'clock now, Colonel—you'll come on first thing   800
    in the morning.
LUKYN Come on? At what court?
MESSITER Mulberry Street.
AGATHA [*with a scream*] Ah! The magistrate?
MESSITER Mr Posket, mum.   805
        *Agatha sinks into a chair, Charlotte at her feet; Lukyn,
        overcome, falls on Vale's shoulders.* [*Messiter throws open the
        door. There are two or three policemen outside*]

    CURTAIN

Act Three

IT CRUMBLES

Scene One

*The first scene is the magistrate's room° at Mulberry Street
Police Court, with a doorway covered by curtains leading
directly into the Court, and a door opening into a passage. It is
the morning after the events of the last act. Police Sergeant
Lugg, a middle-aged man with a slight country dialect, enters
with The Times newspaper, and proceeds to cut it° and glance
at its contents, while he hums a song. MR Wormington, an
elderly, trim and precise man, enters*

WORMINGTON Good-morning, Lugg.

LUGG Morning, Mr Wormington.

WORMINGTON Mr Posket not arrived yet?

LUGG Not yet, sir. Hullo! [*Reading*] 'Raid on a West End Hotel. At
an early hour this morning—'   5

WORMINGTON [*hanging up his coat*] Yes, I've read that—a case of
assault upon the police.

LUGG Why, these must be the folks who've been so precious
rampageous all night.

WORMINGTON Very likely.   10

LUGG Yes, sir, protestin' and protestin' till they protested every-
body's sleep away. Nice-looking women, too, though, as I tell Mrs
Lugg, nowadays there's no telling who's the lady and who isn't.
Who's got this job, sir?

WORMINGTON Inspector Messiter.   15

LUGG [*with contempt*] Messiter! That's luck! Why he's the worst
elocutionist in the force, sir.° (*As he arranges the newspaper upon the
table, he catches sight of Mr Wormington's necktie, which is bright red*)
Well, I—excuse me, Mr Wormington, but all the years I've had
the honour of knowin' you, sir, I've never seen you wear a necktie   20
with, so to speak, a dash of colour in it.

WORMINGTON Well, Lugg, no, that's true, but today is an exceptional occasion with me. It is, in fact, the twenty-fifth anniversary
of my marriage, and I thought it due to Mrs Wormington to vary,
in some slight degree, the sombreness of my attire. I confess I am   25
a little uneasy in case Mr Posket should consider it at all
disrespectful to the Court.

48

LUGG Not he, sir.

WORMINGTON I don't know. Mr Posket is punctiliousness itself in
dress, and his cravat's invariably black. However, it is not every   30
man who has a silver wedding day.

LUGG It's not every one as wants one, sir.

> *Wormington goes out; at the same moment Posket enters quickly,*
> *and leans on his chair as if exhausted. His appearance is*
> *extremely wretched; he is still in evening dress, but his clothes*
> *are muddy, and his linen soiled and crumpled, while across the*
> *bridge of his nose he has a small strip of black plaster*

POSKET (*faintly*) Good-morning, Lugg.

LUGG Good-morning to you, sir. Regretting the liberty I'm taking,
sir—I've seen you look more strong and hearty.   35

POSKET I am fairly well, thank you, Lugg. [*Sitting, centre stage*] My
night was rather—rather disturbed. Lugg!

LUGG Sir?

POSKET Have any inquiries been made about me, this morning—any
messenger from Mrs Posket, for instance, to ask how I am?   40

LUGG No, sir.

POSKET Oh! My child, my stepson, young Mr Farringdon, has not
called, has he?

LUGG No, sir.

POSKET (*to himself*) Where can that boy be? (*To Lugg*) Thank you,   45
that's all.

> *Lugg, who has been eyeing Posket with astonishment, goes to the*
> *door, and then touches the bridge of his nose*

LUGG [*sympathetically*] Nasty cut while shavin', sir?

> *Lugg goes out*

POSKET Where can that boy have got to? If I could only remember
how, when, and where we parted! I think it was at Kilburn. Let
me think—first, the kitchen. (*Putting his hand to his side as if*   50
severely bruised) Oh! Cis was all right, because I fell underneath; I
felt it was my duty to do so. Then what occurred? A dark room,
redolent of onions and cabbages and paraffin oil, and Cis dragging
me over the stone floor, saying, 'We're in the scullery, Guv; let's
try and find the tradesmen's door.' Next, the night air—oh, how   55
refreshing! 'Cis, my boy, we will both learn a lesson from
tonight—never deceive.' Where are we? In Argyll Street.° 'Look
out, Guv, they're after us.' [*Rising in agitation*] Then—then, as Cis
remarked when we were getting over the railings of Portman
Square—then the fun began. We over into the square—they after   60
us. Over again, into Baker Street. Down Baker Street. Curious

recollections, whilst running, of my first visit, as a happy child, to
Madame Tussaud's, and wondering whether her removal had
affected my fortunes. 'Come on, Guv—you're getting blown.'
Where are we? Park Road. What am I doing? Getting up out of a   65
puddle. St John's Wood. The cricket ground. 'I say, Guv, what a
run this would be at Lord's, wouldn't it? And no fear of being run
out either, more fear of being run in.' 'What road is this, Cis?'
Maida Vale. Good gracious! A pious aunt of mine once lived in
Hamilton Terrace; she never thought I should come to this. 'Guv?'   70
'Yes, my boy.' 'Let's get this kind-hearted coffee-stall keeper to
hide us.' We apply. 'Will you assist two unfortunate gentlemen?'
'No, blowed if I will.' 'Why not?' 'Cos I'm agoin' to join in the
chase after you.' Ah! Off again, along Maida Vale! On, on, heaven
knows how or where, 'till at last, no sound of pursuit, no Cis, no   75
breath, and the early Kilburn buses starting to town. [*He sinks in
a chair and wipes his forehead. Rising, after a pause*] Then I came
back again, and not much too soon for the Court. (*Going up to the
washstand and looking into the little mirror, with a low groan*) Oh,
how shockingly awful I look, and how stiff and sore I feel! (*Taking*   80
off his coat and hanging it on a peg, then washing his hands) What a
weak and double-faced creature to be a magistrate! I really ought
to get some member of Parliament to ask a question about me in
the House. Where's the soap? I shall put five pounds and costs into
the poor's box tomorrow. But I deserve a most severe caution. Ah,   85
perhaps I shall get that from Agatha. (*He takes off his white tie, rolls*
it up and crams it into his pocket) When Wormington arrives I will
borrow some money and send out for a black cravat! All my pocket
money is in my overcoat at the Hôtel des Princes. If the police
seize it there is some consolation in knowing that that money will   90
never be returned to me. (*There is a knock at the door*) Come in!
        Lugg enters
LUGG Your servant, Mr Wyke, wants to see you, sir.
POSKET Bring him in.
        Lugg goes out
     Wyke! From Agatha! From Agatha!
        Lugg re-enters with Wyke
WYKE Ahem! Good-morning, sir.   95
POSKET Good-morning, Wyke. Ahem! Is Master Farringdon quite well?
WYKE He hadn't arrived home, when I left, sir.
POSKET Oh! Where is that boy? (*To Wyke*) How's your mistress this
     morning, Wyke?

WYKE Very well, I hope, sir; *she* ain't come home yet, either.   100

POSKET Not returned—nor Miss Verrinder?

WYKE No, sir—neither of them.

POSKET (*to himself*) Lady Jenkins is worse, they are still nursing her!
Good women, true women!

WYKE (*to himself*) That's eased his deceivin' old mind.   105

POSKET (*to himself*) Now, if the servants don't betray me and Cis
returns safely, the worst is over. To what a depth I have fallen
when I rejoice at Lady Jenkins' indisposition!

WYKE Cook thought you ought to know that the mistress hadn't
come home, sir.   110

POSKET Certainly. Take a cab at once to Campden Hill and bring
me back word how poor Lady Jenkins is. Tell Mrs Posket I will
come on the moment the Court rises.

WYKE Yes, sir.

POSKET And, Wyke. It is not at all necessary that Mrs Posket should   115
know of my absence with Master Farringdon from home last night.
Mrs Posket's present anxieties are more than sufficient. Inform
Cook, and Popham, and the other servants that I shall recognise
their discretion in the same spirit I have already displayed towards
you.   120

WYKE (*with sarcasm*) Thank you, sir. I will. (*He produces from his
waistcoat pocket a small packet of money done up in newspaper, which
he throws down upon the table*) Meanwhile, sir, I thought you would
like to count up the little present of money you gave me last night,
and in case you thought you'd been over-liberal, sir, you might   125
halve the amount. It isn't no good spoiling of us all, sir.

> *Lugg enters*

POSKET You are an excellent servant, Wyke; I am very pleased. I will
see you when you return from Lady Jenkins's. Be quick.

WYKE Yes, sir. (*To himself*) He won't give me twopence again in a
hurry.   130

> *He goes out; Lugg is about to follow*

POSKET Oh, Lugg, I want you to go to the nearest hosier's and
purchase me a neat cravat.

LUGG (*looking inquisitively at Posket*) A necktie, sir?

POSKET Yes. (*Turning up his coat collar to shield himself from Lugg's
gaze*) A necktie—a necktie.   135

LUGG What sort of a kind of one, sir?

POSKET Oh, one like Mr Wormington's.

LUGG One like he's wearing this morning, sir?

POSKET Of course, of course, of course.

LUGG (*to himself*) Fancy him being jealous of Mr Wormington, now.   140
Very good, sir—what price, sir?

POSKET The best. (*To himself*) There now, I've no money. (*Seeing
the packet on table*) Oh, pay for it with this, Lugg.

LUGG Yes, sir.

POSKET And keep the change for your trouble.   145

LUGG Thank you, sir; thank you, sir—very much obliged to you, sir.
(*To himself*) That's like a liberal gentleman.

> *Lugg goes out as Wormington enters through the curtains with
> the charge-sheet in his hand. Wormington, on seeing Posket,
> uneasily tucks his pocket handkerchief in his collar so as to hide
> his necktie*

WORMINGTON H'm! Good-morning.

POSKET Good-morning, Wormington.

WORMINGTON The charge-sheet.   150

POSKET Sit down.

> *Wormington puts on his spectacles; Posket also attempts to put on
> his spectacles, but hurts the bridge of his nose, winces, and desists*

POSKET (*to himself*) My nose is extremely painful. (*To Wormington*)
You have a bad cold I am afraid, Wormington—bronchial?

WORMINGTON Ahem! Well—ah—the fact is—you may have noticed
how very chilly the nights are.   155

POSKET Very, very.

WORMINGTON [*turning over his papers*] The only way to maintain the
circulation is to run as fast as one can.

POSKET To run—as fast as one can—yes—quite so.

WORMINGTON (*to himself, looking at Posket's shirt-front*) How very   160
extraordinary—he is wearing no cravat whatever!

POSKET (*buttoning up his coat to avoid Wormington's gaze*) Anything
important this morning?

WORMINGTON Nothing particular after the first charge, a serious
business arising out of the raid on the Hôtel des Princes.   165

POSKET (*starting*) Hôtel des Princes?

WORMINGTON Inspector Messiter found six persons supping there
at one o'clock this morning. Two contrived to escape.

POSKET Dear me—I am surprised—I mean, did they?

WORMINGTON But they left their overcoats behind them, and it is   170
believed they will be traced.

POSKET Oh, do you—do you think it is worth while? The police have
a great deal to occupy them just now.

WORMINGTON But surely if the police see their way to capture anybody we had better raise no obstacle.   175

POSKET No—no—quite so—never struck me.

WORMINGTON (*referring to charge-sheet*) The remaining four it was found necessary to take into custody.

POSKET Good gracious! What a good job the other two didn't wait. I beg your pardon—I mean—you say we have four?   180

WORMINGTON Yes, on the charge of obstructing the police. The first assault occurred in the supper-room—the second in the four-wheeled cab on the way to the station. There were five persons in the cab at the time—the two women, the two men, and the Inspector.   185

POSKET Dear me, it must have been a very complicated assault. Who are the unfortunate people?

WORMINGTON The men are of some position. (*Reading*) 'Alexander Lukyn, Colonel'—

POSKET Lukyn! I—I—know Colonel Lukyn; we are old schoolfel-   190
lows.

WORMINGTON Very sad! (*Reading*) The other is 'Horace, etc. etc. Vale—Captain—Shropshire Fusiliers.'

POSKET And the ladies?

WORMINGTON Call themselves, 'Alice Emmeline Fitzgerald and   195
Harriet Macnamara.'

POSKET (*to himself*) Which is the lady who was under the table with me?

WORMINGTON They are not recognised by the police at present, but they furnish incorrect addresses, and their demeanour is generally   200
violent and unsatisfactory.

POSKET (*to himself*) Who pinched me—Alice or Harriet?

WORMINGTON I mention this case because it seems to be one calling for most stringent measures.

POSKET Wouldn't a fine, and a severe warning from the Bench to the   205
two persons who have got away—

WORMINGTON I think not. Consider, Mr Posket, not only defying the licensing laws, but obstructing the police!

POSKET That's true—it is hard, when the police are doing anything, that they should be obstructed.   210

    Lugg enters

LUGG (*attempting to conceal some annoyance*) Your necktie, sir.

POSKET S—ssh!

WORMINGTON (*to himself*) Then he *came* without one—dear me!

53

LUGG (*clapping down a paper parcel on the table*)   As near like Mr
Wormington's as possible—brighter if anything.   215

POSKET (*opening the parcel, and finding a very common, gaudy necker-
chief*) Good gracious! What a horrible affair!

LUGG [*stolidly*] According to my information, sir—like Mr Wormington's.

POSKET Mr Wormington would never be seen in such an abominable   220
colour.

WORMINGTON Well—really—I—(*Removing the handkerchief from his
throat*) I am extremely sorry.

POSKET My dear Wormington!

WORMINGTON I happen to be wearing something similar—the first   225
time for five-and-twenty years.

POSKET Oh, I beg your pardon. (*To himself*) Everything seems
against me.

LUGG One-and-nine it come to, sir. (*Producing the paper packet of
money and laying it upon the table*) And I brought back all the   230
money you gave me, thinking you'd like to look over it quietly.
Really, sir, I never showed up smaller in any shop in all my life!

POSKET Upon my word. First one and then another! What *is* wrong
with the money? (*Opens the packet*) Twopence! ([*Aghast,*] *to himself*)
That man Wyke will tell all to Agatha! Oh, everything is against me.   235

*Lugg has opened the door, taken a card from someone outside,
and handed it to Wormington.*

WORMINGTON (*handing the card to Posket*) From cell no. 3.

POSKET (*reading*) 'Dear Posket, for the love of goodness see me
before the sitting of the Court. Alexander Lukyn.' Poor dear
Lukyn! What on earth shall I do?

WORMINGTON Such a course would be most unusual.   240

POSKET Everything is unusual. Your cravat is unusual. This prisoner
is invited to dine at my house today—that's peculiar. He is my
wife's first husband's only child's godfather—that's a little out of
the ordinary.

WORMINGTON The charge is so serious!   245

POSKET But I am a man as well as a magistrate, advise me,
Wormington, advise me!

WORMINGTON Well—you can apply to yourself for permission to
grant Colonel Lukyn's request.

POSKET (*hastily scribbling on Lukyn's card*) I do—I do—and after   250
much conflicting argument I consent to see Colonel Lukyn here,
immediately.

*Hands the card to Wormington, who passes it to Lugg, who then
goes out*

Don't leave me, Wormington—you must stand by me to see that
I remain calm, firm, and judicial.

*He hastily puts on the red necktie in an untidy manner; [it sticks
out grotesquely]*

Poor Lukyn, I must sink the friend in the magistrate, and in   255
dealing with his errors apply the scourge to myself. (*To Wormington*) Wormington, tap me on the shoulder when I am inclined to
be more than usually unusual.

*Wormington stands behind him, and Lugg enters with Lukyn.
Lukyn's dress clothes are much soiled and disordered, and he, too,
has a small strip of plaster upon the bridge of his nose. There is
a constrained pause, Lukyn and Posket both cough*

LUKYN (*to himself*) Poor Posket!

POSKET (*to himself*) Poor Lukyn!   260

LUKYN (*to himself*) I suppose he has been sitting up for his wife all
night, poor devil! (*To Posket*) Ahem! How are you, Posket?

Wormington touches Posket's shoulder

POSKET I regret to see you in this terrible position, Colonel Lukyn.

LUKYN By George, old fellow, I regret to find myself in it. (*Sitting,
and taking up newspaper*) I suppose they've got us in *The Times*,   265
confound 'em!

*While Lukyn is reading the paper, Posket and Wormington hold
a hurried consultation respecting Lukyn's behaviour.*

POSKET H'm! (*To Lugg*) Sergeant, I think Colonel Lukyn may be
accommodated with a chair.

LUGG He's in it sir.

LUKYN (*rising and putting down paper*) Beg your pardon, forgot where   270
I was. I suppose everything must be formal in this confounded
place?

POSKET I am afraid, Colonel Lukyn, it will be necessary even here
to preserve strictly our unfortunate relative positions. (*Lukyn bows*)
Sit down. (*Lukyn sits again. Posket takes up the charge-sheet*)   275
Colonel Lukyn! In addressing you now, I am speaking, not as a
man, but as an instrument of the law. As a man I may, or may not,
be a weak, vicious, despicable creature.

LUKYN Certainly—of course.

POSKET But as a magistrate I am bound to say you fill me with pain   280
and astonishment.

LUKYN Quite right—every man to his trade; go on, Posket.

POSKET (*turning his chair to face Lukyn*) Alexander Lukyn—when I
look at you—when I look at you—(*He attempts to put on his
spectacles* [*and hurts his nose. To himself*]) Ah—my nose. (*To Lukyn,* 285
[*holding his spectacles a little away from his face*]) I say, when I look
at you, Alexander Lukyn, I confront a most mournful spectacle. A
military officer, trained in the ways of discipline and smartness,
now, in consequence of his own misdoings, lamentably bruised and
battered, shamefully disfigured by plaster, with his apparel soiled 290
and damaged—all terrible evidence of a conflict with that power of
which I am the representative.

LUKYN (*turning his chair to face Posket*) Well, Posket, if it comes to
that, when I look at you, when I look at you—(*He attempts to fix
his glass in his eye*) Confound my nose! (*To Posket*) When I look at 295
you, *you* are not a very imposing object, this morning.

POSKET Lukyn!

LUKYN You look quite as shaky as I do—and you're not quite
innocent of court plaster.°

POSKET Lukyn! Really! 300

LUKYN And as for our attire, we neither of us look as if we had
slipped out of a bandbox.

POSKET Don't, Lukyn, don't! Pray respect my legal status
          Wormington leads Posket, who has risen, back to his seat
Thank you, Wormington. Alexander Lukyn, I have spoken. It
remains for you to state your motive in seeking this painful 305
interview.

LUKYN Certainly! H'm! You know, of course, that I am not alone in
this affair?

POSKET (*referring to charge-sheet*) Three persons appear to be charged
with you. 310

LUKYN Yes. Two others got away. Cowards! If ever I find them, I'll
destroy them!

POSKET Lukyn!

LUKYN I will! Another job for you, Posket.

POSKET (*with dignity*) I beg your pardon; in the event of such a 315
deplorable occurrence, I should not occupy my present position.
Go on, sir.

LUKYN Horace Vale and I are prepared to stand the brunt of our
misdeeds. But, Posket, there are ladies in the case.

POSKET In the annals of the Mulberry Street Police Court such a 320
circumstance is not unprecedented.

LUKYN Two helpless, forlorn ladies.

POSKET (*referring to charge-sheet*) Alice Emmeline Fitzgerald and Harriet Macnamara. Oh, Lukyn, Lukyn!

LUKYN Pooh! I ask no favour for myself or Vale, but I come to you, 325
Posket, to beg you to use your power to release these two ladies without a moment's delay.

Wormington touches Posket's shoulder

POSKET Upon my word, Lukyn! Do you think I am to be undermined?

LUKYN Undermine the devil, sir! Don't talk to me! Let these ladies 330
go, I say! Don't bring them into Court, don't see their faces—don't hear their voices—if you do, you'll regret it!

POSKET Colonel Lukyn!

LUKYN (*leaning across the table and gripping Posket by the shoulder*)
Posket, do you know that one of these ladies is a married lady? 335

POSKET Of course I don't, sir. I blush to hear it.

LUKYN And do you know that from the moment this married lady steps into your confounded Court, the happiness, the contentment of a doting husband, become a confounded wreck and ruin?

POSKET Then, sir, let it be my harrowing task to open the eyes of 340
this foolish doting man to the treachery, the perfidy, which nestles upon his very hearthrug!

LUKYN Oh, lor'! Be careful, Posket! By George, be careful!

POSKET Alexander Lukyn, you are my friend. Amongst the personal property taken from you when you entered these precincts may 345
have been found a memorandum of an engagement to dine at my house tonight at a quarter to eight o'clock. But, Lukyn, I solemnly prepare you, you stand in danger of being late for dinner! I go further—I am not sure, after this morning's proceedings, that Mrs Posket will be ready to receive you. 350

LUKYN I'm confoundedly certain she *won't*!

POSKET Therefore, Lukyn, as an English husband and father, it will be my duty to teach you and your disreputable companions—
(*Referring to charge-sheet*) Alice Emmeline Fitzgerald and Harriet Macnamara, some rudimentary notions of propriety and decorum. 355

LUKYN Confound you, Posket—listen!

POSKET I am listening, sir, to the guiding voice of Mrs Posket—that newly-made wife still blushing from the embarrassment of her second marriage, and that voice says, 'Strike for the sanctity of hearth and home, for the credit of the wives of England—no mercy!' 360

WORMINGTON It is time to go into Court, sir. The charge against Colonel Lukyn is first on the list.

LUKYN Posket, I'll give you one last chance! If I write upon a scrap
of paper the real names of these two unfortunate ladies, will you
shut yourself up for a moment, away from observation, and read   365
these names before you go into Court?

POSKET Certainly not, Colonel Lukyn! I cannot be influenced by
private information in dealing with an offence which is, in my
opinion, as black as—as my cravat! Ahem!

*Wormington and Posket look at each other's necktie and turn up
their collars hastily*

LUKYN (*to himself*) There's no help for it. (*To Posket*) Then, Posket,   370
you must have the plain truth where you stand, by George! The
two ladies who are my companions in this affair are—

POSKET Sergeant! Colonel Lukyn will now join his party.

Lugg steps up to Lukyn sharply

LUKYN (*boiling with indignation*) What, sir? What?

POSKET Lukyn, I think we both have engagements—will you excuse   375
me?

LUKYN [*choking*] Posket! You've gone too far! If you went down on
your knees, which you appear to have been recently doing, and
begged the names of these two ladies, you shouldn't have 'em! No
sir, by George, you shouldn't.   380

POSKET Good-morning, Colonel Lukyn.

LUKYN You've lectured me, pooh-poohed me, snubbed me—a soldier, sir—a soldier! But when I think of your dinner party tonight,
with my empty chair, like Banquo, by George, sir—and the chief
dish composed of a well-browned, well-basted, family skeleton,   385
served up under the best silver cover, I pity you, Posket! Good-
morning!

He marches out with Lugg

POSKET [*leaning exhausted on the back of a chair*] Ah! Thank
goodness that ordeal is passed. Now, Wormington, I think I am
ready to face the duties of the day! Shall we go into Court?   390

WORMINGTON Certainly, sir.

*Wormington gathers up papers from the table. Posket, with a
shaking hand, pours out water from carafe and drinks*

POSKET [*to himself*] My breakfast. (*To Wormington*) I hope I
defended the sanctity of the Englishman's hearth, Wormington?

WORMINGTON You did, indeed. As a married man, I thank you.

POSKET Give me your arm, Wormington! I am not very well this   395
morning, and this interview with Colonel Lukyn has shaken me. I
think your coat-collar is turned up, Wormington.

WORMINGTON So is yours, I fancy, sir.

POSKET Ahem!

> *They turn their collars down, Posket takes Wormington's arm.*
> *They are going towards the curtains when Wyke enters hurriedly*
> *at the door*

WYKE Excuse me, sir.   400

WORMINGTON Hush! hush! Mr Posket is just going into Court.

WYKE Lady Jenkins has sent me back to tell you that she hasn't seen
the missis for the last week or more.

POSKET Mrs Posket went to Campden Hill with Miss Verrinder last
night!   405

WYKE They haven't arrived there, sir.

POSKET Haven't arrived!

WYKE No sir—and even a slow four-wheeler won't account for that.

POSKET Wormington! There's something wrong! Mrs Posket quitted
a fairly happy home last night and has not been seen or heard of   410
since!

WORMINGTON [*taking his arm again*] Pray don't be anxious, sir, the
Court is waiting.

POSKET [*in a frenzy, shaking him off*] But I am anxious! Tell Sergeant
Lugg to look over the Accident-Book, this morning's Hospital   415
Returns, List of Missing Children, Suspicious Pledges, People
Left Chargeable to the Parish, Attend to your Window Fasten-
ings°—! I—I—Wormington, Mrs Posket and I disagreed last night.

WORMINGTON Don't think of it, sir! You should hear me and Mrs
Wormington! Pray do come into Court.   420

POSKET Court! I'm totally unfit for business! Totally unfit for
business!

> *Wormington hurries him off through the curtains. Lugg enters,*
> *almost breathless [and wiping his face]*

LUGG We've got Charge One in the dock—all four of 'em. (*Seeing*
Wyke) Hallo! You back again!

WYKE Yes—seems so. (*They stand facing each other, dabbing their*   425
foreheads with their handkerchiefs) Phew! You seem warm.

LUGG Phew! You don't seem so cool.

WYKE I've been lookin' after two ladies.

LUGG So have I.

WYKE I haven't found 'em.   430

LUGG If I'd known, I'd a been pleased to lend you our two.

> *From the other side of the curtains there is the sound of a shriek*
> *from Agatha and Charlotte*

WYKE Lor'! What's that!

LUGG That *is* our two. Don't notice them—they're hystericals. They're mild now to what they have been. I say, old fellow—is your guv'nor all right in his head?   435

WYKE I suppose so—why?

LUGG I've a partickler reason for asking. Does he ever tell you to buy him anything and keep the change?

WYKE What d'yer mean?

LUGG Well, does he ever come down handsome for your extry   440
exertion—do you ever get any tips?

WYKE Rather. What do you think he made me a present of last night?

LUGG Don't know.

WYKE Twopence—to buy a new umbrella.   445

LUGG Well, I'm blessed! And he gave me the same sum to get him a silk necktie. It's my opinion he's got a softening of the brain

> *Another shriek from the two women, a cry from Posket, and then a hubbub are heard. Lugg runs up to the curtains and looks through*

Hallo! What's wrong? Here! I told you so—he's broken out, he's broken out.

WYKE Who's broken out?   450

LUGG The lunatic. Keep back, I'm wanted.

> *He goes through the curtains*

WYKE (*looking after him*) Look at the guv'nor waving his arms and going on anyhow at the prisoners! Prisoners! Gracious goodness—it's the missis!

> *Amid a confused sound of voices, Posket is brought in, through the curtains, by Wormington. Lugg follows. [Posket is placed in a chair and Wormington holds a glass of water to his lips]*

POSKET Wormington! Wormington! The two ladies! The two ladies!   455
I know them!

WORMINGTON It's all right, sir, it's all right—don't be upset, sir!

POSKET I'm not well; what shall I do?

WORMINGTON Nothing further, sir. What you have done is quite in form.   460

POSKET What I *have* done?

WORMINGTON Yes, sir—you did precisely what I suggested—took the words from me. They pleaded guilty.

POSKET Guilty!

WORMINGTON Yes, sir—and you sentenced them.   465

POSKET Sentenced them! The ladies!

WORMINGTON Yes, sir. You've given them seven days, without the option of a fine.

> Posket collapses into Wormington's arms

CURTAIN

Scene Two

> The scene changes to Posket's drawing-room, as in the first act. [Daylight. On the writing-table, a little flower-vase, with fresh flowers.] Beatie enters timidly, dressed in simple walking-costume

BEATIE How dreadfully early. Eleven o'clock, and I'm not supposed to come till four. I wonder why I want to instruct Cis all day. [Thoughtfully] I'm not nearly so enthusiastic about the two little girls I teach in Russell Square.

> Popham enters. Her eyes are red, as if from crying

POPHAM (drawing back on seeing Beatie) That music person again. I   5
beg your pardon—I ain't got no instructions to prepare no drawing-room for no lessons till four o'clock.

BEATIE [haughtily] I wish to see Mrs Posket.

POPHAM She hasn't come home.

BEATIE Oh, then—er—um—Master Farringdon will do.   10

POPHAM (in tears) He haven't come home either!

BEATIE Oh, where is he?

POPHAM No one knows! His wicked old stepfather took him out late last night and hasn't returned him. Such a night as it was, too, and him still wearing his summer undervests.   15

BEATIE Mr Posket?

POPHAM Mr Posket—no, my Cis!

BEATIE How dare you speak of Master Farringdon in that familiar way?

POPHAM How dare I? Because me and him formed an attachment   20
before ever you darkened our doors. (Taking a folded printed paper from her pocket) You may put down the iron 'eel too heavy, Miss Tomlinson. I refer you to Bow Bells—'First Love is Best Love; or, The Earl's Choice'.

> As Popham offers the paper, Cis enters, looking very pale, worn-out, and dishevelled. [The two girls give a small scream at

61

*his first appearance. His condition is as deplorable as Posket's in
the previous scene*]

POPHAM and BEATIE Oh!   25

CIS (*staggering to a chair*) Where's the mater?

POPHAM Not home yet.

CIS Thank giminy!

BEATIE He's ill!

POPHAM Oh!   30

*Beatie, assisted by Popham, quickly wheels the large armchair
forward. They catch hold of Cis° and place him in it; he submits
limply*

BEATIE (*taking Cis's hand*) What is the matter, Cis dear? Tell Beatie.

POPHAM (*taking his other hand*) Well, I'm sure! Who's given you
raisins and ketchup from the store cupboard? Come back to Emma!

Cis, with his eyes closed, gives a murmur

BEATIE He's whispering!

They both bob their heads down to listen

POPHAM He says his head's a-whirling.   35

BEATIE Put him on the sofa.

*They take off his boots, loosen his necktie, and dab his forehead
with water out of the flower-vase*

CIS [*indistinctly*] I—I—I wish you two girls would leave off.

[*They bob their heads down as before*]

BEATIE He's speaking again. He hasn't had any breakfast! He's hungry!

POPHAM Hungry! I thought he looked thin! Wait a minute, dear!
Emma Popham knows what her boy fancies!   40

She runs out of the room

CIS Oh, Beatie, hold my head while I ask you something.

BEATIE [*bending over him and holding his hand*] Yes, darling!

CIS No lady would marry a gentleman who had been a convict, would
she?

BEATIE No; certainly not!   45

CIS I thought not! Well, Beatie, I've been run after by a policeman.

BEATIE (*leaving him*) Oh!

CIS Not caught, you know, only run after; and, walking home from
Hendon this morning, I came to the conclusion that I ought to
settle down in life. Beatie—could I write out a paper promising to   50
marry you when I'm one-and-twenty?

BEATIE Don't be a silly boy—of course you could.

CIS Then I shall; and when I feel inclined to have a spree, I shall
think of that paper and say, 'Cis Farringdon, if you ever get locked
up, you'll lose the most beautiful girl in the world.'   55

BEATIE And so you will.
     He goes to the writing-table
CIS I'd better write it now, before my head gets well again.
     He writes; she bends over him [and kisses him]
BEATIE You simple, foolish, Cis! If your head is so queer, shall I tell
    you what to say?
     Popham enters, carrying a tray with breakfast dishes
POPHAM (*to herself*) He won't think so much of *her* now. His   60
    breakfast is my triumph. (*To* CIS) Coffee, bacon, and a teacake.
BEATIE [*raising her head*] Hush! Master Farringdon is writing some-
    thing very important.
POPHAM (*going to the window*) That's a cab at our door.
CIS It must be the mater—I'm off!   65
     He picks up his boots and goes out quickly
BEATIE (*following him with the paper and inkstand*) Cis! Cis! You
    haven't finished the promise! You haven't finished the promise!
LUGG (*heard outside*) All right, sir—I've got you—I've got you.
     Popham opens the door
POPHAM The master and a policeman!
     Lugg enters supporting Posket, who sinks into an armchair with
     a groan
Oh, what's the matter?   70
LUGG All right, my good girl, you run downstairs and fetch a drop
    of brandy and water.
     Popham hurries off °
POSKET [*groaning again*] Oh!
LUGG Now don't take on so, sir. It's what might happen to any
    married gentleman. Now, you're all right now, sir. And I'll hurry   75
    back to the Court to see whether they've sent for Mr Bullamy.
POSKET My wife! My wife!
LUGG Oh, come now, sir, what *is* seven days! Why, many a married
    gentleman in your position, sir, would have been glad to have made
    it fourteen.   80
POSKET Go away—leave me.
LUGG Certainly, sir.
     Popham re-enters with a small tumbler of brandy and water; he
     takes it from her and drinks it
It's not wanted. I'm thankful to say he's better.
POPHAM (*to Lugg*) If you please, Cook presents her compliments,
    and she would be glad of the pleasure of your company downstairs,   85
    before leavin'.
     They go out

POSKET Agatha and Lukyn! Agatha and Lukyn supping together at the Hôtel des Princes, while I was at home and asleep—while I ought to have been at home and asleep! It's awful!

CIS (*looking in at the door and entering*) Hallo, Guv! 90

POSKET (*starting up*) Cis!

CIS Where did you fetch, Guv?

POSKET Where did I fetch! You wretched boy! I fetched Kilburn, and I'll fetch you a sound whipping when I recover my composure. 95

CIS What for?

POSKET For leading me astray, sir. Yours is the first bad companionship I have ever formed! Evil communication° with you, sir, has corrupted me! (*Taking Cis by the collar and shaking him*) Why did you abandon me at Kilburn? 100

CIS Because you were quite done, and I branched off to draw the crowd away from you after me.

POSKET Did you, Cis, did you? (*Putting his hand on Cis's shoulder*) My boy—my boy! Oh, Cis, we're in such trouble!

CIS You weren't caught, Guv? 105

POSKET No—but do you know who the ladies are who were supping at the Hôtel des Princes?

CIS No—do you?

POSKET Do I? They were your mother and Aunt Charlotte.

CIS The mater and Aunt Charlotte! Ha, ha, ha! (*Laughing and dancing with delight*) Ha! ha! Oh, I say, Guv, what a lark! 110

POSKET A lark! They were taken to the police station!

CIS (*changing his tone*) My mother?

POSKET They were brought before the magistrate and sentenced.

CIS Sentenced? 115

POSKET To seven day's imprisonment.

CIS Oh!

He puts his hat on fiercely

POSKET What are you going to do?

CIS Get my mother out first, and then break every bone in that magistrate's body. 120

POSKET Cis! Cis! He's an unhappy wretch and he did his duty.

CIS His duty! To send another magistrate's wife to prison! Guv, I'm only a boy, but I know what professional etiquette is! Come along! Which is the police station?

POSKET Mulberry Street. 125

CIS Who's the magistrate?

POSKET I am!

CIS You! (*Seizing Posket by the collar and shaking him*) You dare to lock up my mother! Come with me and get her out!

>He is dragging Posket towards the door, when Bullamy enters breathlessly

BULLAMY My dear Posket!   130

CIS (*seizing Bullamy and dragging him with Posket to the door*) Come with me and get my mother out.

BULLAMY Leave me alone, sir! She *is* out! I managed it.

POSKET and CIS How?

BULLAMY Wormington sent to me when you were taken ill. When I   135
arrived at the Court, he had discovered, from your manservant, Mrs Posket's awful position.

CIS You leave my mother alone! Go on!

BULLAMY Said I to myself, 'This won't do, I must extricate these people somehow!' (*To Posket*) I'm not so damned conscientious as   140
you are, Posket.

CIS Bravo! Go on!

BULLAMY (*producing his jujube box*) The first thing I did was to take a jujube.

CIS (*snatching the jujube box from him [and stamping his foot]*) Will you   145
make haste?

BULLAMY Then said I to Wormington, 'Posket was *non compos mentis*°
when he heard this case—I'm going to reopen the matter!'

CIS Hurrah!

BULLAMY And I did! And what do you think I found out from the   150
proprietor of the hotel?

POSKET and CIS What?

BULLAMY That this young scamp, Mr Cecil Farringdon, hires a room at the Hôtel des Princes.

CIS I know that.   155

BULLAMY And that Mr Farringdon was there last night with some low stockbroker of the name of Skinner.

CIS Go on—go on! (*Offering him the jujube box*) Take a jujube!

BULLAMY (*taking a jujube*) Now the law, which seems to me quite perfect, allows a man who rents a little apartment at an inn to eat   160
and drink with his friends all night long.

CIS Well?

BULLAMY So said I from the bench, 'These ladies and gentlemen appear to be friends or relatives of a certain lodger in the Hôtel des Princes.'   165

CIS So they are!

BULLAMY 'They were all discovered in one room.'

POSKET So we were—I mean, so they were!

BULLAMY 'And I shall adjourn the case for a week to give Mr
Farringdon an opportunity of claiming these people as his guests.'   170

CIS [*jumping on the sofa and waving his handkerchief*] Three cheers for
Bullamy.

BULLAMY So I censured the police for their interference and released
the ladies on their own recognisances.

POSKET (*taking Bullamy's hand*) And the men?   175

BULLAMY Well, unfortunately, Wormington took upon himself to
despatch the men to the House of Correction before I arrived.

POSKET I'm glad of it! They are dissolute villains! I'm glad of it.
        Popham enters

POPHAM Oh, sir! Here's the missis and Miss Verrinder! In such a
plight!   180

CIS The mater! Guv, you explain!
        He hurries out. Posket rapidly retires into the window recess.
        Agatha and Charlotte enter, pale, red-eyed, and agitated. [They
        carry their hats or bonnets, which are much crushed.] Popham
        goes out

AGATHA and CHARLOTTE (*falling on to Bullamy's shoulders*) O—o—
h—h!

BULLAMY My dear ladies!

AGATHA Preserver!   185

CHARLOTTE Friend!

AGATHA How is my boy?

BULLAMY Never better.

AGATHA And the man who condemned his wife and sister-in-law to
the miseries of a gaol!   190

BULLAMY Ahem! Posket—oh—he—

AGATHA Is he well enough to be told what that wife thinks of him?

BULLAMY It might cause a relapse!

AGATHA It is my duty to risk that.

CHARLOTTE (*raising the covers of the dishes on the table*; [*with an*   195
hysterical cry]) Food!

AGATHA Ah!
        Agatha and Charlotte begin to devour a teacake voraciously

POSKET (*advancing with an attempt at dignity*) Agatha Posket.

AGATHA (*rising, with her mouth full, and a piece of teacake in her hand*)
Sir!   200

66

Charlotte takes the tray and everything on it from the table and goes towards the door

BULLAMY (*going to the door*) There's going to be an explanation.

CHARLOTTE (*at the door*) There's going to be an explanation.

Charlotte and Bullamy go out quietly

POSKET How dare you look me in the face, madam?

AGATHA How dare you look at anybody in any position, sir? You send your wife to prison for pushing a mere policeman.   205

POSKET I didn't know what I was doing.

AGATHA Not when you requested two ladies to raise their veils and show their faces in the dock? We shouldn't have been discovered but for that.

POSKET It was my duty.   210

AGATHA Duty! You don't go to the Police Court again alone! I guess now, Aeneas Posket, why you clung to a single life so long. *You liked it!*

POSKET I wish I had.

AGATHA Why didn't you marry till you were fifty?   215

POSKET Perhaps I hadn't met a widow, madam.

AGATHA Paltry excuse. You revelled in a dissolute bachelorhood!

POSKET Hah! Whist every evening!

AGATHA You can't play whist *alone*. You're an expert at hiding too!

POSKET If I were I should thrash your boy!   220

AGATHA When you wished to conceal yourself last night, you selected a table with a lady under it.

POSKET [*rubbing his arm*] Ah, did you pinch me, or did Charlotte?

AGATHA I did—Charlotte's a single girl.

POSKET I fancy, madam, you found my conduct under that table   225
perfectly respectful?

AGATHA I don't know—I was too agitated to notice.

POSKET Evasion—you're like all the women.

AGATHA Profligate! You oughtn't to know that!

POSKET No wife of mine sups, unknown to me, with dissolute   230
military men; we will have a judicial separation, Mrs Posket.

AGATHA Certainly—I suppose you'll manage that at your Police Court, too?

POSKET I shall send for my solicitor at once.

AGATHA Aeneas! Mr Posket! Whatever happens, you shall not have   235
the custody of my boy.

POSKET Your boy! *I* take charge of *him?* Agatha Posket, he has been my evil genius! He has made me a gambler at an atrocious game

called 'Fireworks'—he has tortured my mind with abstruse specu-
lations concerning Sillikin and Butterscotch for the St Leger°—he   240
has caused me to cower before servants, and to fly before the
police.

AGATHA He! My Cis?
     Cis enters, having changed his clothes

CIS (*breezily*) Hallo, mater—got back?

AGATHA You wicked boy! You dare to have apartments at the Hôtel   245
des Princes!

POSKET Yes—and it was to put a stop to that which induced me to
go to Meek Street last night.

CIS Don't be angry, mater! I've got you out of your difficulties.

POSKET But you got me into mine!   250

CIS Well, I know I did—one can't be always doing the right thing! It
isn't Guv's fault—there!

POSKET Swear it!

AGATHA No, he doesn't know the nature of an oath! I believe him!
Aeneas, I see now, this is all the result of a lack of candour on my   255
part. Tell me, have you ever particularly observed this child?

POSKET Oh!

AGATHA Has it ever struck you he is a little forward?

POSKET Sometimes.

AGATHA You are wrong; he is awfully backward. (*Taking Posket's   260
hand*) Aeneas; men always think they are marrying angels, and
women would be angels if they never had to grow old. That warps
their dispositions. I have deceived you, Aeneas.

POSKET [*clenching his fists*] Ah! Lukyn!

AGATHA No—no—you don't understand! Lukyn was my boy's god-   265
father in 1866.

POSKET 1866?°

CIS 1866?

CIS and POSKET (*together, reckoning rapidly upon their fingers*) 1866.

AGATHA S—s—s—h! Don't count! Cis, go away! (*To Posket*) When   270
you proposed to me in the Pantheon at Spa, you particularly
remarked, 'Mrs Farringdon, I love you for yourself *alone*.'

POSKET I know I did.

AGATHA Those were terrible words to address to a widow with a son
of nineteen. (*Cis and Posket again reckon rapidly upon their fingers*) 275
Don't count, Aeneas, don't count! Those words tempted me. I
glanced at my face in a neighbouring mirror, and I said 'Aeneas is
fifty—why should I—a mere woman, compete with him on the

question of age? He has already the advantage—I will be generous—I will add to it!' I led you to believe I had been married only   280
fifteen years ago, I deceived you and my boy as to his real age, and
I told you I was but one-and-thirty.

POSKET It wasn't the truth?

AGATHA Ah! I merely lacked woman's commonest fault, exaggeration.

POSKET But—Lukyn?   285

AGATHA Knows the real facts. I went to him last night to beg him
not to disturb an arrangement which had brought happiness to all
parties. Look. In place of a wayward, troublesome child, I now
present you with a youth old enough to be a joy, comfort, and
support!   290

CIS Oh, I say, mater, this is a frightful sell for a fellow.

AGATHA Go to your room, sir.

CIS I always thought there was something wrong with me. Blessed if
I'm not behind the age!

    Cis goes out

AGATHA Forgive me, Aeneas. Look at my bonnet! A night in   295
Mulberry Street, without even a powder-puff, is an awful expi-
ation.

POSKET Agatha! How do I know Cis won't be five-and-twenty
tomorrow?

AGATHA No—no—you know the worst, and as long as I live, I'll   300
never deceive you again—except in little things.

    Lukyn and Vale enter

LUKYN (*boiling with rage*) By George, Posket!

POSKET My dear Lukyn!

LUKYN Do you know I am a confounded gaolbird, sir?

POSKET An accident!   305

LUKYN And do you know what has happened to me in gaol—a
soldier, sir—an officer?

POSKET No!

LUKYN I have been washed by the authorities.

POSKET Lukyn, no!   310

    Charlotte has entered, and she rushes across to Vale

CHARLOTTE Horace! Horace! Not you, too?

VALE By Jove, Charlotte, I would have died first.

    Bullamy enters quickly

BULLAMY Mr Posket, I shall choke, sir! Inspector Messiter is
downstairs and says that Isidore, the waiter, swears that you are
the man who escaped from Meek Street last night.   315

LUKYN What?

BULLAMY This is a public scandal, sir!

LUKYN Your game is up, sir!

BULLAMY You have brought a stain upon a spotless Police Court!

LUKYN And lectured me upon propriety and decorum.   320

POSKET Gentlemen, gentlemen, when you have heard my story you will pity me.

LUKYN and BULLAMY (*laughing ironically*) Ha! ha!

POSKET You will find your old friend a man, a martyr, and a magistrate!   325

    Cis enters, pulling Beatie after him

CIS Come on, Beatie! Guv—mater! Here's news! Beatie and I have made up our minds to be married.

AGATHA Oh!

    Popham enters with champagne and glasses

POSKET What's this?

CIS Bollinger—'74—extra dry—to drink our health and happiness.   330

CHARLOTTE Champagne! It may save my life!

AGATHA Miss Tomlinson, go home!

POSKET [*firmly*] Stop! Cis Farringdon, my dear boy, you are but nineteen at present, but you were only fourteen yesterday, so you are a growing lad; on the day you marry and start for Canada, I   335
will give you a thousand pounds!

POPHAM (*putting her apron to her eyes*) Oh!

CIS (*embracing Beatie*) Hurrah! We'll be married directly.

AGATHA He's an infant!° I forbid it!

POSKET I am his legal guardian. Gentlemen, bear witness! I solemnly   340
consent to that little wretch's marriage!

    Agatha sinks into a chair [as the curtain falls]

CURTAIN

THE SCHOOLMISTRESS
A Farce in Three Acts

The play was first staged at the Court Theatre, London, on 27 March 1886, with the following cast:

The Hon. Vere Queckett	*Mr Arthur Cecil*
Rear-Admiral Archibald Rankling, CB° (of HM Flagship *Pandora*)	*Mr John Clayton*
Lieut. John Mallory (of HM Flagship *Pandora*)	*Mr F. Kerr*
Mr Saunders (Mr Mallory's nephew, of the training-ship *Dexterous*)	*Mr Edwin Victor*
Mr *Reginald* Paulover	*Mr H. Eversfield*
Mr Otto Bernstein (a popular composer)	*Mr Chevalier*
Tyler (a servant)	*Mr W. Phillips*
Goff	*Mr Fred Cape*
Jaffray	*Mr Lugg*
Mrs Rankling	*Miss Emily Cross*
Miss Dyott (Principal of Volumnia College° for the Daughters of Gentlemen)	*Mrs John Wood*
Dinah Rankling	*Miss Cudmore*
Gwendolen Hawkins	*Miss Viney*
Ermyntrude Johnson	*Miss La Coste*
Peggy Hesslerigge (an articled pupil°)	*Miss Norreys*
Jane Chipman	*Miss Roche*

Act One

THE MYSTERY

Scene One

The scene is the reception room at Miss Dyott's seminary for young ladies, known as Volumnia College, Volumnia House, near Portland Place.° The windows look on to the street. A large door at the further end of the room opens to the hall, where there are some portmanteaus standing, and there is another door on the spectator's right. Jane Chipman, a stout, middle-aged servant, and Tyler, an unhealthy-looking youth, wearing a page's jacket, enter the room, carrying between them a huge travelling-trunk [lettered 'C. D.']

TYLER (*breathlessly*) 'Old 'ard—'old 'ard! Phew!

They rest the trunk on the floor. Tyler then dabs his forehead with a small, dirty handkerchief, which he afterwards passes on to Jane.

Excuse me not offering it to you first, Jane.

JANE (*dabbing the palms of her hands*) Don't name it, Tyler. Do you 'appen to know what time Missus starts?

TYLER Two-thirty, I 'eard say.

JANE It's a queer thing her going away like this alone—not to say nothing of a schoolmistress leaving a lot of foolish young gals for a month or six weeks.

TYLER (*sitting despondently on the trunk*) Cook and the parlour-maid got rid of too—it's not much of a Christmas vacation we shall get, you and me, Jane.

JANE You're right. (*Sitting on the sofa*) Let's see—how many of our young ladies 'aven't gone home for their 'olidays?

TYLER [*reckoning on his fingers*] Well, there's Miss 'Awkins.

JANE Her people is in India.

TYLER Miss Johnson.

JANE Her people is in the Divorce Court.

TYLER Miss Hesslerigge.

JANE Oh, she ain't got no 'ome. She's a orphan, studying for to be a governess.

TYLER Then there's this new girl, Miss Ranklin'.

JANE Dinah Ranklin'?

73

TYLER Yes, Dinah Ranklin'. Now, why is *she* to spend her Xmas at
    our College? She's the daughter of Admiral Ranklin', and the
    Ranklin's live jest round the corner at Collin'wood 'Ouse.°   25

JANE Oh, she's been fallin' in love or something, and has got to be
    locked up.

TYLER Well then, last but not least, there's the individual who is
    kicking his 'eels about the 'ouse, and giving himself the airs of the
    'aughty.   30

JANE (*mysteriously*) What—Missus's husband?

TYLER Yes—Missus's husband.

JANE Ah! Mark my word, if ever there was a Mystery, there's one.

TYLER *Who* is he? Missus brings him 'ome about a month ago, and
    doesn't introduce him to us or to nobody. The order is she's still   35
    to be called Miss Dyott, and we don't know even his nasty name.

JANE (*returning to the trunk*) She calls him Ducky.

TYLER Yes, but *we* can't call him Ducky. (*Pointing to the handkerchief
    which Jane has left upon the sofa*) My 'andkerchief, please. I don't
    let *anybody* use it.   40

JANE (*returning the handkerchief*) Excuse me. (*In putting the handker-
    chief into his breast-pocket, he first removes a handful of cheap-looking
    squibs*) Lor'! You will carry them deadly fireworks about with you,
    Tyler.

TYLER (*regarding them fondly*) Fireworks is my only disserpation.   45
    There ain't much danger unless anybody lunges at me. (*Producing
    some dirty crackers from his trouser pockets, and regarding them with
    gloomy relish*) Friction is the risk I run.

JANE (*palpitating*) Oh, don't, Tyler! How can you 'ave such a
    'ankering?   50

TYLER (*intensely*) It's more than a 'ankering. I love to 'oard 'em and
    meller° 'em. Today they're damp—tomorrow they're dry. And
    when the time comes for to let them off—

JANE Then they don't go off.

TYLER (*putting the fireworks away*) P'r'aps not—and it's their 'orrible   55
    uncertainty wot I crave after. Lift your end, Jane.

        *They take up the trunk as Gwendoline Hawkins and Ermyn-
        trude Johnson, two pretty girls, the one gushing, the other
        haughty in demeanour, appear in the hall*

GWENDOLINE Here are Miss Dyott's boxes; she is really going
    today. I am so happy!

ERMYNTRUDE What an inexpressible relief! Oh, Tyler, I am dis-
    satisfied with the manner in which my shoes are polished.   60

GWENDOLINE Yes—and, Tyler, you never fed my mice last night.

TYLER It ain't my place. Birds and mice is Jane's place.

GWENDOLINE [*shaking Tyler*] You are an inhuman boy!

ERMYNTRUDE You are a creature!

JANE Don't shake him, Miss, don't shake him!   65

> *Peggy Hesslerigge enters through the hall, and comes between Tyler and Gwendoline. Peggy is a shabbily dressed, untidy girl, with wild hair and inky fingers. Her voice is rather shrewish and her actions are jerky. Altogether she has the appearance of an over-wise and neglected child*

PEGGY Leave the boy alone, Gwendoline Hawkins! What has he done?

GWENDOLINE He won't feed my darling pets.

ERMYNTRUDE And he is generally a Lower Order.

PEGGY Go away, Tyler.   70

> *Tyler and Jane deposit the trunk in the hall with the other baggage, and disappear*

You silly girls! To make an enemy of the boy at the very moment we depend upon his devotion! [*Pointing*] It's just like you, Ermyntrude Johnson!

ERMYNTRUDE Don't you threaten me with your inky finger, Miss Hesslerigge, please!   75

PEGGY Ugh! Haven't we sworn to help Dinah Rankling with our last breath? Haven't we sworn to free her from the chains of tyranny and oppression, and never to eat much till we have seen her safely and happily by her husband's side?

ERMYNTRUDE Yes, but we can't truckle to a pale and stumpy boy, you know.   80

PEGGY We can—we've got to! If Dinah's husband is ever to enter this house, we must crouch before the instrument who opens the door—however short, however pasty.

DINAH (*calling outside*) Are you there, girls?   85

PEGGY (*jumping, and clapping her hands*) Here's Dinah!

ERMYNTRUDE and GWENDOLINE (*calling*) Dinah!

> *They run up to the door to receive and embrace Dinah, who enters through the hall. Dinah is an exceedingly pretty, simple-looking girl of about sixteen*

GWENDOLINE We've been waiting for you, Dinah.

PEGGY And now you're going to keep your promise to us, ain't you?

DINAH My promise?   90

PEGGY To tell us all about it from beginning to end.

DINAH (*bashfully*) Oh, I can't—I don't like to.

PEGGY You must; we've only heard your story in bits.

DINAH But where's Miss Dyott?

PEGGY Out—out—out.   95

DINAH And where is *he*—Miss Dyott's husband?

PEGGY What—the Mystery? (*Skipping across to the right-hand door,
and going down on her knees and peering through the keyhole*) It's all
right. One o'clock in the day, and he's not down yet—the imp! I'd
cold-sponge him if I were Miss Dyott. Places, young ladies.   100
      *Ermyntrude sits with Dinah on the sofa, Gwendoline being at
      Dinah's feet. Peggy perches on the edge of the table, with her feet
      on a chair*
H'm! Now then, Mrs—What's your name, Dinah?

DINAH (*drooping her eyelids*) Paulover—Mrs Reginald Paulover.

PEGGY Attention for Mrs Paulover's narrative. Chapter One.

DINAH [*shyly*] Well, dears, I met him at a party—at Mrs St
Dunstan's in the Cromwell Road.° He was presented to Mamma   105
and me by Major Padgate.

PEGGY Vote of thanks to Major Padgate; I wish *we* knew him, young
ladies. Well?

DINAH I bowed, of course, and then Mr Paulover—Mr Paulover
asked me whether I didn't think the evening was rather warm.   110

PEGGY He soon began to rattle on, then. It was his conversation that
attracted you, I suppose?

DINAH Oh no, love came very gradually. We were introduced at
about ten o'clock, and I didn't feel really drawn to him till long
after eleven. The next day, being Ma's 'At Home' day,° Major   115
Padgate brought him to tea.

PEGGY Young ladies, what is your opinion of Major Padgate?

ERMYNTRUDE I think he must be awfully considerate.

DINAH He's not—he called my *Reginald* a 'young shaver'.

PEGGY That's contemptible enough. How old is your Reginald?   120

DINAH He is much my senior—he was seventeen in November. Well,
the following week Reginald proposed to me in the conservatory.
He spoke very sensibly about settling down, and how we were not
growing younger; and how he'd seen a house in Park Lane which
wasn't to let, but which very likely would be to let some day. And 125
then we went into the drawing-room and told Mamma.

PEGGY, ERMYNTRUDE, and GWENDOLINE Well, well?

DINAH (*breaking down and putting her handkerchief to her eyes*) Oh, I
shall never forget the scene! I never shall.

PEGGY Don't cry, Dinah!   130
    They all try to console her

DINAH Mamma, who is very delicate, went into violent hysterics and
tore at the hearthrug with her teeth. But a day or two afterwards
she grew a little calmer, and promised to write to Papa, who was
with his ship at Malta.

PEGGY And did she?   135

DINAH Yes. Papa, you know, is Admiral Rankling. His ship, the
Pandora,° has never run into anything, and so Papa is a very
distinguished man.

GWENDOLINE And what was his answer?

DINAH He telegraphed home one terrible word—'Bosh!'   140

PEGGY, ERMYNTRUDE, and GWENDOLINE (*indignantly*) Oh!

PEGGY He ought to be struck into a Flying Dutchman!°

DINAH The telegraphic rate from Malta necessitates abruptness, but
I can never forgive the choice of such a phrase. But it decided our
fate. Three weeks ago, when I was supposed to be selecting wools   145
at Whiteley's,° *Reginald* and I were secretly united at the Registry
Office.

GWENDOLINE Oh, how lovely!

ERMYNTRUDE How romantic!

DINAH We declared we were much older than we really are, but, as   150
Reginald said, trouble had aged us, so it wasn't a story. At the
doors of the Registry Office we parted.

ERMYNTRUDE How horrible!

GWENDOLINE I couldn't have done that!

DINAH And when I reached home there was a letter from Papa   155
ordering Mamma to have me locked up at once in a boarding-
school; and here I am—torn from my husband, my letters opened
by Miss Dyott, quite friendless and alone.

PEGGY No, that you're not, Dinah. Listen to me! Miss Dyott is going
out of town today, and I'm left in charge. I'm a poor governess, but 160
playing gaoler over bleeding hearts is not in my articles,° and if your
husband comes to Volumnia House and demands his wife, he
doesn't go away without you—does he, young ladies?

GWENDOLINE and ERMYNTRUDE No.

PEGGY We will do as we would be done by—won't we?   165

GWENDOLINE and ERMYNTRUDE Yes!

    The street doorbell is heard, the girls cling to each other

PEGGY, ERMYNTRUDE, and GWENDOLINE (*in a whisper*) Oh!

DINAH (*trembling*) Miss Dyott!

Tyler is seen crossing the hall. Peggy runs to the window, and looks out

PEGGY No, it isn't—it's the postman.

DINAH A letter from Reginald!   170

Tyler enters with three letters

PEGGY (*sweetly*) Anything for us, Tyler dear?

TYLER (*looking at the letters, which he guards with one arm*) One for Miss Dinah Ranklin'!

DINAH (*snatching at her letter, which Tyler quickly slips into his pocket*) Oh!   175

TYLER My orders is to hand Miss Ranklin's letters to the Missus. (*Handing a letter to Peggy*) Miss Hesslerigge.

PEGGY (*surprised*) For me?

TYLER (*looking at the third letter*) Oh, look 'ere, here's a go!

GIRLS What's that?   180

TYLER (*dancing with delight*) Oh, crikey! This must be for *him*!

PEGGY Miss Dyott's husband!

GIRLS The Mystery!

The Girls gather round Tyler and look over his shoulder

PEGGY (*reading the address*) It's readdressed from the Junior Amalgamated Club, St James's Street.° (*Snatching the letter from Tyler*) 185
Gracious! 'The Honourable° Vere Queckett'!

GWENDOLINE The Honourable!

ERMYNTRUDE The Honourable!

TYLER What's that mean?

PEGGY Young ladies, we have been entertaining a swell unawares!° 190
(*Returning letter to Tyler*) Take it up.

TYLER Swell or no swell, the person who siles° two pairs of boots *per diem* daily° is no friend o' mine.

Tyler goes out

PEGGY (*opening her letter*) Oh! From Dinah's Reginald!

DINAH No, no!   195

PEGGY Addressed to me. (*Referring to the signature*) 'Reginald Percy Paulover'!

DINAH Read it, read it!

Peggy sits on the sofa, the three girls clustering round her and Dinah kneeling at her feet expectantly

PEGGY (*reading*) 'Montpelier Square, West Brompton. Dear Miss Hesslerigge, Heaven will reward you. The letter wrapped round a 200
stone which you threw me last night from an upper window of Volumnia House was handed to me after I had compensated the

78

person upon whose head it unfortunately alighted. The news that
Dinah has one friend in Volumnia House enabled me to get a little
rest between half-past five and six this morning.'   205

GWENDOLINE *One* friend!

ERMYNTRUDE What about us?

          Dinah kisses them

DINAH Go on!

PEGGY (*reading*) 'Not having closed my eyes for eleven nights, sleep
     was of distinct value. Now, dear Miss Hesslerigge, inform Dinah   210
     that our apartments are quite ready—'

GWENDOLINE and ERMYNTRUDE Oh!

PEGGY 'And that I shall present myself at Volumnia College, to fetch
     away the dear love of my heart, tonight at half-past nine.' Tonight!

GWENDOLINE and ERMYNTRUDE Tonight!   215

DINAH Oh, I've come over so frightened!

PEGGY (*waving the letter and dancing round with delight*) Tonight!

GWENDOLINE Finish the letter.

          [*During the continuation of the letter, Peggy and the others wipe
          tears from their eyes with pocket handkerchiefs of various
          colours*]

PEGGY (*resuming her seat, and reading with emotion*) 'Please assure
     Dinah that I shall love her till death, and that the piano is now   220
     moving in. Dinah is my one thought. The former is on the three
     years' system.° Kiss my angel for me. Our carpet is Axminster and,
     I regret to say, second-hand. But, oh! Our life will be a blessed,
     blessed dream—the worn part going well under the centre table.
     This evening at half-past nine. Gratefully yours, Reginald Percy   225
     Paulover. PS. I shall be closely muffled up, as the corner lamppost
     under which I stand is visible from the window of Admiral
     Rankling's dining-room. You will know me by my faithful, trusty
     respirator.'° Oh! I'm so excited! I wish somebody was coming for
     me!   230

ERMYNTRUDE I know—we shall be frustrated by Jane!

GWENDOLINE Or Tyler!

PEGGY Leave them to me—I'll manage 'em!

DINAH But there's Miss Dyott's husband!

PEGGY What! Let the mysterious person who has won Miss Dyott   235
     pause before he steps between a young bride and bridegroom!
     Ladies, Miss Dyott's husband is ours for the holidays. One frown
     from him and his dinners shall be wrecked, his wine watered, his
     cigars dampened. He shall find us not girls but Gorgons!°

> *A loud knock and ring are heard at the front door. Jane crosses the hall*

ERMYNTRUDE, GWENDOLINE, and DINAH (*under their breath*) Miss   240
Dyott! Miss Dyott!

> *They quickly disappear. Peggy remains, hastily concealing the letter. Miss Dyott enters. She is a good-looking, dark woman of dignified presence and rigid demeanour, her dress and manner being those of the typical schoolmistress. [She wears a sombre black silk gown and mantle, and carries an umbrella and a handbag]*

MISS DYOTT Is that Miss Hesslerigge?

PEGGY (*demurely*) Yes, Miss Dyott.

MISS DYOTT How have the young ladies been employing themselves?   245

PEGGY I have been reading aloud to them, Miss Dyott.

MISS DYOTT Is Mr Que—is my husband down yet?

PEGGY I've not had the pleasure of seeing him, Miss Dyott.

MISS DYOTT You can join the young ladies, thank you.

PEGGY Thank you, Miss Dyott.   250

> *In the doorway she waves Reginald's letter defiantly, but quickly disappears as Miss Dyott turns round*

MISS DYOTT Now, if Vere will only remain upstairs a few moments
longer!

> *She goes hurriedly to the right-hand door, listens, and turns the key; then to the centre door, listens again and appears satisfied; after which she throws open the window and, waving her handkerchief, calls in a loud whisper*

Mr Bernstein! Mr Bernstein! I have left the door on the latch.
Come in, please.

> *She closes the window. Very shortly afterwards, Otto Bernstein, a little, elderly German,° with the air of a musician, enters the room*

Thank you for following me so quickly.   255

> *She shuts the centre door and turns the key.*

BERNSTEIN You seemed so agitated that I came after your cab mit
anoder.

MISS DYOTT Agitated, yes. Tell me—miserable woman that I am—
tell me, what did I sound like at rehearsal this morning?

BERNSTEIN Cabital—cabital. Your voice comes out rich and peauti-   260
ful. Marks my vord—you will make a hit tonight. Have you seen
your new name in de pills?

MISS DYOTT The pills?

BERNSTEIN The blaypills.

MISS DYOTT I should drop flat on the pavement, if I did.   265

BERNSTEIN It looks very vine. (*Quoting*) 'Miss Gonstance Delaporte
as Queen Honorine, in Otto Bernstein's new gomic opera, *Pier-
rette*, her vurst abbearance in London.'

MISS DYOTT Oh, how disgraceful!

BERNSTEIN Disgraceful! To sing such melodies! No, no, please.   270
Disgraceful! Vy did you appeal to me, dree weeks ago, to put you
in the vay of getting through the Christmas vocation?

MISS DYOTT (*tearfully*) You don't know everything. Sit down. I can
trust you. You are my oldest friend, and were a pupil of my late
eminent father. Mr Bernstein, I am no longer a single woman.   275

BERNSTEIN Oh, I am very bleased. I wish you many happy returns
of the—eh—no—I congratulate you.

MISS DYOTT I am married secretly—secretly, because my husband
could never face the world of fashion as the consort of the
proprietress of a scholastic establishment. You will gather from   280
this that my husband is a gentleman.

BERNSTEIN H'm! So—is he?

MISS DYOTT It had been a long-cherished ambition with me, if ever
I married, to wed no one but a gentleman. I do not mean a
gentleman in a mere parliamentary sense;° I mean a man of birth,   285
blood, and breeding. Respect my confidence—I have wedded the
Honourable Vere Queckett.

BERNSTEIN (*unconcernedly*) Ah! Is he a very nice man?

MISS DYOTT Nice! Mr Bernstein, you are speaking of a brother of
Lord Limehouse!   290

BERNSTEIN Oh, am I? Lord Limehouse—let me tink—he is very—
very—vot you gall it?—very popular just now. Yah—yah—he is in
the Bankruptcy Court!

MISS DYOTT (*with pride*) Certainly. So is Harold Archideckne Queckett, Vere's youngest brother. So is Loftus Martineau Queckett,   295
Vere's cousin. They have always been a very united family. But,
dear Mr Bernstein, you have accidentally probed the one—I won't
say fault—the one most remarkable attribute of these great Saxon
Quecketts.

BERNSTEIN Oh, yes, I see; you have to pay your husband's leedle   300
pills.

MISS DYOTT Quite so—that is it. I have the honour of being
employed in the gradual discharge of liabilities incurred by

Mr Vere Queckett since the year 1876. I am also engaged in the noble task of providing Mr Queckett with the elaborate necessities of his present existence.   305

BERNSTEIN I know now vy you vanted mine help.

MISS DYOTT Ah, yes! Volumnia College is not equal to the grand duty imposed upon it. It is absolutely necessary that I should increase my income. In my despair at facing this genial season I   310 wrote to you.

BERNSTEIN Proposing to turn your cabital voice to account, eh?

MISS DYOTT Quite so, and suggesting that I should sing in your new oratorio.

BERNSTEIN Well, you are going to do zo.   315

MISS DYOTT What! When you have induced me to figure in a comic opera!

BERNSTEIN Yah, yah—but I have told you I have used the music of my new oratorio for my new gomic opera.

MISS DYOTT Ah, yes, that is my only consolation.   320

BERNSTEIN Vill your goot gentleman be in the stalls tonight?

MISS DYOTT In the stalls—at the theatre! Hush, Mr Bernstein, it is a secret from Vere. Lest his suspicions should be aroused by my leaving home every evening, I have led him to think that I am visiting a clergyman's wife at Hereford. I shall really be lodging in   325 Henrietta Street, Covent Garden.

BERNSTEIN Oh, vy not tell him all about it?

MISS DYOTT Nonsense! Vere is a gentleman; he would insist upon attending me to and from the theatre.

BERNSTEIN Vell, I should hope so.   330

MISS DYOTT No, no. He is himself a graceful dancer. A common chord of sympathy would naturally be struck between him and the *coryphées*.° Oh, there is so much variety in Vere's character.

BERNSTEIN Vell, you are a plucky woman; you deserve to be happy zome day.   335

MISS DYOTT Happy! Think of the deception I am practising upon dear Vere! Think of the people who believe in the rigid austerity of Caroline Dyott, Principal of Volumnia College. Think of the precious confidence reposed in me by the parents and relations of twenty-seven innocent pupils. Give an average of eight and a half   340 relations to each pupil; multiply eight and a half by twenty-seven and you approximate the number whose trust I betray this night!

BERNSTEIN Yes, but tink of the audience you will delight tonight in my oratorio—I mean my gomic opera. Oh, that reminds me.

(*Taking out a written paper from a pocketbook*) Here are two new   345
verses of the Bolitical Song for you to commit to memory before
this evening. They are extremely goot.

MISS DYOTT (*looking at the paper*) Mr Bernstein, surely here is a
veiled allusion to—yes, I thought so. Oh, the unwarrantable
familiarity! I can't—I can't—even vocally allude to a perfect   350
stranger as the Grand Old Man!°

BERNSTEIN Oh, now, now—he von't mind dat!

MISS DYOTT But the tendency of the chorus—(*Reading*) 'Doesn't he
wish he may get it!' is opposed to my stern political convictions!°
Oh! what am I coming to?   355

    Queckett's voice is heard

QUECKETT (*calling outside*) Caroline! Caroline!

MISS DYOTT Here's Vere! (*Hurriedly to Bernstein*) Goodbye, dear Mr
Bernstein. You understand why I cannot present you.

BERNSTEIN (*bustling*) Goodbye—till tonight. Marks my vord, you
vill make a great hit.   360

QUECKETT (*calling*) Caroline!

MISS DYOTT (*unlocking the centre door*) Go—let yourself out.

BERNSTEIN Goot luck to you!

MISS DYOTT (*opening the door*) Yes, yes.

BERNSTEIN And success to my new oratorio—I mean my gomic   365
opera.

MISS DYOTT Oh, go!

    She pushes him out and closes the door, leaning against it faintly

QUECKETT (*rattling the other door*) I say, Caroline!

MISS DYOTT (*calling to him*) Is that my darling Vere?

QUECKETT (*outside*) Yes.   370

    She comes to the other door, unlocks and opens it. vere Queckett
    enters.° He is a fresh, breezy, dapper little gentleman of about
    forty-five, with fair, curly hair, a waxed moustache, and a
    simple, boyish manner. He is dressed in the height of fashion,
    wears an orchid in his buttonhole, and a glass in his eye

QUECKETT Good-morning, Caroline, good-morning.

MISS DYOTT How is my little pet today? (*Kissing his cheek, which he*
turns to her for the purpose) Naughty Vere is down later than usual.

QUECKETT It isn't my fault, dear; the florist was late in sending my
flower.   375

MISS DYOTT What a shame!

QUECKETT (*shaking out a folded silk handkerchief*) Oh, by the bye,
Carrie, I want some fresh scent in my bottles.

MISS DYOTT My Vere shall have it.

QUECKETT Thank you, thank you. (*Sitting before the fire, opening the*   380
newspaper, and humming a tune) Let me see—let me see. Ah, here
we are—'Court of Bankruptcy. Before the Official Receiver.'
Limehouse came up again for hearing yesterday. How they bother
him! They bothered me in '75. Now, here's a coincidence, Carrie.
In 1875 my assets were *nil*, in 1885 dear old Bob's assets are *nil*.   385
That's deuced funny.

MISS DYOTT Vere, dear, have you forgotten what today is?

QUECKETT (*referring to the head of paper*) December the twenty-
second.

MISS DYOTT Yes, but it's the day on which I am to quit my Verey.   390

QUECKETT Oh, you've stuck to going, then! Well, I daresay you're
right, you know. You've a very bad cold. Nothing like change for
a bad cold—change of scene, change of pocket handkerchiefs, and
so on.

MISS DYOTT But you don't say anything about your own lonely   395
Christmas. I have married a man who is too unselfish.

The centre door opens slightly, and the heads of the three girls,
Peggy, Gwendoline, and Ermyntrude, appear one above the
other, spying

QUECKETT (*putting down his paper*) Lonely? By Jove, these inquisitive pupils of yours won't let a fellow be lonely! Upon my soul,
they are vexing girls.

MISS DYOTT But they are a source of income, dear.   400

QUECKETT They are a source of annoyance. I've never had the
measles—I've half a mind to catch it and give it to 'em. Now if I
could only while away my evenings somewhere, these vexing girls
wouldn't so much matter.

He rises; the heads disappear, and the door closes
(*Listening*) What was that?   405

MISS DYOTT The front door, I think.

QUECKETT I thought it might be those vexing girls—they're always
prying about. I was going to say, Carrie, why not let me withdraw
my resignation at the Junior Amalgamated Club and continue my
membership?   410

MISS DYOTT Ten guineas a year for such an object I cannot afford,
and will not pay, Vere.

QUECKETT Upon my soul, I might just as well be nobody, the way
I'm treated.

MISS DYOTT Oh, my king, don't say that! Have you thought about   415
the Christmas expenses?

QUECKETT Frankly, my dear, I have not.

MISS DYOTT Have you forgotten that my rent is due on Friday?

QUECKETT Completely.

MISS DYOTT And then think—only think of your boots!   420

QUECKETT Oh, dash it all—what man of any position ever thinks of
his boots? (*Producing a letter*) The fact is, Caroline, I have had a
note—sent on to me from the Club—from my friend, Jack
Mallory. He is First Lieutenant on the *Pandora*, you know, and
just home after four years at Malta. He reached London yesterday,   425
and writes me—(*Reading*) 'Now, old chap, do let's have one of our
old rollicking nights together, and—'

MISS DYOTT What!

QUECKETT Eh? (*Correcting himself*) He writes me—(*Referring to the
letter*) 'Now, old chap, do let me give you the details of our new   430
self-loading eighty-ton gun.' Well, Carrie, what the deuce am I to
do? It seems a nice gun. (*She shrugs her shoulders*) Carrie, what is
your Vere to do?

> *She makes no answer; he approaches her and touches her on the
> shoulder*

Carrie. Carrie, look at your Vere. Vere speaks to you. (*He sits on
her lap, she looks up affectionately*) Carrie, darling, you know old   435
Jack is such a devil—

MISS DYOTT Eh?

QUECKETT A nice devil, you know—an exceedingly nice devil. Now
I can't show up at the Club after sending in my resignation—
they'd quiz me awfully. But I must entertain poor old Jack.   440
(*Coaxingly*) Eh? Resignation sent in through misunderstanding,
eh? (*Pinching her cheek*) Ten little ginny-winnies, eh?

MISS DYOTT Not a ginny-winny! For a club, not half a ginny-winny!

QUECKETT Caroline, you forget what is due to me.

MISS DYOTT I wish I could forget what is due to everybody. Don't   445
be cross, Vere. I'll fetch your hat and coat, and Vere shall go out
for his little morning stroll. And if he promises not to be angry
with his Caroline, there are five shillings to spend.

> *She gives him some silver; he looks up beamingly again.*

QUECKETT My darling!

MISS DYOTT (*taking his face between her hands, and kissing him*)   450
Um—you spoilt boy!

> *She runs out*

QUECKETT Now what am I to do about Jack? I can't ask him here.
Carrie would never allow it, and if she would I couldn't stand the
chaff about marrying a boarding-school. No, I can't ask Jack here.

Why can't I ask Jack here? Everybody in bed at nine o'clock—   455
square the boy Tyler to wait. Bachelor lodgings, near Portland
Place. Extremely good address. Jack *shall* give me the details of
that eighty-ton gun. Yes, and we'll load it, too. While I'm out I'll
send this wire to Jack. (*Taking a telegraph form from the stationery
cabinet, and writing*) 'Come up tonight, dear old boy—nine-thirty   460
sharp—diggings° of humble bachelor—80, Duke Street, Portland
Place—bring two or three good fellows. Vere.' How much does
that come to? (*Counting the words° rapidly*) One—two—three—
four—five—no. (*Getting confused*) One—two—three—four—five—
six—no. One—two—three—four—five—six. (*Counting to the end*)   465
I think it is one and something halfpenny—but it's all luck with
these young ladies at the post office. Oh, and I haven't addressed
it! Where's Jack's letter?
> *He takes the letter from his pocket. Peggy enters quietly. Seeing*
> *Queckett, she draws back, watching him*

PEGGY (*to herself*) What is he doing now—the Guy Fawkes?°
QUECKETT (*referring to the letter*) Ah, 'Rovers' Club'! (*Addressing the*   470
telegram) 'John Mallory, Rovers' Club'. Let me see—that's in
Green Street, Piccadilly. (*Writing*) 'Green Street, Piccadilly'. Or am
I thinking of the 'Stragglers'?° I've a Club list upstairs—I'll go and
look at it. (*Humming an air, he shuts up the telegraph form in the
blotting-book, and rises, still with his back to Peggy*) I feel so happy!   475
> *He goes out*

PEGGY (*advances to the blotting-book, carrying some luggage labels*)
Miss Dyott has sent me to address her luggage labels. I am
compelled to open that blotting-book. (*She sits on the chair lately
vacated by Queckett, and opens the blotting-book mischievously with
her forefinger and thumb. Seeing the telegraph form*) Ah! (*Reading it*   480
greedily with exclamations) Oh! 'Dear old boy'! Oh! 'Diggings of
humble bachelor'! Oh! 'Bring two or three good fellows'! Oh—oh!
(*Sticking the telegraph form prominently against the stationery cabinet,
facing her, and addressing a luggage label*) 'Miss Dyott, passenger to
Hereford'.   485
QUECKETT (*re-entering gaily*) It *is* in Green Street, Piccadilly.
> *He sees Peggy, and stands perplexed, twisting his little moustache*

PEGGY (*writing solemnly*) 'Miss Dyott, passenger to Hereford'.
QUECKETT (*coughing anxiously*) H'm! I fancy I left an eighty-ton
gun—I mean, I think I've mislaid a—er—(*Without looking up,
Peggy readjusts the telegraph form against the cabinet*) Oh! h'm!   490
That's it.

He makes one or two fidgety attempts to take it, when Peggy
rises with it in her hand. She reads it silently, forming the words
with her lips

Oh, you vexing girl! What do you think of doing about it? (*She*
commences to fold the form very neatly) You know I shan't send it.
I never meant to send it. I say, I shall not send it. (*Nervously*
holding out his hand) Shall I? (*Peggy doubles up the form into another*
fold without speaking) You *are* a vexing girl.

MISS DYOTT (*calling outside*) Miss Hesslerigge!

    Peggy quietly slips the telegraph form into her pocket

QUECKETT Oh! You won't tell my wife! You will not *dare* to tell my
wife! (*Mildly*) Will you?

MISS DYOTT (*calling again*) Miss Hesslerigge!

QUECKETT (*in agony*) Oh! (*Between his teeth*) Do you—do you know
any bad language?

PEGGY I went to the Lord Mayor's Show° once; I heard a little.

QUECKETT Then I regret to say I use it to you, Miss Hesslerigge—I
use it to you!

    Miss Dyott enters, carrying Queckett's hat, gloves, and overcoat

MISS DYOTT You can address the labels in another room, Miss
Hesslerigge, please.

QUECKETT (*to himself*) Will she tell?

PEGGY (*to herself*) He is in our power!

    Peggy goes out

MISS DYOTT (*putting the hat on Queckett's head*) You look sickly, my
Vere.

QUECKETT I shall be better after my stroll, Caroline.

    A knock and ring are heard

MISS DYOTT (*assisting Queckett with his overcoat*) As you have some
solitary evenings before you, you may lay in a few cigars, Vere
darling.

QUECKETT Thank you, Carrie.

MISS DYOTT (*helping him to put on his gloves like a child*) But, for
the sake of our depressed native industries, I beg that you will
order those of purely British origin° and manufacture.

    Tyler enters carrying a large, common, black tea tray upon
    which is a solitary visiting-card

Where's the salver, you bad boy!

TYLER (*pointing to Queckett, sullenly*) 'E slopped his choc'late over it.

MISS DYOTT (*taking the card*) Admiral and Mrs Rankling—Dinah's
parents! I must see them.

QUECKETT (*hastily turning up his collar to conceal his face*) No, no!
They know me—they are old friends of my family!   525
   Tyler shows in Admiral and Mrs rankling.° Mrs rankling is a
   thin, weak-looking, faded lady with a pale face and anxious
   eyes. She is dressed in too many colours, and nothing seems to fit
   very well. Admiral Rankling is a stout, fine old gentleman, with
   short, crisp grey hair and fierce black eyebrows. He appears to
   be suffering inwardly from intense anger

MISS DYOTT My dear Mrs Rankling.
   The ladies shake hands. Tyler goes out

MRS RANKLING (*pointing to Rankling*) This is Admiral Rankling.
   Miss Dyott bows ceremoniously. Rankling returns a slight bow
   and glares at her

MISS DYOTT (*to Mrs Rankling*) Pray sit by the fire.
   As the ladies move to the fire, Queckett, who has been watching
   his opportunity, creeps round at the back and goes out

MRS RANKLING (*warming her feet at the fire*) The Admiral has called
upon you, Miss Dyott, with reference to our child, Dinah.   530
   Rankling, with a smothered exclamation of rage, sits on the sofa

MISS DYOTT Whom we find the charming daughter of charming
parents.
   Rankling gives her a fierce look, which frightens Miss Dyott,
   who is most anxious to conciliate the Admiral.

MRS RANKLING Dinah's obstinacy is a very serious shock to the
Admiral, who is naturally unused to insubordination.

MISS DYOTT Naturally.   535
   Rankling glares at her again; she puts her hand to her heart

MRS RANKLING The Admiral has been stationed with his ship at
Malta for a long period; in fact, the Admiral has not brightened
our home for over four years.

MISS DYOTT How more than delightful to have him with you again!
   Rankling gives Miss Dyott a fearful look; she clutches her chair

MRS RANKLING The Admiral has one of those fine English tem-   540
pers—generous but impetuous. You may guess the sad impression
Dinah's ingratitude has produced upon him. It is an open secret
that the Admiral made three wills yesterday, and read King Lear's
curse° after dinner in place of Thanksgiving.

RANKLING (*sharply*) Emma!   545

MRS RANKLING (*starting*) Yes, Archibald.

RANKLING Leave the fire—you'll be chilled when we go. Come over
here.

MRS RANKLING Yes, Archibald.

*She crosses the room in a flutter and sits beside Rankling, who
makes insufficient room for her*

Thank you, Archibald. I have been sitting up with the Admiral all   550
night, and it is owing to my entreaties that he has consented to
give Dinah one last chance of reconciliation.

RANKLING (*who has been eyeing her*) Emma!

MRS RANKLING Yes, Archibald.

RANKLING Your bonnet's on one side again.   555

MRS RANKLING (*adjusting it*) Thank you, Archibald. We leave town
for the holidays tomorrow; it rests with Dinah whether she spends
Christmas in her papa's society or not.

RANKLING Don't twitch your fingers, Emma—don't twitch your
fingers.   560

MRS RANKLING (*nervously*) It's a habit, Archibald.

RANKLING It's a very bad one.

MRS RANKLING All we require is that Dinah should personally
assure us that she has banished every thought of the foolish young
gentleman she met at Mrs St Dunstan's.   565

MISS DYOTT (*rising and ringing the bell*) If I am any student of the
passing fancies of a young girl's mind—

RANKLING Speak louder, ma'am—your voice doesn't travel.

MISS DYOTT (*nervously—with a gulp*) If I am any student of the
passing—fancies—(*Rankling puts his hand to his ear*) Oh, don't   570
make me so nervous!

> *Jane enters, looking untidy, her sleeves turned up, and wiping
> her hands on her apron*

MISS DYOTT (*shocked*) Where is the manservant?

JANE On a herring,° ma'am.

MISS DYOTT Ask Miss Dinah Rankling to be good enough to step
downstairs.   575

> *Jane goes out. Rankling rises, with Mrs Rankling clinging to his
> arm*

MRS RANKLING You will be calm, Archibald—you will be moderate
in tone. (*With a little nervous cough*) Oh, dear! poor Dinah!

RANKLING Stop that fidgety cough, Emma.

> *He stalks about the room, his wife following him*

MRS RANKLING Even love-matches are sometimes very happy. Ours
was a love-match, Archibald.   580

RANKLING Be quiet! We're exceptions.

> *He paces up to the door; it opens and Peggy presents herself.
> Directly he sees Peggy, he catches her by the shoulders and gives
> her a good shaking*

MISS DYOTT Admiral!

MRS RANKLING Archibald!

PEGGY (*being shaken*) Oh—oh—oh—oh!

RANKLING (*panting, and releasing Peggy*) You good-for-nothing girl!   585
Do you know you have upset your mother?

MRS RANKLING Archibald, that isn't Dinah!

MISS DYOTT That is another young lady.

RANKLING (*aghast*) What—not—? Who—who has led me into this
unpardonable error of judgment?   590

MRS RANKLING (*to Peggy, who is rubbing her shoulders and looking
vindictively at Rankling*) Oh, my dear young lady, pray think of
this only as an amusing mistake. The Admiral has been away for
more than four years; Dinah was but a child when he last saw her.
(*Weeping*) Oh, dear me!   595

RANKLING Be quiet, Emma—you'll make a scene.

MISS DYOTT (*to Peggy*) Where is Miss Rankling?

PEGGY Miss Rankling presents her compliments to Miss Dyott,
and her love to her papa and mamma, and, as her mind is quite
made up, she would rather not cause distress by granting an   600
interview.

> *Rankling sinks into a chair*

MRS RANKLING Archibald!

MISS DYOTT (*to Peggy*) The port wine!

> *Peggy advances with the cake and wine*

MRS RANKLING (*kneeling to Rankling*) Archibald, be yourself! Remember, you have to respond for the Navy° at a banquet tonight.   605
Think of your reputation as a genial after-dinner speaker.

RANKLING (*rising with forced calmness*) Thank you, Emma. (*To Miss
Dyott*) Madam, my daughter is in your charge till you receive
instructions from my solicitor. (*Glaring at Peggy*) A short written
apology shall be sent to this young lady in the course of the   610
afternoon. (*To his wife*) Emma, your hair's rough—come home.

> *He gives Mrs Rankling his arm. They go out. Miss Dyott sinks
> exhausted on sofa. Peggy offers her a glass of wine*

MISS DYOTT Oh, my goodness! (*Declining the wine*) No, no—not
that. It has been decanted since Midsummer.

> *Queckett, his coat-collar turned up, appears at the door, looking
> back over his shoulder*

QUECKETT What's the matter with the Ranklings? (*Seeing Miss Dyott
and Peggy*) Oh! Has that vexing girl told Caroline?   615

> *The clock strikes two*

MISS DYOTT (*to herself*) Two o'clock—I must remove to Henrietta
    Street. (*Seeing Queckett*) My darling.

QUECKETT My love. (*To himself*) All right.

MISS DYOTT I am going to prepare for my journey—the train leaves
    Paddington at three.　　　　　　　　　　　　　　　　　　　　620

> *As Miss Dyott goes towards the centre door, Jane enters carrying
> about twenty boxes of cigars, which she deposits on the floor and
> then goes out*

MISS DYOTT What is this?

QUECKETT H'm! My cigars, Carrie—brought 'em with me in a cab.

MISS DYOTT [*faintly*] Oh! (*Reading the label of one of the boxes*) 'Por
    Carolina'.° Ah, poor Caroline.

> *She goes out. Directly she is gone, Peggy and Queckett, by a
> simultaneous movement, rush to the two doors and close them*

QUECKETT Now, Miss Hesslerigge!　　　　　　　　　　　　　　625

PEGGY Sir.

QUECKETT We will come to a distinct understanding.

PEGGY If you please.

QUECKETT In the first place, you will return me my telegram.

PEGGY I can't.　　　　　　　　　　　　　　　　　　　　　　630

QUECKETT You mean you won't.

PEGGY No, I can't.

QUECKETT Why not?

PEGGY I have just sent it to the telegraph office by Tyler.

QUECKETT Despatched it!　　　　　　　　　　　　　　　　　635

PEGGY Despatched it. It was one and fourpence.

QUECKETT Oh, you—you—you vexing girl! Mr Mallory will be here
    tonight.

PEGGY Yes, and will 'bring two or three good fellows'. At least we
    hope so.　　　　　　　　　　　　　　　　　　　　　　　640

QUECKETT [*sitting in a daze beside the table*] Hope so!

PEGGY (*standing over him with her arms folded*) Listen, Mr Vere
    Queckett. (*He starts*) We ladies are going to give a little party
    tonight to celebrate a serious event in the life of one of us. We
    have invited only one young gentleman; your friends will be　645
    welcome.

QUECKETT Oh!

PEGGY Without us your party must fail, for we command the
    servants. Let it be a compact—your soirée shall be our soirée, and
    our soirée your soirée.　　　　　　　　　　　　　　　　650

QUECKETT And if I indignantly decline?

PEGGY (*solemnly*) Consider, Mr Queckett—your Christmas holidays are to be passed with us. Think in which direction your
comfort and freedom lie, in friendship or in enmity? Even now,
Ermyntrude Johnson is trimming the holly with one of your   655
razors.

QUECKETT But what explanation could I give Mr Mallory of your
presence here?

PEGGY Every detail has been considered. You are our bachelor uncle.

QUECKETT Uncle!   660

PEGGY We are your four nieces.

    Queckett looks up—is tickled by the idea, and bursts out
    laughing. Peggy joins in

QUECKETT I don't see why that shouldn't be rather jolly.

PEGGY (*roguishly*) D'ye consent?

QUECKETT Can't help myself, can I?

PEGGY (*delighted*) That you can't.   665

QUECKETT Let's be friends, then, shall we? Have you girls got any
money?

PEGGY No. Have you?

QUECKETT No—that is, all mine's invested.

MISS DYOTT (*outside*) Tyler, fetch a cab.   670

    Queckett makes a bolt from the room. Peggy vigorously re-
    arranges the furniture as Miss Dyott enters, dressed as if for a
    journey, and carrying her umbrella and handbag

Where is my husband?

PEGGY (*looking about her*) Your handbag, Miss Dyott?

    Queckett re-enters

MISS DYOTT Still in your overcoat, dear?

QUECKETT Of course, Carrie. I'll drive with you to Paddington.

MISS DYOTT No, no, I insist on going alone.   675

QUECKETT (*taking off his coat with alacrity*) Oh, Carrie, I *am*
disappointed!

    Dinah, Gwendoline, and Ermyntrude come through the hall into
    the room, and form a group. Jane appears in the hall. Tyler joins
    her there

MISS DYOTT Miss Hesslerigge—young ladies. I regret to say I am
compelled to—to quit Volumnia House for a time. The length of
my absence depends upon how long it runs—[*Correcting herself in*   680
confusion] upon how long it runs to it,° to employ a colloquialism
of the vulgar. But I depart with a light heart, because I leave my
husband in authority. He will find a trusty lieutenant in Miss

Hesslerigge. Ladies, to abandon for the moment our mother
tongue, Je vous embrasse de tout mon coeur—soyez sages!°   685
GIRLS (*together*) Au revoir, Mademoiselle Dyott! Bon voyage, Mademoiselle Dyott!

> [*Soft, sentimental music is played in the orchestra.*] *Peggy joins
> the girls and they talk earnestly. A cabman is seen carrying out
> the boxes from the hall, assisted by Tyler. Miss Dyott produces
> some paper packets of money from her handbag*

MISS DYOTT (*as she gives the packets to Queckett*) Vere, the house-
agent will apply for the rent—there it is. Our fire insurance expired
yesterday—post the premium to the Eagle office° at once. Jane's   690
wages are due next week—deduct for the broken water-bottle.
When you need exercise, dear one, tidy up the back yard—the
recreation ground. A charwoman assists Jane on Fridays—three-
quarters of a day, and leaves before her tea. Goodbye, Vere.
TYLER The cab's a-waitin', ma'am.   695

> *Miss Dyott takes Queckett's arm*

GIRLS Goodbye, Miss Dyott.

> *Miss Dyott and Queckett go out through the hall.* [*The music
> changes to a bright galop.*] *Peggy, Ermyntrude, and Gwendoline
> run over to the windows and look out. Dinah sits apart, thinking*

ERMYNTRUDE There they are!
GWENDOLINE Miss Dyott's in the cab!
PEGGY She's off!
THE THREE Hurrah! Hurrah!   700

> *Queckett returns, the girls surround him demonstratively*

PEGGY Dinah—young ladies—(*Pointing to Queckett*) Uncle Vere!
ERMYNTRUDE and GWENDOLINE (*together*) Uncle Vere! Uncle Vere!

> *Queckett tries to maintain his dignity, and pushes the girls from
> him. Tyler, with Jane, is seen letting off a squib in the hall*

CURTAIN

Act Two

THE PARTY

Scene One

The scene is a plain-looking schoolroom at Miss Dyott's. Outside the two windows runs a narrow balcony, and beyond are seen the upper stories and roofs of the opposite houses. There are two doors facing each other. The room is decorated for the occasion with holly and evergreen, and a table is laid with supper. Peggy is standing on a chair, with a large hammer in her hand, nailing up holly

PEGGY (*surveying her work*) There! I'm sure *Miss Dyott* wouldn't recognise the dull old classrooms. (*Descending*) I think it's time I dressed.

   Queckett enters slowly; he is in a perfectly-fitting evening dress, with a flower in his buttonhole, but looks much depressed. He and Peggy regard each other for a moment silently

Oh, I'm so glad you're ready early! How good it makes one feel, giving pleasure to others—doesn't it? Aren't you well?   5

QUECKETT Yes—no. I deeply regret plunging into the vortex of these festivities.

PEGGY Oh, I suppose you're nervous in society.

QUECKETT (*drawing himself up*) Nervous in society, Miss Hesslerigge?   10

PEGGY What do you think of the decorations? Artistic, aren't they?

QUECKETT [*disgusted*] A treat at a Sunday school!

PEGGY Then you shouldn't have locked up the rooms downstairs.

QUECKETT I daren't allow the neighbours to see the house lighted up downstairs. I wish I could have locked up all you vexing   15
girls.

PEGGY [*with dignity*] That's not the spirit to give a party in! (*Contemplating the table*) How many do you think your friend, Mr Mallory, will bring?

QUECKETT I don't think Mr Mallory will find his way here at all.   20
Have you observed the fog?

PEGGY Is it foggy?

QUECKETT You can't see your hand before you outside. I sincerely hope my friend will *not* come.

94

PEGGY There's hospitality! Ours will.   25

QUECKETT Who *is* your friend?

PEGGY Mr Paulover.

QUECKETT And who the devil is—?

PEGGY I don't think that's the language for a party, Mr Queckett!

QUECKETT I beg your pardon. Who is Paulover?   30

> *Tyler enters with a bill in his hand, his hair stiffly brushed and greased, and wearing an expression of intense wonderment*

What's this?

TYLER A beautiful large lobster salid is come, sir.

QUECKETT (*looking at Peggy*) *I* haven't ordered a lobster salad. (*In an undertone*) You know, this is getting extremely vexing. (*He takes from his pocket the packets of money previously given him by Miss Dyott*) I've already paid a bill for some oysters and a pâté de foie gras. Jane's wages went for that. (*Opening a packet*) Now, here's a salad. That breaks into next week's household expenses.   35

> *He hands the money to Tyler, who goes out*

PEGGY We're only girls, you know. And you seem to forget you're our uncle.   40

QUECKETT (*irritably*) I am *not* your uncle.

PEGGY Tonight you are. But you needn't be our uncle tomorrow.

QUECKETT (*gloomily*) Somebody will have to be *my* uncle° tomorrow. Then I understand there's a lark pudding ordered for half-past nine. I can't allow the account to be sent in to—to—   45

PEGGY [*slyly*] To Auntie?

QUECKETT Well—to—to Auntie. Who pays for the lark pudding?

PEGGY You couldn't well ask girls to do it. Besides, it's your party.

QUECKETT It is *not* my party, and it is *your* lark pudding.

PEGGY It may be our lark, but it's your pudding.   50

> *Tyler enters, still much astonished, with another bill*

QUECKETT (*taking the bill*) What's that?

TYLER Sich a lot of champagne's come, sir!

PEGGY Champagne! Who ordered that? *I* didn't.

QUECKETT Hush! I did—I did—I did.

PEGGY Then it *is* your party?   55

QUECKETT Part of the party is my party. (*Opening another packet*) I've broken into the rent.

> *He hands Tyler the bill and some money, pocketing the remainder. Tyler goes out*

The fire insurance alone remains intact. (*Opening the last packet*) Postal orders for three pounds ten. I'll despatch that, at any rate.

*He sits at the writing-table and begins to write. Peggy hammers
up the last piece of holly as Queckett tries to write*

Oh, you vexing girl!   60

PEGGY Beg pardon; this is the last blow.

*She gives another knock as Jane enters, carrying a large
ornamental wedding cake. Jane is in a black gown and smart
cap and apron; her eyes are wide open with pleasure and
astonishment. Jane deposits the cake upon the writing-table
before Queckett*

JANE 'Scuse me, sir; the confectioner's jest brought the things.

QUECKETT What's that? *That* isn't the lark pudding.

JANE Oh, lor', no, sir!

She goes out

PEGGY Oh, that's the wedding cake.   65

QUECKETT Oh, come! It isn't my wedding cake.

PEGGY (*laughing*) Oh, don't, you funny man! No, it's Mr Paulover's.

QUECKETT Who the dev—?

PEGGY Hush!

QUECKETT Let's settle one thing at a time. Who is Paulover?   70

PEGGY Dear Dinah's husband.

QUECKETT [*blankly*] Dear Dinah?

PEGGY Your niece—Dinah Rankling.

QUECKETT Married?

PEGGY Secretly. To Mr Paulover.   75

Queckett puts his hand to his brow

QUECKETT Oh, that's old Paulover, is it?

PEGGY *Young* Paulover. They were married really three weeks ago,
but without any breakfast—I don't mean a bacon breakfast, I mean
a proper breakfast. But we girls think they ought to have a wedding
cake and everything complete to start them in life together: and   80
that's why you're giving this party, you know.

QUECKETT Now, understand me, I will not be dragged into such a
conspiracy!

PEGGY But you're in it.

QUECKETT The Ranklings are acquaintances of mine, almost relat-   85
ives; Admiral Rankling's cousin married the sister of the man who
bought my brother's horses. (*Rubbing his hands together*) I wash my
hands of all you vexing girls.

PEGGY Don't fret about it, please. Nothing can ever make Mrs
Paulover Miss Rankling again. I'll go and dress while you finish   90
your letter.

QUECKETT (*impatiently*) Oh!

> *He resumes writing at the table*

PEGGY (*going to the door*) The girls will be here directly. Be nice, won't you?

> *She goes out. Jane enters with tarts and confectionery on dishes which she places on the table before Queckett*

JANE S'cuse me, sir. 95

> *Queckett rises with his letter and the inkstand, and goes impatiently over to the other side of the room, where he continues writing on the top of piano*

QUECKETT They won't let me write to the insurance office.

> *Tyler enters with some boxes of bon-bons. The writing-table being crowded, Jane waves him over to the piano and goes out. Tyler puts the bon-bons on the top of the piano before Queckett, who again snatches up his letter and the inkstand and goes to the centre table*

QUECKETT I *will* write to the insurance office.

> *Tyler goes out as Jane re-enters*

JANE (*presenting a bill*) The pastry-cook's bill, sir.

QUECKETT Great Scot! (*Diving his hand into his pocket, bringing out some loose money and giving it to Jane*) There! 100

> *Jane goes out*

I've written to the insurance office. (*Sealing the letter*) My mind's easy—done my duty to poor Caroline.

> *He puts the letter in his breast-pocket as Tyler enters*

TYLER (*more astonished than ever, announcing*) Miss Gwendoline Hawkins.

> *Gwendoline enters, dressed in a simple and pretty party dress. Tyler goes out*

GWENDOLINE (*bashfully, seeing nobody but Queckett*) Oh, I'm first; I 105 shall come back again.

> *She starts to go*

QUECKETT Come in—come in. How d'ye do? (*Gwendoline advances. Queckett shakes hands with her*) Extremely pleased to see you—so glad you've come—won't you sit down? (*To himself with satisfaction*) Illustrations of Deportment and the Restrictions of Society— 110 Vere Queckett.° Carrie would be delighted.

> *Tyler re-enters, still more astonished*

TYLER Miss Hermyntrude Johnson, and—and—and Mrs Reginald Paulover!

QUECKETT This is a little too vexing!

> *Ermyntrude and Dinah enter, both prettily dressed—Dinah in*
> *white. Tyler goes out*

(*Angrily*) How d'ye do—so glad you've come—won't you sit down? 115

DINAH We're very well, thank you.

ERMYNTRUDE Awfully well.

> *They sit, the three girls in a row—Dinah in the centre,*
> *Gwendoline and Ermyntrude taking her hands*

QUECKETT (*to himself*) Instructions in Polite Conversation. (*Brusque-*
ly to Dinah) How is Paulover?

DINAH I think he's very well, thank you. 120

QUECKETT (*to himself*) Carrie would be pleased. (*To the girls*) H'm!
I suppose you young ladies distinctly understand that I occupy a
painfully false position this evening?

DINAH I am sure it is very, very kind of you to give this party.

QUECKETT (*to himself*) Well, now, that's exceedingly appropriate, 125
the way in which that is put. Carrie really does do her duty to the
parents of these girls.

GWENDOLINE Peggy says you insist on our calling you Uncle.

QUECKETT Does she! (*To himself*) Peggy is the one I've turned
against. 130

ERMYNTRUDE We think you'll be an awfully jolly uncle.

QUECKETT (*pleased*) Thank ye—thank ye. (*To himself*) I begin to like
helping Carrie with the pupils.

> *Peggy enters. She is quaintly but untidily dressed in poor, much-*
> *worn, and old-fashioned finery. In her hand she carries a pair*
> *of soiled, long white gloves*

Hallo!

> *Without speaking a word, Peggy hurries across the room and*
> *goes out at the other door*

What is the matter with that vexing girl now? 135

> *Peggy re-enters with Tyler, pushing him forward*

TYLER (*announcing*) Miss Margaret Hesslerigge.

> *Peggy advances to Queckett, holding out her hand*

PEGGY How do you do?

QUECKETT (*savagely*) How d'ye do? Delighted to see you. For
goodness' sake, sit down!

> *He turns away to the fire. The three girls rise to greet Peggy*

DINAH (*anxiously*) I don't think it's nearly half-past nine yet. 140

PEGGY (*rather proudly, produces a huge old-fashioned watch*) Twenty
to ten.

DINAH I thought it was.

*Dinah, Gwendoline, and Ermyntrude run to a window, pull
aside the blind, and look out. Peggy goes to the other window,
pulls up the blind, and opens the window*

QUECKETT What are you doing?

PEGGY I can just see him, under his lamppost. 145

DINAH The fog will hurt him.

PEGGY Hush! I told him we'd whistle twice.

DINAH Do it!

Peggy makes two or three ineffectual attempts to whistle

PEGGY Girls, it's ominous—my whistle has left me. (*To Queckett,
taking his arm*) Come and whistle! 150

QUECKETT No, no.

PEGGY (*leading Queckett to the open window*) Whistle, or you'll catch
cold.

*Queckett whistles twice, desperately, then returns to the fireplace,
annoyed*

He's heard it. (*She closes the window and pulls down the blind*)
Now, listen. (*To Gwendoline and Ermyntrude*) You two girls count 155
five.

GWENDOLINE One.

ERMYNTRUDE Two.

DINAH Oh, how slowly you count!

GWENDOLINE Three. 160

ERMYNTRUDE Four.

DINAH (*clasping her hands*) Five!

*There is a distant ring at the bell; with a little cry, Dinah runs
out. Peggy begins to put her gloves on. Ermyntrude and
Gwendoline go to the door, open it and listen*

PEGGY (*to Queckett*) Thank you for whistling. I shall never make a
'whistling woman',° shall I?

QUECKETT A wide knowledge of humanity, in its highest and lowest 165
grades, Miss Hesslerigge, does not enable me even to conjecture
the possibilities of your future.

PEGGY No compliments, please. Thank you.

*She holds out her gloved hand for him to button the glove. After
a look of astonishment he complies*

You know my idea about my future, don't you?

QUECKETT No. 170

PEGGY That I only need one essential to become a Duchess.

QUECKETT What is that?

PEGGY A Duke.

GWENDOLINE They're coming upstairs!

PEGGY (*to Queckett*) Now you'll see Mr Paulover. Oh, I do hope he'll   175
take to you!

QUECKETT Well, really, I'm—

> *He walks angrily away as Dinah enters with Reginald Paulover,*
> *a good-looking lad, rather sheepish in repose, but fiery and*
> *demonstrative when out of temper. He is in evening dress,*
> *overcoat, and muffler, and wears a respirator, which he removes*
> *on entering*

DINAH (*introducing the three girls*) Reggie, these are my three dear
friends—Miss Hawkins—Miss Johnson—

REGINALD (*bowing*) Awfully pleased to meet you.   180

DINAH And Miss Hesslerigge.

> *Peggy advances and shakes hands with Reginald*

REGINALD Thank you very much for being so kind to—my wife.

ERMYNTRUDE (*to Gwendoline, disappointed*) No whiskers or moustache! Oh!

PEGGY (*to Reginald*) Had you been waiting long?   185

REGINALD Ten minutes. I was jolly glad to hear my wife's dear little
whistle. I should know it from a thousand.

PEGGY H'm! Dinah dear, make Mr Paulover and Mr Queckett
known to each other.

> *Queckett comes forward with a disagreeable look. Reginald*
> *glares at him*

DINAH (*timidly*) Reggie dear, this is Mr Queckett.   190

> *Queckett bows stiffly. Reginald nods angrily*

REGINALD (*to Dinah*) Dinah, what is a man doing here? You know I
can't bear you to talk to a man.

DINAH Oh, Reggie, why are you always so jealous?

PEGGY Mr Queckett is giving the party.

REGINALD What party?   195

PEGGY Your wedding party.

REGINALD Is he! (*To Queckett, angrily*) I'm much obliged to Mr
Queckett.

PEGGY (*pacifying Reginald*) Mr Queckett is so nice—he calls himself
Dinah's uncle.   200

REGINALD Does he! Then it's a liberty—that's all I can say.

QUECKETT Do you know you're in my house, sir?

REGINALD I'm not in your house, sir! Come away, Dinah!

PEGGY Hush! Mr Queckett is Miss Dyott's—

QUECKETT Be quiet—mind your own business.   205

REGINALD (*to Queckett*) At any rate it's my business, sir.

QUECKETT I'm afraid you're a cub,° sir.

REGINALD What!

DINAH Oh, Reggie, don't!

> *A loud knock and ring are heard*

PEGGY (*to Queckett*) Your friend.   210

REGINALD Whose friend?

QUECKETT *My* friend.

REGINALD Another man, I suppose! Dinah!

PEGGY Ladies, do explain everything to Mr Paulover.

> *Dinah seizes Reginald's arm. Gwendoline and Ermyntrude*
> *gather round them, Reginald protesting*

REGINALD (*handing his card as he passes Queckett*) My card, sir.°   215

QUECKETT Pooh, sir!

> *He throws the card in the fire. The three girls hurry Reginald*
> *out of the room*

PEGGY (*to Queckett*) I'm so sorry—he *hasn't* taken to you.

QUECKETT He needn't trouble himself! Upon my soul, this is going
to be a nice party!

> *Tyler enters*

TYLER Three gentlemen, sir: I was to say the name of Mallory.   220

QUECKETT *Three* gentlemen!

PEGGY (*delighted, to Queckett*) Oh, he's brought some good fellows!
(*Reckoning on her fingers*) That's one for Ermyntrude—and one for
me—and one for—

QUECKETT (*to Peggy*) Be quiet. (*To Tyler*) I'll come down.   225

MALLORY (*outside*) Queckett!

QUECKETT Yes, Jack!

> *Jack Mallory enters. He is a good-looking, jovial fellow of about*
> *thirty-six, with a bronzed face. He is in evening dress and*
> *overcoat. Tyler goes out*

MALLORY (*shaking hands heartily with Queckett*) Ah, Queckett, dear
old chap! Well, I am glad to see you.

QUECKETT [*constrained*] How are you, Jack?   230

MALLORY Quaint diggings you have up here. The hanging committee have skied you,° though, haven't they? (*Seeing Peggy*) I beg
your pardon.

QUECKETT (*confused*) Oh—ah—yes. I didn't mention it. I have
my—my—nieces spending Christmas with me.   235

MALLORY (*bowing to Peggy*) Delighted. (*To Queckett*) Did you say
niece or nieces?

QUECKETT Nieces. (*Softly to Peggy, quickly*) How many? I forget.

PEGGY (*to Queckett*) Three.

QUECKETT Three.   240

PEGGY Three, not counting me.

QUECKETT Three, not counting me. I mean three, not counting that vexing girl—Peggy—Margaret.

MALLORY (*bowing*) It would be impossible not to count Miss—Margaret.   245

PEGGY (*simpering*) Oh!

> *Queckett assists Mallory to take off his overcoat, first darting an angry look at Peggy*

PEGGY (*to herself*) I shall give Gwendoline and Ermyntrude the two that are downstairs.

QUECKETT H'm! You're not alone, are you, Jack?

MALLORY No—they're coming up.   250

QUECKETT (*grimly*) Are they?

MALLORY The old gentleman takes his time with the stairs.

QUECKETT (*with forced ease*) Poor old gentleman! Who the deuce—?

MALLORY The fact is, there's been a big Navy dinner tonight at the Whitehall Rooms. The enthusiasm became rather forced—'Britan-   255
nia rules the waves',° and all that sort of thing—so I gladly thought of finishing up with you. I've brought my nephew—hallo, here he is!

> *Mr Saunders enters. He is a pretty boy, almost a child, in the uniform of a naval cadet*

My nephew—Horatio Nelson Drake Saunders, of the training-ship *Dexterous*.   260

SAUNDERS (*with the airs of a little man, but in a treble voice*) How do you do? Awfully pleased to come here.

QUECKETT Glad to see you, Mr. Saunders.

MALLORY (*laughing, to Saunders*) I say, you shouldn't have left the old gentleman.   265

SAUNDERS (*laughing*) He sent me up to count how many more stairs there were.

QUECKETT (*impatiently*) Jack, I don't put the question on theological grounds, but who *is* 'the old gentleman'?°

MALLORY Oh, I beg your pardon—and his. We persuaded an old   270
acquaintance of yours to join us—Admiral Rankling.

QUECKETT (*aghast*) What!

MALLORY Do you mind?

QUECKETT Mind!

RANKLING (*outside*) Mr Saunders!   275

SAUNDERS Here, sir.

> *Peggy makes a bolt out of the room. Saunders goes to the door,*
> *and returns with Rankling. Rankling is in evening dress,*
> *overcoat, and muffler, and is much out of breath*

RANKLING Ah, Mr Queckett, how do you do? We haven't met
anywhere lately; I've been away, you know.

QUECKETT I am delighted to renew our acquaintance, Admiral
Rankling.   280

RANKLING (*puffing*) Mr Mallory suggested that we should smoke our
last cigar at your lodgings. I can't stay long, for I've a considerable
distance to drive home. At least, I suppose I have, for I really don't
know quite where we are. What quarter of London have you
brought me to, Mr Mallory? Oh, thank ye!   285

> *He turns to Saunders, who is offering to remove his overcoat.*
> *The door is slightly opened, and the heads of all the girls are seen*

QUECKETT (*hastily to Mallory*) He doesn't know where he is!

MALLORY The fog's as thick as a board outside.

QUECKETT He isn't aware he lives a hundred and fifty yards off!

MALLORY No—does he?

QUECKETT Hush, don't tell him! Jack, don't tell him! I'll explain why   290
by and by.

> *Queckett turns to assist Saunders who, mounted on a chair, is*
> *struggling ineffectually to relieve Rankling of his overcoat*

RANKLING Thank ye—bits o' boys, bits o' boys.

MALLORY (*to himself*) There's a wild look about poor Queckett I
don't like. It's his lonely bachelor life, I suppose. Curious place,
too. He used to be such a swell in the Albany.°   295

> *He looks about him. The door shuts and the heads disappear*

RANKLING (*to Queckett*) Thank ye—thank ye. (*Panting*) Ouf!

> *Rankling sits down; Mallory talks to him. Saunders has seated*
> *himself on the sofa and is dozing, quite tired out*

QUECKETT Oh, what a party!

> *The door opens, and Peggy's head appears*

PEGGY (*hurriedly to Queckett*) Who'd have thought of this?

QUECKETT [*faintly*] It might be worse; he doesn't recognise the
house he is in.   300

PEGGY Doesn't he?

QUECKETT Get rid of his daughter and that horrid Paulover.

PEGGY Certainly not; I know he won't recognise his daughter.

QUECKETT Won't recognise his own dau—! You'll drive me mad!

They continue to talk in undertones. Saunders is now fast asleep

RANKLING (*to Mallory*) No, *I* don't like the look of poor Queckett.   305

MALLORY He seems altered.

RANKLING Altered! He glares like the devil! He's not married, is he?

MALLORY No.

RANKLING Then, what does he mean by it? Queer rooms, too.
(*Catching sight of the wedding cake on the table*) Lord, look there!   310

MALLORY (*looking at the cake*) Hallo!

RANKLING Why, it's like the thing we had at my wedding breakfast.
Phew! I shall go.

MALLORY No, no! The fact is poor old Queckett has some nieces
staying with him.   315

RANKLING Nieces?

MALLORY Four of 'em. I've seen one, and I fancy, by the look of her
mischievous little face, that they're too much for him.

PEGGY (*to Queckett*) Leave everything to me. Don't spoil the party,
Uncle.   320

QUECKETT Dash the party!

*Peggy retiring hastily, the door bangs, at which Rankling and
Mallory look round*

RANKLING Oh, Queckett, where are your nieces?

QUECKETT Nieces—nieces? Oh, they retire at eight o'clock. Early to
bed, early to rise—

Gwendoline and Ermyntrude enter, visibly pushed on by Peggy

RANKLING (*rising*) H'm! This doesn't look like early to bed.   325

QUECKETT (*weakly*) Just got up, I suppose. Gwendoline—Ermyntrude—my dears—Admiral Rankling—Mr Mallory—(*Looking
about for Saunders*) Mr—Mr—oh, Mr Saunders is asleep.

Ermyntrude and Gwendoline advance to Rankling

RANKLING (*to the girls*) How do you do? And whose daughters are
you?   330

*Gwendoline and Ermyntrude look frightened, and shake their
heads*

QUECKETT Oh, these are my sister Isabel's girls.

RANKLING Why, all your sister Isabel's children were boys.

QUECKETT *Were* boys, yes.

RANKLING (*irritably*) *Are* boys, sir.

QUECKETT Are *men*, now. H'm! I should have said these are my   335
sister Janet's children.

RANKLING Oh! I've never heard of your sister Janet.

QUECKETT No—quiet, retiring woman, Janet.

RANKLING Well, then, whom did Janet marry?

QUECKETT Whom *didn't* Janet marry! I mean, whom *did* Janet 340
marry? Why, Finch Griffin of the Berkshire Royals!°

RANKLING Dear me, we're going to meet Major Griffin and his wife
on Christmas Day at the Trotwells'.

QUECKETT *Are* you? (*To Gwendoline and Ermyntrude*) Go away!
    Peggy enters
Oh—ahem! This is Margaret—Peggy. 345

RANKLING Oh, another of Mrs Griffin's?

QUECKETT Yes, yes.

RANKLING Large family.

QUECKETT Rapid—two a year.

RANKLING (*eyeing Peggy*) Why, we've met before today! 350

QUECKETT Eh! where?

RANKLING At a miserable school near my house in Portland Place.

PEGGY Oh, yes. Our holidays began this afternoon.

RANKLING Why, Queckett, my daughter Dinah and Miss Griffin are
schoolfellows! 355

QUECKETT No!

RANKLING Yes!

QUECKETT No!

RANKLING Yes, sir.

QUECKETT How small the world is! 360

RANKLING Do you happen to know anything about the person who
keeps that school? What's the woman's name—Miss—Miss—?

QUECKETT Miss—Miss—Miss—

PEGGY Miss Dyott. Oh, yes, Uncle knows her to speak to.

RANKLING What about her, Queckett? 365

QUECKETT (*looking vindictively at Peggy*) Er—um—rather not haz-
ard an opinion.
    He hastily joins Mallory, Gwendoline, and Ermyntrude

RANKLING (*confidentially to Peggy*) H'm! My dear Miss Griffin, did
you receive a short but ample apology from me this afternoon,
addressed 'To the young lady who was shaken'? 370

PEGGY Yes; and, oh, I shall always prize it!

RANKLING No, no, don't! You haven't bothered your uncle about it,
have you, dear?

PEGGY No, not yet.

RANKLING I shouldn't, then; I shouldn't. He seems worried enough. 375
Shall I take you and your sisters to see the pantomime?

PEGGY Yes, please.

RANKLING Then you'd better give me back that apology.

PEGGY Oh, no—you'd use it again.

RANKLING One—two—three. Mr Mallory says you have *four* nieces   380
with you, Mr Queckett.

QUECKETT Ah, but Jack's been dining, you know. I beg your pardon,
Jack.

PEGGY Oh, yes, there is one more. Mrs—Mrs—Parkinson is here
with her husband.   385

QUECKETT H'm! My brother Tankerville's eldest girl.

RANKLING I've never heard of your brother Tankerville!

QUECKETT No—he's Deputy Inspector of Prisons in British Guiana.
Quiet, retiring chap.

PEGGY I'll go and fetch them.   390
She runs out

QUECKETT (*to Rankling*) To make a clean breast of it, the girls have
been preparing a little festival tonight in honour of Mr and
Mrs—Mr and Mrs—the name Peggy mentioned. My niece was
married, very quietly, some weeks ago to a charming young
fellow—a charming young fellow—and these foolish children insist   395
on cutting a wedding cake and all that sort of nonsense. I didn't
want to disturb you with their chatter—

RANKLING You forget, Queckett, you are speaking to a father, sir.

QUECKETT [*wiping his brow*] No—I don't, indeed.
Peggy re-enters, followed by Reginald and Dinah

PEGGY My cousin and Mr Parkinson.   400

RANKLING How do you—? (*Staring*) What an extraordinary likeness
to my brother Ned! (*Taking her hand slowly, still looking at her*)
And how do you do?

DINAH (*palpitating*) Thank you, I am very well.

RANKLING Do you know, your voice is exceedingly like my sister   405
Rachel's!

REGINALD (*thrusting himself between Dinah and Rankling*) I am sorry
to differ; I think my wife resembles no one but herself.

RANKLING (*hotly*) I beg your pardon, sir.

REGINALD (*hotly*) Pray don't.   410

RANKLING (*to himself*) That's not a charming young fellow!

PEGGY (*presenting Mallory to Dinah*) Mr Mallory.

MALLORY (*gallantly, to Dinah*) I am delighted to have the opportunity of congratulating my old friend's niece upon her recent
marriage. (*Taking her hand*) I think myself especially fortunate in   415
being present on such—

REGINALD (*thrusting himself between Dinah and Mallory, and giving Dinah his arm*) How do you do, sir?

PEGGY Mr Mallory—Mr Parkinson.

> *They bow abruptly, glaring at each other*

MALLORY (*to himself*) Is *that* a charming young fellow?   420

> *Dinah expostulates in undertones with Reginald. He replies by gesticulating violently and by glaring at Rankling, who meanwhile is muttering comments on Dinah's resemblance to various members of his family. Peggy endeavours to pacify Mallory, who is evidently annoyed, and altogether there is much hubbub with signs of general ill-feeling*

QUECKETT (*sinking back in his chair*) Oh, what a party!

> *Jane enters*

JANE (*quietly to Queckett*) The pudding is in the arey,° sir, waiting to be paid.

QUECKETT I'll come to it.

> *Jane goes out*

(*To Peggy*) Margaret, show Admiral Rankling and Mr Mallory   425
where the cigarettes are. They may like—(*To himself*) Years are going off my life!

> *He goes out*

PEGGY (*to Mallory*) May I take you to the cigarettes?

MALLORY (*to Peggy*) You may take me anywhere.

PEGGY (*bashfully*) Oh! (*To Rankling*) The cigarettes are in the next   430
room, Admiral Rankling.

RANKLING (*not hearing Peggy, but still eyeing Dinah*) That girl has a look of Emma's sister Susan.

> *Peggy and Mallory go out. Reginald, seeing Rankling is still looking at Dinah, abruptly takes her over to the door, glaring at Rankling as he passes*

REGINALD (*to Dinah, fiercely*) Come away, Dinah!

DINAH (*to Reginald, tearfully*) Oh, Reggie, dear Reggie, you are so   435
different when people are not present.

> *They go out. Rankling watches them through the doorway. Gwendoline has meanwhile seated herself beside Saunders, whose head has gradually fallen till it rests upon her shoulder. She is now sitting quite still, looking down upon the boy's face*

ERMYNTRUDE (*watching them enviously*) Well, considering that Mr Saunders was introduced to us asleep, I don't think Gwendoline's behaviour is at all *comme il faut*! (*She bumps gently against Rankling*) Oh!

    440

RANKLING (*looking at Ermyntrude, rather dazed*) My dear, I am quite glad to see somebody who isn't like any of my relations. Come along.

> *They go out. Saunders moves dreamily and murmurs*

SAUNDERS (*waking*) All right, ma dear, I'll come down directly. (*He raises his head and kisses Gwendoline, then opens his eyes and looks at her, startled*) Oh, I've been dreaming about my ma! I—I don't know you, do I?   445

GWENDOLINE It doesn't matter, Mr Saunders. You've had such a good sleep.

> *She kisses his forehead gently*

SAUNDERS Oh, that's just like my ma! Where are the others?   450

GWENDOLINE (*arranging his curls upon his forehead*) I'll take you to them.

SAUNDERS Thank you. What's your name?

GWENDOLINE Gwendoline.

SAUNDERS Gwen's short for that, isn't it? (*Rubbing his eyes with his fists, then offering her his arm*) Permit me, Gwen.   455

> *They go out. Queckett, his hair disarranged, his appearance generally wild, immediately enters, followed by Jane and Tyler*

QUECKETT I can't help it! I am in the hands of fate. Arrange the table. I cannot help it!

> *Tyler and Jane proceed to arrange the table and the seats for supper. Peggy enters quietly*

PEGGY It is supper time. Oh, what's the matter, Uncle Vere?

QUECKETT Well, in the first place, there are no oysters.   460

PEGGY I've seen them!

QUECKETT I've gone further—I've tasted them.

PEGGY Bad?

QUECKETT Well, I should describe them as inland oysters. A long time since *they* had a fortnight at the seaside.   465

PEGGY Oh, dear! Then we must fall back on the lark pudding.

QUECKETT You'll injure yourself seriously if you do.

PEGGY Tell me everything. It has not come small?

QUECKETT It has come ridiculously small.

PEGGY It was ordered for eight persons.   470

QUECKETT Then it is architecturally disproportionate.

PEGGY (*to herself*) Something must be done.

> *She runs to the writing-table and begins to write rapidly on three half-sheets of paper, folding each into a three-cornered note as she finishes it*

The girls must be warned. (*Writing*) 'For goodness' sake, don't taste the pudding.' Poor girls—what an end to a happy day!

QUECKETT (*to himself*) Oh, if the members of my family could see me at this moment! I, whose suppers in the Albany were at one time a proverb! Oh, Caroline, Caroline, even you little know the sacrifice I have made for you! 475

PEGGY (*to Queckett, handing him the notes*)   Quick, please! Quick! Give them these notes. 480

QUECKETT (*taking the notes*) What for?

PEGGY Oh, don't ask; you will see the result.

QUECKETT But you mustn't write to people you—!

PEGGY (*angrily*) Go away!

   He hurries out. Peggy wipes her eyes

JANE Ah, don't be upset, Miss! 485

PEGGY No, I won't, I won't. But I am only a girl, and the responsibility is very great for such young shoulders.

   There is a murmur of voices outside. Jane and Tyler go out as Rankling enters with Ermyntrude, followed by Reggie with Dinah. Reginald is endeavouring to keep her away from Mallory, who comes after them. Saunders and Gwendoline follow next, and Queckett brings up the rear. There is much talking as Queckett indicates the seats they are to occupy

PEGGY (*quietly to Queckett*) Did you give the girls the notes?

QUECKETT (*surprised*) No.

PEGGY Oh! Never mind—I'll whisper to them now. 490

   She whispers hurriedly to Dinah, Gwendoline, and Ermyntrude

QUECKETT (*to himself*) I didn't understand they were for the *girls*.

   He goes to the head of the table as Rankling, Mallory, and Saunders come suddenly together, each carrying a note

RANKLING (*to Mallory*) Mallory, we were right—there is some horrible mystery about Queckett. (*Looking to see they are not observed*) I've had an anonymous warning: 'For Heaven's sake, don't touch the pudding!'

MALLORY I know. 495

RANKLING Tell the boy.

MALLORY (*to Saunders*) I say—don't you say yes to pudding.

SAUNDERS I know. Tell the old gentleman.

MALLORY (*to Saunders*) He knows. (*To Rankling*) He knows. 500

   With a simultaneous gesture they pocket the notes and go to find their seats at table. They all sit. The lobster salad and the pâté have been placed by Tyler at the end of the table. Tyler

now enters carrying nine large plates, which he places before
Queckett

QUECKETT (*with assumed composure and good spirits*)   There is a
spontaneity about our jolly little supper which will perhaps—
ah'm!—atone for any absence of elaboration.

RANKLING   Don't name it, Mr Queckett.

MALLORY   Just as it should be, my dear fellow.   505
Tyler goes out

QUECKETT   The language of the heart is simplicity. Our little supper
is from the heart.

MALLORY   Ah, I shall never forget your little suppers in the Albany.
Where were they from?

QUECKETT   Gunter's,° Jack. (*With a groan*) Oh!   510
Jane, at the door, hands to Tyler a very small pudding in a
silver-plated basin, which he places before Queckett

RANKLING, MALLORY, and SAUNDERS (*to themselves*)   The pudding!
They exhibit great eagerness to get a view of the pudding

PEGGY (*behind Mallory's back*)   Oh, how shameful it looks!

QUECKETT (*falteringly*)   Here is a homely little dish which has
fascinations for many, though I never touch it myself—I never
touch it myself. (*Rankling, Mallory*, and *Saunders exchange signifi-*   515
cant looks) Ah'm! A pudding made of larks. (*He glances round; all*
look down; there is deep silence) A pudding—made—of larks. (*To*
Dinah) My dear—a very little?

DINAH   No, thank you, Uncle.

QUECKETT   Perhaps you're right. Gwendoline, a suggestion?   520

GWENDOLINE   No, thank you, Uncle.

QUECKETT (*to Peggy*)   Margaret, I know what your digestion is—I
won't tempt you. (*To Ermyntrude*) Ermyntrude—the least in the
world?

ERMYNTRUDE   No, thank you, Uncle.   525

QUECKETT (*to himself*)   Ah! How lucky!

PEGGY (*to herself*)   Brave girls! I was afraid they'd falter.

QUECKETT (*heartily*)   Now then—Admiral Rankling?

RANKLING   No, thank you.

QUECKETT   No pudding?   530

RANKLING   I haven't long dined, thank you, Queckett.

QUECKETT (*to Reginald, coldly*)   May I?

REGINALD (*distantly*)   I never eat suppers, thank you.

QUECKETT (*to Saunders*)   My dear Mr Saunders?

SAUNDERS   No, Mr Queckett, thank you.   535

QUECKETT (*getting desperate, to Mallory*) Jack—a lark?

MALLORY No, thanks, old fellow.

QUECKETT Well, I—(*Throwing down his knife and spoon, and leaning back in his chair. To Tyler*) Take it away!

> *Tyler removes the pudding; they all watch its going*

TYLER (*handing it to Jane*) Keep it warm,° Jane.   540

QUECKETT Jack, a lobster salad and a small pâté de foie gras are at your end of the table.

MALLORY (*looking round*) May I?

> *There is a general reply of 'No, thank you', from the ladies*

PEGGY (*to herself*) Poor girls, what sacrifices they make for these men!

MALLORY (*with a plate in his hand*) May I—?   545

RANKLING, SAUNDERS, and REGINALD (*together*) No, thank you.

QUECKETT (*to himself*) What a supper party! Tyler, the champagne.

> *Tyler fetches a bottle of champagne, and proceeds to open it*

RANKLING (*behind Ermyntrude and Peggy, to Mallory*) If we see the cork drawn, shall we risk it?

MALLORY (*to Rankling*) Risk it.   550

RANKLING Risk it.

> *Reginald has risen from the table and is seen tapping Saunders upon the shoulder and speaking to him rapidly and excitedly.*

SAUNDERS No, I have not!

> *Talking together, Reginald and Saunders go out hurriedly*

MALLORY What's the matter with that charming young fellow now? (*To the table*) Excuse me.

> *He follows them out*

DINAH (*tearfully to Gwendoline*) Reginald's jealousy gets worse and   555
worse. I am sure it will cloud our future.

GWENDOLINE (*to Dinah*) Mr Saunders wasn't looking at you, I am positive. The poor little fellow was stroking my hand.

> *Mallory returns with Saunders and Reginald, who both look excited, and their hair is disarranged*

REGINALD (*to Mallory and Saunders*) I beg your pardon; I may have been mistaken. I imagined that Mr Saunders was regarding   560
my wife in a way which overstepped the borders of ordinary admiration.

> *They hastily shake hands all round and hurry back to their seats. Tyler has poured out the champagne, and now departs. Admiral Rankling rises. queckett taps the table for silence*

QUECKETT Please—please.

RANKLING Ah'm!

MALLORY (*to himself*) I thought the old gentleman wouldn't resist   565
the temptation.

RANKLING My dear Mr Queckett, it would ill become an old
man—himself the father of a daughter, nearly, if not quite, of the
age of the young lady opposite me—to lose an opportunity of
saying a few words on the pleasant, the—the extremely pleasant—   570
condition of the British Naval Forces—ah'm! No—

MALLORY (*to himself*) I knew that would happen.

RANKLING Pardon me, I have been speaking on other subjects
tonight—I should say, the extremely pleasant occasion which
brings us together.   575

QUECKETT Certainly, my dear Rankling; how nice of you!

RANKLING Not only am I the commander—the father—of a ship—of
a daughter whom it is my ambition to see happily wedded to the
man of her choice—

PEGGY Hear, hear!   580

QUECKETT (*in an undertone, glaring at her*) You vexing girl!

RANKLING But I am also the husband of a heavily plated cruiser—
er—um—h'm!—of a dear lady to whose affection and society I owe
the greatest happiness of my life.

PEGGY (*to herself*) How different some gentlemen are when their   585
wives are not present.

RANKLING If I have the regret of knowing that my acquaintance with
Mrs—Mrs—

PEGGY Parkinson.

RANKLING Thank you, I know—Parkinson—has begun only tonight,   590
I have also the pleasure of inaugurating a friendship with that
delightful young lady, which on my side shall be little less than
paternal. I—I—I—

MALLORY Oh, gracious!

RANKLING I—I cannot sit down—   595

MALLORY (*wearily [to himself]*) Why not!

RANKLING I will not sit down without adding a word of congratula-
tion to Mr—Mr—

PEGGY Parkinson.

RANKLING Thank you, I know—Parkinson—the young gentleman   600
whose ingenious construction and seagoing qualities—

MALLORY No, no.

RANKLING Er—um—whose amiability and genial demeanour have
so favourably impressed us. As an old married man I welcome this
recruit to the service.   605

PEGGY Hear, hear!

RANKLING It is one of hardship and danger, of stiff breezes and dismal night watches. But it is because Englishmen never know when they are beaten—

MALLORY No, no.   610

RANKLING Yes, sir—it is because Englishmen never know when they are beaten that they occasionally find conjugal happiness. I ask you all to drink to the Navy—to—to Mr and Mrs—thank you, I know—Jenkinson.

> *All except Dinah and Reginald rise and drink the toast, 'Mr and Mrs Parkinson'; then, as they resume their seats, Reginald rises sulkily*

REGINALD Admiral Rankling—   615

> *Jane appears at the door, wildly beckoning to Queckett*

JANE (*in a whisper*) Sir—Sir—!

QUECKETT (*angrily*) Not now—not now—go away!

GIRLS Hush!

> *The girls motion Jane away; she retires*

QUECKETT (*to Reginald*) I beg pardon.

REGINALD All I have to say is that the highest estimate Admiral   620
Rankling can form of me will not do justice to my devotion to my wife.

PEGGY (*sotto voce*) Oh, beautiful!

REGINALD (*fiercely*) And I should like to know the individual, old or young, who would take my wife from me!   625

MALLORY (*to himself*) Many a husband would like to know *that* person.

REGINALD In conclusion—as for Admiral Rankling's offer of a paternal friendship, I trust he will remember that offer if ever we should have occasion to remind him of it. (*Looking at his watch*)   630
And now I regret to say—

> *The girls rise, the men follow*

PEGGY No, no—not before we have danced one quadrille.

GWENDOLINE and ERMYNTRUDE Oh, yes—oh, yes! A quadrille!

PEGGY Uncle Vere will play for us.

QUECKETT No, Uncle Vere will not!   635

MALLORY Oh, yes, you will, Queckett, old fellow—eh?

QUECKETT Well—I—with pleasure, Jack. (*To himself*) How dare they!

PEGGY Clear the floor!

> *Saunders and Mallory, assisted by Ermyntrude and Gwendoline, put back the table and chairs*

RANKLING (*getting very good-humoured*) Upon my soul, I never saw
such girls in my life! I wonder whether my Dinah is anything like   640
'em!

    Dinah and Reginald are having a violent altercation

DINAH A wife shouldn't dance with her husband—it is horrible
form!

REGINALD I can't see you led out by a stranger.

DINAH It is merely a quadrille.°   645

REGINALD Merely a quadrille! Woman, do you think I am marble!

DINAH (*distractedly, turning to Rankling*) Admiral Rankling, are you
going to dance?

RANKLING (*gallantly*) If you do me the honour, my dear madam.

    She takes his arm

REGINALD (*madly, to Dinah*) Ah, flirt!   650

QUECKETT (*to Peggy*) Get rid of them soon, or I shall become a
gibbering idiot!

MALLORY (*slapping Queckett on the back*) Now then, Queckett.

    Queckett goes to the piano

(*To Peggy*) Will you make me happy, dear Miss Peggy?

PEGGY Thank you, Mr Mallory, I never dance. (*Taking his arm*) But   655
I don't mind this once. Uncle!

QUECKETT (*to himself*) I wash my hands of the entire party!

    He plays the first figure of a quadrille, while they dance—Rank-
    ling and Dinah, Saunders and Gwendoline, Mallory and Peggy,
    Ermyntrude and Reginald. They dance with brightness and
    animation, but whenever Reginald encounters dinah there is a
    violent altercation. As the figure ends, Jane enters again, and
    runs to Queckett at the piano

QUECKETT What is it?

JANE Oh, sir, do come downstairs—as far down as you can get!

QUECKETT What do you mean?   660

JANE That boy, Tyler, sir!

QUECKETT Tyler—well?

JANE He went off bang in the kitchen, sir, about ten minutes ago.
Them fireworks!

QUECKETT Fireworks! Where is he?   665

JANE Gone for the engines, sir.

QUECKETT (*rising*) The engines!

ERMYNTRUDE Uncle!

GWENDOLINE Uncle Vere!

PEGGY Now then, Uncle!   670

QUECKETT Excuse me—let somebody take my place at the piano. I—I'll be back in a moment!

> *Jane hurries out, he following her*

PEGGY (*running to the piano and commencing a waltz*) A waltz! Change partners!

> *Rankling dances with Ermyntrude, Saunders with Gwendoline. reginald is left out, but is wildly following Dinah, who is dancing with Mallory*

RANKLING (*puffing*) Not so fast, Miss Griffin—not so fast!   675

REGINALD (*in Dinah's ear*) I shall require some explanation, Madam.

DINAH Oh, Reginald!

> *There is the sound of a prolonged knocking at the street door, followed by a bell ringing violently.*

PEGGY (*playing*) Somebody wants to come in, evidently.

> *Suddenly the music and the dancing stop and everybody listens; then they all run to the windows and look out.*

RANKLING What's that?

MALLORY What's wrong?   680

SAUNDERS Oh, look there!

PEGGY Oh, there's such a crowd at our house!

> *Queckett re-enters with Jane, who sinks into a chair. Queckett looks very pale and frightened*

QUECKETT Listen to me, please.

ALL What's the matter?

QUECKETT Don't be alarmed. Look at me. Imitate my self-posses-   685
sion.

ALL What *is* the matter?

QUECKETT The matter? The weather is so unfavourable that the boy Tyler has been compelled to display fireworks on the premises.

GIRLS Oh!   690

MEN What has happened?

QUECKETT Pray don't be disturbed. There is not the slightest occasion for alarm. We have now the choice of one alternative.

RANKLING and MALLORY What's that?

QUECKETT To get out without unnecessary delay.   695

GIRLS (*clustering together*) Oh!

RANKLING (*assuming the tone of a commander*) Mr Mallory! Mr Saunders!

MALLORY Yes, sir.

SAUNDERS Yes, sir.   700

> *Mallory and Saunders place themselves beside Rankling*

RANKLING Ladies, fetch your cloaks and wraps preparatory to
breaking up our pleasant little party. Who volunteers to assist the
ladies?

MALLORY I, sir!

SAUNDERS I, sir!   705

REGINALD I do!

QUECKETT I do!

RANKLING Mr Mallory, tell off° Mr Queckett and Mr Jenkinson to
help the ladies.

The girls run out, followed by Reginald, Queckett, and Jane

RANKLING Mr Mallory! Mr Saunders!   710

MALLORY and SAUNDERS Yes, sir.

RANKLING Our respective coats.

*They bustle about to get their coats as the door quietly opens and
Jaffray, a fireman,° appears*

JAFFRAY Good-evening, gentlemen. Can you tell me where I'll find
the ladies?

MALLORY They're putting on their hats and cloaks.   715

JAFFRAY Thank you, gentlemen, I'm much obliged to you.

*He goes to the window, pulls up the blind, and throws the
window open; the top of a ladder is seen against the balcony*

Are you coming up, Mr Goff?

GOFF (*out of sight*) Yes, Mr Jaffray.

*Goff, a middle-aged, jolly-looking fireman, [wearing a helmet,]
enters by the balcony and the window*

JAFFRAY Gentlemen, Mr Goff—one of the oldest and most respected
members of the Brigade. Mr Goff tells some most interesting   720
stories, gentlemen.

RANKLING (*impatiently*) Stories, sir! Call the ladies, Mr Mallory.

Mallory goes out

GOFF I shouldn't hurry them, sir—ladies like to take their time. Now
I remember an instance in October '78—

RANKLING Confound it, sir, you're not going to relate anecdotes   725
now!

JAFFRAY I beg your pardon, sir—Mr Goff is one of the most
experienced and entertaining members of the Brigade.

RANKLING I tell you I don't care about that just now! Where are the
ladies?   730

Saunders goes out

JAFFRAY Excuse me, sir, Mr Goff's reminiscences are well worth
hearing while you wait.

116

RANKLING But I don't wish to wait!

> *Mallory and Peggy, Saunders and Gwendoline, Reginald and Dinah, followed by Jane, enter. The girls are hastily attired in all sorts of odd apparel and carrying bonnet-boxes, parcels, and small handbags. Ermyntrude carries, amongst other things, a cage of white mice, Gwendoline a bird in a cage, Dinah a black cat, and Peggy a pair of skates and a brush and comb*

GIRLS We're ready. Take us away!

JAFFRAY I must really ask you, ladies and gentlemen, to take it quietly for a few minutes.   735

ALL Take it quietly! What for?

JAFFRAY The staircase isn't just the thing for ladies and gentlemen at the present moment. I shall have to ask the ladies and gentlemen to use the Escape.   740

ALL (*turning to the window*) The escape! Where is it?

JAFFRAY It'll be here in two minutes. In the mean time, I think Mr Goff could wile away the time very pleasantly with a reminiscence or two. Ladies, Mr Goff—

GIRLS Oh, take us away! Take us away!   745

> *Mallory, Saunders, and Reginald soothe the ladies; Jaffray goes to the window and looks out*

GOFF (*pleasantly seating himself and taking off his helmet*) Well, ladies, I don't know that I can tell you much to amuse you. However—

RANKLING Be quiet, sir—we will not be entertained!

JAFFRAY (*carrying a hose from the window to the door*) Really, gentlemen, I must say I've never heard Mr Goff treated so hasty at any conflagration.   750

> *He carries the hose out*

RANKLING A fireman full of anecdote! I decline to appreciate any reminiscence whatever. So do we all!

REGINALD Certainly!   755

MALLORY All of us!

GOFF It was in July '79, ladies—my wife had just brought my tea to the Chandos Street Station—

> *Jaffray re-enters, and goes to the window*

MALLORY Will you be silent, sir?

REGINALD Get up and do something!   760

SAUNDERS Go away!

JAFFRAY The escape, ladies and gentlemen. That window—one at a time.

There is a general movement and hubbub. Goff rises; he and Jaffray disappear by the window on the left. Mallory throws open the other window, and Jaffray appears outside and receives Dinah, Gwendoline, Ermyntrude, Peggy, and Jane as they escape

RANKLING Mr Mallory—Mr Saunders—good-evening!

Reginald disappears by the right-hand window. Saunders goes after him. Mallory is about to follow when Queckett enters hurriedly. Queckett is in a tall hat, a short covert coat,° and carries gloves and an umbrella. He is flourishing a letter

QUECKETT (*pulling Mallory back*) Jack—Jack!   765

MALLORY Hallo!

QUECKETT I'm going back to save some valuables. Directly you get down, post that letter. Oh, Jack, it's so important.

MALLORY (*looking at the letter*) To the Eagle Fire Insurance Company.

QUECKETT Quite so—slipped my memory.   770

Mallory disappears. Jaffray follows him

RANKLING (*hurrying to Queckett*) My dear Queckett, it is the commander's duty to be the last to leave the ship—you are master here. Thank you for your hospitality. Good-night.

QUECKETT My dear Rankling, thank *you* for coming to see me. Good-night.   775

Jaffray appears at the window

JAFFRAY It's all right, gentlemen; there's a kind lady down below who is taking everybody into her house for the night—Mrs Rankling of Portland Place.

RANKLING Mrs Rankling! That's my wife!

Queckett disappears

JAFFRAY Is she, sir? Glad to hear it. Then they are all your visitors   780
till tomorrow.

RANKLING Confound it, sir, where do I live?

JAFFRAY Just at the corner here, sir—a hundred yards off.

RANKLING Then where am I now?

JAFFRAY Miss Dyott's boarding-school, sir—Volumnia College.   785

RANKLING What!

He and Jaffray go out by the window on the right as Goff enters by the window on the left

GOFF Where is he? (*Calling at the door*) Sir, here's the lady of the house—rode up on an engine from Piccadilly. Make haste—she says she will come up the ladder.

Queckett enters quickly, dragging after him several boxes of cigars

QUECKETT A lady! What lady?
> *Miss Dyott appears at the window. She is in the gorgeous dress of an opera-buffa queen, with a flaxen wig, much disarranged, and a crown on one side. [She makes for Queckett]*

(*Recoiling*) Caroline!

MISS DYOTT (*taking him by the collar*) Come down!
> *She drags him towards the window [as the curtain falls]*

CURTAIN

Act Three

NIGHTMARE

Scene One

The scene is a well-furnished, tastefully decorated room in the house of Admiral Rankling. At the further end of the room there are two double doors facing each other, one with glazed panels opening to a conservatory, the other admitting to a dark chamber. There are two other doors, also facing each other, nearer to the spectator. All is darkness, save for a faint glow from the fire and a blue light coming from the conservatory. Peggy, dressed as before, enters quietly, looking about her

PEGGY (*in a whisper*) Where have I got to now, I wonder? What a dreadful wilderness of a house to wander about in, in the dark, all alone. Oh, for the daylight! (*Looking at her watch*) Half-past six. Why, gracious! Here's a spark of fire! Oh, joy!

She goes down on her knees, and replenishes the fire with coal from the scuttle. The door opens, and Gwendoline peeps in

GWENDOLINE (*in a whisper*) What room is this? (*Entering noiselessly*) 5
Will the day never break? (*Frightened and retreating, as Peggy makes a noise in blowing up the fire*) Oh!

PEGGY (*frightened*) Oh! Who is that? (*Looking round*) Gwendoline!

GWENDOLINE Peggy!

PEGGY Are you wandering about too? 10

GWENDOLINE Yes. I can't sleep—can you?

PEGGY (*shivering*) Sleep! No. As if I could sleep in a strange bed in a strange house, in one of Admiral Rankling's nightgowns! You didn't meet any daylight on the stairs, did you?

Another door opens, and Ermyntrude enters noiselessly

GWENDOLINE (*clinging to Peggy*) Oh, look there! 15

ERMYNTRUDE (*in a whisper*) I wonder where I am now.

PEGGY Ermyntrude!

ERMYNTRUDE (*clinging to a chair*) Ah!

PEGGY Be quiet! It's we—it's us—it's her and me! Oh, my grammar's going now! 20

ERMYNTRUDE Can't you girls get to sleep?

GWENDOLINE I should think not.

PEGGY There wasn't any daylight in your room when you came down, was there?

ERMYNTRUDE I thought I saw a glimmer through the window on the first-floor landing.   25

PEGGY Ah, perhaps that's some of yesterday's. I know! I've made up the fire; let us bivouac here till daybreak. Two by the fire, and take it in turns for the sofa. (*Picking up a bearskin rug and carrying it to the sofa*) Who's first for the sofa?   30

GWENDOLINE Ermyntrude.

ERMYNTRUDE Gwendoline.

PEGGY Come along, Gwendoline. (*Gwendoline puts herself upon the sofa, and Peggy covers her with the bearskin*) There—as soon as you drop off to sleep it will be Ermyntrude's turn. (*Looking through the conservatory doors*) Oh, how the snow is coming down!   35

> She joins Ermyntrude, who is warming her hands by the fire, and sits in an armchair

ERMYNTRUDE Peggy, do you know what has become of poor Dinah?

PEGGY Yes, she's locked up upstairs till the morning. Admiral Rankling locked her up.

GWENDOLINE (*from the sofa*) It's a shame!   40

PEGGY Go to sleep! Oh, what a scene there was! Admiral Rankling foamed at the mouth. It was lucky they got Mr Queckett away from him in time.

GWENDOLINE (*sleepily*) Where is Mr Queckett?

PEGGY Go to sleep.   45

ERMYNTRUDE (*leaning against Peggy's knees*) Mr Queckett is locked up too, isn't he?

PEGGY Of course he is—till the morning. Miss Dyott locked *him* up—very properly I think.

ERMYNTRUDE And where's Miss Dyott?   50

PEGGY Upstairs, in the room next to mine, in hysterics. Hush! I do believe Gwendoline has gone off. Are you pretty comfortable?

ERMYNTRUDE (*her head on Peggy's lap, sleepily*) Yes, thank you.

PEGGY (*wearily*) Oh!

> The door quietly opens, and Saunders appears. Peggy and Ermyntrude are hidden from him by the armchair

SAUNDERS (*sleepily*) I can't sleep in my room. Where have they   55
put Uncle Jack, I wonder? (*Seeing Gwendoline, who is sleeping with the light from the conservatory windows upon her*) Oh! What's that? (*Going softly up to Gwendoline, and looking at her*) Why, here's my Gwen. I wonder if she'd mind my sitting near her.

(*Turning up his coat-collar, he sits gently on the footstool and*   60
leans against the head of the sofa, drowsily) Now if any burglars
wanted to hurt Gwen, I could kill them. (*Closing his eyes wearily*)
Oh!

> *Soon there is a sound of heavy regular breathing from the four*
> *sleeping figures. The door opens, and Mallory enters*

MALLORY (*shivering*) Can't get a blessed wink of sleep. Where
have I wandered to? Why, this is the room where the awful row   65
was. (*Seeing Gwendoline*) Hallo, here's one of those schoolgirls—
(*Discovering Saunders*) And—well, this nephew of mine is a
devil of a fellow! That isn't a glimmer of fire, surely. (*Walking
towards the fireplace, he nearly stumbles over Ermyntrude*) More
girls!   70

> *He accidentally knocks over the scuttle. They all wake with a*
> *start*

PEGGY and ERMYNTRUDE What's that?

GWENDOLINE and SAUNDERS Who is it?

MALLORY Hush, don't be frightened! It's only I.

PEGGY Mr Mallory!

MALLORY I've been wandering about—can't sleep.   75

PEGGY No, we can't sleep either.

MALLORY Well, I don't know about that.

> *Ermyntrude lights the candles on the mantelpiece*

PEGGY Why haven't you and Mr Saunders gone home? You're not
burnt out.

MALLORY Perhaps not; but Admiral Rankling asked me to remain,   80
and, if he hadn't, I'm not going to leave this house till my friend
Queckett is out of danger.

PEGGY Out of danger?

MALLORY Yes. Are you aware that you young ladies have brought
very grave difficulties upon that unfortunate gentleman?   85

PEGGY (*crying*) He encouraged us! He's a man!

MALLORY Now, pray don't cry, my dear Miss—what is your name
this morning?

PEGGY Hesslerigge, and I wish I'd never been born!

MALLORY Hesslerigge, and you wish you'd never been born.   90
(*Taking her hand*) Well, Miss Hesslerigge, the serious aspect of
the affair is that Admiral Rankling has a most violent, ungovernable temper.

PEGGY (*tearfully*) I know. I've never seen a gentleman foam at the
mouth before. It's quite a new experience.   95

MALLORY (*soothingly*) Of course, of course; and therefore I'm appre-
hensive for poor Mr Queckett's bodily safety. Meanwhile I won't
disturb you any longer. Come along, Saunders.

PEGGY Where are you going?

MALLORY To the front door—to speak a word or two of encourage-   100
ment to that young fellow, Paulover.

PEGGY Oh, he is outside still? In the snow!

MALLORY Why, he has been walking up and down on the other side
of the way all night.

PEGGY (*indignantly*) And you haven't let him in!   105

MALLORY How could I! You forget that our host has forbidden him
the house.

PEGGY No, I don't; I saw them roll out into the road together. Girls,
shall we open the front door, or shall we remain the mere slaves
of etiquette?   110

GWENDOLINE I should like to let him in.

ERMYNTRUDE Certainly—why not?

SAUNDERS Come along—I know the way.

> *Saunders, Gwendoline, and Ermyntrude go out quietly*

MALLORY (*to Peggy*), Well, you'll perhaps pardon my saying that
you are a devil-may-care little schoolgirl!   115

PEGGY You make a great mistake. I am not a schoolgirl; I am
struggling to be a governess.

MALLORY Ah, I hope you'll make your way in your profession.

> *Peggy has discovered the spirit-stand on the sideboard and now*
> *places it on the table*

MALLORY What are you going to do now?

PEGGY Brew poor Mr Paulover something hot. (*Bringing the kettle*   120
and spirit-lamp to the table) Light this lamp for me, please. (*He*
lights the lamp) If you can recommend me at any time to a lady
with young daughters I shall be grateful.

MALLORY I will—I will.

PEGGY I think I am almost capable of finishing° any young lady now.   125

MALLORY I am sure you are. (*Looking at the spirit-lamp*) Is that
alight? (*They put their heads down close together to look at the lighted*
lamp) That's all right.

PEGGY Seems so.

> *They rise and look at one another*

MALLORY We'd better watch it, perhaps, in case it goes out.   130

> *They bob down again with their heads together, and both sit on*
> *the same chair*

You'll get into an awful scrape over your share in last night's business, won't you?

PEGGY Frightful; the thought depresses me.

MALLORY Do you think Miss Dyott, or Mrs Queckett, or whatever she is, will send you home?   135

PEGGY She can't—she's got me for ever. She took me, years ago, for a bad debt.

MALLORY How can she punish you then?

PEGGY I think she will withdraw her confidence from me.

MALLORY You won't despair, will you?   140

PEGGY I'll try not to.

MALLORY What a jolly little sailor's wife you'd make—brewing grog like this.

PEGGY I hope I should do my duty in any station of life to which I might be called.   145

MALLORY *I'm* a sailor, you know.

PEGGY No—are you?

MALLORY (*taking her hand and putting it to his lips*) You know I am.

PEGGY (*suddenly*) It's going to boil over! (*They jump up quickly; Mallory retreats*) Oh, no, it isn't.   150

> *Gwendoline and Ermyntrude enter, leading Reginald, with Saunders following. Reginald is in a deplorable condition, covered with snow and icicles. His face is white, and his nose red*

Oh, poor Mr Paulover!

SAUNDERS He's frostbitten!

PEGGY Thaw him by degrees.

> *Peggy mixes the grog. Gwendoline and Ermyntrude lead Reginald to a chair before the fire, he uttering some violent but incoherent exclamations*

ERMYNTRUDE He's annoyed with Admiral Rankling.

> *The girls chafe his hands, while he still mutters with rolling eyes*

PEGGY (*putting the glass of grog to his lips*) It's a good job his language   155
is frozen.

REGINALD (*reviving*) Thank you. Take my hat off, please—I bought it from a cabman. (*Gwendoline removes his hat, which is very shabby*) Good-morning! Where's my wife Dinah?

PEGGY She's quite safe.   160

REGINALD I must see her—speak to her!

PEGGY You can't—she's locked up.

REGINALD [*on his feet, wildly*] Then I must push a long letter under her door. She *must*, she *shall* know that I am going to walk up and

down outside this house all my life! (*Faintly*) Bring writing   165
materials?

MALLORY I'll hunt for the pen and ink.

SAUNDERS So will I.

REGINALD (*to Peggy*) No, no; you do it. These men are bachelors—
they can't feel for me!   170

MALLORY Here's a writing-table.
> *Peggy runs to Mallory and opens the lid of the writing-table*

PEGGY Notepaper and envelopes. Where's the——? (*Opening one of the
small drawers, she starts back with a cry*) Oh!
> *They all turn and look at her*

ALL What's the matter?

PEGGY (*taking from the drawer a large bunch of keys, each with a small*   175
label, which she examines breathlessly) Duplicate keys of all the
rooms in the house! What gross carelessness—to leave keys in an
open drawer! Girls, why should not we impress this fact upon
Admiral Rankling by releasing Dinah immediately?

GWENDOLINE and ERMYNTRUDE Oh, yes, yes!   180

REGINALD (*seizing Peggy's hand*) Oh, Miss Hesslerigge, my father-
in-law is entertaining an angel unawares.°

MALLORY Oh, stop, stop, stop! I don't think we're quite justified—

REGINALD (*scornfully*) Hah, I told you he was merely a bach-   185
elor! (*Pointing to Saunders*) So is his companion. Give *me* the
keys!

PEGGY No, no; I take the responsibility of this. I am a girl! (*Going
towards the door, and looking at Mallory and Saunders as they make
way for her*) I hope you will repent your line of conduct,   190
gentlemen.
> *She goes out*

MALLORY I think we *all* shall.
> *There is a sudden noise, as of someone falling down a couple of*
> *stairs. They start and listen*

GIRLS Oh!

MALLORY What's that?

ERMYNTRUDE (*looking out at door*) Here's Admiral Rankling!   195
> *There is a suppressed exclamation from everybody, and a silent*
> *scamper to the further end of the room*

MALLORY (*indignantly*) What the deuce does a respectable man want
out of bed at this unearthly hour?

RANKLING (*in a rage, outside the door*) Confound that!

GIRLS Oh!

REGINALD (*opening the door leading to the dark room*) Here's a room   200
here. Shall we condescend to hide?

ALL Yes.

> *They disappear hastily as Rankling appears in a dressing-gown,
> his face pale and his eyes red and wild*

RANKLING Hallo!° Someone has been sitting up. Candles—and a
fire. Ah!

> *Sniffing and walking about the room, he goes straight to the
> mantelpiece, upon which Reginald's grog has been left, and takes
> up the tumbler*

It's Mallory. (*With suppressed passion*) It's against the rules for   205
anybody to sit up in my house! (*Calmly*) But I don't mind
Mallory—I don't—(*Looking at sofa*) Hallo! Mallory has been
turning in here. (*Going to the sofa and sitting there, shaking with
anger*) Are we never going to have any more daylight? How long
am I to wait till that miserable schoolmistress releases the worm   210
Queckett! Queckett! *Uncle Vere!* The reptile who has made a fool
of me in the eyes of my wife and daughter! Ugh! But I must
husband my strength for Queckett. I have been a very careful man
all my life; so far as muscular economy goes, Queckett shall have
the savings of a lifetime. (*Lying down and pulling the rug over*   215
him) Uncle Vere! Ah, I was a wild, impetuous, daring lad once—
(*Going to sleep*) And I can be unpleasant even now. I can! The
Admiralty doesn't know it—Emma doesn't know it—Queckett
shall know it.

> *He breathes heavily. The others have been peeping from their
> hiding-place, and as they close the door, Peggy enters alone,
> quickly but silently. She looks for the others, then almost falls
> over Rankling on the sofa, at which she retreats with a
> suppressed screech of horror. Mallory opens the farther door and
> gesticulates to her violently to be silent*

PEGGY (*petrified*) Oh, my goodness gracious!   220

> *Mallory advances and bends over Rankling, listening to his
> breathing; he then goes to Peggy.*

MALLORY He's dropped off. Where is Mrs Paulover?

PEGGY She's not on that side of the house.

MALLORY I've a plan for disposing of the old gentleman. Try the
other side.

PEGGY I'm going to. (*Turning and clutching Mallory*) But, oh, Mr   225
Mallory, what *do* you think I've done?

MALLORY That's impossible to conjecture.

PEGGY I've made a mistake about the doors and—I have unlocked Mr Queckett!

> *She goes out quickly; Mallory thinks for a moment, then bursts into a fit of silent laughter*

MALLORY I love that girl!   230

> *Reginald appears at the farther door, gesticulating*

REGINALD (*in a hoarse whisper*) Where is my wife? I cannot live longer without her! Where is Dinah!

MALLORY Hush! She'll be here in a minute. Come out of there and lend me a hand.

> *Saunders, Gwendoline, and Ermyntrude enter on tiptoe*

(*To Reginald*) Now then—gently.   235

> *Mallory and Reginald each take an end of the sofa and carry Rankling out through the door into the dark room*

GWENDOLINE (*breathlessly*) If they bump him, all's lost!

> *Mallory and Reginald reappear*

REGINALD I feel warmer now.

MALLORY Turn the key.

> *Reginald turns the key as Dinah and Peggy enter cautiously*

GWENDOLINE and ERMYNTRUDE Dinah!

DINAH Reggie!   240

REGINALD My wife!

> *Reginald rushes to Dinah and embraces her frantically. There is a general cry of relief as Mallory embraces Peggy and Gwendoline throws her arms round Saunders. Suddenly there is the sound of someone stumbling downstairs, accompanied by a smothered exclamation.*

ALL (*listening*) What's that?

ERMYNTRUDE (*peeping out at the door*) Here's Uncle Vere got loose. He has fallen downstairs.

REGINALD Oh, bother! Come along, Dinah.   245

> *Reginald and Dinah, Saunders, Ermyntrude, and Gwendoline go out quickly*

PEGGY (*to Mallory*) Rather bad taste of your nephew and those girls to run after a newly married couple, isn't it?

MALLORY Yes; *we* won't do it.

PEGGY No; but we don't want to be bothered with your old friend, Queckett, do we?   250

MALLORY No; he's an awful bore. Is the conservatory heated?

PEGGY (*taking his arm*) I don't mind if it isn't.

They disappear into the conservatory. The door opens, and Queckett, his face pale and haggard, enters, still wearing his hat and the short covert coat over his evening dress, and carrying his gloves and umbrella

QUECKETT To whom am I indebted for being let out? Was it by way of treachery, I wonder? Somebody has been sitting up late, or rising early! Who is it? (*Sniffing and looking about him, then going to the mantelpiece and taking up the tumbler and smelling the contents*) I am anxious not to do anyone an injustice, but that's Peggy. Oh, what a night I've passed! I have no hesitation in saying that the extremely bad behaviour of Caroline—of the lady I have married—and the ungovernable rage of Rankling, are indelibly impressed upon me. (*Looking round nervously*) Good gracious! I am actually in the room in which Rankling announced his intention of ultimately dislocating my vertebrae. I shall certainly not winter in England. (*The clock strikes seven; he looks at his watch*) Seven. It will be wise to remain here for the first gleam of daylight, and then leave the house—unostentatiously. I will exchange *no* explanations with Caroline. I shall simply lay the whole circumstances of my injudicious, boyish marriage before my brother Bob and the other members of my family. Any allowance which Caroline may make me shall come through them. (*There is a sound of something falling and breaking outside the room*) The deuce! What's that? (*Going on tiptoe over to the door, and peeping out*) Somebody has knocked something over. (*Snatching up his hat, gloves, and umbrella*) I shan't wait till daybreak if they're breaking other things.

He hurries to another door, opens it, looks out, and closes it quickly

People sitting on the stairs! Is this a plot to surround me? The conservatory?

He goes quickly to the conservatory door, opens it, then draws back, closing it quickly

Two persons under a palm tree. (*There is a knock at the door on the right*) Oh! (*Seeing the door leading to the dark room*) Where does that lead to?

He tries the door, unlocks it and looks in

A dark room! Oh, I'm so thankful!

He disappears, closing the door after him. The knocking outside is repeated, then the door opens and Miss Dyott enters. She is dressed in her burlesque costume, her face pale. She carries the head, broken off at the neck, of a terracotta bust of a woman

MISS DYOTT I have broken a bust now. It is an embarrassing thing
to break a bust in the house of comparative strangers. Oh, will it
never be daylight? Does the milkman *never* come to Portland Place!
I have been listening at the keyhole of Vere's room—not a sound.
He can sleep with the ruin of Volumnia College upon his   285
conscience while I—(*Sinking into a chair*) Ah, I realise now the
correctness of the poet's observation—'Uneasy lies the head that
wears a crown!'°

Queckett comes quietly from the dark room, much terrified

QUECKETT Rankling's in there—asleep. In the dark I sat on him. Oh,
what a narrow escape I've had! (*Coming behind Miss Dyott and*   290
suddenly seeing her) Caroline! Scylla and Charybdis!°

He bolts back into the dark room

MISS DYOTT (*rising, alarmed*) What's that?

Mrs Rankling enters, in a peignoir°

MRS RANKLING I heard something fall. (*Seeing Miss Dyott*) Mrs
Queckett! (*Distantly*) Instructions were given that everybody
should be called at eight. I had arranged that a more appropriate   295
costume should be placed at your disposal. (*Seeing the broken bust*)
Ah, what has happened?

MISS DYOTT I knocked over the pedestal.

MRS RANKLING (*distressed*) Oh! Bust of myself by Belt! I saw him
working on it! Oh, Mrs Queckett, is there no end to the trouble   300
you have brought upon us?°

MISS DYOTT The trouble *you* have brought upon me.

MRS RANKLING What! Why didn't you tell us you had a husband?

MISS DYOTT Why didn't you tell me that Dinah had a husband?

MRS RANKLING We didn't know it.   305

MISS DYOTT Well, if you didn't know your own daughter was
married, how can you wonder at your ignorance of other people's
domestic complications?

MRS RANKLING But that's not all. You have informed us that you are
now actually contributing to a nightly entertainment of a volatile   310
description—that you are positively being laughed at in public.

MISS DYOTT Isn't it better to be laughed at in public, and paid for
it, than to be sniggered at privately for nothing!

MRS RANKLING Mrs Queckett, you are revealing your true character.

MISS DYOTT It is the same as your own—an undervalued wife. Let   315
me open your eyes as mine are opened. We have engaged to love
and to honour two men.

MRS RANKLING *I* have done nothing of the kind.

MISS DYOTT I mean one each.

MRS RANKLING Oh—excuse me.   320

MISS DYOTT Now—looking at him microscopically—is there much to love and to honour in Admiral Rankling?

MRS RANKLING He is a genial after-dinner speaker.

MISS DYOTT Hah!

MRS RANKLING It is true he is rather austere.   325

MISS DYOTT An austere sailor! All bows abroad and stern at home. Well then—knowing what occurred last night—is there anything to love and to honour in Mr Queckett?

MRS RANKLING Nothing whatever.

MISS DYOTT (*annoyed*) And yet he is undoubtedly the superior of   330
Admiral Rankling. Very well then, do as I mean to do—put your foot down. If Heaven has gifted you with a large one, so much the better.

    The voices of Queckett and Rankling are heard suddenly raised in the adjoining room

RANKLING (*outside*) Queckett!

QUECKETT (*outside*) My dear Rankling!

MISS DYOTT Vere!   335

MRS RANKLING The Admiral has released your husband.

RANKLING (*in the distance*) I'll trouble you, sir!

QUECKETT Certainly, Rankling.

MISS DYOTT (*to Mrs Rankling*) Come away, and I will advise you. Bring your head with you.   340

    Miss Dyott and Mrs Rankling, carrying the broken bust, hurry out as Queckett enters quickly, followed by Rankling

QUECKETT Admiral Rankling, I shall mark my opinion of your behaviour—through the post.

RANKLING Sit down.

QUECKETT Thank you, I've been sitting. I sat on you, on the sofa.

RANKLING Sit down! (*Queckett sits promptly*) As an old friend of your   345
family, Mr Queckett, I am going to have a quiet chat with you on family matters.

    Rankling wheels the armchair near Queckett

QUECKETT (*to himself*) I don't like his calmness—I don't like his calmness.

    Rankling sits bending forward, and glaring at Queckett

RANKLING (*grimly*) How is your sister Janet? Quite well, eh? (*Fiercely*)   350
Tell me—without a moment's delay, sir—how is Janet?

QUECKETT Permit me to say, Admiral Rankling, that whatever your standing may be with other members of my family, you have *no* acquaintance with the lady you mention.

RANKLING Oh, haven't I? (*Drawing his chair nearer Queckett*) Very 355
well, then. Is Griffin quite well—Finch-Griffin of the Berkshire
Royals?

QUECKETT I do not know how Major Griffin is, and I feel I do not
care.

RANKLING Oh, you don't. Very well, then. (*Drawing his chair still* 360
nearer Queckett) Will you answer me one simple but important
question?

QUECKETT If it be a question a gentleman may answer—certainly.

RANKLING How often do you hear from your brother Tankerville?

QUECKETT Oh! 365

RANKLING (*clutching Queckett's knee*) He's Deputy Inspector of
Prisons in British Guiana, you know. Doesn't have time to write
often, does he?

QUECKETT Admiral Rankling, you will permit me to remind you that
in families of long standing and complicated interests there are 370
regrettable estrangements which should be lightly dealt with.
(*Affected*) You have recalled memories. (*Rising*) Excuse me.

RANKLING (*rising*) No, sir, I will not excuse you!

QUECKETT Where are my gloves?

RANKLING Because, Mr Queckett, I have your assurance as a 375
gentleman that your brother Tankerville's daughter is married
to a charming young fellow of the name of Parkinson. Now I've
discovered that Parkinson is really a charming young fellow of
the name of Paulover; so that, as Paulover has married my
daughter as well as Tankerville's, Paulover must be prosecuted for 380
bigamy, and as you knew that Paulover was Parkinson, and
Parkinson Paulover, you connived at the crime, inasmuch as
knowing Paulover was Tankerville's daughter's husband, you
deliberately aided Parkinson in making my child Dinah his wife.
But that's not the worst of it! 385

QUECKETT Oh!

RANKLING (*continuing rapidly and excitedly*) Because I have since
received your gentlemanly assurance that Tankerville's daughter is
my daughter. Now, either you mean to say that I've behaved like
a blackguard to Tankerville—which is a libel; or that Tankerville 390
has conducted himself with less than common fairness to me—
which will be a divorce. And, in either case, without wishing to
anticipate the law, I shall personally chastise you, because,
although I've been a sailor on the high seas for five-and-forty years,
I have *never* during the whole of that period listened to such a yarn 395
of mendacious fabrications as you spun me last night!

QUECKETT (*beginning to carefully put on his gloves*) It would be idle
　　to deny that this affair has now assumed its most unpleasant aspect.
　　Admiral Rankling, the time has come for candour on both sides.

RANKLING Be quick, sir!　　　　　　　　　　　　　　　　　400

QUECKETT I am being quick, Rankling. I admit, with all the rapidity
　　of utterance of which I am capable, that my assurances of last night
　　were founded upon an airy basis.

RANKLING In plain words—lies, Mr Queckett.

QUECKETT A habit of preparing election manifestos for various　405
　　members of my family may have impaired a fervent admiration for
　　truth, in which I yield to no man.

RANKLING (*advancing in a determined manner*) Very well, sir!

QUECKETT (*retreating*) One moment, Rankling. One moment—*if not
　　two!* I glean that you are prepared to assault—　　　　　410

RANKLING To chastise!

QUECKETT Well, to inconvenience a man at whose table you feasted
　　last night. Do so!

RANKLING I will do so!

QUECKETT I say, do so. But the triumph, when you kneel upon my　415
　　body—for I am bound to tell you that I shall lie down—the
　　triumph will be mine!

RANKLING You are welcome to it, sir. Put down that umbrella!

QUECKETT What for?

RANKLING *I* haven't an umbrella.　　　　　　　　　　　　420

QUECKETT You haven't? Allow me to leave this room, my dear
　　Rankling, and I'll beg your acceptance of this one.

　　　　　Rankling advances fiercely; Queckett retreats; Miss Dyott enters

QUECKETT Caroline!

MISS DYOTT Stop, Admiral Rankling, if you please! Any reprimand,
　　physical or otherwise, will be administered to Mr Queckett at my　425
　　hands.

QUECKETT (*to himself*) I would have preferred Rankling. Rankling I
　　could have winded.

　　　　　He goes out quickly, Miss Dyott following in pursuit

MISS DYOTT (*as she goes*) Vere!

RANKLING I am in my own house, madam—　　　　　　　　430

　　　　　Mrs Rankling enters, carrying the broken bust

RANKLING Emma, go back to bed.

MRS RANKLING Archibald Rankling, attend to me. Don't roll your
　　eyes, but attend to me.

RANKLING Emma, your tone is dictatorial.

MRS RANKLING It is meant to be so, because, after seventeen years   435
of married life, I am going to speak my mind, at last. (*Holding up
the head before him*) Archibald, look at that.

RANKLING What is it?

MRS RANKLING Myself, less than ten years ago—the sculptor's
earliest effort.   440

RANKLING Broken—made of bad stuff—send it back.

MRS RANKLING It is your memory I wish to send back. Ah,
Archibald, do you see how round and plump those cheeks are?

RANKLING People alter. You were stout then.

MRS RANKLING I was.   445

RANKLING In those days I was thin.

MRS RANKLING Frightfully.

RANKLING Very well, then—the average remains the same. Some
day we may return to the old arrangement.

MRS RANKLING If you ever find yourself a spare man again,   450
Archibald, it won't be because I have worried and fretted you with
my peevish ill-humour—

RANKLING Emma!

MRS RANKLING As you have worried and worn me with yours.

RANKLING Emma, you have completely lost your head. (*She raises*   455
the broken bust) I don't mean that confounded bust. That was ideal.

MRS RANKLING And if a mere sculptor could make your wife ideal,
why shouldn't you try? So, understand me finally, Archibald—I will
not be ground down any longer. Unless some arrangement is arrived
at for the happiness of dear Dinah and Mr Paulover, I leave you.   460

RANKLING Leave me!

MRS RANKLING This very day.

RANKLING Wantonly desert your home and husband, Emma.

MRS RANKLING Yes.

RANKLING (*with emotion*) And I don't know where to put my hand   465
upon even a necktie!

    [*He sits, covering his face with his handkerchief*]

MRS RANKLING All the world shall learn how highly you thought of
Dinah's marriage at Mr Queckett's party last night.

RANKLING (*to himself*) Oh!

MRS RANKLING And what a very different man you have always   470
been in your own home. (*Beginning to cry*) And take care,
Archibald, that the verdict of posterity is not that you were less a
husband and father than a tyrant and oppressor.

    Queckett enters, with Miss Dyott in pursuit; she follows him out

133

MISS DYOTT (*as she goes*) Vere!
> *Rankling blows his nose and wipes his eyes, and looks at Mrs*
> *Rankling*

RANKLING (*in a conciliatory tone*) Emma! Emma!   475

MRS RANKLING (*weeping*) Oh, dear, oh, dear!

RANKLING Emma. (*Irritably*) Don't tuck your head under your arm in that way! (*She puts the broken bust on the table*) Emma, there have been grave faults on both sides. Yours I will endeavour to overlook.   480

MRS RANKLING Ah, now you are your dear old self again.

RANKLING But, Emma, you are occasionally an irritating woman to live with.

MRS RANKLING You are the first who has ever said that.

RANKLING So I should hope, Emma.   485

MRS RANKLING And poor Dinah—you will forgive her?

RANKLING On condition that she doesn't see Paulover's face again for five years.

MRS RANKLING Oh, there will be no difficulty about that.
> *Reginald and Dinah enter; she is dressed for flight*

DINAH Papa!   490

REGINALD My father-in-law!
> *They retreat hastily*

RANKLING (*madly*) Who let you out? Who let you in?
> *He goes out after them; Mrs Rankling follows*

MRS RANKLING (*as she goes out*) Archibald! Continue your dear old self!
> *Queckett enters by another door, Miss Dyott following him—*
> *both out of breath. [He sits on the right, she on the left.] They*
> *look at each other, recovering themselves*

QUECKETT [*adjusting his collar*] I understand that you wish to speak   495
to me, Caroline.

MISS DYOTT Oh, you—you paltry little man! You mean, ungrateful little creature! You laced-up heap of pompous pauperism! You—you—! I cannot adequately describe you. Wretch!

QUECKETT (*putting on his gloves again*) Have you finished with me,   500
Caroline?

MISS DYOTT Finished with you! I shall never have finished with you! Never till you leave me!

QUECKETT (*rising*) Till I leave you?

MISS DYOTT Till you leave me a widow.   505

QUECKETT (*resuming his seat, disappointed*) Oh!

MISS DYOTT You don't think I expect you to leave me anything else. Oh, what could I have seen in you!

QUECKETT I take it, Caroline, that, in the language of the hunting-field, you 'scented' a gentleman.   510

MISS DYOTT Scented a gentleman! In the few weeks of our marriage I have scented you and cigaretted you, wined you and liqueured you, tailored and hatted and booted you. I have darned and mended and washed you—gruelled you with a cold, tinctured you with a toothache, and linimented you with the gout. ([*Rising,*]   515 *fiercely*) Have I not? Have I not?

QUECKETT You certainly have had exceptional privileges. Familiarity appears to have fulfilled its usual functions and bred—

MISS DYOTT The most utter contempt. [*Pacing up and down*] Have I not paid your debts?   520

QUECKETT (*promptly*) Not at my suggestion.

MISS DYOTT And all for what?

QUECKETT I assume, for love's dear sake, Carrie.

MISS DYOTT For the sake of having the vestal seclusion of Volumnia College telegraphically denominated as 'bachelor diggings'!   525
    [*She sits at the table*]

QUECKETT Any collection of young ladies may be so described.° The description is happy but harmless. As for the subsequent confla-gration—

MISS DYOTT Don't talk about it!

QUECKETT I say with all sincerity that from the moment the fire   530 broke out till I escaped no one regretted it more than myself. *That* was Tyler!

MISS DYOTT [*rising*] Tyler! What Tyler!° I make no historical reference when I say what Tyler was it who abruptly tore aside the veil of mystery which had hitherto shrouded the existence of   535 champagne and lobster salad from four young girls! It was you!

QUECKETT No, it wasn't, Carrie, upon my word!

MISS DYOTT Bah!

QUECKETT Upon my honour!

MISS DYOTT (*witheringly*) Hah!   540

QUECKETT Those vexing pupils played the very devil with me. After you left, the pupils, as it were, dilated.

MISS DYOTT [*walking up the stage*] Yes, and you ordered them champagne glasses, I suppose! Oh, deceiver!

QUECKETT [*walking down stage*] You talk of deception! What about   545 the three o'clock train from Paddington?

MISS DYOTT [*walking down on the opposite side*] It was the whole truth—there was one.

QUECKETT But you didn't travel in it! What about the clergyman's wife at Hereford?   550

MISS DYOTT Go there—you will find several!

QUECKETT But you're not staying with them. Oh, Carrie, how can you meet my fearless glance when you recall that my last words yesterday were: 'Cabman, drive to Paddington—the lady will pay your fare'?   555

MISS DYOTT I cannot deny that it is by accident you have discovered that I am Queen Honorine in Otto Bernstein's successful comic opera.

QUECKETT And what do you think my family would think of that?

MISS DYOTT It is true that the public now know me as Miss   560
Constance Delaporte.

QUECKETT (*indignantly*) Oh! Miss Constance Delaporte!

MISS DYOTT The new and startling contralto—her first appearance.

QUECKETT [*sinking into a chair*] And have I, a Queckett, after all, gone and married a Connie?°   565

MISS DYOTT You have! It is true, too, that last night, while you and my pupils were dilating, I was singing—ay, and at one important juncture, dancing!

QUECKETT (*rising, with horror*) No, no—not dancing!

MISS DYOTT Madly, desperately, hysterically, dancing!   570

QUECKETT And to think—if there was any free list°—that my brother Bob may have been there.

    [*He sits, shading his eyes*]

MISS DYOTT But do you guess the one thought that prompted me, buoyed me up, guided my steps, and ultimately produced a lower G of exceptional power.   575

QUECKETT (*with a groan*) No.

MISS DYOTT The thought that every note I sang might bring a banknote to my lonely Vere at home.

QUECKETT [*looking up*] Carrie!

MISS DYOTT [*dramatically*] I went through the performance in a   580
dream! The conductor's baton beat nothing but, 'Vere, Vere, Vere', into my brain. Someone applauded me! I thought, 'Ah, that's worth a new hat to Vere!' I sang my political verse—a man very properly hissed. 'He has smashed Vere's new hat,' I mur-mured. At last came my important solo. I drew a long breath, saw   585
a vision of you reading an old copy of *The Rock*° by the fireside at

home, and opened my mouth. I remember nothing more till I found myself wildly dancing to the refrain of my song. The audience yelled with approbation; I bowed again and again, and then tottered away to sink into the arms of the prompter with the words, 'Vere, catch your Carrie'!

[*She sinks into a chair; Queckett rises*]

QUECKETT But my family—my brother Bob—

MISS DYOTT What have they ever done for you? While I—it was my ambition to devote every penny of my salary to your little wants.

QUECKETT And isn't it?

MISS DYOTT No, Vere Albany Bute Queckett, it isn't. The moment I dragged you down that ladder last night, and left behind me the smouldering ruins of Volumnia College, I became an altered woman.

QUECKETT Then I will lay the whole affair before my family.

MISS DYOTT [*rising*] Do, and tell them to what your selfishness has brought you—that where there was love there is disdain, where there was claret there will be beer, where there were cigars there will be pipes, and where there was Poole there will be Kino!°

QUECKETT Oh, why didn't I wait and marry a lady?

MISS DYOTT You *did* marry a lady! But scratch the lady and you find a hard-working comic actress!

QUECKETT Be silent, madam!

MISS DYOTT [*coming down stage, centre*] Ha! Ha! This is my revenge, Vere Queckett! Tonight I will dance more wildly, more demonstratively than ever!

QUECKETT I forbid it!

MISS DYOTT *You* forbid it! *You* dictate to Constance Delaporte—the hit of the opera! I am Queen Honorine!

She slaps her hands and sings with great abandonment, and in the pronounced manner of the buffa queen, the song she is supposed to sing in Bernstein's opera. [*The air must be tuneful and vigorous*]

> 'Rine, 'Rine, Honorine!
> Mighty, whether wife or queen;
> Firmer ruler never seen,
> Than 'Rine, 'Rine! La!°

QUECKETT (*indignantly*) I will write to my married sisters!

MISS DYOTT [*putting her face near his*] Do—and I will call upon
them! (*Singing*)

> Man's a boasting, fretting fumer,
> Smoking alcohol consumer,
> Quick of temper, ill of humour!

QUECKETT Oh, you shall sing this to my family!   620
MISS DYOTT I will! (*Singing, with her hands upon her hips*)

> Woman has no petty vices;
> Cuts her sins in good thick slices,
> With a smile that sweet and nice is!

QUECKETT (*writhing*) Oh!
MISS DYOTT (*boisterously*) Refrain! (*Singing and dancing*)

> 'Rine, 'Rine, Honorine!
> Mighty, whether wife or queen,
> Firmer ruler never seen,
> Than 'Rine, 'Rine! La!

> With a burst of hysterical laughter she sinks into a chair

QUECKETT Oh, I will tell my brother of you!
> *Daylight appears through the conservatory doors. Mrs Rankling
> and Dinah enter. Mallory and Peggy enter from the conserva-
> tory, 'spooning'.*°

MRS RANKLING My dear Mrs Queckett, I owe everything to you—   625
my treatment of the dear Admiral has had wonderful results. What
do you think! The Admiral and Mr Paulover are quite reconciled
and understand each other perfectly.
> *Rankling and Paulover enter, glaring at each other and quar-
> relling violently in undertones*

Look—the Admiral already regards him as his own child.
> *Saunders, Ermyntrude, and Gwendoline enter and join Peggy
> and Mallory*

DINAH (*sobbing*) But we are to be separated for five years. Oh, Reggie,   630
you trust me implicitly, don't you?
REGINALD (*fiercely*) I do. And that is why I warn you never to let
me hear of you addressing another man.
DINAH Oh, Reggie!
> *They embrace*

RANKLING Don't do that! You don't see me behaving in that way to   635
Mrs Rankling—and we've been married for years.

MRS RANKLING (*to Dinah*) But you and Mr Paulover are to be allowed to meet once every quarter.

REGINALD Yes! In the presence of Admiral Rankling and a policeman!
Mrs Rankling, Rankling, Dinah, and Reginald join the others. Otto Bernstein enters quickly and excitedly, carrying a quantity of newspapers

BERNSTEIN I beg your pardon. I must see Miss Constance Dela-   640
porte—I mean, Miss Dyott.

MISS DYOTT Mr Bernstein.

BERNSTEIN Your house is burnt down. It does not madder. You have made a gread hit in my new oratorio—I mean my gomic opera. I have been walking up and down Fleet Street waiting for the babers   645
to gome out. (*Handing round all the newspapers*) Der *Dimes*—Der *Delegraph*—Der *Daily News*—Der *Standard*—Der *Bost*—Der *Ghronicle*! Dey are all gomplimentary except one, and dat I gave to the gabman.

MISS DYOTT (*reading*) 'Miss Delaporte—a decided acquisition'.   650

BERNSTEIN Go on!

QUECKETT (*reading*) 'Miss Delaporte—an imposing figure'. (*Indignantly*) What do they know about it?

BERNSTEIN (*excitedly*) Go on! Go on! I always say I do not read the babers, but I *do!* (*To Miss Dyott*) You will get fifty bounds a week   655
in my next oratorio—I mean, my gomic opera.

QUECKETT Fifty pounds a week! My Carrie! I shall be able to snap my fingers at my damn family.

MRS RANKLING How very pleasing! (*Reading*) 'A voice of great purity, a correct intonation, and a lower G of decided volume,   660
rendered attractive some music not remarkable for grace or originality.'

Bernstein takes the paper from Mrs Rankling

BERNSTEIN I did not see dat; I will give *dat* to the gabman. Goobye—I cannot stay. I am going to have a Turkish bath till the evening babers gome out. I always say I do not read the evening   665
babers, but I *do!*

He bustles out

MRS RANKLING Mrs Queckett, I shall book stalls at once to hear your singing.

RANKLING No, Emma—dress circle.

MRS RANKLING Stalls, Archibald.   670

RANKLING (*glaring*) Dress circle!

MRS RANKLING Stalls, Archibald, or I leave you for ever!

RANKLING (*mildly*) Very well, Emma. I have no desire but to please you.

QUECKETT I take this as a great compliment, my dear Rankling. 675
Carrie and I thank you. But I can't hear of it. I insist on offering you both a seat in my box.

MISS DYOTT *Your* box!

QUECKETT (*softly to her*) Hush! Carrie, my darling! Your Vere's private box! 680

MISS DYOTT [*to everybody*] Mr Queckett's private box, during my absence at night, will be our lodgings, where he will remain under lock and key.
Peggy laughs at Queckett

QUECKETT (*to Peggy*) Oh, you vexing girl!°

MALLORY (*annoyed*) Excuse me, my dear Queckett, but while look- 685
ing at the plants in the conservatory, I became engaged to Miss Hesslerigge.
There is a general exclamation of surprise

REGINALD (*to Mallory*) Ah, coward, you haven't to wait five years!
Jane enters

JANE Oh, if you please ma'am, Tyler—

MISS DYOTT, QUECKETT, PEGGY, and DINAH Tyler! 690

JANE Tyler wants to know who is to pay him the reward for being the first to fetch the fire-engines last night?
[*Music in the orchestra*]

QUECKETT (*threateningly*) I will!

MISS DYOTT No—I will. Tyler has rendered me a signal service. He has demolished Volumnia College. From the ashes of that estab- 695
lishment rises the phoenix of my new career. Miss Dyott is extinct—Miss Delaporte is alive and, during the evening, kicking. I hope none will regret the change—I shall not, for one, while the generous public allow me to remain a favourite!

CURTAIN

THE SECOND
MRS TANQUERAY

A Play in Four Acts

The play was first staged at the St James's Theatre, London, on 27 May 1893, with the following cast:

Aubrey Tanqueray	*Mr George Alexander*
Sir George Orreyed, Bt.	*Mr. A. Vane-Tempest*
Captain Hugh Ardale	*Mr Ben Webster*
Cayley Drummle	*Mr Cyril Maude*
Frank Misquith, QC, MP	*Mr Nutcombe Gould*
Gordon Jayne, MD	*Mr Murray Hathorn*
Morse	*Mr Alfred Holles*
Lady Orreyed	*Miss Edith Chester*
Mrs Cortelyon	*Miss Amy Roselle*
Paula	*Mrs Patrick Campbell*
Ellean	*Miss Maude Millett*

Act One

Scene One

The scene is set in November, in Aubrey Tanqueray's chambers in the Albany—a richly and tastefully decorated room, elegantly and luxuriously furnished: on the right a large pair of doors opening into another room, on the left, at the further end of the room, a small door leading to a bedchamber. A circular table is laid for a dinner for four persons, which has now reached the stage of dessert and coffee. Everything in the apartment suggests wealth and refinement. The fire is burning brightly. Aubrey Tanqueray, Misquith, and Jayne are seated at the dinner table. Aubrey is forty-two, handsome, winning in manner, his speech and bearing retaining some of the qualities of young manhood. Misquith is about forty-seven, genial and portly. Jayne is a year or two Misquith's senior; soft-speaking and precise—in appearance a type of the prosperous town physician. Morse, Aubrey's servant, places a little cabinet of cigars and the spirit-lamp on the table beside Aubrey, and goes out

MISQUITH Aubrey, it is a pleasant yet dreadful fact to contemplate, but it's nearly fifteen years since I first dined with you. You lodged in Piccadilly in those days, over a hat-shop. Jayne, I met you at that dinner, and Cayley Drummle.

JAYNE Yes, yes. What a pity it is that Cayley isn't here to-night.   5

AUBREY Confound the old gossip! His empty chair has been staring us in the face all through dinner. I ought to have told Morse to take it away.

MISQUITH Odd, his sending no excuse.

AUBREY I'll walk round to his lodgings later on and ask after him.   10

MISQUITH I'll go with you.

JAYNE So will I.

AUBREY (*opening the cigar-cabinet*) Doctor, it's useless to tempt you, I know. Frank—(*Misquith and Aubrey smoke*) I particularly wished Cayley Drummle to be one of us tonight. You two fellows and   15
Cayley are my closest, my best friends—

MISQUITH My dear Aubrey!

JAYNE I rejoice to hear you say so.

AUBREY And I wanted to see the three of you round this table. You can't guess the reason.   20

MISQUITH You desired to give us a most excellent dinner.

JAYNE Obviously.

AUBREY (*hesitatingly*) Well—I—(*Glancing at the clock*) Cayley won't turn up now.

JAYNE H'm, hardly.   25

AUBREY Then you two shall hear it. Doctor, Frank, this is the last time we are to meet in these rooms.

JAYNE The last time?

MISQUITH You're going to leave the Albany?

AUBREY Yes. You've heard me speak of a house I built in the country   30
years ago, haven't you?

MISQUITH In Surrey.

AUBREY Well, when my wife died I cleared out of that house and let it. I think of trying the place again.

MISQUITH But you'll go raving mad if ever you find yourself down   35
there alone.

AUBREY Ah, but I shan't be alone, and that's what I wanted to tell you. I'm going to be married.

JAYNE Going to be married?

MISQUITH Married?   40

AUBREY Yes—tomorrow.

JAYNE Tomorrow?

MISQUITH You take my breath away! My dear fellow, I—I—of course, I congratulate you.

JAYNE And—and so do I—heartily.   45

AUBREY Thanks—thanks.

There is a moment or two of embarrassment

MISQUITH Er—ah—this is an excellent cigar.

JAYNE Ah—um—your coffee is remarkable.

AUBREY Look here; I daresay you two old friends think this treatment very strange, very unkind. So I want you to understand me.   50
You know a marriage often cools friendships. What's the usual
course of things? A man's engagement is given out, he is congra-
tulated, complimented upon his choice; the church is filled with
troops of friends, and he goes away happily to a chorus of good
wishes. He comes back, sets up house in town or country, and   55
thinks to resume the old associations, the old companionships. My
dear Frank, my dear good doctor, it's very seldom that it can be
done. Generally, a worm has begun to eat its way into those hearty,
unreserved, pre-nuptial friendships; a damnable constraint sets in
and acts like a wasting disease; and so, believe me, in nine cases   60

out of ten a man's marriage severs for him more close ties than it forms.

MISQUITH Well, my dear Aubrey, I earnestly hope—

AUBREY I know what you're going to say, Frank. I hope so, too. In the mean time let's face dangers. I've reminded you of the *usual* course of things, but my marriage isn't even the conventional sort of marriage likely to satisfy society. Now, Cayley's a bachelor, but you two men have wives. By the bye, my love to Mrs Misquith and to Mrs Jayne when you get home—don't forget that. Well, your wives may not—like—the lady I'm going to marry.

JAYNE Aubrey, forgive me for suggesting that the lady you are going to marry may not like our wives—mine at least; I beg your pardon, Frank.

AUBREY Quite so; then I must go the way my wife goes.

MISQUITH Come, come, pray don't let us anticipate that either side will be called upon to make such a sacrifice.

AUBREY Yes, yes, let us anticipate it. And let us make up our minds to have no slow bleeding-to-death of our friendship. We'll end a pleasant chapter here tonight, and after tonight start afresh. When my wife and I settle down at Willowmere it's possible that we shall all come together. But if this isn't to be, for Heaven's sake let us recognise that it is simply because it *can't* be, and not wear hypocritical faces and suffer and be wretched. Doctor, Frank— (*Holding out his hands, one to Misquith, the other to Jayne*) Good luck to all of us!

MISQUITH But—but—do I understand we are to ask nothing? Not even the lady's name, Aubrey?

AUBREY The lady, my dear Frank, belongs to the next chapter, and in that her name is Mrs Aubrey Tanqueray.

JAYNE (*raising his coffee-cup*) Then, in an old-fashioned way, I propose a toast. Aubrey, Frank, I give you 'The Next Chapter!'
They drink the toast, saying, 'The Next Chapter!'

AUBREY Doctor, find a comfortable chair; Frank, you too. As we're going to turn out by and by, let me scribble a couple of notes now while I think of them.

MISQUITH and JAYNE Certainly—yes, yes.

AUBREY It might slip my memory when I get back.
Aubrey sits at a writing-table at the other end of the room,° and writes

JAYNE (*to Misquith, in a whisper*) Frank—(*Misquith quietly leaves his chair and sits nearer to Jayne*) What is all this? Simply a

morbid crank of Aubrey's with regard to ante-nuptial acquaintances?   100

MISQUITH H'm! Did you notice *one* expression he used?

JAYNE Let me think—

MISQUITH 'My marriage is not even the conventional sort of marriage likely to satisfy society.'

JAYNE Bless me, yes! What does that suggest?   105

MISQUITH That he has a particular rather than a general reason for
anticipating estrangement from his friends, I'm afraid.

JAYNE A horrible *mésalliance!* A dairymaid who has given him a glass
of milk during a day's hunting, or a little anaemic shopgirl! Frank,
I'm utterly wretched!   110

MISQUITH My dear Jayne, speaking in absolute confidence, I have
never been more profoundly depressed in my life.

Morse enters

MORSE (*announcing*) Mr Drummle.

*Cayley Drummle enters briskly. He is a neat little man of about
five-and-forty, in manner bright, airy, debonair, but with an
undercurrent of seriousness. Morse retires*

DRUMMLE I'm in disgrace; nobody realises that more thoroughly
than I do. Where's my host?   115

AUBREY (*who has risen*) Cayley.

DRUMMLE (*shaking hands with him*) Don't speak to me till I have
tendered my explanation. A harsh word from anybody would
unman me.

Misquith and Jayne shake hands with Drummle

AUBREY Have you dined?   120

DRUMMLE No—unless you call a bit of fish, a cutlet, and a pancake
dining.

AUBREY Cayley, this is disgraceful.

JAYNE Fish, a cutlet, and a pancake will require a great deal of
explanation.   125

MISQUITH Especially the pancake. My dear friend, your case looks
miserably weak.

DRUMMLE Hear me! hear me!

JAYNE Now then!

MISQUITH Come!   130

AUBREY Well!

DRUMMLE It so happens that tonight I was exceptionally early in
dressing for dinner.

MISQUITH For which dinner—the fish and cutlet?

DRUMMLE For *this* dinner, of course—really, Frank! At a quarter to   135

eight, in fact, I found myself trimming my nails, with ten minutes
to spare. Just then enter my man with a note—would I hasten, as
fast as cab could carry me, to old Lady Orreyed in Bruton
Street—'sad trouble'. Now, recollect, please, I had ten minutes on
my hands, old Lady Orreyed was a very dear friend of my   140
mother's, and was in some distress.

AUBREY Cayley, come to the fish and cutlet?

MISQUITH and JAYNE Yes, yes, and the pancake!

DRUMMLE Upon my word! Well, the scene in Bruton Street beggars
description; the women servants looked scared, the men drunk;   145
and there was poor old Lady Orreyed on the floor of her boudoir
like Queen Bess among her pillows.°

AUBREY What's the matter?

DRUMMLE (to everybody) You know George Orreyed?

MISQUITH Yes.   150

JAYNE I've met him.

DRUMMLE Well, he's a thing of the past.

AUBREY Not dead!

DRUMMLE Certainly, in the worst sense. He's married Mabel
Hervey.   155

MISQUITH What!

DRUMMLE It's true—this morning. The poor mother showed me his
letter—a dozen curt words, and some of those ill-spelt.

MISQUITH (walking up to the fireplace) I'm very sorry.

JAYNE Pardon my ignorance—who was Mabel Hervey?   160

DRUMMLE You don't—? Oh, of course not. Miss Hervey—Lady
Orreyed, as she now is—was a lady who would have been, perhaps
has been, described in the reports of the police or the Divorce
Court as an actress. Had she belonged to a lower stratum of our
advanced civilisation, she would, in the event of judicial inquiry,   165
have defined her calling with equal justification as that of a
dressmaker.° To do her justice, she is a type of a class which
is immortal. Physically, by the strange caprice of creation,
curiously beautiful; mentally, she lacks even the strength of
deliberate viciousness. Paint her portrait, it would symbolise a   170
creature perfectly patrician; lance a vein of her superbly
modelled arm, you would get the poorest *vin ordinaire*! Her
affections, emotions, impulses, her very existence—a burlesque!
Flaxen, five-and-twenty, and feebly frolicsome; anybody's, in less
gentle society I should say everybody's, property! That, doctor,   175
was Miss Hervey who is the new Lady Orreyed. Dost thou like
the picture?

MISQUITH Very good, Cayley! Bravo!

AUBREY (*laying his hand on Drummle's shoulder*) You'd scarcely
believe it, Jayne, but none of us really know anything about this   180
lady, our gay young friend here, I suspect, least of all.

DRUMMLE Aubrey, I applaud your chivalry.

AUBREY And perhaps you'll let me finish a couple of letters which
Frank and Jayne have given me leave to write. (*Returning to the
writing-table*) Ring for what you want, like a good fellow!   185

> *Aubrey resumes his writing*

MISQUITH (*to Drummle*) Still, the fish and cutlet remain unex-
plained.

DRUMMLE Oh, the poor old woman was so weak that I insisted upon
her taking some food, and felt there was nothing for it but to sit
down opposite her. The fool! The blackguard!   190

MISQUITH Poor Orreyed! Well, he's gone under for a time.

DRUMMLE For a time! My dear Frank, I tell you he has absolutely
ceased to be.

> *Aubrey, who has been writing busily, turns his head towards the
> speakers and listens. His lips are set, and there is a frown upon
> his face.*

For all practical purposes you may regard him as the late George
Orreyed. Tomorrow the very characteristics of his speech, as we   195
remember them, will have become obsolete.

JAYNE But surely, in the course of years, he and his wife will
outlive—

DRUMMLE No, no, doctor, don't try to upset one of my settled
beliefs. You may dive into many waters, but there is *one* social   200
Dead Sea—!

JAYNE Perhaps you're right.

DRUMMLE Right! Good God! I wish you could prove me otherwise!
Why, for years I've been sitting, and watching and waiting.

MISQUITH You're in form tonight, Cayley. May we ask where you've   205
been in the habit of squandering your useful leisure?

DRUMMLE Where? On the shore of that same sea.

MISQUITH And, pray, what have you been waiting for?

DRUMMLE For some of my best friends *to come up*.

> *aubrey utters a half-stifled exclamation of impatience; then he
> hurriedly gathers up his papers from the writing-table. The three
> men turn to him*

Eh?   210

AUBREY Oh, I—I'll finish my letters in the other room if you'll
excuse me for five minutes. Tell Cayley the news.

0e4f91

He goes out

DRUMMLE (*hurrying to the door*) My dear fellow, my jabbering has disturbed you! I'll never talk again as long as I live!

MISQUITH Close the door, Cayley.   215

Drummle shuts the door

JAYNE Cayley—

DRUMMLE (*advancing to the dinner table*) A smoke, a smoke, or I perish!

Selects a cigar from the little cabinet

JAYNE Cayley, marriages are in the air.

DRUMMLE Are they? Discover the bacillus, doctor, and destroy it.   220

JAYNE I mean, among our friends.

DRUMMLE Oh, Nugent Warrinder's engagement to Lady Alice Tring. I've heard of that. They're not to be married till the spring.

JAYNE Another marriage that concerns us a little takes place tomorrow.   225

DRUMMLE Whose marriage?

JAYNE Aubrey's.

DRUMMLE Aub—! (*Looking towards Misquith*) Is it a joke?

MISQUITH No.

DRUMMLE (*looking from Misquith to Jayne*) To whom?   230

MISQUITH He doesn't tell us.

JAYNE We three were asked here tonight to receive the announcement. Aubrey has some theory that marriage is likely to alienate a man from his friends, and it seems to me he has taken the precaution to wish us goodbye.   235

MISQUITH No, no.

JAYNE Practically, surely.

DRUMMLE (*thoughtfully*) Marriage in general, does he mean, or *this* marriage?

JAYNE That's the point. Frank says—   240

MISQUITH No, no, no; I feared it suggested—

JAYNE Well, well. (*To Drummle*) What do you think of it?

DRUMMLE (*after a slight pause*) Is there a light there? (*Lighting his cigar*) He—wraps the lady—in mystery—you say?

MISQUITH Most modestly.   245

DRUMMLE Aubrey's—not—a very—young man.

JAYNE Forty-three.

DRUMMLE Ah! *L'âge critique!*

MISQUITH A dangerous age—yes, yes.

DRUMMLE When you two fellows go home, do you mind leaving me   250 behind here?

MISQUITH Not at all.

JAYNE By all means.

DRUMMLE All right. (*Anxiously*) Deuce take it, the man's second
marriage mustn't be another mistake!   255

> *With his head bent he walks up to the fireplace*

JAYNE You knew him in his short married life, Cayley. Terribly
unsatisfactory, wasn't it?

DRUMMLE Well—(*Looking at the door*) I quite closed that door?

MISQUITH Yes.

> *Settles himself on the sofa; Jayne is seated in an armchair*

DRUMMLE (*smoking, with his back to the fire*) He married a Miss   260
Herriott; that was in the year eighteen—confound dates—twenty
years ago. She was a lovely creature—by Jove, she was; by religion
a Roman Catholic. She was one of your cold sort, you know—all
marble arms and black velvet. I remember her with painful
distinctness as the only woman who ever made me nervous.   265

MISQUITH [*softly*] Ha, ha!

DRUMMLE He loved her—to distraction, as they say. Jupiter, how
fervently that poor devil courted her! But I don't believe she
allowed him even to squeeze her fingers. She *was* an iceberg! As
for kissing, the mere contact would have given him chapped lips.   270
However, he married her and took her away, the latter greatly to
my relief.

JAYNE Abroad, you mean?

DRUMMLE Eh? Yes. I imagine he gratified her by renting a villa in
Lapland, but I don't know. After a while they returned, and then   275
I saw how woefully Aubrey had miscalculated results.

JAYNE Miscalculated—?

DRUMMLE He had reckoned, poor wretch, that in the early days of
marriage she would thaw. But she didn't. I used to picture him
closing his doors and making up the fire in the hope of seeing her   280
features relax. Bless her, the thaw never set in! I believe she kept
a thermometer in her stays° and always registered ten degrees
below zero. However, in time a child came—a daughter.

JAYNE Didn't that—?

DRUMMLE Not a bit of it; it made matters worse. Frightened at her   285
failure to stir up in him some sympathetic religious belief, she
determined upon strong measures with regard to the child. He
opposed her for a miserable year or so, but she wore him down,
and the insensible little brat was placed in a convent, first in
France, then in Ireland. Not long afterwards the mother died,   290

strangely enough, of fever, the only warmth, I believe, that ever came to that woman's body.

MISQUITH Don't, Cayley!

JAYNE The child is living, we know.

DRUMMLE Yes, if you choose to call it living. Miss Tanqueray—a   295
young woman of nineteen now—is in the Loretto convent at Armagh.° She professes to have found her true vocation in a religious life, and within a month or two will take final vows.

MISQUITH He ought to have removed his daughter from the convent when the mother died.   300

DRUMMLE Yes, yes, but absolutely at the end there was reconciliation between husband and wife, and she won his promise that the child should complete her conventual education. He reaped his reward. When he attempted to gain his girl's confidence and affection he was too late; he found he was dealing with   305
the spirit of the mother. You remember his visit to Ireland last month?

JAYNE Yes.

DRUMMLE That was to wish his girl goodbye.

MISQUITH Poor fellow!   310

DRUMMLE He sent for me when he came back. I think he must have had a lingering hope that the girl would relent—would come to life, as it were—at the last moment, for, for an hour or so, in this room, he was terribly shaken. I'm sure he'd clung to that hope from the persistent way in which he kept breaking off in his talk   315
to repeat one dismal word, as if he couldn't realise his position without dinning this damned word into his head.

JAYNE What word was that?

DRUMMLE Alone—alone.

Aubrey enters°

AUBREY [*advancing to the fire*] A thousand apologies!   320

DRUMMLE (*gaily*) We are talking about you, my dear Aubrey.

During the telling of the story, Misquith has risen and gone to the fire, and Drummle has thrown himself full-length on the sofa. Aubrey now joins Misquith and Jayne

AUBREY Well, Cayley, are you surprised?

DRUMMLE Surp—! I haven't been surprised for twenty years.

AUBREY And you're not angry with me?

DRUMMLE Angry! (*Rising*) Because you considerately withhold the   325
name of a lady with whom it is now the object of my life to become acquainted? My dear fellow, you pique my curiosity, you give zest

to my existence! And as for a wedding, who on earth wants to
attend that familiar and probably draughty function? Ugh! My
cigar's out.   330

AUBREY Let's talk about something else.

MISQUITH (*looking at his watch*) Not tonight, Aubrey.

AUBREY My dear Frank!

MISQUITH I go up to Scotland tomorrow, and there are some little
matters—   335

JAYNE I am off too.

AUBREY No, no.

JAYNE I must: I have to give a look to a case in Clifford Street on
my way home.

AUBREY (*going to the door*) Well!   340
        Misquith and Jayne exchange looks with Drummle
(*Opening the door and calling*) Morse, hats and coats! I shall write
to you all next week from Genoa or Florence. Now, doctor, Frank,
remember, my love to Mrs Misquith and to Mrs Jayne!
        Morse enters with hats and coats

MISQUITH and JAYNE Yes, yes—yes, yes.

AUBREY And your young people!   345
        *As Misquith and Jayne put on their coats, there is the clatter of
        careless talk*

JAYNE Cayley, I meet you at dinner on Sunday.

DRUMMLE At the Stratfields'. That's very pleasant.

MISQUITH (*putting on his coat with Aubrey's aid*) Ah—h!

AUBREY What's wrong?

MISQUITH A twinge. Why didn't I go to Aix in August?°   350

JAYNE (*shaking hands with Drummle*) Good-night, Cayley.

DRUMMLE Good-night, my dear doctor!

MISQUITH (*shaking hands with Drummle*) Cayley, are you in town for
long?

DRUMMLE Dear friend, I'm nowhere for long. Good-night.   355

MISQUITH Good-night.
        *Aubrey, Jayne, and Misquith go out, followed by Morse; the
        hum of talk is continued outside*

AUBREY A cigar, Frank?

MISQUITH No, thank you.

AUBREY Going to walk, doctor?

JAYNE If Frank will.   360

MISQUITH By all means.

AUBREY It's a cold night.

*The door is closed. Drummle remains standing with his coat on
his arm and his hat in his hand*

DRUMMLE (*to himself, thoughtfully*) Now then! What the devil—!
    Aubrey returns

AUBREY (*eyeing Drummle a little awkwardly*) Well, Cayley?

DRUMMLE Well, Aubrey?   365
    Aubrey walks up to the fire and stands looking into it

AUBREY You're not going, old chap?
    [*Drummle deliberately puts his hat and coat on the sofa and sits*]

DRUMMLE No.

AUBREY (*after a slight pause, with a forced laugh*) Hah! Cayley, I
    never thought I should feel—shy—with you.

DRUMMLE Why do you?   370

AUBREY Never mind.

DRUMMLE Now, I can quite understand a man wishing to be married
    in the dark, as it were.

AUBREY You can?

DRUMMLE In your place I should very likely adopt the same course.   375

AUBREY You think so?

DRUMMLE And if I intended marrying a lady not prominently in
    Society,° as I presume you do—as I presume you do—

AUBREY Well?

DRUMMLE As I presume you do, I'm not sure that *I* should tender   380
    her for preliminary dissection at afternoon-tea tables.

AUBREY No?

DRUMMLE In fact, there is probably only one person—were I in your
    position tonight—with whom I should care to chat the matter over.

AUBREY Who's that?   385

DRUMMLE Yourself, of course. (*Going to Aubrey and standing beside
    him*) Of course, yourself, old friend.

AUBREY (*after a pause*) I must seem a brute to you, Cayley. But there
    are some acts which are hard to explain, hard to defend—

DRUMMLE To defend—?   390

AUBREY Some acts which one must trust to time to put right.
    *Drummle watches him for a moment, then takes up his hat and
    coat*

DRUMMLE Well, I'll be moving.

AUBREY Cayley! Confound you and your old friendship! Do you
    think I forget it? Put your coat down! Why did you stay behind
    here? Cayley, the lady I am going to marry is the lady—who is   395
    known as—Mrs Jarman

There is a pause

DRUMMLE (*in a low voice*) Mrs Jarman! Are you serious?
   He walks up to the fireplace, where he leans upon the mantel-
   piece uttering something like a groan

AUBREY As you've got this out of me I give you leave to say all you
   care to say. Come, we'll be plain with each other. You know Mrs
   Jarman?   400

DRUMMLE I first met her at—what does it matter?

AUBREY Yes, yes, everything! Come!

DRUMMLE I met her at Homburg,° two—three seasons ago.

AUBREY Not as Mrs Jarman?

DRUMMLE No.   405

AUBREY She was then—?

DRUMMLE Mrs Dartry.

AUBREY Yes. She has also seen you in London, she says.

DRUMMLE Certainly.

AUBREY In Aldford Street. Go on.   410

DRUMMLE Please!

AUBREY I insist.

DRUMMLE (*with a slight shrug of the shoulders*) Sometime last year I
   was asked by a man to sup at his house, one night after the theatre.

AUBREY Mr Selwyn Ethurst—a bachelor.   415

DRUMMLE Yes.

AUBREY You were surprised therefore to find Mr Ethurst aided in
   his cursed hospitality° by a lady.

DRUMMLE I was unprepared.

AUBREY The lady you had known as Mrs Dartry? (*Drummle inclines*   420
   his head silently) There is something of a yachting cruise in the
   Mediterranean too, is there not?

DRUMMLE I joined Peter Jarman's yacht at Marseilles, in the spring,
   a month before he died.

AUBREY Mrs Jarman was on board?   425

DRUMMLE She was a kind hostess.

AUBREY And an old acquaintance?

DRUMMLE Yes.

AUBREY You have told your story.

DRUMMLE With your assistance.   430

AUBREY I have put you to the pain of telling it to show you that this
   is not the case of a blind man entrapped by an artful woman. Let
   me add that Mrs Jarman has no legal right to that name, that she
   is simply Miss Ray—Miss Paula Ray.

DRUMMLE (*after a pause*) I should like to express my regret, Aubrey,   435
for the way in which I spoke of George Orreyed's marriage.

AUBREY You mean you compare Lady Orreyed with Miss Ray?
(*Drummle is silent°*) Oh, of course! To you, Cayley, all women who
have been roughly treated, and who dare to survive by borrowing
a little of our philosophy, are alike. You see in the crowd of the   440
ill-used only one pattern; you can't detect the shades of goodness,
intelligence, even nobility there. Well, how should you? The crowd
is dimly lighted! And, besides, yours is the way of the world.

DRUMMLE My dear Aubrey, I *live* in the world.

AUBREY The name we give our little parish of St James's.°   445

DRUMMLE (*laying a hand on Aubrey's shoulder*) And you are quite
prepared, my friend, to forfeit the esteem of your little parish?

AUBREY I avoid mortification by shifting from one parish to another.
I give up Pall Mall for the Surrey hills; leave off varnishing my
boots and double the thickness of the soles.   450

DRUMMLE And your skin—do you double the thickness of that also?

AUBREY I know you think me a fool, Cayley—you needn't infer that
I'm a coward into the bargain. No! I know what I'm doing, and I
do it deliberately, defiantly. I'm alone; I injure no living soul by
the step I'm going to take; and so you can't urge the one argument   455
which might restrain me. Of course, I don't expect you to think
compassionately, fairly even, of the woman whom I—whom I am
drawn to—

DRUMMLE My dear Aubrey, I assure you I consider Mrs—Miss
Jarman—Mrs Ray—Miss Ray—delightful. But I confess there is a   460
form of chivalry which I gravely distrust, especially in a man
of—our age.

AUBREY Thanks. I've heard you say that from forty till fifty a man
is at heart either a stoic or a satyr.

DRUMMLE (*protestingly*) Ah! Now—   465

AUBREY I am neither. I have a temperate, honourable affection for
Mrs Jarman. She has never met a man who has treated her well—I
intend to treat her well. That's all. And in a few years, Cayley, if
you've not quite forsaken me, I'll prove to you that it's possible to
rear a life of happiness, of good repute, on a—miserable foundation.   470

DRUMMLE (*offering his hand*) Do prove it!

AUBREY (*taking his hand*) We have spoken too freely of—of Mrs
Jarman. I was excited—angry. Please forget it!

DRUMMLE My dear Aubrey, when we next meet I shall remember
nothing but my respect for the lady who bears your name.   475

Morse enters, closing the door behind him carefully

AUBREY What is it?

MORSE (*hesitatingly*) May I speak to you, sir? (*In an undertone*) Mrs Jarman, sir.

AUBREY (*softly to Morse*) Mrs Jarman! Do you mean she is at the lodge° in her carriage?   480

MORSE No, sir—here.° (*Aubrey looks towards Drummle, perplexed*) There's a nice fire in your—in that room, sir. (*Glancing in the direction of the door leading to the bedroom*)

AUBREY (*between his teeth, angrily*) Very well.

       Morse retires

DRUMMLE (*looking at his watch*) A quarter to eleven—horrible! 485
(*Taking up his hat and coat*) Must get to bed—up late every night this week. (*Aubrey assists Drummle with his coat*) Thank you. Well, good-night, Aubrey. I feel I've been dooced serious,° quite out of keeping with myself; pray overlook it.

AUBREY (*kindly*) Ah, Cayley!   490

DRUMMLE (*putting on a neck-handkerchief°*) And remember that, after all, I'm merely a spectator in life; nothing more than a man at a play, in fact; only, like the old-fashioned playgoer, I love to see certain characters happy and comfortable at the finish. You understand?   495

AUBREY I think I do.

DRUMMLE Then, for as long as you can, old friend, will you—keep a stall° for me?

AUBREY Yes, Cayley.

DRUMMLE (*gaily*) Ah, ha! Good-night! (*Bustling to the door*) Don't 500
bother! I'll let myself out! Good-night! God bless yer!

       He goes out; Aubrey follows him. Morse enters by the other door, carrying some unopened letters which, after a little consideration, he places on the mantelpiece against the clock. Aubrey returns

AUBREY Yes?

MORSE You hadn't seen your letters that came by the nine o'clock post, sir; I've put 'em where they'll catch your eye by and by.

AUBREY Thank you.   505

MORSE (*hesitatingly*) Gunter's cook and waiter° have gone, sir. Would you prefer me to go to bed?

AUBREY (*frowning*) Certainly not.°

MORSE Very well, sir.

       He goes out

AUBREY (*opening the upper door*) Paula! Paula!   510
     Paula enters and throws her arms round his neck. She is a young
     woman of about twenty-seven: beautiful, fresh, innocent-looking.
     She is in superb evening dress

PAULA Dearest!

AUBREY Why have you come here?

PAULA Angry?

AUBREY Yes—no. But it's eleven o'clock.

PAULA (*laughing*) I know.   515

AUBREY What on earth will Morse think?

PAULA Do you trouble yourself about what servants *think*?

AUBREY Of course.

PAULA Goose! They're only machines made to wait upon people—
and to give evidence in the Divorce Court. (*Looking round*) Oh,   520
indeed! A snug little dinner!

AUBREY Three men.

PAULA (*suspiciously*) Men?

AUBREY Men.

PAULA (*penitently*) Ah! (*Sitting at the table*) I'm so hungry.   525

AUBREY Let me get you some game pie, or some—

PAULA No, no, hungry for this. What beautiful fruit! I love fruit
when it's expensive.
     He clears a space on the table, places a plate before her, and
     helps her to fruit
I haven't dined, Aubrey dear.

AUBREY My poor girl! Why?   530

PAULA In the first place, I forgot to order any dinner, and my cook,
who has always loathed me, thought he'd pay me out before he
departed.

AUBREY The beast!

PAULA That's precisely what I—   535

AUBREY No, Paula!

PAULA What I told my maid to call him. What next will you think
of me?

AUBREY Forgive me. You must be starved.

PAULA (*eating fruit*) *I* didn't care. As there was nothing to eat, I sat   540
in my best frock, with my toes on the dining-room fender, and
dreamt, oh, such a lovely dinner party.

AUBREY Dear, lonely, little woman!

PAULA It was perfect. I saw you at the end of a very long table,
opposite me, and we exchanged sly glances now and again over the   545

flowers. We were host and hostess, Aubrey, and had been married about five years.

AUBREY (*kissing her hand*) Five years.

PAULA And on each side of us was the nicest set imaginable—you know, dearest, the sort of men and women that can't be imitated.   550

AUBREY Yes, yes. Eat some more fruit.

PAULA But I haven't told you the best part of my dream.

AUBREY Tell me.

PAULA Well, although we had been married only such a few years, I seemed to know by the look on their faces that none of our guests   555 had ever heard anything—anything—anything peculiar about the fascinating hostess.

AUBREY That's just how it will be, Paula. The world moves so quickly. That's just how it will be.

PAULA (*with a little grimace*) I wonder! (*Glancing at the fire*) Ugh! Do   560 throw another log on.

AUBREY (*mending the fire*) There. But you mustn't be here long.

PAULA Hospitable wretch! I've something important to tell you. No, stay where you are. (*Turning from him, her face averted*) Look here, that was my dream, Aubrey; but the fire went out while I was   565 dozing, and I woke up with a regular fit of the shivers. And the result of it all was that I ran upstairs and scribbled you a letter.

AUBREY Dear baby!

PAULA Remain where you are. (*Taking a letter from her pocket*) This is it. I've given you an account of myself, furnished you with a list   570 of my adventures since I—you know. (*Weighing the letter in her hand*) I wonder if it would go for a penny. Most of it you're acquainted with; *I've* told you a good deal, haven't I?

AUBREY Oh, Paula!

PAULA What I haven't told you, I daresay you've heard from others.   575 But in case they've omitted anything—the dears—it's all here.

AUBREY In Heaven's name, why must you talk like this tonight?

PAULA It may save discussion by and by, don't you think? (*Holding out the letter*) There you are.

AUBREY No, dear, no.   580

PAULA Take it. (*He takes the letter*) Read it through after I've gone, and then—read it again, and turn the matter over in your mind finally. And if, even at the very last moment, you feel you—oughtn't to go to church with me, send a messenger to Pont Street,° any time before eleven tomorrow, telling me that you're   585 afraid, and I—I'll take the blow.

158

AUBREY Why, what—what do you think I am?

PAULA That's it. It's because I know you're such a dear good fellow
that I want to save you the chance of ever feeling sorry you married
me. I really love you so much, Aubrey, that to save you that I'd   590
rather you treated me as—as the others have done.

AUBREY (*turning from her with a cry*) Oh!

PAULA (*after a slight pause*) I suppose I've shocked you. I can't help
it if I have.

> She sits, with assumed languor and indifference. He turns to her,
> advances, and kneels by her

AUBREY My dearest, you don't understand me. I—I can't bear to   595
hear you always talking about—what's done with. I tell you I'll
never remember it; Paula, can't you dismiss it? Try. Darling, if we
promise each other to forget, to forget, we're bound to be happy.
After all, it's a mechanical matter; the moment a wretched thought
enters your head, you quickly think of something bright—it   600
depends on one's will. Shall I burn this, dear? (*Referring to the
letter he holds in his hand*) Let me, let me!

PAULA (*with a shrug of the shoulders*) I don't suppose there's much
that's new to you in it—just as you like.

> He goes to the fire and burns the letter

AUBREY There's an end of it. (*Returning to her*) What's the matter?   605

PAULA (*rising, coldly*) Oh, nothing! I'll go and put my cloak on.

AUBREY (*detaining her*) What *is* the matter?

PAULA Well, I think you might have said, 'You're very generous,
Paula', or at least, 'Thank you, dear', when I offered to set you free.

AUBREY (*catching her in his arms*) Ah!   610

PAULA Ah! Ah! Ha, ha! It's all very well, but you don't know what
it cost me to make such an offer. I do so want to be married.

AUBREY But you never imagined—?

PAULA Perhaps not. And yet I *did* think of what I'd do at the end of
our acquaintance if you had preferred to behave like the rest.   615

> She takes a flower from her bodice

AUBREY Hush!

PAULA Oh, I forgot!

AUBREY What would you have done when we parted?

PAULA Why, killed myself.

AUBREY Paula, dear!   620

PAULA It's true. (*Putting the flower in his buttonhole*) Do you know, I
feel certain I should make away with myself if anything serious
happened to me.

AUBREY Anything serious! What, has nothing ever been serious to
you, Paula?   625
PAULA Not lately; not since a long while ago. I made up my mind
then to have done with taking things seriously. If I hadn't,
I—However, we won't talk about that.
AUBREY But now, now, life will be different to you, won't it—quite
different? Eh, dear?   630
PAULA Oh yes, now. Only, Aubrey, mind you keep me always happy.
AUBREY I will try to.
PAULA I know I couldn't swallow a second big dose of misery. I
know that if ever I felt wretched again—truly wretched—I should
take a leaf out of Connie Tirlemont's book. You remember? They   635
found her—(*With a look of horror*)
AUBREY For God's sake, don't let your thoughts run on such things!
PAULA (*laughing*) Ha, ha, how scared you look! There, think of the
time! Dearest, what will my coachman say! My cloak!
> *She runs off, gaily, by the upper door. Aubrey looks after her
> for a moment, then he walks up to the fire and stands warming
> his feet at the bars. As he does so he raises his head and observes
> the letters upon the mantelpiece. He takes one down quickly*
AUBREY Ah! Ellean! (*Opening the letter and reading*) 'My dear father,   640
A great change has come over me. I believe my mother in Heaven
has spoken to me, and counselled me to turn to you in your
loneliness. At any rate, your words have reached my heart, and I
no longer feel fitted for this solemn life. I am ready to take my
place by you. Dear father, will you receive me? Ellean.'   645
> *Paula re-enters, dressed in a handsome cloak. He stares at her
> as if he hardly realised her presence*
PAULA What are you staring at? Don't you admire my cloak?
AUBREY Yes.
PAULA Couldn't you wait till I'd gone before reading your letters?
AUBREY (*putting the letter away*) I beg your pardon.
PAULA Take me downstairs to the carriage.   650
> *(Slipping her arm through his)*
How I tease you! Tomorrow! I'm so happy!
> *They go out*

CURTAIN

Act Two

Scene One

The scene is morning-room in Aubrey Tanqueray's house, Highercoombe, near Willowmere, Surrey—a bright and prettily furnished apartment of irregular shape, with double doors opening into a small hall at the back, another door on the left, and a large recessed window through which is obtained a view of extensive grounds. Everything about the room is charming and graceful. The fire is burning in the grate, and a small table is tastefully laid for breakfast. It is a morning in early spring the following year, and the sun is streaming in through the window. Aubrey and Paula are seated at breakfast, and Aubrey is silently reading his letters. Two servants, a man and a woman, hand dishes and then retire. After a little while Aubrey puts his letters aside and looks across to the window

AUBREY Sunshine! Spring!

PAULA (*glancing at the clock*) Exactly six minutes.

AUBREY Six minutes?

PAULA Six minutes, Aubrey dear, since you made your last remark.

AUBREY I beg your pardon; I was reading my letters. Have you seen   5
Ellean this morning?

PAULA (*coldly*) Your last observation but one was about Ellean.

AUBREY Dearest, what shall I talk about?

PAULA Ellean breakfasted two hours ago, Morgan tells me, and then
went out walking with her dog.   10

AUBREY She wraps up warmly, I hope; this sunshine is deceptive.

PAULA I ran about the lawn last night, after dinner, in satin shoes.
Were you anxious about me?

AUBREY Certainly.

PAULA (*melting*) Really?   15

AUBREY You make me wretchedly anxious; you delight in doing
incautious things. You are incurable.

PAULA Ah, what a beast I am! (*Going to him and kissing him, then
glancing at the letters by his side*) A letter from Cayley?

AUBREY He is staying very near here, with Mrs—very near here.   20

PAULA With the lady whose chimneys we have the honour of
contemplating from our windows?

AUBREY With Mrs Cortelyon—yes.

PAULA Mrs Cortelyon! The woman who might have set the example of calling on me when we first threw out roots in this deadly lively soil! Deuce take Mrs Cortelyon! 25

AUBREY Hush! My dear girl!

PAULA (*returning to her seat*) Oh, I know she's an old acquaintance of yours—and of the first Mrs Tanqueray. And she joins the rest of 'em in slapping the second Mrs Tanqueray in the face. However, I have my revenge—she's six-and-forty, and I wish nothing worse to happen to any woman. 30

AUBREY Well, she's going to town, Cayley says here, and his visit's at an end. He's coming over this morning to call on you. Shall we ask him to transfer himself to us? Do say yes. 35

PAULA Yes.

AUBREY (*gladly*) Ah, ha! Old Cayley!

PAULA (*coldly*) He'll amuse *you*.

AUBREY And you too.

PAULA Because you find a companion, shall I be boisterously hilarious? 40

AUBREY Come, come! He talks London, and you know you like that.

PAULA London! London or Heaven! Which is farther from me!

AUBREY Paula!

PAULA Oh! Oh, I am so bored, Aubrey! 45

AUBREY (*gathering up his letters and going to her, leaning over her shoulder*) Baby, what can I do for you?

PAULA I suppose, nothing. You have done all you can for me.

AUBREY What do you mean?

PAULA You have married me. 50

He walks away from her thoughtfully, to the writing-table. As he places his letters on the table, he sees an addressed letter, stamped for the post, lying on the blotting-book; he picks it up

AUBREY (*in an altered tone*) You've been writing this morning before breakfast?

PAULA (*looking at him quickly, then away again*) Er—that letter.

AUBREY (*with the letter in his hand*) To Lady Orreyed. Why?

PAULA Why not? Mabel's an old friend of mine. 55

AUBREY Are you—corresponding?

PAULA I heard from her yesterday. They've just returned from the Riviera. She seems happy.

AUBREY (*sarcastically*) That's good news.

PAULA Why are you always so cutting about Mabel? She's a kind-   60
hearted girl. Everything's altered; she even thinks of letting her
hair go back to brown. She's Lady Orreyed. She's married to
George. What's the matter with her?

AUBREY (*turning away*) Oh!

PAULA You drive me mad sometimes with the tone you take about   65
things! Great goodness, if you come to that, George Orreyed's wife
isn't a bit worse than yours! (*He faces her suddenly*) I suppose I
needn't have made that observation.

AUBREY No, there was scarcely a necessity.

   He throws the letter on to the table, and takes up the newspaper

PAULA I am very sorry.

AUBREY All right, dear.   70

PAULA (*trifling with the letter*) I—I'd better tell you what I've written.
I meant to do so, of course. I—I've asked the Orreyeds to come
and stay with us. (*He looks at her and lets the paper fall to the ground
in a helpless way*) George was a great friend of Cayley's; I'm sure   75
he would be delighted to meet them here.

AUBREY (*laughing mirthlessly*) Ha, ha, ha! They say Orreyed has taken
to tippling at dinner. Heavens above!

PAULA Oh! I've no patience with you! You'll kill me with this life!
(*She selects some flowers from a vase on the table, cuts and arranges   80
them, and fastens them in her bodice*) What is my existence, Sunday
to Saturday? In the morning, a drive down to the village, with the
groom, to give my orders to the tradespeople. At lunch, you and
Ellean. In the afternoon, a novel, the newspapers; if fine, another
drive—*if* fine! Tea—you and Ellean. Then two hours of dusk; then   85
dinner—you and Ellean. Then a game of bezique,° you and I,
while Ellean reads a religious book in a dull corner. Then a yawn
from me, another from you, a sigh from Ellean; three figures
suddenly rise—'Good-night, good-night, good-night!' (*Imitating a
kiss*) 'God bless you!' Ah!   90

AUBREY Yes, yes, Paula—yes, dearest—that's what it is *now*. But, by
and by, if people begin to come round us—

PAULA Hah! That's where we've made the mistake, my friend
Aubrey! (*Pointing to the window*) Do you believe these people will
ever come round us? Your former crony, Mrs Cortelyon? Or the   95
grim old vicar, or that wife of his whose huge nose is positively
indecent? Or the Ullathornes, or the Gollans, or Lady William
Petres? I know better! And when the young ones gradually take the
place of the old, there will still remain the sacred tradition that the

dreadful person who lives at the top of the hill is never, under any   100
circumstances, to be called upon! And so we shall go on here, year
in and year out, until the sap is run out of our lives, and we're
stale and dry and withered from sheer, solitary respectability.
Upon my word, I wonder we didn't see that we should have been
far happier if we'd gone in for the devil-may-care, café-living sort   105
of life in town! After all, *I* have a set and you might have joined
it. It's true I did want, dearly, dearly, to be a married woman, but
where's the pride in being a married woman among married
women who are—married! If—(*Seeing that Aubrey's head has sunk
into his hands*) Aubrey! My dear boy! You're not—crying?   110

> [*She puts an arm round his neck.*] *He looks up, with a flushed
> face. Ellean enters, dressed very simply for walking. She is a
> low-voiced, grave girl of about nineteen, with a face somewhat
> resembling a Madonna. Towards Paula her manner is cold and
> distant*

AUBREY (*in an undertone*) Ellean!

ELLEAN Good-morning, Papa. Good-morning, Paula.

> *Paula puts her arms round Ellean and kisses her. Ellean makes
> little response*

PAULA Good-morning. (*Brightly*) We've been breakfasting this side
of the house, to get the sun.

> *She sits at the piano and rattles at a gay melody. Seeing that
> Paula's back is turned to them, Ellean goes to Aubrey and kisses
> him; he returns the kiss almost furtively. As they separate, the
> servants re-enter, and proceed to carry out the breakfast table*

AUBREY (*to Ellean*) I guess where you've been: there's some gorse   115
clinging to your frock.

ELLEAN (*removing a sprig of gorse from her skirt*) Rover and I walked
nearly as far as Black Moor. The poor fellow has a thorn in his
pad; I am going upstairs for my tweezers.

AUBREY Ellean! (*She returns to him*) Paula is a little depressed—out   120
of sorts. She complains that she has no companion.

ELLEAN I am with Paula nearly all the day, Papa.

AUBREY Ah, but you're such a little mouse. Paula likes cheerful
people about her.

ELLEAN I'm afraid I am naturally rather silent; and it's so difficult to   125
seem to be what one is not.

AUBREY I don't wish that, Ellean.

ELLEAN I will offer to go down to the village with Paula this
morning—shall I?

AUBREY (*touching her hand gently*) Thank you—do.   130
ELLEAN When I've looked after Rover, I'll come back to her.
    She goes out; Paula ceases playing, and turns on the music stool,
    looking at Aubrey.
PAULA Well, have you and Ellean had your little confidence?
AUBREY Confidence?
PAULA Do you think I couldn't feel it, like a pain between my
    shoulders?   135
AUBREY Ellean is coming back in a few minutes to be with you.
    (*Bending over her*) Paula, Paula dear, is this how you keep your
    promise?
PAULA Oh! (*Rising impatiently and crossing swiftly to the settee, where*
    she sits, moving restlessly) I *can't* keep my promise; I *am* jealous; it   140
    won't be smothered. I see you looking at her, watching her; your
    voice drops when you speak to her. I know how fond you are of
    that girl, Aubrey.
AUBREY What would you have? I've no other home for her. She is
    my daughter.   145
PAULA She is your saint. Saint Ellean!
AUBREY You have often told me how good and sweet you think her.
PAULA Good—yes! Do you imagine *that* makes me less jealous?
    (*Going to him and clinging to his arm*) Aubrey, there are two sorts
    of affection—the love for a woman you respect, and the love for a   150
    woman you—love. She gets the first from you: I never can.
AUBREY Hush, hush! You don't realise what you say.
PAULA If Ellean cared for me only a little, it would be different. I
    shouldn't be jealous then. Why doesn't she care for me?
AUBREY She—she—she will, in time.   155
PAULA You can't say that without stuttering.
AUBREY Her disposition seems a little unresponsive; she resembles
    her mother in many ways; I can see it every day.
PAULA She's marble. It's a shame. There's not the slightest excuse;
    for all she knows, I'm as much a saint as she—only married.   160
    Dearest, help me to win her over!
AUBREY Help you?
PAULA You can. Teach her that it is her duty to love me; she hangs
    on to every word you speak. I'm sure, Aubrey, that the love of a
    nice woman who believed me to be like herself would do me a   165
    world of good. You'd get the benefit of it as well as I. It would
    soothe me; it would make me less horribly restless; it would take
    this—this—mischievous feeling from me. (*Coaxingly*) Aubrey!

AUBREY Have patience; everything will come right.

PAULA Yes, if you help me.   170

AUBREY In the mean time you will tear up your letter to Lady
Orreyed, won't you?

PAULA (*kissing his hand*) Of course I will—anything!

AUBREY Ah, thank you, dearest! (*Laughing*) Why, good gracious—ha,
ha!—just imagine 'Saint Ellean' and that woman side by side!   175

PAULA (*going back with a cry*) Ah!

AUBREY What?

PAULA (*passionately*) It's Ellean you're considering, not me? It's all
Ellean with you! Ellean! Ellean!

    Ellean re-enters

ELLEAN Did you call me, Paula?   180

    Clenching his hands, Aubrey turns away and goes out

Is Papa angry?

PAULA [*shrugging her shoulders*] I drive him distracted sometimes.
There, I confess it!

    [*She walks away to the settee and sits down, petulantly*]

ELLEAN [*advancing*] Do you? Oh, why do you?

PAULA Because I—because I'm jealous.   185

ELLEAN Jealous?

PAULA Yes—of you. (*Ellean is silent*) Well, what do you think of that?

ELLEAN I knew it; I've seen it. It hurts me dreadfully. What do you
wish me to do? Go away?

PAULA Leave us! (*Beckoning her with a motion of the head*) Look here!   190
(*Ellean goes to Paula slowly and unresponsively*) You could cure me
of my jealousy very easily. Why don't you—like me?

ELLEAN What do you mean by—like you? I don't understand.

PAULA Love me.

ELLEAN Love is not a feeling that is under one's control. I shall alter   195
as time goes on, perhaps. I didn't begin to love my father deeply
till a few months ago, and then I obeyed my mother.

PAULA [*dryly*] Ah, yes, you dream things, don't you—see them in
your sleep? You fancy your mother speaks to you?

ELLEAN When you have lost your mother it is a comfort to believe   200
that she is dead only to this life, that she still watches over her
child. I do believe that of my mother.

PAULA Well, and so you haven't been bidden to love *me*?

ELLEAN (*after a pause, almost inaudibly*) No.

PAULA Dreams are only a hash-up of one's day-thoughts, I suppose   205
you know. Think intently of anything, and it's bound to come back
to you at night. I don't cultivate dreams myself.

ELLEAN Ah, I knew you would only sneer!

PAULA I'm not sneering; I'm speaking the truth. I say that if you
cared for me in the daytime I should soon make friends with those   210
nightmares of yours. Ellean, why don't you try to look on me as
your second mother? Of course there are not many years between
us, but I'm ever so much older than you—in experience. I shall
have no children of my own, I know that; it would be a real
comfort to me if you would make me feel we belonged to each   215
other. Won't you? Perhaps you think I'm odd—not nice. Well, the
fact is I've two sides to my nature, and I've let the one almost
smother the other. A few years ago I went through some trouble,
and since then I haven't shed a tear. I believe if you put your arms
round me just once I should run upstairs and have a good cry.   220
There, I've talked to you as I've never talked to a woman in my
life. Ellean, you seem to fear me. Don't! Kiss me!

> *With a cry, almost of despair, Ellean turns from Paula and sinks
> on to the settee, covering her face with her hands*

(*Indignantly*) Oh! Why is it! How dare you treat me like this? What
do you mean by it? What do you mean?

> *A servant enters*

SERVANT Mr Drummle, ma'am.   225

> *Cayley Drummle, in riding dress, enters briskly. The servant
> retires*

PAULA (*recovering herself*) Well, Cayley!

DRUMMLE (*shaking hands with her cordially*) How are you? (*Shaking
hands with Ellean, who rises*) I saw you in the distance an hour ago,
in the gorse near Stapleton's.

ELLEAN I didn't see you, Mr Drummle.   230

DRUMMLE My dear Ellean, it is my experience that no charming
young lady of nineteen ever does see a man of forty-five. (*Laughing*) Ha, ha!

ELLEAN (*going to the door*) Paula, Papa wishes me to drive down to
the village with you this morning. Do you care to take me?   235

PAULA (*coldly*) Oh, by all means. Pray tell Watts to balance the cart
for three.°

> *Ellean goes out*

DRUMMLE How's Aubrey?

PAULA Very well—when Ellean's about the house.

DRUMMLE And you? I needn't ask.   240

PAULA (*walking away to the window*) Oh, a dog's life, my dear Cayley,
mine.

DRUMMLE Eh?

PAULA Doesn't that define a happy marriage? I'm sleek, well-kept,
well-fed, never without a bone to gnaw and fresh straw to lie upon.   245
(*Gazing out of the window*) Oh, dear me!

DRUMMLE H'm! Well, I heartily congratulate you on your kennel.
The view from the terrace here is superb.

PAULA Yes, I can see London.

DRUMMLE London! Not quite so far, surely?   250

PAULA *I* can. Also the Mediterranean, on a fine day. I wonder what
Algiers looks like this morning from the sea! (*Impulsively*)
Oh, Cayley, do you remember those jolly times on board Peter
Jarman's yacht when we lay off—? (*Stopping suddenly, seeing
Drummle staring at her*) Good gracious! What are we talking   255
about!

> *Aubrey enters*

AUBREY (*to Drummle*) Dear old chap! Has Paula asked you?

PAULA Not yet.

AUBREY We want you to come to us, now that you're leaving Mrs
Cortelyon—at once, today. Stay a month, as long as you please—   260
eh, Paula?

PAULA As long as you can possibly endure it—do, Cayley.

DRUMMLE (*looking at Aubrey*) Delighted. (*To Paula*) Charming of
you to have me.

PAULA My dear man, you're a blessing. I must telegraph to London   265
for more fish! A strange appetite to cater for! Something to do, to
do, to do!

> *She goes out in a mood of almost childish delight*

DRUMMLE (*eyeing Aubrey*) Well?

AUBREY (*with a wearied, anxious look*) Well, Cayley?

DRUMMLE How are you getting on?   270

AUBREY My position doesn't grow less difficult. I told you, when I
met you last week, of this feverish, jealous attachment of Paula's
for Ellean?

DRUMMLE Yes. I hardly know why, but I came to the conclusion that
you don't consider it an altogether fortunate attachment.   275

AUBREY Ellean doesn't respond to it.

DRUMMLE These are early days. Ellean will warm towards your wife
by and by.

AUBREY Ah, but there's the question, Cayley!

DRUMMLE What question?   280

AUBREY The question which positively distracts me. Ellean is so
different from—most women; I don't believe a purer creature

exists out of Heaven. And I—I ask myself, am I doing right in
exposing her to the influence of poor Paula's light, careless nature?

DRUMMLE My dear Aubrey! 285

AUBREY That shocks you! So it does me. I assure you I long to urge
my girl to break down the reserve which keeps her apart from
Paula, but somehow I can't do it—well, I don't do it. How can I
make you understand? But when you come to us you'll understand
quickly enough. Cayley, there's hardly a subject you can broach on 290
which poor Paula hasn't some strange, out-of-the-way thought to
give utterance to; some curious, warped notion. They are not mere
worldly thoughts—unless—good God!—they belong to the little
hellish world which our blackguardism has created: no, her ideas
have too little calculation in them to be called worldly. But it 295
makes it the more dreadful that such thoughts should be ready,
spontaneous; that expressing them has become a perfectly natural
process; that her words, acts even, have almost lost their proper
significance for her, and seem beyond her control. Ah, and the pain
of listening to it all from the woman one loves, the woman one 300
hoped to make happy and contented, who is really and truly a good
woman, as it were, maimed! Well, this is my burden, and I
shouldn't speak to you of it but for my anxiety about Ellean.
Ellean! What is to be her future? It is in my hands; what am I to
do? Cayley, when I remember how Ellean comes to me, from 305
another world I always think, when I realise the charge that's laid
on me, I find myself wishing, in a sort of terror, that my child were
safe under the ground!

DRUMMLE My dear Aubrey, aren't you making a mistake?

AUBREY Very likely. What is it? 310

DRUMMLE A mistake, not in regarding your Ellean as an angel, but
in believing that, under any circumstances, it would be possible for
her to go through life without getting her white robe—shall we say,
a little dusty at the hem? Don't take me for a cynic. I am sure there
are many women upon earth who are almost divinely innocent; but 315
being on earth, they must send their robes to the laundry
occasionally. Ah, and it's right that they should have to do so, for
what can they learn from the checking of their little washing-bills
but lessons of charity? Now I see but two courses open to you for
the disposal of your angel. 320

AUBREY Yes?

DRUMMLE You must either restrict her to a paradise which is, like
every earthly paradise, necessarily somewhat imperfect, or treat her

as an ordinary flesh-and-blood young woman, and give her the
advantages of that society to which she properly belongs.   325

AUBREY Advantages?

DRUMMLE My dear Aubrey, of all forms of innocence mere ignorance is the least admirable. Take my advice, let her walk and talk
and suffer and be healed with the great crowd. Do it, and hope
that she'll some day meet a good, honest fellow who'll make her   330
life complete, happy, secure. Now you see what I'm driving at.

AUBREY A sanguine programme, my dear Cayley! Oh, I'm not
pooh-poohing it. Putting sentiment aside, of course I know that a
fortunate marriage for Ellean would be the best—perhaps the
only—solution of my difficulty. But you forget the danger of the   335
course you suggest.

DRUMMLE Danger?

AUBREY If Ellean goes among men and women, how can she escape
from learning, sooner or later, the history of—poor Paula's—old
life?   340

DRUMMLE H'm! You remember the episode of the Jeweller's Son in
the *Arabian Nights*?° Of course you don't. Well, if your daughter
lives, she *can't* escape—what you're afraid of. (*Aubrey gives a
half-stifled exclamation of pain*) And when she does hear the story,
surely it would be better that she should have some knowledge of   345
the world to help her to understand it.

AUBREY To understand!

DRUMMLE To understand, to—to philosophise.

AUBREY To philosophise?

DRUMMLE Philosophy is toleration, and it is only one step from   350
toleration to forgiveness.

AUBREY You're right, Cayley; I believe you always are. Yes, yes. But,
even if I had the courage to attempt to solve the problem of
Ellean's future in this way, I—I'm helpless.

DRUMMLE How?   355

AUBREY What means have I now of placing my daughter in the
world I've left?

DRUMMLE Oh, some friend—some woman friend.

AUBREY I have none; they're gone.

DRUMMLE You're wrong there; I know one—   360

AUBREY (*listening*) That's Paula's cart. Let's discuss this again.

DRUMMLE (*going up to the window and looking out*) It isn't the
dogcart. (*Turning to Aubrey*) I hope you'll forgive me, old chap.

AUBREY What for?

DRUMMLE Whose wheels do you think have been cutting ruts in   365
your immaculate drive?
    A servant enters
SERVANT (*to Aubrey*) Mrs Cortelyon, sir.
AUBREY Mrs Cortelyon! (*After a short pause*) Very well.
    The servant withdraws
What on earth is the meaning of this?
DRUMMLE Ahem! While I've been our old friend's guest, Aubrey, we   370
have very naturally talked a good deal about you and yours.
AUBREY Indeed, have you?
DRUMMLE Yes, and Alice Cortelyon has arrived at the conclusion
that it would have been far kinder had she called on Mrs
Tanqueray long ago. She's going abroad for Easter before settling   375
down in London for the season,° and I believe she has come over
this morning to ask for Ellean's companionship.
AUBREY Oh, I see! (*Frowning*) Quite a friendly little conspiracy, my
dear Cayley!
DRUMMLE Conspiracy! Not at all, I assure you. (*Laughing*) Ha, ha!   380
    Ellean enters from the hall with Mrs Cortelyon, a handsome,
    good-humoured, spirited woman of about forty-five.
ELLEAN Papa—
MRS CORTELYON (*to Aubrey, shaking hands with him heartily*) Well,
Aubrey, how are you? I've just been telling this great girl of yours
that I knew her when she was a sad-faced, pale baby. How is Mrs
Tanqueray? I have been a bad neighbour, and I'm here to beg   385
forgiveness. Is she indoors?
AUBREY She's upstairs putting on a hat, I believe.
MRS CORTELYON (*sitting comfortably*) Ah! (*She looks round: Drummle*
and Ellean are talking together in the hall) We used to be very frank
with each other, Aubrey. I suppose the old footing is no longer   390
possible, eh?
AUBREY If so, I'm not entirely to blame, Mrs Cortelyon.
MRS CORTELYON Mrs Cortelyon? H'm! No, I admit it. But you must
make some little allowance for me, *Mr Tanqueray*. Your first wife
and I, as girls, were like two cherries on one stalk,° and then I was   395
the confidential friend of your married life. That post, perhaps,
wasn't altogether a sinecure. And now—well, when a woman gets
to my age I suppose she's a stupid, prejudiced, conventional creature. However, I've got over it and—(*Giving him her hand*) I hope
you'll be enormously happy and let me be a friend once more.   400
AUBREY Thank you, Alice.

MRS CORTELYON That's right. I feel more cheerful than I've done
for weeks. But I suppose it would serve me right if the second Mrs
Tanqueray showed me the door. Do you think she will?

AUBREY (*listening*) Here is my wife.   405
      Mrs Cortelyon rises, and Paula enters, dressed for driving; she
      stops abruptly on seeing Mrs Cortelyon
Paula dear, Mrs Cortelyon has called to see you.
      Paula starts, looks at Mrs Cortelyon irresolutely, then after a
      slight pause barely touches Mrs Cortelyon's extended hand

PAULA (*whose manner now alternates between deliberate insolence and*
assumed sweetness) Mrs—? What name, Aubrey?

AUBREY Mrs Cortelyon.

PAULA Cortelyon? Oh, yes. Cortelyon.   410

MRS CORTELYON (*carefully guarding herself throughout against any*
expression of resentment) Aubrey ought to have told you that Alice
Cortelyon and he are very old friends.

PAULA Oh, very likely he has mentioned the circumstance. I have
quite a wretched memory.   415

MRS CORTELYON You know we are neighbours, Mrs Tanqueray.

PAULA Neighbours? Are we really? Won't you sit down? (*They both*
sit) Neighbours! That's most interesting!

MRS CORTELYON Very near neighbours. You can see my roof from
your windows.   420

PAULA I fancy I *have* observed a roof. But you have been away from
home; you have only just returned.

MRS CORTELYON I? What makes you think that?

PAULA Why, because it is two months since we came to Highercoombe, and I don't remember your having called.   425

MRS CORTELYON Your memory is now terribly accurate. No, I've
not been away from home, and it is to explain my neglect that I
am here, rather unceremoniously, this morning.

PAULA Oh, to explain—quite so. (*With mock solicitude*) Ah, you've
been very ill; I ought to have seen that before.   430

MRS CORTELYON Ill!

PAULA You look dreadfully pulled down. We poor women show
illness so plainly in our faces, don't we?

AUBREY (*anxiously*) Paula dear, Mrs Cortelyon is the picture of
health.   435

MRS CORTELYON (*with some asperity*) I have never *felt* better in my life.

PAULA (*looking round innocently*) Have I said anything awkward?
Aubrey, tell Mrs Cortelyon how stupid and thoughtless I always am!

MRS CORTELYON (*to Drummle, who is now standing close to her*)
Really, Cayley—! (*He soothes her with a nod and smile and a motion*   440
of his finger to his lip) Mrs Tanqueray, I am afraid my explanation
will not be quite so satisfactory as either of those you have just
helped me to. You may have heard—but, if you have heard, you
have doubtless forgotten—that twenty years ago, when your
husband first lived here, I was a constant visitor at Highercoombe.   445
PAULA Twenty years ago—fancy! I was a naughty little child then.
MRS CORTELYON Possibly. Well, at that time, and till the end of her
life, my affections were centred upon the lady of this house.
PAULA Were they? That was very sweet of you.
         Ellean approaches Mrs Cortelyon, listening intently to her
MRS CORTELYON I will say no more on that score, but I must add   450
this: when, two months ago, you came here, I realised, perhaps for
the first time, that I was a middle-aged woman, and that it had
become impossible for me to accept without some effort a break-
ing-in upon many tender associations. There, Mrs Tanqueray, that
is my confession. Will you try to understand it and pardon me?   455
PAULA (*watching Ellean, sneeringly*)   Ellean dear, you appear to be
very interested in Mrs Cortelyon's reminiscences; I don't think I
can do better than make you my mouthpiece—there is such
sympathy between us. What do you say—can we bring ourselves
to forgive Mrs Cortelyon for neglecting us for two weary months?   460
MRS CORTELYON (*to Ellean, pleasantly*)   Well, Ellean?
         With a little cry of tenderness Ellean impulsively sits beside Mrs
         Cortelyon and takes her hand
My dear child!
PAULA (*in an undertone to Aubrey*) Ellean isn't so very slow in taking
to Mrs Cortelyon!
MRS CORTELYON (*to Paula and Aubrey*)   Come, this encourages me   465
to broach my scheme. Mrs Tanqueray, it strikes me that you two
good people are just now excellent company for each other, while
Ellean would perhaps be glad of a little peep into the world you
are anxious to avoid. Now, I'm going to Paris tomorrow for a week
or two before settling down in Chester Square,° so—don't gasp,   470
both of you!—if this girl is willing, and you have made no other
arrangements for her, will you let her come with me to Paris, and
afterwards remain with me in town during the season? (*Ellean*
utters an exclamation of surprise. Paula is silent) What do you say?
AUBREY Paula—Paula dear. (*Hesitatingly*) My dear Mrs Cortelyon,   475
this is wonderfully kind of you; I am really at a loss to—eh, Cayley?

DRUMMLE (*watching Paula apprehensively*)   Kind! Now I must say I don't think so! I begged Alice to take *me* to Paris, and she declined. I am thrown over for Ellean! Ha! Ha!

MRS CORTELYON (*laughing*) What nonsense you talk, Cayley!   480
The laughter dies out. Paula remains quite still

AUBREY Paula dear.

PAULA (*slowly collecting herself*) One moment. I—I don't quite—(*To Mrs Cortelyon*) You propose that Ellean leaves Highercoombe almost at once and remains with you some months?

MRS CORTELYON It would be a mercy to me. You can afford to be   485 generous to a desolate old widow. Come, Mrs Tanqueray, won't you spare her?

PAULA Won't *I* spare her? (*Suspiciously*) Have you mentioned your plan to Aubrey—before I came in?

MRS CORTELYON No, I had no opportunity.   490

PAULA Nor to Ellean?

MRS CORTELYON Oh, no.

PAULA (*looking about her, in suppressed excitement*) This hasn't been discussed at all, behind my back?

MRS CORTELYON My dear Mrs Tanqueray!   495

PAULA Ellean, let us hear your voice in the matter!

ELLEAN I should like to go with Mrs Cortelyon—

PAULA Ah!

ELLEAN That is, if—if—

PAULA If—if what?   500

ELLEAN (*looking towards Aubrey, appealingly*) Papa?

PAULA (*in a hard voice*) Oh, of course—I forgot. (*To Aubrey*) My dear Aubrey, it rests with you, naturally, whether I am—to lose—Ellean.

AUBREY Lose Ellean! (*Advancing to Paula*) There is no question of   505 losing Ellean. You would see Ellean in town constantly when she returned from Paris; isn't that so, Mrs Cortelyon?

MRS CORTELYON Certainly.

PAULA (*laughing softly*) Oh, I didn't know I should be allowed that privilege.   510

MRS CORTELYON Privilege, my dear Mrs Tanqueray!

PAULA Ha, ha! That makes all the difference, doesn't it?

AUBREY (*with assumed gaiety*) All the difference? I should think so! (*To Ellean, laying his hand upon her head, tenderly*) And you are quite certain you wish to see what the world is like on the other   515 side of Black Moor?

ELLEAN If you are willing, Papa, I am quite certain.

AUBREY (*looking at Paula irresolutely, then speaking with an effort*)
Then I—I am willing.

PAULA (*rising and striking the table lightly with her clenched hand*)   520
That decides it!
> *There is a general movement*

(*Excitedly to Mrs Cortelyon, who advances towards her*) When do
you want her?

MRS CORTELYON We go to town this afternoon at five o'clock, and
sleep tonight at Bayliss's.° There is barely time for her to make   525
her preparations.

PAULA I will undertake that she is ready.

MRS CORTELYON I've a great deal to scramble through at home too,
as you may guess. Goodbye!

PAULA (*turning away*) Mrs Cortelyon is going.   530
> *Paula stands looking out of the window, with her back to those
> in the room*

MRS CORTELYON (*to Drummle*) Cayley—

DRUMMLE (*to her*) Eh?

MRS CORTELYON I've gone through it, for the sake of Aubrey and
his child, but I—I feel a hundred. Is that a madwoman?

DRUMMLE Of course; all jealous women are mad.   535
> *He goes out with Aubrey*°

MRS CORTELYON (*hesitatingly, to Paula*) Goodbye, Mrs Tanqueray.
> *Paula inclines her head with the slightest possible movement, then
> resumes her former position. Ellean comes from the hall and takes
> Mrs Cortelyon out of the room. After a brief silence, Paula turns
> with a fierce cry, and hurriedly takes off her coat and hat, and
> tosses them upon the settee*

PAULA Oh! Oh! Oh! (*She drops into the chair as Aubrey returns;*° *he
stands looking at her*) Who's that?

AUBREY I. You have altered your mind about going out?

PAULA Yes. Please to ring the bell.   540

AUBREY (*touching the bell*) You are angry about Mrs Cortelyon and
Ellean. Let me try to explain my reasons—

PAULA Be careful what you say to me just now! I have never felt like
this—except once—in my life. Be careful what you say to me!
> *A servant enters*

PAULA (*rising*) Is Watts at the door with the cart?   545

SERVANT Yes, ma'am.

PAULA Tell him to drive down to the post office directly, with this.

She picks up the letter which has been lying upon the table

AUBREY With that?

PAULA Yes. My letter to Lady Orreyed.

She gives the letter to the servant, who goes out

AUBREY Surely you don't wish me to countermand any order of   550
yours to a servant? Call the man back—take the letter from him!

PAULA I have not the slightest intention of doing so.

AUBREY I must, then.

*He goes to the door. She snatches up her hat and coat and
follows him*

What are you going to do?

PAULA If you stop that letter, walk out of the house.   555

He hesitates, then leaves the door

AUBREY I am right in believing that to be the letter inviting George
Orreyed and his wife to stay here, am I not?

PAULA Oh yes—quite right.

AUBREY Let it go; I'll write to him by and by.

PAULA (*facing him*) You dare!   560

AUBREY Hush, Paula!

PAULA Insult me again and, upon my word, I'll go straight out of the
house!

AUBREY Insult you?

PAULA Insult me! What else is it? My God! What else is it? What do   565
you mean by taking Ellean from me?

AUBREY Listen—!

PAULA Listen to *me!* And how do you take her? You pack her off in
the care of a woman who has deliberately held aloof from me,
who's thrown mud at me! Yet this Cortelyon creature has only to   570
put foot here once to be entrusted with the charge of the girl you
know I dearly want to keep near me!

AUBREY Paula dear! Hear me—!

PAULA Ah! Of course, of course! I can't be so useful to your daughter
as such people as this; and so I'm to be given the go-by for any   575
town friend of yours who turns up and chooses to patronise us!
Hah! Very well, at any rate, as you take Ellean from me you justify
my looking for companions where I can most readily find 'em.

AUBREY You wish me to fully appreciate your reason for sending that
letter to Lady Orreyed?   580

PAULA Precisely—I do.

AUBREY And could you, after all, go back to associates of that order?
It's not possible!

PAULA (*mockingly*) What, not after the refining influence of these
intensely respectable surroundings? (*Going to the door*) We'll see! 585
AUBREY Paula!
PAULA (*violently*) We'll see!
    She goes out. He stands still looking after her

CURTAIN

Act Three

Scene One

The scene is the drawing-room at Highercoombe. Facing the spectator are two large french windows, sheltered by a veranda, leading into the garden; on the right is a door opening into a small hall. The fireplace, with a large mirror above it, is on the left-hand side of the room, and higher up in the same wall are double doors, recessed. The room is richly furnished, and everything betokens taste and luxury. The windows are open, and there is moonlight in the garden. Lady Orreyed, a pretty, affected doll of a woman with a mincing voice and flaxen hair, is sitting on the ottoman,° her head resting against the drum, and her eyes closed. Paula, looking pale, worn, and thoroughly unhappy, is sitting at a table. Both are in sumptuous dinner-gowns

LADY ORREYED (*opening her eyes*) Well, I never! I dropped off! (*Feeling her hair*) Just fancy! Where are the men?

PAULA (*icily*) Outside, smoking.

A servant enters with coffee, which he hands to Lady Orreyed. Sir George Orreyed comes in by the window. He is a man of about thirty-five, with a low forehead, a receding chin, a vacuous expression, and an ominous redness about the nose

LADY ORREYED (*taking coffee*) Here's Dodo.

SIR GEORGE I say, the flies under the veranda make you swear. 5

The servant hands coffee to Paula, who declines it, then to Sir George, who takes a cup

Hi! Wait a bit! (*He looks at the tray searchingly, then puts back his cup*) Never mind. (*Quietly to Lady Orreyed*) I say, they're dooced sparin' with their liqueur, ain't they?

The servant goes out at window

PAULA (*to Sir George*) Won't you take coffee, George?

SIR GEORGE No, thanks. It's gettin' near time for a whisky and 10
potass.° (*Approaching Paula, regarding Lady Orreyed admiringly*) I say, Birdie looks rippin' tonight, don't she?

PAULA Your wife?

SIR GEORGE Yaas—Birdie.

PAULA Rippin'? 15

SIR GEORGE Yaas.

PAULA Quite—quite rippin'.

> *He moves round to the settee. Paula watches him with distaste,
> then rises and walks away. Sir George falls asleep on the settee
> [by the fireplace]*

LADY ORREYED Paula love, I fancied you and Aubrey were a little
more friendly at dinner. You haven't made it up, have you?

PAULA We? Oh, no. We speak before others, that's all.   20

LADY ORREYED And how long do you intend to carry on this game,
dear?

PAULA (*turning away impatiently*) I really can't tell you.

LADY ORREYED Sit down, old girl; don't be so fidgety.

> *Paula sits on the upper seat of the ottoman, with her back to
> Lady Orreyed*

Of course, it's my duty, as an old friend, to give you a good   25
talking-to—(*Paula glares at her suddenly and fiercely*) But really I've
found one gets so many smacks in the face through interfering in
matrimonial squabbles that I've determined to drop it.

PAULA I think you're wise.

LADY ORREYED However, I must say that I do wish you'd look at   30
marriage in a more solemn light—just as I do, in fact. It is such a
beautiful thing—marriage, and if people in our position don't
respect it, and set a good example by living happily with their
husbands, what can you expect from the middle classes? When did
this sad state of affairs between you and Aubrey actually begin?   35

PAULA Actually, a fortnight and three days ago; I haven't calculated
the minutes.

LADY ORREYED A day or two before Dodo and I turned up—
arrived.

PAULA Yes. One always remembers one thing by another; we left   40
off speaking to each other the morning I wrote asking you to
visit us.

LADY ORREYED Lucky for you I was able to pop down, wasn't it,
dear?

PAULA (*glaring at her again*) Most fortunate.   45

LADY ORREYED A serious split with your husband without a pal on
the premises—I should say, without a friend in the house—would
be most unpleasant.

PAULA (*turning to her abruptly*) This place must be horribly doleful
for you and George just now. At least you ought to consider him   50
before me. Why don't you leave me to my difficulties?

LADY ORREYED Oh, we're quite comfortable, dear, thank you—both of us. George and me are so wrapped up in each other, it doesn't matter where we are. I don't want to crow over you, old girl, but I've got a perfect husband.   55

>   *Sir George is now fast asleep, his head thrown back and his mouth open, looking hideous*

PAULA (*glancing at Sir George*) So you've given me to understand.

LADY ORREYED Not that we don't have our little differences. Why, we fell out only this very morning. You remember the diamond and ruby tiara Charley Prestwick gave poor dear Connie Tirlemont years ago, don't you?   60

PAULA No, I do not.

LADY ORREYED No? Well, it's in the market. Benjamin of Piccadilly has got it in his shop-window, and I've set my heart on it.

PAULA You consider it quite necessary?

LADY ORREYED Yes, because what I say to Dodo is this—a lady of   65
my station must smother herself with hair ornaments. It's different with you, love—people don't look for so much blaze from you, but I've got rank to keep up; haven't I?

PAULA Yes.

LADY ORREYED Well, that was the cause of the little set-to between   70
I and Dodo this morning. He broke two chairs, he was in such a rage. I forgot, they're your chairs; do you mind?

PAULA No.

LADY ORREYED You know, poor Dodo can't lose his temper without smashing something; if it isn't a chair, it's a mirror; if it isn't that,   75
it's china—a bit of Dresden for choice. Dear old pet! He loves a bit of Dresden when he's furious. He doesn't really throw things *at* me, dear; he simply lifts them up and drops them, like a gentleman. I expect our room upstairs will look rather wrecky°
before I get that tiara.   80

PAULA Excuse the suggestion, perhaps your husband can't afford it.

LADY ORREYED Oh, how dreadfully changed you are, Paula! Dodo can always mortgage something, or borrow of his ma. What *is* coming to you!

PAULA Ah!   85

>   *She sits at the piano and touches the keys*

LADY ORREYED Oh, yes, do play! That's the one thing I envy you for.

PAULA What shall I play?

LADY ORREYED What was that heavenly piece you gave us last night, dear?

PAULA A bit of Schubert. Would you like to hear it again?   90

LADY ORREYED You don't know any comic songs, do you?

PAULA I'm afraid not.

LADY ORREYED I leave it to you, then.

> *Paula plays. Aubrey and Cayley Drummle appear outside the window; they look into the room*

AUBREY (*to Drummle*) You can see her face in that mirror. Poor girl, how ill and wretched she looks.   95

DRUMMLE When are the Orreyeds going?

AUBREY (*entering the room*) Heaven knows!

DRUMMLE (*following Aubrey*) But *you're* entertaining them; what's it to do with Heaven?

AUBREY Do you know, Cayley, that even the Orreyeds serve a useful 100 purpose? My wife actually speaks to me before our guests—think of that! I've come to rejoice at the presence of the Orreyeds!

DRUMMLE I dare say; we're taught that beetles are sent for a benign end.

AUBREY Cayley, talk to Paula again tonight.   105

DRUMMLE Certainly, if I get the chance.

AUBREY Let's contrive it. George is asleep; perhaps I can get that doll out of the way.

> *As they advance into the room, Paula abruptly ceases playing and finds interest in a volume of music. Sir George is now nodding and snoring apoplectically*

Lady Orreyed, whenever you feel inclined for a game of billiards, I'm at your service.   110

LADY ORREYED (*jumping up*) Charmed, I'm sure! I really thought you'd forgotten poor little me. Oh, look at Dodo!

AUBREY No, no, don't wake him; he's tired.

LADY ORREYED I must, he looks so plain. (*Rousing Sir George*) Dodo! Dodo!   115

SIR GEORGE (*stupidly*) 'Ullo!

LADY ORREYED Dodo, dear, you were snoring.

SIR GEORGE Oh, I say, you could 'a told me that by and by.

AUBREY You want a cigar, George; come into the billiard-room. (*Giving his arm to Lady Orreyed*) Cayley, bring Paula.   120

> *Aubrey and Lady Orreyed go out*

SIR GEORGE (*rising*) Hey, what! Billiard-room! (*Looking at his watch*) How goes the—? Phew! 'Ullo, 'Ullo! Whisky and potass!

> *He goes rapidly after Aubrey and Lady Orreyed. Paula resumes playing*

PAULA (*after a pause*) Don't moon about after me, Cayley; follow the
  others.

DRUMMLE Thanks, by and by. (*Sitting*) That's pretty.   125

PAULA (*after another pause, still playing*) I wish you wouldn't stare so.

DRUMMLE Was I staring? I'm sorry.

> *She plays a little longer, then stops suddenly, rises, and goes to
> the window, where she stands looking out. Drummle moves from
> the ottoman to the settee*

A lovely night.

PAULA (*startled*) Oh! (*Without turning to him*) Why do you hop about
  like a monkey?   130

DRUMMLE Hot rooms play the deuce with the nerves. Now, it would
  have done you good to have walked in the garden with us after
  dinner and made merry. Why didn't you?

PAULA You know why.

DRUMMLE Ah, you're thinking of the—difference between you and   135
  Aubrey?

PAULA Yes, I *am* thinking of it.

DRUMMLE Well, so am I. How long—?

PAULA Getting on for three weeks.

DRUMMLE Bless me, it must be! And this would have been such a   140
  night to have healed it! Moonlight, the stars, the scent of flowers;
  and yet enough darkness to enable a kind woman to rest her hand
  for an instant on the arm of a good fellow who loves her. Ah, ha!
  It's a wonderful power, dear Mrs Aubrey, the power of an offended
  woman! Only realise it! Just that one touch—the mere tips of her   145
  fingers—and, for herself and another, she changes the colour of the
  whole world!

PAULA (*turning to him, calmly*) Cayley, my dear man, you talk exactly
  like a very romantic old lady.

> *She leaves the window and sits playing with the knick-knacks
> on the table*

DRUMMLE (*to himself*) H'm, that hasn't done it! [*Rising and coming*   150
  down] Well—ha, ha!—I accept the suggestion. An old woman, eh?

PAULA Oh, I didn't intend—

DRUMMLE But why not? I've every qualification—well, almost. And
  I confess it would have given this withered bosom a throb of
  grandmotherly satisfaction if I could have seen you and Aubrey at   155
  peace before I take my leave tomorrow.

PAULA Tomorrow, Cayley!

DRUMMLE I must.

PAULA Oh, this house is becoming unendurable.

DRUMMLE You're very kind. But you've got the Orreyeds. 160

PAULA (*fiercely*) The Orreyeds! I—I hate the Orreyeds! I lie awake at night, hating them!

DRUMMLE Pardon me, I've understood that their visit is, in some degree, owing to—hem!—your suggestion.

PAULA Heavens! That doesn't make me like them better. Somehow 165 or another, I—I've outgrown these people. This woman—I used to think her 'jolly'!—sickens me. I can't breathe when she's near me: the whiff of her handkerchief turns me faint! And she patronises me by the hour, until I—I feel my nails growing longer with every word she speaks! 170

DRUMMLE My dear lady, why on earth don't you say all this to Aubrey?

PAULA Oh, I've been such an utter fool, Cayley!

DRUMMLE (*soothingly*) Well, well, mention it to Aubrey!

PAULA No, no, you don't understand. What do you think I've done? 175

DRUMMLE Done! What, *since* you invited the Orreyeds?

PAULA Yes; I must tell you—

DRUMMLE Perhaps you'd better not.

PAULA Look here. I've intercepted some letters from Mrs Cortelyon and Ellean to—him. (*Producing three unopened letters from the bodice* 180 *of her dress*) There are the accursed things! From Paris—two from the Cortelyon woman, the other from Ellean!

DRUMMLE But why—why?

PAULA I don't know. Yes, I do! I saw letters coming from Ellean to her father; not a line to me—not a line. And one morning it 185 happened I was downstairs before he was, and I spied this one lying with his heap on the breakfast-table, and I slipped it into my pocket—out of malice, Cayley, pure devilry! And a day or two afterwards I met Elwes the postman at the Lodge, and took the letters from him, and found these others amongst 'em. I felt simply 190 fiendish when I saw them—fiendish! (*Returning the letters to her bodice*) And now I carry them about with me, and they're scorching me like a mustard plaster!°

DRUMMLE Oh, this accounts for Aubrey not hearing from Paris lately!

PAULA That's an ingenious conclusion to arrive at! Of course it does! 195 (*With an hysterical laugh*) Ha, ha!

DRUMMLE Well, well! (*Laughing*) Ha, ha, ha!

PAULA (*turning upon him*) I suppose it *is* amusing!

DRUMMLE I beg pardon.

PAULA   Heaven knows I've little enough to brag about! I'm a bad lot,   200
but not in mean tricks of this sort. In all my life this is the most
caddish thing I've done. How am I to get rid of these letters—
that's what I want to know? How am I to get rid of them?

DRUMMLE   If I were you, I should take Aubrey aside and put them
into his hands as soon as possible.   205

PAULA   What! And tell him to his face that I—! No, thank you. I
suppose *you* wouldn't like to—

DRUMMLE   No, no; I won't touch 'em!

PAULA   And you call yourself my friend?

DRUMMLE   (*good-humouredly*) No, I don't!   210

PAULA   Perhaps I'll tie them together and give them to his man in
the morning.

DRUMMLE   That won't avoid an explanation.

PAULA   (*recklessly*) Oh, then he must miss them—

DRUMMLE   And trace them.   215

PAULA   (*throwing herself upon the ottoman*) I don't care!

DRUMMLE   I know you don't; but let me send him to you now,
may I?

PAULA   Now! What do you think a woman's made of? I couldn't
stand it, Cayley. I haven't slept for nights; and last night there was   220
thunder, too! I believe I've got the horrors.

DRUMMLE   (*taking the little hand-mirror from the table*) You'll sleep
well enough when you deliver those letters. Come, come, Mrs
Aubrey—a good night's rest! (*Holding the mirror before her face*) It's
quite time.   225

> She looks at herself for a moment, then snatches the mirror from
> him

PAULA   You brute, Cayley, to show me that!

DRUMMLE   Then—may I? Be guided by a fr—a poor old woman!
May I?

PAULA   You'll kill me, amongst you!

DRUMMLE   What do you say?   230

PAULA   (*after a pause*) Very well.

> He nods his head and goes out rapidly. She looks after him for
> a moment, and calls 'Cayley! Cayley!' Then she again produces
> the letters, deliberately, one by one, fingering them with aversion.
> Suddenly she starts, turning her head towards the door

Ah!

> Aubrey enters quickly°

AUBREY   Paula!

PAULA (*handing him the letters, her face averted*) There! (*He examines the letters, puzzled, and looks at her inquiringly*) They are many days old. I stole them, I suppose to make you anxious and unhappy. 235

He looks at the letters again, then lays them aside on the table

AUBREY (*gently*) Paula, dear, it doesn't matter.

PAULA (*after a short pause*) Why—why do you take it like this?

AUBREY What did you expect?

PAULA Oh, but I suppose silent reproaches are really the severest. 240 And then, naturally, you are itching to open your letters.

She crosses the room as if to go

AUBREY Paula! (*She pauses*) Surely, surely it's all over now?

PAULA All over! (*Mockingly*) Has my stepdaughter returned then? When did she arrive? I haven't heard of it!

AUBREY You can be very cruel. 245

PAULA That word's always on a man's lips; he uses it if his soup's cold. (*With another movement as if to go*) Need we—

AUBREY I know I've wounded you, Paula. But isn't there any way out of this?

PAULA When does Ellean return? Tomorrow? Next week? 250

AUBREY (*wearily*) Oh! Why should we grudge Ellean the little pleasure she is likely to find in Paris and in London?

PAULA I grudge her nothing, if that's a hit at me. But with that woman—!

AUBREY It must be that woman or another. You know that at present 255 we are unable to give Ellean the opportunity of—of—

PAULA Of mixing with respectable people.

AUBREY The opportunity of gaining friends, experience, ordinary knowledge of the world. If you are interested in Ellean, can't you see how useful Mrs Cortelyon's good offices are? 260

PAULA May I put one question? At the end of the London season, when Mrs Cortelyon has done with Ellean, is it quite understood that the girl comes back to us? (*Aubrey is silent*) Is it? Is it?

AUBREY Let us wait till the end of the season—

PAULA Oh! I knew it. You're only fooling me; you put me off with 265 any trash. I believe you've sent Ellean away, not for the reasons you give, but because you don't consider me a decent companion for her, because you're afraid she might get a little of her innocence rubbed off in my company. Come, isn't that the truth? Be honest! Isn't that it? 270

AUBREY Yes.

There is a moment's silence on both sides

PAULA (*with uplifted hands as if to strike him*) Oh!

AUBREY (*taking her by the wrists*) Sit down. Sit down. (*He puts her into a chair; she shakes herself free with a cry*) Now listen to me. Fond as you are, Paula, of harking back to your past, there's one chapter of it you always let alone. I've never asked you to speak of it; you've never offered to speak of it. I mean the chapter that relates to the time when you were—like Ellean. (*She attempts to rise; he restrains her*) No, no.

PAULA I don't choose to talk about that time. I won't satisfy your curiosity.

AUBREY My dear Paula, I have no curiosity—I know what you were at Ellean's age. I'll tell you. You hadn't a thought that wasn't a wholesome one, you hadn't an impulse that didn't tend towards good, you never harboured a notion you couldn't have gossiped about to a parcel of children. (*She makes another effort to rise: he lays his hand lightly on her shoulder*) And this was a very few years back—there are days now when you look like a schoolgirl—but think of the difference between the two Paulas. You'll have to think hard, because after a cruel life one's perceptions grow a thick skin. But, for God's sake, do think till you get these two images clearly in your mind, and then ask yourself what sort of a friend such a woman as you are today would have been for the girl of seven or eight years ago.

PAULA (*rising*) How dare you? I could be almost as good a friend to Ellean as her own mother would have been, had she lived. I know what you mean. How dare you?

AUBREY You say that; very likely you believe it. But you're blind, Paula; you're blind. You! Every belief that a young, pure-minded girl holds sacred—that you once held sacred—you now make a target for a jest, a sneer, a paltry cynicism. I tell you, you're not mistress any longer of your thoughts or your tongue. Why, how often, sitting between you and Ellean, have I seen her cheeks turn scarlet as you've rattled off some tale that belongs by right to the club or the smoking-room!° Have you noticed the blush? If you have, has the cause of it ever struck you? And this is the girl you say you love, I admit that you *do* love, whose love you expect in return! Oh, Paula, I make the best, the only, excuse for you when I tell you you're blind!

PAULA Ellean—Ellean blushes easily.

AUBREY You blushed as easily a few years ago.

PAULA (*after a short pause*) Well! Have you finished your sermon?

AUBREY (*with a qesture of despair*) Oh, Paula!
>   *He goes up to the window and stands with his back to the room*

PAULA (*to herself*) A few—years ago!
>   *She walks slowly towards the door, then suddenly drops upon the ottoman in a paroxysm of weeping*

O God! A few years ago!   315

AUBREY (*going to her*) Paula!

PAULA (*sobbing*) Oh, don't touch me!

AUBREY Paula!

PAULA Oh, go away from me!
>   *He goes back a few steps, and after a little while she becomes calmer and rises unsteadily; then in an altered tone*

Look here—!   320
>   *He advances a step; she checks him with a quick gesture*

Look here! Get rid of these people—Mabel and her husband—as soon as possible! I—I've done with them!

AUBREY (*in a whisper*) Paula!

PAULA And then—then—when the time comes for Ellean to leave Mrs Cortelyon, give me—give me another chance!   325
>   *He advances again, but she shrinks away*

No, no!
>   *She goes out by the door on the right. He sinks on to the settee, covering his eyes with his hands. There is a brief silence, then a servant enters*

SERVANT Mrs Cortelyon, sir, with Miss Ellean.
>   *Aubrey rises to meet Mrs Cortelyon, who enters, followed by Ellean, both being in travelling-dresses. The servant withdraws*

MRS CORTELYON (*shaking hands with Aubrey*) Oh, my dear Aubrey!

AUBREY Mrs Cortelyon! (*Kissing Ellean*) Ellean dear!

ELLEAN Papa, is all well at home?   330

MRS CORTELYON We're shockingly anxious.

AUBREY Yes, yes, all's well. This is quite unexpected (*To Mrs Cortelyon*) You've found Paris insufferably hot?

MRS CORTELYON Insufferably hot! Paris is pleasant enough. We've had no letter from you!   335

AUBREY I wrote to Ellean a week ago.

MRS CORTELYON Without alluding to the subject I had written to you upon.

AUBREY (*thinking*) Ah, of course—

MRS CORTELYON And since then we've both written and you've been absolutely silent. Oh, it's too bad!   340

AUBREY (*picking up the letters from the table*) It isn't altogether my fault. Here are the letters—

ELLEAN Papa!

MRS CORTELYON They're unopened.   345

AUBREY An accident delayed their reaching me till this evening. I'm afraid this has upset you very much.

MRS CORTELYON Upset me!

ELLEAN (*in an undertone to Mrs Cortelyon*) Never mind. Not now, dear—not tonight.   350

AUBREY Eh?

MRS CORTELYON (*to Ellean aloud*) Child, run away and take your things off. She doesn't look as if she'd journeyed from Paris today.

AUBREY (*taking Ellean's hands*) I've never seen her with such a colour.   355

ELLEAN (*to Aubrey, in a faint voice*) Papa, Mrs Cortelyon has been so very, very kind to me, but I—I have come home.

      She goes out

AUBREY Come home! (*To Mrs Cortelyon*) Ellean returns to us, then?

MRS CORTELYON That's the very point I put to you in my letters, and you oblige me to travel from Paris to Willowmere on a warm   360
day to settle it. I think perhaps it's right that Ellean should be with you just now, although I—My dear friend, circumstances are a little altered.

AUBREY Alice, you're in some trouble.

MRS CORTELYON Well—yes, I *am* in trouble. You remember pretty   365
little Mrs Brereton who was once Caroline Ardale?

AUBREY Quite well.

MRS CORTELYON She's a widow now, poor thing. She has the entresol° of the house where we've been lodging in the Avenue de Friedland. Caroline's a dear chum of mine; she formed a great   370
liking for Ellean.

AUBREY I'm very glad.

MRS CORTELYON Yes, it's nice for her to meet her mother's friends. Er—that young Hugh Ardale the papers were full of some time ago—he's Caroline Brereton's brother, you know.   375

AUBREY No, I didn't know. What did he do? I forget.

MRS CORTELYON Checked one of those horrid mutinies at some faraway station in India, marched down with a handful of his men and a few faithful natives, and held the place until he was relieved. They gave him his company and a VC° for it.   380

AUBREY And he's Mrs Brereton's brother?

MRS CORTELYON Yes. He's with his sister—*was*, rather—in Paris. He's home—invalided. Good gracious, Aubrey, why don't you help me out? Can't you guess what has occurred?

AUBREY Alice!   385

MRS CORTELYON Young Ardale—Ellean!

AUBREY An attachment?

MRS CORTELYON Yes, Aubrey. (*After a little pause*) Well, I suppose I've got myself into sad disgrace. But really I didn't foresee anything of this kind. A serious, reserved child like Ellean, and a   390 boyish, high-spirited soldier—it never struck me as being likely.

Aubrey paces to and fro thoughtfully

I did all I could directly Captain Ardale spoke—wrote to you at once. Why on earth don't you receive your letters promptly, and when you do get them, why can't you open them? I endured the anxiety till last night, and then made up my mind—home! Of   395 course, it has worried me terribly. My head's bursting. Are there any salts about?

Aubrey fetches a bottle from the cabinet and hands it to her

We've had one of those hateful smooth crossings that won't let you be properly indisposed.

AUBREY My dear Alice, I assure you I've no thought of blaming you.   400

MRS CORTELYON That statement always precedes a quarrel.

AUBREY I don't know whether this is the worst or the best luck. How will my wife regard it? Is Captain Ardale a good fellow?

MRS CORTELYON My dear Aubrey, you'd better read up the accounts of his wonderful heroism. Face to face with death for a   405 whole week; always with a smile and a cheering word for the poor helpless souls depending on him! Of course, it's that that has stirred the depths of your child's nature. I've watched her while we've been dragging the story out of him, and if angels look different from Ellean at that moment, I don't desire to meet any,   410 that's all!

AUBREY If you were in my position—? But you can't judge.

MRS CORTELYON Why, if I had a marriageable daughter of my own and Captain Ardale proposed for her, naturally I should cry my eyes out all night—but I should thank Heaven in the morning.   415

AUBREY You believe so thoroughly in him?

MRS CORTELYON Do you think I should have only a headache at this minute if I didn't! Look here, you've got to see me down the lane; that's the least you can do, my friend. Come into my house for a moment and shake hands with Hugh.   420

189

AUBREY What, is he here?

MRS CORTELYON He came through with us, to present himself
formally tomorrow. Where are my gloves? (*Aubrey fetches them
from the ottoman*) Make my apologies to Mrs Tanqueray, please.
She's well, I hope? (*Going towards the door*) I can't feel sorry she   425
hasn't seen me in this condition.

  Ellean enters

ELLEAN (*to Mrs Cortelyon*) I've been waiting to wish you good-night.
I was afraid I'd missed you.

MRS CORTELYON Good-night, Ellean.

ELLEAN (*in a low voice, embracing Mrs Cortelyon*) I can't thank you.   430
Dear Mrs Cortelyon!

MRS CORTELYON (*her arms round Ellean, in a whisper to Aubrey*)
Speak a word to her.

  Mrs Cortelyon goes out

AUBREY (*to Ellean*) Ellean, I'm going to see Mrs Cortelyon home.
(*Going to the door*) Tell Paula where I am; explain, dear.   435

ELLEAN (*her head drooping*) Yes. ([*He looks at her steadily for a
moment then walks towards the door.*] *Quickly*) Father! [*He turns
towards her*] You are angry with me—disappointed?

AUBREY Angry? No.

ELLEAN Disappointed?   440

AUBREY (*smiling and going to her and taking her hand*) If so, it's only
because you've shaken my belief in my discernment. I thought you
took after your poor mother a little, Ellean; but there's a look on
your face tonight, dear, that I never saw on hers—never, never.

ELLEAN (*leaning her head on his shoulder*) Perhaps I ought not to have   445
gone away?

AUBREY Hush! You're quite happy?

ELLEAN Yes.

AUBREY That's right. Then, as you are quite happy, there is
something I particularly want you to do for me Ellean.   450

ELLEAN What is that?

AUBREY Be very gentle with Paula. Will you?

ELLEAN You think I have been unkind.

AUBREY (*kissing her upon the forehead*) Be very gentle with Paula.
  *He goes out and she stands looking after him, then, as she turns
  thoughtfully from the door, a rose is thrown through the window
  and falls at her feet. She picks up the flower wonderingly and
  goes to the window*

ELLEAN (*starting back*) Hugh!   455

Hugh Ardale, a handsome young man of about seven-and-twenty, with a boyish face and manner, appears outside the window

HUGH Nelly! Nelly dear!

ELLEAN What's the matter?

HUGH Hush! Nothing. It's only fun. (*Laughing*) Ha, ha, ha! I've found out that Mrs Cortelyon's meadow runs up to your father's plantation; I've come through a gap in the hedge.   460

ELLEAN Why, Hugh?

HUGH I'm miserable at The Warren; it's so different from the Avenue de Friedland. Don't look like that! Upon my word I meant just to peep at your home and go back, but I saw figures moving about here, and came nearer, hoping to get a glimpse of you. (*Entering the room*) Was that your father?   465

ELLEAN Yes.

HUGH Isn't this fun! A rabbit ran across my foot while I was hiding behind that old yew.

ELLEAN You must go away; it's not right for you to be here like this.   470

HUGH But it's only fun, I tell you. You take everything so seriously. Do wish me good-night.

ELLEAN We have said good-night.

HUGH In the hall at The Warren before Mrs Cortelyon and a manservant. Oh, it's so different from the Avenue de Friedland!   475

ELLEAN (*giving him her hand hastily*) Good-night, Hugh.

HUGH Is that all? We might be the merest acquaintances.

He momentarily embraces her, but she releases herself

ELLEAN It's when you're like this that you make me feel utterly miserable. (*Throwing the rose from her angrily*) Oh!

HUGH I've offended you now, I suppose?   480

ELLEAN Yes.

HUGH Forgive me, Nelly. Come into the garden for five minutes; we'll stroll down to the plantation.

ELLEAN No, no.

HUGH For two minutes—to tell me you forgive me.   485

ELLEAN I forgive you.

HUGH Evidently. I shan't sleep a wink tonight after this. What a fool I am! Come down to the plantation. Make it up with me.

ELLEAN There is somebody coming into this room. Do you wish to be seen here?   490

HUGH I shall wait for you behind that yew tree. You must speak to me. Nelly!

He disappears. Paula enters

PAULA Ellean!

ELLEAN You—you are very surprised to see me, Paula, of course.

PAULA Why are you here? Why aren't you with—your friend?   495

ELLEAN I've come home—if you'll have me. We left Paris this morning; Mrs Cortelyon brought me back. She was here a minute or two ago; Papa has just gone with her to The Warren. He asked me to tell you.

PAULA There are some people staying with us that I'd rather you didn't   500
meet. It was hardly worth your while to return for a few hours.

ELLEAN A few hours?

PAULA Well, when do you go to London?

ELLEAN I don't think I go to London, after all.

PAULA (*eagerly*) You—you've quarrelled with her?   505

ELLEAN No, no, no, not that; but—Paula! (*In an altered tone*) Paula!

PAULA (*startled*) Eh? (*Ellean goes deliberately to Paula and kisses her*) Ellean!

ELLEAN Kiss me.

PAULA What—what's come to you?   510

ELLEAN I want to behave differently to you in the future. Is it too late?

PAULA Too—late! (*Impulsively kissing Ellean and crying*) No—no—no! No—no!

ELLEAN Paula, don't cry.

PAULA (*wiping her eyes*) I'm a little shaky; I haven't been sleeping.   515
It's all right—talk to me.

ELLEAN There is something I want to tell you—

PAULA Is there—is there?

They sit together on the ottoman, Paula taking Ellean's hand

ELLEAN Paula, in our house in the Avenue de Friedland, on the floor below us, there was a Mrs Brereton. She used to be a friend of my   520
mother's. Mrs Cortelyon and I spent a great deal of our time with her.

PAULA (*suspiciously*) Oh! (*Letting Ellean's hand fall*) Is this lady going to take you up in place of Mrs Cortelyon?

ELLEAN No, no. Her brother is staying with her—*was* staying with   525
her. Her brother—(*Breaking off in confusion*)

PAULA [*looking into her face*] Well?

ELLEAN (*almost inaudibly*) Paula—

She rises and walks away, Paula following her

PAULA Ellean! (*Taking hold of her*) You're not in love!

Ellean looks at Paula appealingly

PAULA Oh! *You* in love! You! Oh, this is why you've come home! Of 530
course, you can make friends with me now! You'll leave us for
good soon, I suppose; so it doesn't much matter being civil to me
for a little while!

ELLEAN Oh, Paula!

PAULA Why, how you have deceived us—all of us! We've taken you 535
for a cold-blooded little saint. The fools you've made of us! Saint
Ellean! Saint Ellean!

ELLEAN Ah, I might have known you'd only mock me!

PAULA (*her tone changing*) Eh?

ELLEAN I—I can't talk to you. (*Sitting on the settee*) You do nothing 540
else but mock and sneer, nothing else.

PAULA Ellean dear! Ellean! I didn't mean it. I'm so horribly jealous,
it's a sort of curse on me. (*Kneeling beside Ellean and embracing her*)
My tongue runs away with me. I'm going to alter, I swear I am.
I've made some good resolutions, and, as God's above me, I'll keep 545
them! If you are in love, if you do ever marry, that's no reason
why we shouldn't be fond of each other. Come, you've kissed me
of your own accord—you can't take it back. Now we're friends
again, aren't we? Ellean dear! I want to know everything, everything. Ellean dear, Ellean! 550

ELLEAN Paula, Hugh has done something that makes me very angry.
He came with us from Paris today, to see Papa. He is staying with
Mrs Cortelyon and—I ought to tell you—

PAULA Yes, yes. What?

ELLEAN He has found his way by The Warren meadow through the 555
plantation up to this house. He is waiting to bid me good-night.
(*Glancing towards the garden*) He is—out there.

PAULA Oh!

ELLEAN What shall I do?

PAULA Bring him in to see me! Will you? 560

ELLEAN No, no.

PAULA But I'm dying to know him. Oh, yes, you must. I shall meet
him before Aubrey does. (*Excitedly running her hands over her hair*)
I'm so glad.

 Ellean goes out by the window

The mirror—mirror. What a fright I must look! 565

 *Not finding the hand-glass on the table, she jumps on to the
 settee, and surveys herself in the mirror over the mantelpiece,
 then sits quietly down and waits*

Ellean! Just fancy! Ellean!

> *After a pause Ellean enters by the window with Hugh*

ELLEAN Paula, this is Captain Ardale—Mrs Tanqueray.

> *Paula rises and turns, and she and Hugh stand staring blankly at each other for a moment or two; then Paula advances and gives him her hand*

PAULA (*in a strange voice, but calmly*) How do you do?

HUGH How do you do?

PAULA (*to Ellean*) Mr Ardale and I have met in London, Ellean.   570
Er—Captain Ardale, now?

HUGH Yes.

ELLEAN In London?

PAULA They say the world's very small, don't they?

HUGH Yes.   575

PAULA Ellean, dear, I want to have a little talk about you to Mr Ardale—Captain Ardale—alone. (*Putting her arms round Ellean, and leading her to the door*) Come back in a little while.

> *Ellean nods to Paula with a smile and goes out, while Paula stands watching her at the open door*

In a little while—in a little—(*Closing the door and then taking a seat facing Hugh*)   580
Be quick! Mr Tanqueray has only gone down to The Warren with Mrs Cortelyon. What is to be done?

HUGH (*blankly*) Done?

PAULA Done—done. Something must be done.

HUGH I understood that Mr Tanqueray had married a Mrs—Mrs—   585

PAULA Jarman?

HUGH Yes.

PAULA I'd been going by that name. You didn't follow my doings after we separated.

HUGH No.   590

PAULA (*sneeringly*) No.

HUGH I went out to India.

PAULA What's to be done?

HUGH Damn this chance!

PAULA Oh, my God!   595

HUGH Your husband doesn't know, does he!

PAULA That you and I—?

HUGH Yes.

PAULA No. He knows about others.

HUGH Not about me. How long were we—?   600

PAULA I don't remember, exactly.

HUGH Do you—do you think it matters?

PAULA His—his daughter.

> *With a muttered exclamation, he turns away and sits with his head in his hands*

What's to be done?

HUGH I wish I could think.   605

PAULA Oh! Oh! What happened to that flat of ours in Ethelbert Street?

HUGH I let it.

PAULA All that pretty furniture?

HUGH Sold it.

PAULA I came across the key of the escritoire the other day in an old   610
purse! (*Suddenly realising the horror and hopelessness of her position, and starting to her feet with an hysterical cry of rage*) What am I maundering about?°

HUGH For God's sake, be quiet! Do let me think.

PAULA This will send me mad! (*Suddenly turning and standing over*   615
him) You—you beast, to crop up in my life again like this!

HUGH I always treated you fairly.

PAULA (*weakly*) Oh! I beg your pardon—I know you did—I—

> *She sinks on to the settee, crying hysterically*

HUGH Hush!

PAULA She kissed me tonight! I'd won her over! I've had such a fight   620
to make her love me! And now—just as she's beginning to love me, to bring this on her!

HUGH Hush, hush! Don't break down!

PAULA (*sobbing*) You don't know! I—I haven't been getting on well
in my marriage. It's been my fault. The life I used to lead spoilt   625
me completely. But I'd made up my mind to turn over a new life from tonight. From tonight!

HUGH Paula—

PAULA Don't you call me that!

HUGH Mrs Tanqueray, there is no cause for you to despair in this   630
way. It's all right, I tell you—it *shall* be all right.

PAULA (*shivering*) What are we to do?

HUGH Hold our tongues.

PAULA (*staring vacantly*) Eh?

HUGH The chances are a hundred to one against anyone ever turning   635
up who knew us when we were together. Besides, no one would be such a brute as to split on us. If anybody did do such a thing, we should have to lie! What are we upsetting ourselves like this for, when we've simply got to hold our tongues?

PAULA You're as mad as I am!   640

HUGH Can you think of a better plan?

PAULA There's only one plan possible—let's come to our senses! Mr Tanqueray must be told.

HUGH Your husband! What, and I lose Ellean! I lose Ellean!

PAULA You've got to lose her.   645

HUGH I won't lose her! I can't lose her!

PAULA Didn't I read of your doing any number of brave things in India? Why, you seem to be an awful coward!

HUGH That's another sort of pluck altogether; I haven't this sort of pluck.   650

PAULA Oh, I don't ask *you* to tell Mr Tanqueray. That's my job.

HUGH (*standing over her*) You—you—you'd better! You—!

PAULA (*rising*) Don't bully me! I intend to.

HUGH (*taking hold of her; she wrenches herself free*) Look here, Paula! I never treated you badly—you've owned it. Why should you want   655 to pay me out like this? You don't know how I love Ellean!

PAULA Yes, that's just what I *do* know.

HUGH I say you don't! She's as good as my own mother. I've been downright honest with her too. I told her, in Paris, that I'd been a bit wild at one time, and, after a damned wretched day, she   660 promised to forgive me because of what I'd done since in India. She's behaved like an angel to me! Surely I oughtn't to lose her, after all, just because I've been like other fellows! No; I haven't been half as rackety° as a hundred men we could think of. Paula, don't pay me out for nothing; be fair to me, there's a good girl—be   665 fair to me!

PAULA Oh, I'm not considering you at all! I advise you not to stay here any longer; Mr Tanqueray is sure to be back soon.

HUGH (*taking up his hat*) What's the understanding between us then? What have we arranged to do?   670

PAULA I don't know what you're going to do; I've got to tell Mr Tanqueray.

HUGH (*approaching her fiercely*) By God, you shall do nothing of the sort!

PAULA You shocking coward!   675

HUGH If you dare! (*Going up to the window*) Mind! If you dare!

PAULA (*following him*) Why, what would you do?

HUGH (*after a short pause, sullenly*) Nothing. I'd shoot myself—that's nothing. Good-night.

PAULA Good-night.   680

He disappears. She walks unsteadily to the ottoman, and sits; and as she does so her hand falls upon the little silver mirror, which she takes up, staring at her own reflection

CURTAIN

Act Four

Scene One

The scene is the drawing-room at Highercoombe, the same evening. Paula is still seated on the ottoman, looking vacantly before her, with the little mirror in her hand. Lady Orreyed enters

LADY ORREYED There you are! You never came into the billiard-room. Isn't it maddening—Cayley Drummle gives me sixty out of a hundred and beats me. I must be out of form, because I know I play remarkably well for a lady. Only last month—(*Paula rises*) Whatever is the matter with you, old girl?   5

PAULA Why?

LADY ORREYED (*staring*) It's the light, I suppose. (*Paula replaces the mirror on the table*) By Aubrey's bolting from the billiard-table in that fashion I thought perhaps—

PAULA Yes; it's all right.   10

LADY ORREYED You've patched it up? (*Paula nods*) Oh, I am jolly glad—! [*Kisses her*] I mean—

PAULA Yes, I know what you mean. Thanks, Mabel.

LADY ORREYED Now take my advice; for the future—

PAULA Mabel, if I've been disagreeable to you while you've been   15
staying here, I—I beg your pardon.
        She walks away and sits down

LADY ORREYED You, disagreeable, my dear? I haven't noticed it. Dodo and me both consider you make a first-class hostess, but then you've had such practice, haven't you? (*Dropping on to the ottoman and gaping°*) Oh, talk about being sleepy—!   20

PAULA Why don't you—!

LADY ORREYED Why, dear, I must hang about for Dodo. You may as well know it; he's in one of his moods.

PAULA (*under her breath*) Oh—!

LADY ORREYED Now, it's not his fault; it was deadly dull for him   25
while we were playing billiards. Cayley Drummle did ask him to mark,° but I stopped that; it's so easy to make a gentleman look like a billiard-marker. This is just how it always is; if poor old Dodo has nothing to do, he loses count, as you may say.

PAULA Hark!   30

198

Sir George Orreyed enters, walking slowly and deliberately; he looks pale and watery-eyed

SIR GEORGE (*with mournful indistinctness*) I'm 'fraid we've lef' you a grea' deal to yourself tonight, Mrs Tanqueray. Attra'tions of billiards. I apol'gise. I say, where's ol' Aubrey?

PAULA My husband has been obliged to go out to a neighbour's house.   35

SIR GEORGE I want his advice on a rather pressing matter connected with my family—my family. (*Sitting*) Tomorrow will do just as well.

LADY ORREYED (*to Paula*) This is the mood I hate so—drivelling about his precious family.   40

SIR GEORGE The fact is, Mrs Tanqueray, I am not easy in my min' 'bout the way I am treatin' my poor ol' mother.

LADY ORREYED (*to Paula*) Do you hear that? That's *his* mother, but *my* mother he won't so much as look at!

SIR GEORGE I shall write to Bruton Street° firs' thing in the   45
morning.

LADY ORREYED (*to Paula*) Mamma has stuck to me through every-thing—well, you know!

SIR GEORGE I'll get ol' Aubrey to figure out a letter. I'll drop line to Uncle Fitz too—dooced shame of the ol' feller to chuck me over   50
in this manner. (*Wiping his eyes*) All my family have chucked me over.

LADY ORREYED (*rising*) Dodo!

SIR GEORGE Jus' because I've married beneath me, to be chucked over! Aunt Lydia, the General, Hooky Whitgrave, Lady Sugnall—   55
my own dear sister!—all turn their backs on me. It's more than I can stan'!

LADY ORREYED (*approaching him with dignity*) Sir George, wish Mrs Tanqueray good-night at once and come upstairs. Do you hear me?   60

SIR GEORGE (*rising angrily*) Wha'—

LADY ORREYED Be quiet!

SIR GEORGE You presoom to order me about!

LADY ORREYED You're making an exhibition of yourself!

SIR GEORGE Look 'ere—!   65

LADY ORREYED Come along, I tell you!

He hesitates, utters a few inarticulate sounds, then snatches up a fragile ornament from the table, and is about to dash it on to the ground. Lady Orreyed retreats, and Paula goes to him

PAULA George!

>*He replaces the ornament*

SIR GEORGE *(shaking Paula's hand)* Good ni', Mrs Tanqueray.

LADY ORREYED *(to Paula)* Good-night, darling. Wish Aubrey good-
night for me. Now, Dodo?   70

>*She goes out*

SIR GEORGE *(to Paula)* I say, are you goin' to sit up for ol' Aubrey?

PAULA Yes.

SIR GEORGE Shall *I* keep you comp'ny?

PAULA No, thank you, George.

SIR GEORGE Sure?   75

PAULA Yes, sure.

SIR GEORGE *(shaking hands)* Good-night again.

PAULA Good-night.

>*She turns away. He goes out, steadying himself carefully.*
>*Drummle appears outside the window, [with a cap on his head,*
>*and] smoking*

DRUMMLE *(looking into the room, and seeing Paula)* My last cigar.
Where's Aubrey?   80

PAULA Gone down to The Warren, to see Mrs Cortelyon home.

DRUMMLE *(entering the room)* Eh? Did you say Mrs Cortelyon?

PAULA Yes. She has brought Ellean back.

DRUMMLE Bless my soul! Why?

PAULA I—I'm too tired to tell you, Cayley. If you stroll along the   85
lane you'll meet Aubrey. Get the news from him.

DRUMMLE *(going up to the window)* Yes, yes. *(Returning to Paula)* I
don't want to bother you, only—the anxious old woman, you
know. Are you and Aubrey—?

PAULA Good friends again?   90

DRUMMLE *(nodding)* Um.

PAULA *(giving him her hand)* Quite, Cayley, quite.

DRUMMLE *(retaining her hand)* That's capital. As I'm off so early
tomorrow morning, let me say now—thank you for your hospitality.   95

>*He bends over her hand gallantly, then goes out by the window*

PAULA *(to herself)* 'Are you and Aubrey—?' 'Good friends again?'
'Yes'. 'Quite, Cayley, quite'.

>*There is a brief pause, then Aubrey enters hurriedly, wearing a*
>*light overcoat and carrying a cap*

AUBREY Paula dear! Have you seen Ellean?

PAULA I found her here when I came down.

AUBREY She—she's told you?   100

PAULA Yes, Aubrey.

AUBREY It's extraordinary, isn't it! Not that somebody should fall in
love with Ellean or that Ellean herself should fall in love. All that's
natural enough and was bound to happen, I suppose, sooner or
later. But this young fellow! You know his history?   105

PAULA [*startled*] His history?

AUBREY You remember the papers were full of his name a few
months ago?

PAULA Oh, yes.

AUBREY The man's as brave as a lion, there's no doubt about that;   110
and, at the same time, he's like a big good-natured schoolboy, Mrs
Cortelyon says. Have you ever pictured the kind of man Ellean
would marry some day?

PAULA I can't say that I have.

AUBREY A grave, sedate fellow I've thought about—hah! She has   115
fallen in love with the way in which Ardale practically laid down
his life to save those poor people shut up in the Residency. (*Taking
off his coat*) Well, I suppose if a man can do that sort of thing, one
ought to be content. And yet—(*Throwing his coat on the settee*) I
should have met him tonight, but he'd gone out. Paula dear, tell   120
me how you look upon this business.

PAULA Yes, I will—I must. To begin with, I—I've seen Mr Ardale.

AUBREY Captain Ardale?

PAULA Captain Ardale.

AUBREY Seen him?   125

PAULA While you were away he came up here, through our grounds,
to try to get a word with Ellean. I made her fetch him in and
present him to me.

AUBREY (*frowning*) Doesn't Captain Ardale know there's a lodge and
a front door to this place? Never mind! What is your impression   130
of him?

PAULA Aubrey, do you recollect my bringing you a letter—a letter
giving you an account of myself—to the Albany late one night—
the night before we got married?

AUBREY A letter?   135

PAULA You burnt it; don't you know?

AUBREY Yes; I know.

PAULA His name was in that letter.

AUBREY (*going back from her slowly, and staring at her*) I don't
understand.   140

PAULA Well—Ardale and I once kept house together. (*He remains silent, not moving*) Why don't you strike me? Hit me in the face—I'd rather you did! Hurt me! Hurt me!

AUBREY (*after a pause*) What did you—and this man—say to each other—just now?   145

PAULA I—hardly—know.

AUBREY Think!

PAULA The end of it all was that I—I told him I must inform you of—what had happened . . . he didn't want me to do that . . . I declared that I would . . . he dared me to. (*Breaking down*) Let me   150
alone! Oh!

AUBREY Where was my daughter while this went on?

PAULA I—I had sent her out of the room . . . that is all right.

AUBREY Yes, yes—yes, yes.
        He turns his head towards the door

PAULA Who's that?   155
        A servant enters with a letter

SERVANT The coachman has just run up with this from The Warren, sir. (*Aubrey takes the letter*) It's for Mrs Tanqueray, sir; there's no answer.
        The servant withdraws. Aubrey goes to Paula and drops the letter into her lap; she opens it with uncertain hands

PAULA (*reading it to herself*) It's from—him. He's going away—or gone—I think. (*Rising in a weak way*) What does it say? I never   160
could make out his writing.
        She gives the letter to Aubrey and stands near him, looking at the letter over his shoulder as he reads

AUBREY (*reading*) 'I shall be in Paris by tomorrow evening. Shall wait there, at Meurice's,° for a week, ready to receive any communication you or your husband may address to me. Please invent some explanation to Ellean. Mrs Tanqueray, for God's sake, do what   165
you can for me.'
        Paula and Aubrey speak in low voices, both still looking at the letter

PAULA Has he left The Warren, I wonder, already?

AUBREY That doesn't matter.

PAULA No, but I can picture him going quietly off. Very likely he's walking on to Bridgeford or Cottering tonight, to get the first train   170
in the morning. A pleasant stroll for him.

AUBREY We'll reckon he's gone, that's enough.

PAULA That isn't to be answered in any way?

AUBREY Silence will answer that.

PAULA He'll soon recover his spirits, I know.   175

AUBREY You know. (*Offering her the letter*) You don't want this, I
suppose?

PAULA No.

AUBREY It's done with—done with.

> *He tears the letter into small pieces. She has dropped the
> envelope; she searches for it, finds it, and gives it to him*

PAULA Here!   180

AUBREY (*looking at the remnants of the letter*) This is no good; I must
burn it.

PAULA Burn it in your room.

AUBREY Yes.

PAULA Put it in your pocket for now.   185

AUBREY Yes.

> *He does so. Ellean enters and they both turn, guiltily, and stare
> at her*

ELLEAN (*after a short silence, wonderingly*) Papa—

AUBREY What do you want, Ellean?

ELLEAN I heard from Willis that you had come in; I only want to
wish you good-night.   190

> *Paula steals away, without looking back*

What's the matter? Ah! Of course, Paula has told you about
Captain Ardale?

AUBREY Well?

ELLEAN Have you and he met?

AUBREY No.   195

ELLEAN You are angry with him; so was I. But tomorrow when he
calls and expresses his regret—tomorrow—

AUBREY Ellean—Ellean!

ELLEAN Yes, Papa?

AUBREY I—I can't let you see this man again.   200

> *He walks away from her in a paroxysm of distress, then, after
> a moment or two, he returns to her and takes her to his arms*

Ellean! My child!

ELLEAN (*releasing herself*) What has happened, Papa? What is it?

AUBREY (*thinking out his words deliberately*) Something has occurred,
something has come to my knowledge, in relation to Captain
Ardale, which puts any further acquaintanceship between you two   205
out of the question.

ELLEAN Any further acquaintanceship . . . out of the question?

AUBREY Yes.

   [*She sits.*] *He advances to her quickly, but she shrinks from him*

ELLEAN No, no—I am quite well. (*After a short pause*) It's not an
   hour ago since Mrs Cortelyon left you and me together here; you   210
   had nothing to urge against Captain Ardale then.

AUBREY No.

ELLEAN You don't know each other; you haven't even seen him this
   evening. Father!

AUBREY I have told you he and I have not met.   215

ELLEAN Mrs Cortelyon couldn't have spoken against him to you just
   now. No, no, no; she's too good a friend to both of us. Aren't you
   going to give me some explanation? You can't take this position
   towards me—towards Captain Ardale—without affording me the
   fullest explanation.   220

AUBREY Ellean, there are circumstances connected with Captain
   Ardale's career which you had better remain ignorant of. It must
   be sufficient for you that I consider these circumstances render him
   unfit to be your husband.

ELLEAN Father!   225

AUBREY You must trust me, Ellean; you must try to understand the
   depth of my love for you and the—the agony it gives me to hurt
   you. You must trust me.

ELLEAN I will, father; but you must trust me a little too. Circumstances connected with Captain Ardale's career?   230

AUBREY Yes.

ELLEAN When he presents himself here tomorrow of course you will
   see him and let him defend himself?

AUBREY Captain Ardale will not be here tomorrow.

ELLEAN Not! You have stopped his coming here?   235

AUBREY Indirectly—yes.

ELLEAN But just now he was talking to me at that window! Nothing
   had taken place then! And since then nothing can have—! Oh!
   Why—you have heard something against him from Paula.

AUBREY From—Paula!   240

ELLEAN She knows him.

AUBREY She has told you so?

ELLEAN When I introduced Captain Ardale to her she said she had
   met him in London. Of course! It is Paula who has done this!

AUBREY (*in a hard voice*) I—I hope you—you'll refrain from rushing   245
   at conclusions. There's nothing to be gained by trying to avoid the
   main point, which is that you must drive Captain Ardale out of your

thoughts. Understand that! You're able to obtain comfort from your religion, aren't you? I'm glad to think that's so. I talk to you in a harsh way, Ellean, but I feel your pain almost as acutely as you do. *(Going to the door)* I—I can't say anything more to you tonight.

ELLEAN Father! *(He pauses at the door)* Father, I'm obliged to ask you this; there's no help for it—I've no mother to go to. Does what you have heard about Captain Ardale concern the time when he led a wild, a dissolute life in London?

AUBREY *(returning to her slowly and staring at her)* Explain yourself!

ELLEAN He has been quite honest with me. One day—in Paris—he confessed to me—what a man's life is—what his life had been.

AUBREY *(under his breath)* Oh!

ELLEAN He offered to go away, not to approach me again.

AUBREY And you—you accepted his view of what a man's life is!°

ELLEAN As far as *I* could forgive him, I forgave him.

AUBREY *(with a groan)* Why, when was it you left us? It hasn't taken you long to get your robe 'just a little dusty at the hem'!

ELLEAN What do you mean?

AUBREY Hah! A few weeks ago my one great desire was to keep you ignorant of evil.

ELLEAN Father, it is impossible to be ignorant of evil. Instinct, common instinct, teaches us what is good and bad. Surely I am none the worse for knowing what is wicked and detesting it!

AUBREY Detesting it! Why, you love this fellow!

ELLEAN Ah, you don't understand! I have simply judged Captain Ardale as we all pray to be judged. I have lived in imagination through that one week in India when he deliberately offered his life back to God to save those wretched, desperate people. In his whole career I see now nothing but that one week; those few hours bring him nearer the saints, I believe, than fifty uneventful years of mere blamelessness would have done! And so, father, if Paula has reported anything to Captain Ardale's discredit—

AUBREY Paula—!

ELLEAN It must be Paula; it can't be anybody else.

AUBREY You—you'll please keep Paula out of the question. Finally, Ellean, understand me—I have made up my mind.

He again goes to the door

ELLEAN But wait—listen! I have made up my mind also.

AUBREY Ah! I recognise your mother in you now!

ELLEAN You need not speak against my mother because you are angry with me!

AUBREY I—I hardly know what I'm saying to you. In the morning—
in the morning—

> *He goes out. She remains standing, and turns her head to listen.*
> *Then, after a moment's hesitation, she goes softly to the window,*
> *and looks out under the veranda*

ELLEAN (*in a whisper*) Paula! Paula!   290

> *Paula appears outside the window and steps into the room; her*
> *face is white and drawn, her hair is a little disordered*

PAULA (*huskily*) Well?

ELLEAN Have you been under the veranda all the while—listening?

PAULA N—no.

ELLEAN You *have* overheard us—I see you have. And it *is* you who
have been speaking to my father against Captain Ardale. Isn't it?   295
Paula, why don't you own it or deny it?

PAULA Oh, I—I don't mind owning it; why should I?

ELLEAN Ah! You seem to have been very very eager to tell your
tale.

PAULA No, I wasn't eager, Ellean. I'd have given something not to   300
have had to do it. I wasn't eager.

ELLEAN Not! Oh, I think you might safely have spared us all for a
little while.

PAULA But, Ellean, you forget I—I am your stepmother. It was
my—my duty—to tell your father what I—what I knew—   305

ELLEAN What you knew! Why, after all, what can you know! You
can only speak from gossip, report, hearsay! How is it possible that
you—!

> *She stops abruptly. The two women stand staring at each other*
> *for a moment; then Ellean backs away from Paula slowly*

Paula!

PAULA What—what's the matter?   310

ELLEAN You—you knew Captain Ardale in London!

PAULA Why—what do you mean?

ELLEAN Oh!

> *She makes for the door, but Paula catches her by the wrist*

PAULA You shall tell me what you mean!

ELLEAN Ah! (*Suddenly looking fixedly in Paula's face*) You know what   315
I mean.

PAULA You accuse me!

ELLEAN It's in your face!

PAULA (*hoarsely*) You—you think I'm—that sort of creature, do you?

ELLEAN Let me go!   320

PAULA Answer me! You've always hated me! (*Shaking her*) Out with it!

ELLEAN You hurt me!

PAULA You've always hated me! You shall answer me!

ELLEAN Well, then, I have always—always—   325

PAULA What?

ELLEAN I have always known what you were!

PAULA Ah! Who—who told you?

ELLEAN Nobody but yourself. From the first moment I saw you I knew you were altogether unlike the good women I'd left;   330 directly I saw you I knew what my father had done. You've wondered why I've turned from you! There—that's the reason! Oh, but this is a horrible way for the truth to come home to everyone! Oh!

PAULA It's a lie! It's all a lie! (*Forcing Ellean down upon her knees*)   335 You shall beg my pardon for it. (*Ellean utters a loud shriek of terror*) Ellean, I'm a good woman! I swear I am! I've always been a good woman! You dare to say I've ever been anything else! It's a lie! (*Throwing her off violently*)

    Aubrey re-enters

AUBREY Paula!   340

    Paula staggers back as Aubrey advances

(*Raising Ellean*) What's this? What's this?

ELLEAN (*faintly*) Nothing. It—it's my fault. Father, I—I don't wish to see Captain Ardale again.

    She goes out, Aubrey slowly following her to the door

PAULA Aubrey, she—she guesses.

AUBREY Guesses?   345

PAULA About me—and Ardale.

AUBREY About you—and Ardale?

PAULA She says she suspected my character from the beginning . . . that's why she's always kept me at a distance . . . and now she sees through—   350

    She falters; he helps her to the ottoman, where she sits

AUBREY (*bending over her*) Paula, you must have said something—admitted something—

PAULA I don't think so. It—it's in my face.

AUBREY What?

PAULA She tells me so. She's right! I'm tainted through and through;   355 anybody can see it, anybody can find it out. You said much the same to me tonight.

AUBREY [*partly to himself, as if dazed*] If she has got this idea into her head we must drive it out, that's all. We must take steps to—What shall we do? We had better—better—(*Sitting and staring before him*) What—what?   360

PAULA Ellean! So meek, so demure! You've often said she reminded you of her mother. Yes, I know now what your first marriage was like.

AUBREY We must drive this idea out of her head. We'll do some-   365
thing. What shall we do?

PAULA She's a regular woman too. She could forgive *him* easily enough—but *me!* That's just a woman!

AUBREY What *can* we do?

PAULA Why, nothing! She'd have no difficulty in following up her   370
suspicions. Suspicions! You should have seen how she looked at me!

> *He buries his head in his hands. There is silence for a time, then she rises slowly, and goes and sits beside him*

Aubrey!

AUBREY Yes.

PAULA I'm very sorry.°   375

> *Without meeting her eyes, he lays his hand on her arm for a moment*

AUBREY Well, we must look things straight in the face. (*Glancing round*) At any rate, we've done with this.

PAULA [*following his glance*] I suppose so. (*After a brief pause*) Of course, she and I can't live under the same roof any more. You know she kissed me tonight, of her own accord.   380

AUBREY I asked her to alter towards you.

PAULA That was it, then.

AUBREY I—I'm sorry I sent her away.

PAULA It was my fault; I made it necessary.

AUBREY Perhaps now she'll propose to return to the convent,—well,   385
she must.

PAULA Would you like to keep her with you and—and leave me?

AUBREY Paula—!

PAULA You needn't be afraid I'd go back to—what I was. I couldn't.

AUBREY Sssh, for God's sake! We—you and I—we'll get out of this   390
place . . . what a fool I was to come here again!

PAULA You lived here with your first wife!

AUBREY We'll get out of this place and go abroad again, and begin afresh.

PAULA Begin afresh?   395

AUBREY There's no reason why the future shouldn't be happy for
us—no reason that I can see—

PAULA Aubrey!

AUBREY Yes?

PAULA You'll never forget this, you know.   400

AUBREY This?

PAULA Tonight, and everything that's led up to it. Our coming here,
Ellean, our quarrels—cat and dog!—Mrs Cortelyon, the Orreyeds,
this man! What an everlasting nightmare for you!

AUBREY Oh, we can forget it, if we choose.   405

PAULA That was always your cry. How *can* one do it?

AUBREY We'll make our calculations solely for the future, talk about
the future, think about the future.

PAULA I believe the future is only the past again, entered through
another gate.   410

AUBREY That's an awful belief.

PAULA Tonight proves it. You must see now that, do what we will,
go where we will, you'll be continually reminded of—what I was.
I see it.

AUBREY You're frightened tonight; meeting this man has frightened   415
you. But that sort of thing isn't likely to recur. The world isn't
quite so small as all that.

PAULA Isn't it! The only great distances it contains are those we
carry within ourselves—the distances that separate husbands and
wives, for instance. And so it'll be with us. You'll do your   420
best—oh, I know that—you're a good fellow. But circumstances
will be too strong for you in the end, mark my words.

AUBREY Paula—!

PAULA Of course I'm pretty now—I'm pretty still—and a pretty
woman, whatever else she may be, is always—well, endurable. But   425
even now I notice that the lines of my face are getting deeper; so
are the hollows about my eyes. Yes, my face is covered with little
shadows that usen't to be there. Oh, I know I'm 'going off'. I hate
paint and dye and those messes, but, by and by, I shall drift the
way of the others; I shan't be able to help myself. And then, some   430
day—perhaps very suddenly, under a queer, fantastic light at night
or in the glare of the morning—that horrid, irresistible truth that
physical repulsion forces on men and women will come to you, and
you'll sicken at me.

AUBREY I—!   435

PAULA You'll see me then, at last, with other people's eyes; you'll
see me just as your daughter does now, as all wholesome folks see
women like me. And I shall have no weapon to fight with—not one
serviceable little bit of prettiness left me to defend myself with! A
worn-out creature—broken up, very likely, some time before I   440
ought to be—my hair bright, my eyes dull, my body too thin or
too stout, my cheeks raddled and ruddled°—a ghost, a wreck, a
caricature, a candle that gutters, call such an end what you like!
Oh, Aubrey, what shall I be able to say to you then? And this is
the future you talk about! I know it—I know it! (*He is still sitting*   445
staring forward; she rocks herself to and fro as if in pain) Oh, Aubrey!
Oh! Oh!

AUBREY (*trying to comfort her*) Paula—!

PAULA (*laying her head upon his shoulder*) Oh, and I wanted so much
to sleep tonight!   450

> *From the distance, in the garden, there comes the sound of*
> *Drummle's voice; he is singing as he approaches the house*

(*Starting up*) That's Cayley, coming back from The Warren. He
doesn't know, evidently. I—I won't see him!

> *She goes out quickly. Drummle's voice comes nearer. Aubrey*
> *rouses himself and snatches up a book from the table, making a*
> *pretence of reading. After a moment or two, Drummle appears*
> *at the window and looks in*

DRUMMLE Aha! My dear chap!

AUBREY Cayley?

DRUMMLE (*coming into the room*) I went down to The Warren after   455
you.

AUBREY Yes?

DRUMMLE Missed you. Well? I've been gossiping with Mrs Cortelyon. Confound you, I've heard the news!

AUBREY What have you heard?   460

DRUMMLE What have I heard! Why—Ellean and young Ardale!
(*Looking at Aubrey keenly*) My dear Aubrey! Alice is under
the impression that you are inclined to look on the affair favourably.

AUBREY (*rising and advancing to Drummle*) You've not—met Captain   465
Ardale?

DRUMMLE No. Why do you ask? By the bye, I don't know that I
need tell you—but it's rather strange. He's not at The Warren
tonight.

AUBREY No?   470

DRUMMLE He left the house half an hour ago, to stroll about the lanes; just now a note came from him, a scribble in pencil, simply telling Alice that she would receive a letter from him tomorrow. What's the matter? There's nothing very wrong, is there! My dear chap, pray forgive me if I'm asking too much.   475

AUBREY Cayley, you—you urged me to send her away!

DRUMMLE Ellean! Yes, yes. But—but—by all accounts this is quite an eligible young fellow. Alice has been giving me the history—

AUBREY Curse him! (*Hurling his book to the floor*) Curse him! Yes, I   480 do curse him—him and his class! Perhaps I curse myself too in doing it. He has only led 'a man's life'—just as I, how many of us, have done! The misery he has brought on me and mine, it's likely enough we, in our time, have helped to bring on others by this leading 'a man's life'! But I do curse him for all that. My God,   485 *I've* nothing more to fear—I've paid *my* fine! And so I can curse him in safety. Curse him! Curse him!

DRUMMLE In Heaven's name, tell me what's happened?

AUBREY (*gripping Drummle's arm*) Paula! Paula!

DRUMMLE What?   490

AUBREY They met tonight here. They—they—they're not strangers to each other.

DRUMMLE Aubrey!

AUBREY Curse him! My poor, wretched wife! My poor, wretched wife!
  The door opens and Ellean appears. The two men turn to her. There is a moment's silence

ELLEAN Father . . . father . . .!   495

AUBREY Ellean?

ELLEAN I—I want you.
  He goes to her
Father . . . go to Paula! (*He looks into her face, startled*) Quickly— quickly!
  He passes her to go out, she seizes his arm, with a cry
No, no; don't go!   500
  He shakes her off and goes. Ellean staggers back towards Drummle

DRUMMLE (*to Ellean*) What do you mean? What do you mean?

ELLEAN I—I went to her room—to tell her I was sorry for something I had said to her. And I *was* sorry—I *was* sorry. I heard the fall. I—I've seen her. It's horrible.

DRUMMLE She—she has—!

ELLEAN Killed herself? Yes—yes. So everybody will say. But I know—I helped to kill her. [*She beats her breast°*] If I had only been merciful!

> *She faints upon the ottoman. He pauses for a moment irresolutely —then he goes to the door, opens it, and stands looking out.°*

CURTAIN

TRELAWNY OF
THE 'WELLS'

A Comedietta° in Four Acts

The play was first staged at the Court Theatre, London, on 20 January 1898, with the following cast:

Theatrical Folk

James Telfer	*Mr Athol Forde*
Augustus Colpoys	*Mr E. M. Robson*
Ferdinand Gadd	*Mr Gerald du Maurier*
Tom Wrench of the Bagnigge Wells Theatre°	*Mr Paul Arthur*
Mrs Telfer (Miss Violet Sylvester)	*Mrs E. Saker*
Avonia Bunn	*Miss Pattie Browne*
Rose Trelawny	*Miss Irene Vanbrugh*
Imogen Parrot (of the Royal Olympic Theatre)	*Miss Hilda Spong*
O'Dwyer	*Mr Richard Purdon*
Members of the company of the Pantheon Theatre	*Mr Vernon, Mr Foster, Mr Melton and Miss Baird*
Hall-keeper at the Pantheon	*Mr W. H. Quinton*

Non-Theatrical Folk

Vice-Chancellor Sir William Gower, Knt.	*Mr Dion Boucicault*
Arthur Gower (his grandson)	*Mr James Erskine*
Clara de Foenix (his granddaughter)	*Miss Eva Williams*
Miss Trafalgar Gower (Sir William's sister)	*Miss Isabel Bateman*
Captain de Foenix (Clara's husband)	*Mr Sam Sothern*
Mrs Mossop	*Miss Le Thiere*
Mr Ablett	*Mr Fred Thorne*
Charles	*Mr Aubrey Fitzgerald*
Sarah	*Miss Polly Emery*

Pinero included the following direction to the stage-manager:

THE costumes and scenic decoration of this little play should follow, to the closest detail, the mode of the early Sixties—the period, in dress, of crinoline and the peg-top trouser; in furniture, of horsehair and mahogany, and the abominable 'walnut-and-rep.'. No attempt should be made to modify such fashions in illustration, to render them less strange, even less grotesque, to the modern eye. On the contrary, there should be an endeavour to reproduce, perhaps to accentuate, any feature which may now seem particularly quaint and bizarre. Thus, lovely youth should be shown decked uncompromisingly as it was at the time indicated, at the risk (which the author believes to be a slight one) of pointing the chastening moral that, while beauty fades assuredly in its own time, it may appear to succeeding generations not to have been beauty at all.

Act One

Scene One

The scene represents a sitting-room on the first floor of a respectable lodging-house at 2, Brydon Crescent, Clerkenwell. On the right are two sash-windows, having Venetian blinds and giving a view of houses on the other side of the street. The grate of the fireplace is hidden by an ornament composed of shavings and paper roses. Over the fireplace is a mirror: on each side there is a sideboard-cupboard. On the left is a door, and a landing is seen outside. Between the windows stand a cottage piano° and a piano stool. Above the sofa, on the left, stands a large black trunk, the lid bulging with its contents and displaying some soiled theatrical finery. On the front of the trunk, in faded lettering, appear the words 'Miss Violet Sylvester, Theatre Royal, Drury Lane'. Under the sofa there are two or three pairs of ladies' satin shoes, much the worse for wear, and on the sofa a white satin bodice, yellow with age, a heap of dog-eared playbooks, and some other litter of a like character. On the top of the piano there is a wig-block, with a man's wig upon it, and in the corners of the room there stand some walking-sticks and a few theatrical swords. In the centre of the stage is a large circular table. There is a clean cover upon it, and on the top of the sideboard-cupboards are knives and forks, plate, glass, cruet-stands, and some gaudy flowers in vases—all suggesting preparations for festivity. The woodwork of the room is grained, the ceiling plainly whitewashed, and the wallpaper is of a neutral tint and much faded. The pictures are engravings in maple frames, and a portrait or two, in oil, framed in gilt. The furniture, curtains, and carpet are worn, but everything is clean and well-kept. The light is that of afternoon in early summer; it is May. Mrs Mossop—a portly, middle-aged Jewish lady, elaborately attired—is laying the table-cloth. Ablett enters hastily, divesting himself of his coat as he does so. He is dressed in rusty black for 'waiting'.

MRS MOSSOP (*in a fluster*) Oh, here you are, Mr Ablett—!

ABLETT Good-day, Mrs Mossop.

MRS MOSSOP (*bringing the cruet-stands*) I declare I thought you'd forgotten me.

ABLETT (*hanging his coat upon a curtain-knob, and turning up his shirt*   5
sleeves) I'd begun to fear I should never escape from the shop,
ma'am. Jest as I was preparin' to clean myself, the 'ole universe
seemed to cry aloud for pertaters.° (*Relieving Mrs Mossop of the*
cruet-stands, and satisfying himself as to the contents of the various
bottles) Now you take a seat, Mrs Mossop. You 'ave but to say 'Mr   10
Ablett, lay for so many,' and the exact number shall be laid for.

MRS MOSSOP (*sinking into the armchair*) I hope the affliction of short
breath may be spared you, Ablett. Ten is the number.

ABLETT (*whipping up the mustard energetically*) Short-breathed you
may be, ma'am, but not short-sighted. That gal of yours is no   15
ordinary gal, but to 'ave set 'er to wait on ten persons would 'ave
been to 'ave caught disaster.

> *He brings knives and forks, glass, etc., and glances round the*
> *room as he does so*

I am in Mr and Mrs Telfer's setting-room, I believe, ma'am?

MRS MOSSOP (*surveying the apartment complacently*)   And what a
handsomely proportioned room it is, to be sure!   20

ABLETT   May I h'ask if I am to 'ave the honour of includin' my triflin'
fee for this job in their weekly book?

MRS MOSSOP   No, Ablett—a separate bill, please. The Telfers kindly
give the use of their apartment, to save the cost of holding the
ceremony at The Clown Tavern; but share and share alike over the   25
expenses is to be the order of the day.

ABLETT   I thank you, ma'am. (*Rubbing up the knives with a napkin*)
You let fall the word 'ceremony', ma'am—

MRS MOSSOP   Ah, Ablett, and a sad one—a farewell cold collation to
Miss Trelawny.   30

ABLETT   Lor' bless me! I 'eard a rumour—

MRS MOSSOP   A true rumour. She's taking her leave of us, the dear.

ABLETT   This will be a blow to the 'Wells', ma'am.

MRS MOSSOP   The best juvenile lady the 'Wells' has known since Mr
Phillips's management.°   35

ABLETT   Report 'as it, a love affair, ma'am.

MRS MOSSOP   A love affair, indeed. And a poem into the bargain,
Ablett, if poet was at hand to write it.

ABLETT   Reelly, Mrs Mossop! (*Polishing a tumbler*) Is the beer to be
bottled or draught, ma'am, on this occasion?   40

MRS MOSSOP   Draught for Miss Trelawny, invariably.°

ABLETT   Then draught it must be all round, out of compliment. Jest
fancy! Nevermore to 'ear customers speak of Trelawny of the

'Wells', except as a pleasin' memory! A non-professional gentleman they give out, ma'am.   45

MRS MOSSOP Yes.

ABLETT Name of Glover.

MRS MOSSOP Gower. Grandson of Vice-Chancellor° Sir William
Gower, Mr Ablett.

ABLETT You don't say, ma'am!   50

MRS MOSSOP No father nor mother, and lives in Cavendish
Square° with the old judge and a great aunt.

ABLETT Then Miss Trelawny quits the Profession, ma'am, for good
and all, I presoom?

MRS MOSSOP Yes, Ablett, she's at the theaytre at this moment,   55
distributing some of her little ornaments and fallals° among the
ballet. She played last night for the last time—the last time on any
stage. (*Rising and going to the sideboard-cupboard*) And without so
much as a line in the bill to announce it. What a benefit° she might
have taken!   60

ABLETT I know one who was good for two box tickets, Mrs
Mossop.

MRS MOSSOP (*bringing the flowers to the table and arranging them, while
Ablett sets out the knives and forks*) But no. 'No fuss', said the
Gower family, 'no publicity. Withdraw quietly'—that was the   65
Gower family's injunctions—'withdraw quietly, and have done
with it.'

ABLETT And when is the weddin' to be, ma'am?

MRS MOSSOP It's not yet decided, Mr Ablett. In point of fact, before
the Gower family positively say yes to the union, Miss Trelawny   70
is to make her home in Cavendish Square for a short term—'short
term' is the Gower family's own expression—in order to habituate
herself to the West End. They're sending their carriage for her at
two o'clock this afternoon, Mr Ablett—their carriage and pair of
bay horses.   75

ABLETT Well, I dessay a West End life has sooperior advantages over
the Profession in some respecks, Mrs Mossop.

MRS MOSSOP When accompanied by wealth, Mr Ablett. Here's
Miss Trelawny but nineteen, and in a month or two's time she'll
be ordering about her own powdered footman, and playing on   80
her grand piano. How many actresses do *that*, I should like to
know!

    Tom Wrench's voice is heard

TOM (*outside the door*) Rebecca! Rebecca, my loved one!

MRS MOSSOP Oh, go along with you, Mr Wrench!

Tom enters, with a pair of scissors in his hand. He is a shabbily dressed, ungraceful man of about thirty, with a clean-shaven face, curly hair, and eyes full of good humour

TOM My own, especial Rebecca!   85

MRS MOSSOP Don't be a fool, Mr Wrench! Now, I've no time to waste. I know you want something—

TOM Everything, adorable. But most desperately do I stand in need of a little skilful trimming at your fair hands.

MRS MOSSOP (*taking the scissors from him and clipping the frayed edges*   90
of his shirt-cuffs and collar) First it's patching a coat, and then it's binding an Inverness!° Sometimes I wish that top room of mine was empty.

TOM And sometimes I wish my heart was empty, cruel Rebecca.

MRS MOSSOP (*giving him a thump*) Now, I really will tell Mossop of   95
you, when he comes home! [*She turns Tom round to trim the back of his collar*] I've often threatened it—

TOM (*to Ablett*) Whom do I see! No—it can't be—but yes—I believe I have the privilege of addressing Mr Ablett, the eminent greengrocer, of Rosoman Street?°   100

ABLETT (*sulkily*) Well, Mr Wrench, and wot of it?

TOM You possess a cart, good Ablett, which may be hired by persons of character and responsibility. 'By the hour or job'—so runs the legend. I will charter it, one of these Sundays, for a drive to Epping.°   105

ABLETT I dunno so much about that, Mr Wrench.

TOM Look to the springs, good Ablett, for this comely lady will be my companion.

MRS MOSSOP Dooce take your impudence! Give me your other hand. Haven't you been to rehearsal this morning with the rest of   110
'em?

TOM I have, and have left my companions still toiling. My share in the interpretation of Sheridan Knowles's immortal work° did not necessitate my remaining after the first act.

MRS MOSSOP Another poor part, I suppose, Mr Wrench?   115

TOM Another, and tomorrow yet another, and on Saturday two others—all equally, damnably rotten.

MRS MOSSOP Ah, well, well! *Somebody* must play the bad parts in this world, on and off the stage. There—(*Returning the scissors*) There's no more edge left to fray; we've come to the soft. (*He*   120
points the scissors at his breast) Ah! don't do that!

TOM You are right, sweet Mossop, I won't perish on an empty stomach. (*Taking her aside*) But tell me, shall I disgrace the feast, eh? Is my appearance too scandalously seedy?

MRS MOSSOP Not *it*, my dear.   125

TOM Miss Trelawny—do you think she'll regard me as a blot on the banquet? (*Wistfully*) Do you, Beccy?

MRS MOSSOP She! La! Don't distress yourself. She'll be too excited to notice *you*.

TOM H'm, yes! Now I recollect, she has always been that. Thanks,   130
Beccy.

>   *A knock, at the front door, is heard. Mrs Mossop hurries to the*
>   *window down the stage*

MRS MOSSOP Who's that? (*Opening the window and looking out*) It's Miss Parrott! Miss Parrott's arrived!

TOM Jenny Parrott? Has Jenny condescended—?

MRS MOSSOP *Jenny!* Where are your manners, Mr Wrench?   135

TOM (*grandiloquently*) Miss Imogen Parrott, of the Olympic Theatre.°

MRS MOSSOP (*at the door, to Ablett*) Put your coat on, Ablett. We are not selling cabbages.

>   *She disappears and is heard speaking in the distance*

Step up, Miss Parrott! Tell Miss Parrott to mind that mat,   140
Sarah—!

TOM Be quick, Ablett, be quick! The élite is below! More dispatch, good Ablett!

ABLETT (*to Tom, spitefully, while struggling into his coat*) Miss Tre-lawny's leavin' will make all the difference to the old 'Wells'. The   145
season'll terminate abrupt, and then the comp'ny'll be h'out, Mr Wrench—h'out, sir!

TOM (*adjusting his necktie, at a mirror over the piano*) Which will lighten the demand for the spongy turnip and the watery marrow, my poor Ablett.   150

ABLETT (*under his breath*) Presumpshus!

>   *He produces a pair of white cotton gloves, and having put one*
>   *on, makes a horrifying discovery*

Two lefts! That's Mrs Ablett all over!

>   *During the rest of the act, he is continually in difficulties,*
>   *through his efforts to wear one of the gloves upon his right hand.*
>   *Mrs Mossop now re-enters, with Imogen Parrott. Imogen is a*
>   *pretty, light-hearted young woman, of about seven-and-twenty,*
>   *daintily dressed*

MRS MOSSOP (*to Imogen*) There, it might be only yesterday you
lodged in my house, to see you gliding up those stairs! And this
the very room you shared with poor Miss Brooker!   155

IMOGEN (*advancing to Tom*) Well, Wrench, and how are you?

TOM (*bringing her a chair, demonstratively dusting the seat of it with his
pocket handkerchief*) Thank you, much the same as when you used
to call me Tom.

IMOGEN Oh, but I have turned over a new leaf, you know, since I   160
have been at the Olympic.

MRS MOSSOP I am sure my chairs don't require dusting, Mr
Wrench.

TOM (*placing the chair below the table, and blowing his nose with his
handkerchief, with a flourish*) My way of showing homage,   165
Mossop.

MRS MOSSOP Miss Parrott has sat on them often enough, when she
was an honoured member of the 'Wells'—haven't you, Miss
Parrott?

IMOGEN (*sitting, with playful dignity*) I suppose I must have done so.   170
Don't remind me of it. I sit on nothing nowadays but down pillows
covered with cloth of gold.

> *Mrs Mossop and Ablett prepare to withdraw.* [*Tom crosses up
> to the fireplace*]

MRS MOSSOP (*at the door, to Imogen*) Ha, ha! Ha! I could fancy
I'm looking at Und*i*ne again—Und*i*ne, the Spirit of the Waters.°
She's not the least changed since she appeared as Und*i*ne—is she,   175
Mr Ablett?

ABLETT (*joining Mrs Mossop*) No—or as Prince Cammyralzyman in
the pantomime.° *I* never 'ope to see a pair o' prettier limbs—

MRS MOSSOP (*sharply*) Now then!

> *She pushes him out; they disappear*

IMOGEN (*after a shiver at Ablett's remark*) In my present exalted   180
station I don't hear much of what goes on at the 'Wells', Wrench.
Are your abilities still—still—?

TOM Still unrecognized, still confined within the almost boundless
and yet repressive limits of Utility—General Utility?° (*Nodding*)
H'm, still.   185

IMOGEN Dear me! A thousand pities! I positively mean it.

TOM Thanks.

IMOGEN What do you think! You were mixed up in a funny dream
I dreamt one night lately.

TOM (*bowing*) Highly complimented.   190

IMOGEN It was after a supper which rather—well, I'd had some strawberries sent me from Hertfordshire.

TOM Indigestion levels all ranks.

IMOGEN It was a nightmare. I found myself on the stage of the Olympic in that wig you—oh, gracious! You used to play your very   195
serious little parts in it—

TOM The wig with the ringlets?

IMOGEN Ugh! Yes.

TOM I wear it tonight, for the second time this week, in a part which is very serious—and very little.   200

IMOGEN Heavens! It *is* in existence then!

TOM And long will be, I hope. I've only three wigs, and this one accommodates itself to so many periods.

IMOGEN Oh, how it used to amuse the gallery-boys!°

TOM They still enjoy it. If you looked in this evening at half-past   205
seven°—I'm done at a quarter to eight—if you looked in at half-past seven, you would hear the same glad, rapturous murmur in the gallery when the presence of that wig is discovered. Not that they fail to laugh at my other wigs, at every article of adornment I possess, in fact! Good God, Jenny—!   210

IMOGEN (*wincing*) Ssssh!

TOM Miss Parrott—if they gave up laughing at me now, I believe I—I believe I should—*miss it*. I believe I couldn't spout my few lines now in silence; my unaccompanied voice would sound so strange to me. Besides, I often think those gallery-boys are really   215
fond of me, at heart. You can't laugh as they do—rock with laughter sometimes!—at what you dislike.

IMOGEN Of course not. *Of course* they like you, Wrench. You cheer them, make their lives happier—

TOM And tonight, by the bye, I also assume that beast of a felt   220
hat—the grey hat with the broad brim, and the imitation wool feathers. You remember it?

IMOGEN Y—y—yes.

TOM I see you do. Well, that hat still persists in falling off, when I most wish it to stick on. It will tilt and tumble tonight—during   225
one of Telfer's pet speeches; I feel it will.

IMOGEN Ha, ha, ha!

TOM And those yellow boots; I wear *them* tonight—

IMOGEN No!

TOM Yes!   230

IMOGEN Ho, ho, ho, ho!

TOM (*with forced hilarity*) Ho, ho! Ha, ha! And the spurs—the spurs that once tore your satin petticoat! You recollect—?

IMOGEN (*her mirth suddenly checked*) Recollect!

TOM You would see those spurs tonight, too, if you patronised us—*and* the red worsted tights. The worsted tights are a little thinner, a little more faded and discoloured, a little more darned— Oh, yes, thank you, I am still, as you put it, still—still—still— 235

  He walks away, going to the mantelpiece and turning his back upon her

IMOGEN (*after a brief pause*) I'm sure I didn't intend to hurt your feelings, Wrench. 240

TOM (*turning, with some violence*) You! You hurt my feelings! Nobody can hurt my feelings! I have no feelings—!

  Ablett re-enters, carrying three chairs of odd patterns. Tom seizes the chairs and places them about the table, noisily

ABLETT Look here, Mr Wrench! If I'm to be 'ampered in performin' my dooties—

TOM More chairs, Ablett! In my apartment, the chamber nearest Heaven, you will find one with a loose leg. We will seat Mrs Telfer upon that. She dislikes me, and she is, in every sense, a heavy woman.° 245

ABLETT (*moving toward the door—dropping his glove*) My opinion, you are meanin' to 'arrass me, Mr Wrench— 250

TOM (*picking up the glove and throwing it to Ablett—singing*) 'Take back thy glove, thou faithless fair!'° Your glove, Ablett.

ABLETT Thank you, sir; it *is* my glove, and you are no gentleman.

  He withdraws

TOM True, Ablett—not even a Walking Gentleman.°

IMOGEN Don't go on so, Wrench. What about your plays? Aren't you trying to write any plays just now? 255

TOM Trying! I am doing more than trying to write plays. I am writing plays. I have written plays.

IMOGEN Well?

TOM My cupboard upstairs is choked with 'em. 260

IMOGEN Won't anyone take a fancy—?

TOM Not a sufficiently violent fancy.

IMOGEN You know, the speeches were so short and had such ordinary words in them, in the plays you used to read to me—no big opportunity for the leading lady, Wrench. 265

TOM Mm. Yes. I strive to make my people talk and behave like live people, don't I—?

IMOGEN (*vaguely*) I suppose you do.

TOM To fashion heroes out of actual, dull, everyday men—the sort
of men you see smoking cheroots in the club windows in St   270
James's Street;° and heroines from simple maidens in muslin
frocks. Naturally, the managers won't stand that.

IMOGEN Why, of course not.

TOM If *they* did, the public wouldn't.

IMOGEN Is it likely?   275

TOM Is it likely? I wonder!

IMOGEN Wonder—what?

TOM Whether they would.

IMOGEN The public!

TOM The public. Jenny, I wonder about it sometimes so hard that   280
that little bedroom of mine becomes a banqueting-hall, and this
lodging-house a castle.

> *There is a loud and prolonged knocking at the front door*

IMOGEN Here they are, I suppose.

TOM (*pulling himself together*) Good Lord! Have I become dishevelled?   285

IMOGEN [*slyly*] Why, are you anxious to make an impression, even
down to the last, Wrench?

TOM (*angrily*) Stop that!

IMOGEN It's no good your being sweet on her any longer, surely?

TOM (*glaring at her*) What cats you all are, you girls!   290

IMOGEN (*holding up her hands*) Oh! Oh, dear! How vulgar—after the
Olympic!

> *Ablett returns, carrying three more chairs*

ABLETT (*arranging these chairs on the left of the table*) They're all
'ome! They're all 'ome!

> *Tom places the four chairs belonging to the room at the table*

(*To Imogen*) She looks 'eavenly, Miss Trelawny does. I was jest   295
takin' in the ale when she floated down the Crescent on her lover's
arm. (*Wagging his head at Imogen admiringly*) There, I don't know
which of you two is the—

IMOGEN (*haughtily*) Man, keep your place!

ABLETT (*hurt*) H'as you please, miss—but you apperently forget I   300
used to serve you with vegetables.

> *He takes up a position at the door as Telfer and Gadd enter.*
> *Telfer is a thick-set, elderly man, with a worn, clean-shaven*
> *face, and iron-grey hair 'clubbed'° in the theatrical fashion of*
> *the time. Sonorous, if somewhat husky, in speech, and elaborate-*

ly dignified in bearing, he is at the same time a little uncertain about his h's. Gadd is a flashily dressed young man of seven-and-twenty, with brown hair arranged à la *Byron and moustache of a deeper tone*

TELFER (*advancing to Imogen, and kissing her paternally*) Ha, my dear child! I heard you were 'ere. Kind of you to visit us. Welcome! I'll just put my 'at down—

> *He places his hat on the top of the piano, and proceeds to inspect the table*

GADD (*coming to Imogen, in an elegant, languishing way*) Imogen, my darling. (*Kissing her*) Kiss Ferdy!   305

IMOGEN Well, Gadd, how goes it—I mean how are you?

GADD (*earnestly*) I'm hitting them hard this season, my darling. Tonight, Sir Thomas Clifford. They're simply waiting for my Clifford.   310

IMOGEN But who on earth is your Julia?°

GADD Ha! Mrs Telfer *goes on* for it—a venerable stopgap. Absurd, of course; but we daren't keep my Clifford from them any longer.

IMOGEN You'll miss Rose Trelawny in business pretty badly, I expect, Gadd?   315

GADD (*with a shrug of the shoulders*) She was to have done Rosalind° for my benefit. Miss Fitzhugh joins on Monday; I must pull *her* through it somehow. I would reconsider my bill, but they're waiting for my Orlando,° waiting for it—

> *Colpoys enters—an insignificant, wizened little fellow, who is unable to forget that he is a low-comedian. He stands at the door squinting hideously at Imogen and indulging in extravagant gestures of endearment, while she continues her conversation with Gadd*

COLPOYS (*failing to attract her attention*) My love! My life!   320

IMOGEN (*nodding to him indifferently*) Good-afternoon, Augustus.

COLPOYS (*ridiculously.*) She speaks! She hears me!

ABLETT (*holding his glove before his mouth, convulsed with laughter*) Ho, ho! Oh, Mr Colpoys! Oh, reelly, sir! Ho, dear!

GADD (*to Imogen, darkly*) Colpoys is not nearly as funny as he was last year. Everybody's saying so. We want a low-comedian badly.   325

> *He retires, deposits his hat on the wig-block, and joins Telfer and Tom*

COLPOYS (*staggering to Imogen and throwing his arms about her neck*) Ah—h—h! After all these years!

IMOGEN (*pushing him away*) Do be careful of my things, Colpoys!

ABLETT (*going out, blind with mirth*) Ha, ha, ha! Ho, ho!   330
    He collides with Mrs Telfer, who is entering at this moment. Mrs
    Telfer is a tall, massive lady of middle age—a faded queen of
    tragedy
    (*As he disappears*) I'm sure I beg your pardon, Mrs Telfer, ma'am.

MRS TELFER Violent fellow! (*Advancing to Imogen and kissing her*
    solemnly) How is it with you, Jenny Parrott?

IMOGEN Thank you, Mrs Telfer, as well as can be. And you?

MRS TELFER (*waving away the inquiry*) I am obliged to you for this   335
    response to my invitation. It struck me as fitting that at such a time
    you should return for a brief hour or two to the company of your
    old associates—(*Becoming conscious of Colpoys, behind her, making*
    grimaces at Imogen) Eh—h—h? (*Turning to Colpoys and surprising*
    him) Oh—h—h! Yes, Augustus Colpoys, you are extremely hu-   340
    morous *off*.

COLPOYS (*stung*) Miss Sylvester—Mrs Telfer!

MRS TELFER *On* the stage, sir, you are enough to make a cat weep.

COLPOYS Madam! From one artist to another! Well, I—! 'Pon my
    soul! (*Retreating and talking under his breath*) Popular favourite!   345
    Draw more money than all the—old guys°—

MRS TELFER (*following him*) What do you say, sir! Do you mutter!
    They explain mutually. Avonia Bunn enters—an untidy, taw-
    drily dressed young woman of about three-and-twenty, with the
    airs of a suburban soubrette.°

AVONIA (*embracing Imogen*) Dear old girl!

IMOGEN Well, Avonia?

AVONIA This is jolly, seeing you again. My eye, what a rig-out! She'll   350
    be up directly. (*With a gulp*) She's taking a last look round at our
    room.

IMOGEN You've been crying, 'Vonia.

AVONIA No, I haven't. (*Breaking down*) If I have, I can't help it. Rose
    and I have chummed together—all this season—and part of   355
    last—and—it's a hateful profession! The moment you make a
    friend—! (*Looking toward the door*) There! Isn't she a dream? I
    dressed her—
    She moves away, as Rose Trelawny and Arthur Gower enter.
    Rose is nineteen, wears washed muslin,° and looks divine. She
    has much of the extravagance of gesture, over-emphasis in
    speech, and freedom of manner engendered by the theatre, but is
    graceful and charming nevertheless. Arthur is a handsome,
    boyish young man—'all eyes' for Rose.

ROSE (*meeting Imogen*) Dear Imogen!

IMOGEN (*kissing her*) Rose, dear!   360

ROSE To think of your journeying from the West to see me make my
exit from Brydon Crescent!° But you're a good sort; you always
were. Do sit down and tell me—oh! Let me introduce Mr Gower.
Mr Arthur Gower—Miss Imogen Parrott. *The* Miss Parrott of the
Olympic.   365

ARTHUR (*reverentially*) I know. I've seen Miss Parrott as Jupiter,°
and as—I forget the name—in the new comedy—
            Imogen and Rose sit, below the table°

ROSE He forgets everything but the parts *I* play, and the pieces *I* play
in—poor child! Don't you, Arthur?

ARTHUR (*standing by Rose, looking down upon her*) Yes—no. Well, of   370
course I do! How can I help it, Miss Parrott? Miss Parrott won't
think the worse of me for that—will you, Miss Parrott?

MRS TELFER I am going to remove my bonnet. Imogen Parrott—?

IMOGEN Thank you, I'll keep my hat on, Mrs Telfer—take care!
            *Mrs Telfer, in turning to go, encounters Ablett, who is entering
            with two jugs of beer. Some of the beer is spilt*

ABLETT I beg your pardon, ma'am.   375

MRS TELFER (*examining her skirts*) Ruffian!°
            She departs

ROSE (*to Arthur*) Go and talk to the boys. I haven't seen Miss Parrott
for ages.
            In backing away from them, Arthur comes against Ablett

ABLETT I beg your pardon, sir.

ARTHUR I beg yours.   380

ABLETT (*grasping Arthur's hand*) Excuse the freedom, sir, if freedom
you regard it as—

ARTHUR Eh—?

ABLETT You 'ave plucked the flower, sir; you 'ave stole our ch'icest
blossom.   385

ARTHUR (*trying to get away*) Yes, yes, I know—

ABLETT Cherish it, Mr Glover—!

ARTHUR I will, I will. Thank you—
            *Mrs Mossop's voice is heard calling 'Ablett!' Ablett releases
            Arthur and goes out. Arthur joins Colpoys and Tom*

ROSE (*to Imogen*) The carriage will be here in half an hour. I've so
much to say to you. Imogen, the brilliant hits you've made! How   390
lucky you have been!

IMOGEN *My* luck! What about *yours*?

ROSE Yes, isn't this a wonderful stroke of fortune for me! Fate,
Jenny! That's what it is—fate! Fate ordains that I shall be a
well-to-do fashionable lady, instead of a popular but toiling actress. 395
Mother often used to stare into my face, when I was little, and
whisper, 'Rosie, I wonder what is to be your—fate.' Poor mother!
I hope she *sees*.

IMOGEN Your Arthur seems nice.

ROSE Oh, he's a dear. Very young, of course—not much more than 400
a year older than me—than I. But he'll grow manly in time, and
have moustaches, and whiskers out to here, he says.

IMOGEN How did you—?

ROSE He saw me act Blanche in *The Pedlar of Marseilles*,° and fell in
love. 405

IMOGEN Do you prefer Blanche—?

ROSE To Celestine? Oh, yes. You see, I got leave to introduce a
song—where Blanche is waiting for Raphael on the bridge. (*Singing dramatically, but in low tones*) 'Ever of thee I'm fondly
dreaming—' 410

IMOGEN I know—

ROSE and IMOGEN [*singing together*] 'Thy gentle voice my spirit can
cheer.'

ROSE It was singing that song that sealed my destiny, Arthur
declares. At any rate, the next thing was he began sending 415
bouquets and coming to the stage-door. Of course, I never spoke
to him, never glanced at him. Poor mother brought me up in that
way, not to speak to anybody, nor look.

IMOGEN Quite right.

ROSE I do hope she sees. 420

IMOGEN And then—?

ROSE Then Arthur managed to get acquainted with the Telfers, and
Mrs Telfer presented him to me. Mrs Telfer has kept an eye on
me all through. Not that it was necessary, brought up as I
was—but she's a kind old soul. 425

IMOGEN And now you're going to live with his people for a time,
aren't you?

ROSE Yes—on approval.

IMOGEN Ha, ha, ha! You don't mean that!

ROSE Well, in a way—just to reassure them, as they put it. The 430
Gowers have such odd ideas about theatres, and actors and
actresses.

IMOGEN Do you think you'll like the arrangement?

228

ROSE It'll only be for a little while. I fancy they're prepared to take
to me, especially Miss Trafalgar Gower—   435

IMOGEN Trafalgar!

ROSE Sir William's sister; she was born Trafalgar year,° and christened after it—

> *Mrs Mossop and Ablett enter, carrying trays on which are a pile
> of plates and various dishes of cold food—a joint, a chicken and
> a tongue, a ham, a pigeon pie, etc. They proceed to set out the
> dishes upon the table*

AVONIA Here comes the food! Oh, we are going to have a jolly
time.   440

> *General chatter. Colpoys takes the pigeon pie and, putting it on
> his head, trots round in front of table to right of it*

Now, Gus, you'll drop it—don't be silly! Put it down!

> *Colpoys puts it on the table, Avonia brings bread to the table.
> Arthur takes joints and vegetables from Mrs Mossop and places
> them on the table. Ablett goes up stage and, assisted by Telfer
> and others, places ham, tongue, vegetables, etc. on the table. Mrs
> Mossop cuts bread. Ablett pours out beer and then puts the jug
> up stage on the left°*

IMOGEN (*cheerfully*) Well, God bless you, my dear. I'm afraid *I*
couldn't give up the stage though, not for all the Arthurs—

ROSE Ah, your mother wasn't an actress.

IMOGEN No.   445

ROSE Mine was, and I remember her saying to me once, 'Rose, if
ever you have the chance, get out of it.'

IMOGEN The Profession?

ROSE Yes. 'Get out of it'. Mother said, 'if ever a good man comes
along, and offers to marry you and to take you off the stage, seize 450
the chance—get out of it.'

IMOGEN Your mother was never popular, was she?

ROSE Yes, indeed she was, most popular—till she grew oldish and
lost her looks.

IMOGEN Oh, *that's* what she meant, then?   455

ROSE Yes, that's what she meant.

IMOGEN (*shivering*) Oh, lor, doesn't it make one feel depressed!

ROSE Poor mother! Well, I hope she sees.

MRS MOSSOP Now, ladies and gentlemen, everything is prepared,
and I do trust to your pleasure and satisfaction.   460

TELFER Ladies and gentlemen, I beg you to be seated.

> *There is a general movement*

Miss Trelawny will sit 'ere, on my right. On my left, my friend
Mr Gower will sit. Next to Miss Trelawny—who will sit beside
Miss Trelawny?

GADD and COLPOYS I will.   465

AVONIA No, do let me!

    Gadd, Colpoys, and Avonia gather round Rose and wrangle for
    the vacant place. [Gadd pushes Avonia up stage]

ROSE (*standing by her chair*) It must be a gentleman, 'Vonia. Now, if
you two boys quarrel—!

GADD Please don't push me, Colpoys!

COLPOYS 'Pon my soul, Gadd—!   470

ROSE I know how to settle it. Tom Wrench—!

TOM (*coming to her*) Yes?

    Colpoys and Gadd move away, arguing

IMOGEN (*seating herself*) Mr Gadd and Mr Colpoys shall sit by me,
one on each side.

    Colpoys sits on Imogen's right, Gadd on her left, Avonia sits
    between Tom and Gadd; Mrs Mossop on the right of
    Colpoys. Amid much chatter,° *the viands are carved by Mrs*
    Mossop, Telfer, and Tom. Some plates of chicken etc. are
    handed round by Ablett, while others are passed about by those
    at the table

TELFER [*holding plate to Arthur*] Mr Gower—°   475

GADD (*quietly to Imogen, during a pause in the hubbub*) Telfer takes the
chair, you observe. Why *he*—more than myself, for instance?

IMOGEN (*to Gadd*) The Telfers have lent their room—

GADD Their stuffy room! That's no excuse. I repeat, Telfer has
thrust himself into this position.   480

IMOGEN He's the oldest man present.

GADD True. And he begins to age in his acting too. His h's! Scarce
as pearls!

IMOGEN Yes, that's shocking. Now, at the Olympic, slip an h and
you're damned for ever.   485

GADD And he's losing all his teeth. To act with him, it makes the
house seem half empty.

    Ablett is now going about pouring out the ale. Occasionally he
    drops his glove, misses it, and recovers it

TELFER (*to Imogen*) Miss Parrott, my dear, follow the counsel of one
who has sat at many a 'good man's feast'°—have a little 'am.

IMOGEN Thanks, Mr Telfer.   490

    Mrs Telfer returns

MRS TELFER Sitting down to table in my absence! (*To Telfer*) How is this, James?

TELFER We are pressed for time, Violet, my love.

ROSE Very sorry, Mrs Telfer.

MRS TELFER (*taking her place, between Arthur and Mrs Mossop, gloomily*) A strange proceeding.   495

ROSE Rehearsal was over so late. (*To Telfer*) You didn't get to the last act till a quarter to one, did you?

AVONIA (*taking off her hat and flinging it across the table to Colpoys*) Gus! Catch! Put it on the sofa, there's a dear boy.   500

> *Colpoys perches the hat upon his head, and behaves in a ridiculous, mincing way. Ablett is again convulsed with laughter. Some of the others are amused also, but more moderately*

Take that off, Gus! Mr Colpoys, you just take my hat off!

> *Colpoys rises, imitating the manners of a woman, and deposits the hat on the sofa*

ABLETT Ho, ho, ho! Oh, don't Mr Colpoys! Oh, don't, sir!

> *Colpoys returns to the table*

GADD (*quietly to Imogen*) It makes me sick to watch Colpoys in private life. He'd stand on his head in the street, if he could get a ragged infant to laugh at him. (*Picking the leg of a fowl furiously*)   505
What I say is this. Why can't an actor, in private life, be simply a gentleman? (*Loudly and haughtily*) More tongue here!°

ABLETT (*hurrying to him*) Yessir, certainly, sir. (*Again discomposed by some antic on the part of Colpoys*) Oh, don't, Mr Colpoys! (*Going to Telfer with Gadd's plate—speaking while Telfer carves a slice of   510
tongue*) I shan't easily forget this afternoon, Mr Telfer. (*Exhausted*)
This'll be something to tell Mrs Ablett. Ho, ho! Oh, dear, oh, dear!

> *Ablett, averting his face from Colpoys, brings back Gadd's plate. By an unfortunate chance, Ablett's glove has found its way to the plate and is handed to Gadd by Ablett*

GADD (*picking up the glove in disgust*) Merciful powers! What's this!

ABLETT (*taking the glove*) I beg your pardon, sir—my error, entirely.

> *A firm rat-tat-tat at the front door is heard. There is a general exclamation. At the same moment Sarah, a diminutive servant in a crinoline, appears in the doorway.*

SARAH (*breathlessly*) The kerridge has just drove up!   515

> *Imogen, Gadd, Colpoys, and Avonia go to the windows, open them, and look out. Mrs Mossop hurries away, pushing Sarah before her*

TELFER Dear me, dear me! Before a single speech has been made.

AVONIA (*at the window*) Rose, do look!

IMOGEN (*at the other window*) Come here, Rose!

ROSE (*shaking her head*) Ha, ha! I'm in no hurry; I shall see it often enough. (*Turning to Tom*) Well, the time has arrived. (*Laying down her knife and fork*) Oh, I'm so sorry, now.   520

TOM (*brusquely*) Are you? I'm glad.

ROSE Glad! That *is* hateful of you, Tom Wrench!

ARTHUR (*looking at his watch*) The carriage is certainly two or three minutes before its time, Mr Telfer.   525

TELFER Two or three—! The speeches, my dear sir, the speeches!
    Mrs Mossop returns, panting

MRS MOSSOP The footman, a nice-looking young man with hazel eyes, says the carriage and pair can wait for a little bit. They must be back by three, to take their lady into the Park—

TELFER (*rising*) Ahem! Resume your seats, I beg. Ladies and gentlemen—   530

AVONIA Wait, wait! We're not ready!
    Imogen, Gadd, Colpoys, and Avonia return to their places.
    Mrs Mossop also sits again. Ablett stands by the door

TELFER (*producing a paper from his breast-pocket*) Ladies and gentlemen, I devoted some time this morning to the preparation of a list of toasts. I now 'old that list in my hand. The first toast—   535
    He pauses, to assume a pair of spectacles

GADD (*to Imogen*) He arranges the toast-list! *He!*

IMOGEN (*to Gadd*) Hush!

TELFER The first toast that figures 'ere is, naturally, that of The Queen. (*Laying his hand on Arthur's shoulder*) With my young friend's chariot at the door, his horses pawing restlessly and   540 fretfully upon the stones, I am prevented from enlarging, from expatiating, upon the merits of this toast. Suffice it, both Mrs Telfer and I have had the honour of acting before Her Majesty upon no less than two occasions.

GADD (*to Imogen*) Tsch, tsch, tsch! An old story!   545

TELFER Ladies and gentlemen, I give you—(*to Colpoys*) The malt is with you,° Mr Colpoys.

COLPOYS (*handing the ale to Telfer*) Here you are, Telfer.

TELFER (*filling his glass*) I give you The Queen, coupling with that toast the name of Miss Violet Sylvester—Mrs Telfer—formerly,   550 as you are aware, of the Theatre Royal, Drury Lane. Miss Sylvester has so frequently and, if I may say so, so nobly impersonated the various queens of tragedy that I cannot but feel she is a fitting person to acknowledge our expression of loyalty. (*Raising his glass*) The Queen! And Miss Violet Sylvester!   555

>   *All rise, except Mrs Telfer, and drink the toast. After drinking,*
>   *Mrs Mossop passes her tumbler to Ablett*

ABLETT The Queen! Miss Vi'lent Sylvester!

>   *He drinks and returns the glass to Mrs Mossop. The company*
>   *being reseated, Mrs Telfer rises. Her reception is a polite one*

MRS TELFER (*heavily*) Ladies and gentlemen, I have played fourteen or fifteen queens in my time—

TELFER Thirteen, my love, to be exact; I was calculating this morning.   560

MRS TELFER Very well, I have played thirteen of 'em. And, as parts, they are not worth a tinker's oath. I thank you for the favour with which you have received me.

>   *She sits; the applause is heartier. During the demonstration*
>   *Sarah appears in the doorway, with a kitchen chair*

ABLETT (*to Sarah*) Wot's all this?

SARAH (*to Ablett*) Is the speeches on?   565

ABLETT H'on! Yes, and you be h'off!

>   *She places the chair against the open door and sits, full of*
>   *determination. At intervals Ablett vainly represents to her the*
>   *impropriety of her proceeding*

TELFER (*again rising*) Ladies and gentlemen. Bumpers, I charge ye! The toast I 'ad next intended to propose was Our Immortal Bard, Shakespeare, and I had meant, myself, to 'ave offered a few remarks in response—   570

GADD (*to Imogen, bitterly*) Ha!

TELFER But with our friend's horses champing their bits, I am compelled—nay, forced—to postpone this toast to a later period of the day, and to give you now what we may justly designate the toast of the afternoon. Ladies and gentlemen, we are about to lose,   575
to part with, one of our companions, a young comrade who came amongst us many months ago, who in fact joined the company of the 'Wells' last February twelve-month, after a considerable experience in the provinces of this great country.

COLPOYS Hear, hear!   580

AVONIA (*tearfully*) Hear, hear! (*With a sob*) I detested her at first.

COLPOYS Order!

IMOGEN Be quiet, 'Vonia!

TELFER Her late mother an actress, herself made familiar with the stage from childhood if not from infancy, Miss Rose Trelawny—   585

for I will no longer conceal from you that it is to Miss Trelawny
I refer—(*Loud applause*) Miss Trelawny is the stuff of which great
actresses are made.

ALL Hear, hear!

ABLETT (*softly*) 'Ear, 'ear!   590

TELFER So much for the actress. Now for the young lady—nay, the
woman, the gyirl.° Rose is a good girl—

> *Loud applause, to which Ablett and Sarah contribute largely.*
> *Avonia rises and impulsively embraces Rose. She is recalled to*
> *her seat by a general remonstrance*

A good girl—

MRS TELFER (*clutching a knife*) Yes, and I should like to hear
anybody, man or woman—!   595

TELFER She is a good girl, and will be long remembered by us as
much for her private virtues as for the commanding authority of
her genius.

> *More applause, during which there is a sharp altercation between*
> *Ablett and Sarah*

And now, what has happened to 'the expectancy and Rose of the
fair state'?°   600

IMOGEN Good, Telfer! Good!

GADD (*to Imogen*) Tsch, tsch! Forced! Forced!

TELFER I will tell you—(*Impressively*) A man has crossed her path.

ABLETT (*in a low voice*) Shame!

MRS MOSSOP (*turning to him*) Mr Ablett!   605

TELFER A man—ah, but also a gentle man. (*Applause*) A gentleman
of probity, a gentleman of honour, and a gentleman of wealth and
station. That gentleman, with the modesty of youth—for I may tell
you at once that 'e is not an old man—comes to us and asks us to
give him this gyirl to wife. And, friends, we have done so. A few   610
preliminaries 'ave, I believe, still to be concluded between Mr
Gower and his family, and then the bond will be signed, the
compact entered upon, the mutual trust accepted. Riches this
youthful pair will possess—but what is gold? May they be rich in
each other's society, in each other's love! May they—I can wish   615
them no greater joy—be as happy in their married life as my—
my—as Miss Sylvester and I 'ave been in ours! (*Raising his glass*)
Miss Rose Trelawny—Mr Arthur Gower!

> *The toast is drunk by the company, upstanding. Three cheers are*
> *called for by Colpoys, and given. Those who have risen then sit*

Miss Trelawny.

ROSE (*weeping*) No, no, Mr Telfer.   620

MRS TELFER (*to Telfer, softly*) Let her be for a minute, James.

TELFER Mr Gower.

> *Arthur rises and is well received*

ARTHUR Ladies and gentlemen, I—I would I were endowed with Mr
Telfer's flow of—of—of splendid eloquence. But I am no orator,
no speaker, and therefore cannot tell you how highly—how deeply   625
I appreciate the—the compliment—

ABLETT You deserve it, Mr Glover!

MRS MOSSOP Hush!

ARTHUR All I can say is that I regard Miss Trelawny in the light of
a—a solemn charge, and I—I trust that, if ever I have the pleasure   630
of—of meeting any of you again, I shall be able to render a
good—a—a—satisfactory—satisfactory—

TOM (*in an audible whisper*) Account.

ARTHUR Account of the way—of the way—in which I—in which—
(*Loud applause*) Before I bring these observations to a conclusion,   635
let me assure you that it has been a great privilege to me to
meet—to have been thrown with—a band of artists—whose
talents—whose striking talents—whose talents—

TOM (*kindly, behind his hand*) Sit down.

ARTHUR (*helplessly*) Whose talents not only interest and instruct   640
the—the more refined residents of this district, but whose
talents—

IMOGEN (*quietly to Colpoys*) Get him to sit down.

ARTHUR The fame of whose talents, I should say—

COLPOYS (*quietly to Mrs Mossop*) He's to sit down. Tell Mother   645
Telfer.

ARTHUR The fame of whose talents has spread to—to regions—

MRS MOSSOP (*quietly to Mrs Telfer*) They say he's to sit down.

ARTHUR To—to quarters of the town—to quarters—

MRS TELFER (*to Arthur*) Sit down!   650

ARTHUR Eh?

MRS TELFER You finished long ago. Sit down.

ARTHUR Thank you. I'm exceedingly sorry. Great Heavens, how
wretchedly I've done it!

> *He sits, burying his head in his hands. More applause*

TELFER Rose, my child.   655

> *Rose starts to her feet. The rest rise with her, and cheer again,*
> *and wave handkerchiefs. She goes from one to the other, round*
> *the table, embracing and kissing and crying over them all*

*excitedly. Sarah is kissed, but upon Ablett is bestowed only a
handshake, to his evident dissatisfaction. Imogen runs to the
piano and strikes up the air of 'Ever of Thee'. When Rose gets
back to the place, she mounts her chair, with the aid of Tom and
Telfer, and faces them with flashing eyes. They pull the flowers
out of the vases and throw them at her*

ROSE Mr Telfer, Mrs Telfer! My friends! Boys! Ladies and
gentlemen! No, don't stop, Jenny! Go on! ([*Imogen plays again.*]
Rose sings, her arms stretched out to them) 'Ever of thee I'm fondly
dreaming, Thy gentle voice—'. You remember! The song I sang
in *The Pedlar of Marseilles*—which made Arthur fall in love with   660
me! Well, I know I shall dream of *you*, of all of you, very often, as
the song says. Don't believe—(*Wiping away her tears*) Oh, don't
believe that, because I shall have married a swell, you and the old
'Wells'—the dear old 'Wells'!—

    Cheers

ROSE You and the old 'Wells' will have become nothing to me! No,   665
many and many a night you will see me in the house, looking down
at you from the circle—me and my husband—

ARTHUR Yes, yes, certainly!

ROSE And if you send for me I'll come behind the curtain to you,
and sit with you and talk of bygone times, these times that end   670
today. And shall I tell you the moments which will be the happiest
to me in my life, however happy I may be with Arthur? Why,
whenever I find that I am recognized by people, and pointed
out—people in the pit of a theatre, in the street, no matter where;
and when I can fancy they're saying to each other, 'Look! That   675
was Miss Trelawny! You remember—Trelawny! Trelawny of the
"Wells"!'—

    *They cry 'Trelawny!' and 'Trelawny of the "Wells"!' and
    again 'Trelawny!' wildly. Then there is the sound of a sharp
    rat-tat at the front door. Imogen leaves the piano and looks out
    of the window*

IMOGEN (*to somebody below*) What is it?

A VOICE Miss Trelawny, ma'am. We can't wait.

ROSE (*weakly*) Oh, help me down—   680

    *They assist her, and gather round her finally, bidding her
    farewell*

CURTAIN

Act Two

Scene One

The scene represents a spacious drawing-room in a house in Cavendish Square. The walls are sombre in tone, the ceiling dingy, the hangings, though rich, are faded, and altogether the appearance of the room is solemn, formal, and depressing. On the right are folding doors admitting to a further drawing-room. Beyond these is a single door. The wall on the left is mainly occupied by three sash-windows. The wall facing the spectators is divided by two pilasters into three panels. On the centre panel is a large mirror, reflecting the fireplace; on the right hangs a large oil painting—a portrait of Sir William Gower in his judicial wig and robes. On the left hangs a companion picture—a portrait of Miss Gower. In the corners of the room there are marble columns supporting classical busts, and between the doors stands another marble column, upon which is an oil lamp. Against the lower window there are two chairs and a card-table. Behind a further table supporting a lamp, stands a threefold screen. The lamps are lighted, but the curtains are not drawn, and outside the windows it is twilight, the month is June. Sir William Gower is seated, near a table, asleep, with a newspaper over his head, concealing his face. Miss Trafalgar Gower is sitting at the further end of a couch, also asleep, and with a newspaper over her head. At the lower end of this couch sits Mrs De Foenix—Clara—a young lady of nineteen, with a 'married' air. She is engaged upon some crochet work. On the other side of the room, near a table, Rose is seated, wearing the look of a boredom which has reached the stony stage. On another couch Arthur sits, gazing at his boots, his hands in his pockets. On the right of this couch stands Captain De Foenix, leaning against the wall, his mouth open, his head thrown back, and his eyes closed. De Foenix is a young man of seven-and-twenty—an example of the heavily whiskered 'swell' of the period.° Everybody is in dinner-dress. After a moment or two Arthur rises and tiptoes down to Rose. Clara raises a warning finger and says 'Hush!' He nods to her, in assent

ARTHUR (*on Rose's left, in a whisper*) Quiet, isn't it?

ROSE (*to him, in a whisper*) Quiet! Arthur—! (*Clutching his arm*) Oh, this dreadful half-hour after dinner, every, *every* evening!

ARTHUR (*creeping across to the right of the table and sitting there*) Grandfather and Aunt Trafalgar must wake up soon. They're longer than usual tonight. 5

ROSE (*to him, across the table*) Your sister Clara, over there, and Captain de Foenix—when they were courting, did they have to go through this?

ARTHUR Yes. 10

ROSE And now that they are married, they still endure it!

ARTHUR Yes.

ROSE And we, when *we* are married, Arthur, shall *we*—?

ARTHUR Yes. I suppose so.

ROSE (*passing her hand across her brow*) Phe—ew! 15

> *De Foenix, fast asleep, is now swaying, and in danger of toppling over. Clara grasps the situation and rises*

CLARA (*in a guttural whisper*) Ah, Frederick! No, no, no!

ROSE and ARTHUR (*turning in their chairs*) Eh—what—? Ah—h— h—h!

> *As Clara reaches her husband, he lurches forward into her arms*

DE FOENIX (*his eyes bolting*) Oh! Who—?

CLARA Frederick dear, wake! 20

DE FOENIX (*dazed*) How did this occur?

CLARA You were tottering, and I caught you.

DE FOENIX (*collecting his senses*) I wemember. I placed myself in an upwight position, dearwest, to prewent myself dozing.

CLARA (*sinking on to the couch*) How you alarmed me! 25

> *Seeing that Rose is laughing, De Foenix comes down to her*

DE FOENIX (*in a low voice*) Might have been a very serwious accident, Miss Trelawny.

ROSE (*seating herself on the footstool*) Never mind! (*Pointing to the chair she has vacated*) Sit down and talk. (*He glances at the old people and shakes his head*) Oh, do, do, do! Do sit down, and let us all have a jolly whisper. (*He sits*) Thank you, Captain Fred. Go on! Tell me something—anything; something about the military— 30

DE FOENIX (*again looking at the old people, then wagging his finger at Rose*) I know; you want to get me into a wow. (*Settling himself into his chair*) Howwid girl! 35

ROSE (*despairingly*) Oh—h—h!

> *There is a brief pause, and then the sound of a street organ, playing in the distance, is heard. The air is 'Ever of Thee'.*

ROSE Hark! (*Excitedly*) Hark!

CLARA, ARTHUR, and DE FOENIX Hush!

ROSE (*heedlessly*) The song I sang in *The Pedlar—The Pedlar of Marseilles!* The song that used to make you cry, Arthur—! 40

> *They attempt vainly to hush her down, but she continues dramatically, in hoarse whispers*

And then Raphael enters—comes on to the bridge. The music continues, softly. 'Raphael, why have you kept me waiting? Man, do you wish to break my heart—(*Thumping her breast*) A woman's hear—r—rt, Raphael?'

> *Sir William and Miss Gower suddenly whip off their newspapers and sit erect. Sir William is a grim, bullet-headed old gentleman of about seventy; Miss Gower a spare, prim lady, of gentle manners, verging upon sixty. They stare at each other for a moment, silently*

SIR WILLIAM What a hideous riot, Trafalgar! 45

MISS GOWER Rose, dear, I hope I have been mistaken—but through my sleep I fancied I could hear you shrieking at the top of your voice.

> *Sir William gets on to his feet; all rise, except Rose, who remains seated sullenly*

SIR WILLIAM Trafalgar, it is becoming impossible for you and me to obtain repose. (*Turning his head sharply*) Ha! Is not that a street 50
organ? (*To Miss Gower*) An organ?

MISS GOWER Undoubtedly. An organ in the Square, at this hour of the evening—singularly out of place!

SIR WILLIAM (*looking round*) Well, well, well, does no one stir?

ROSE (*under her breath*) Oh, don't stop it! 55

> *Clara goes out quickly. With a great show of activity, Arthur and De Foenix hurry across the room and, when there, do nothing*

SIR WILLIAM (*coming upon Rose and peering down at her*) What are ye upon the floor for, my dear? Have we no cheers?° (*To Miss Gower, producing his snuffbox*) Do we lack cheers here, Trafalgar?

MISS GOWER (*going to Rose*) My dear Rose! (*Raising her*) Come, come, come, this is quite out of place! Young ladies do not crouch 60
and huddle upon the ground—do they, William?

SIR WILLIAM (*taking snuff*) A moment ago I should have hazarded the opinion that they do not. (*Chuckling unpleasantly*) He, he, he!

> *Clara returns. The organ music ceases abruptly*

CLARA (*coming to Sir William*) Charles was just running out to stop 65
the organ when I reached the hall, Grandpa.

SIR WILLIAM Ye'd surely no intention, Clara, of venturing, yourself,
into the public street—the open Square—?

CLARA (*faintly*) I meant only to wave at the man from the door—

MISS GOWER Oh, Clara, that would hardly have been in place! 70

SIR WILLIAM (*raising his hands*) In mercy's name, Trafalgar, what *is*
befalling my household?

MISS GOWER (*bursting into tears*) Oh, William—!

> Rose and Clara creep away and join the others. Miss Gower
> totters to Sir William and drops her head upon his breast

SIR WILLIAM Tut, tut, tut, tut!

MISS GOWER (*between her sobs*) I—I—I—I know what is in your 75
mind.

SIR WILLIAM (*drawing a long breath*) Ah—h—h—h!

MISS GOWER Oh, my dear brother, be patient!

SIR WILLIAM Patient!

MISS GOWER Forgive me; I should have said hopeful. Be hopeful 80
that I shall yet succeed in ameliorating the disturbing conditions
which are affecting us so cruelly.

SIR WILLIAM Ye never will, Trafalgar; *I've* tried.

MISS GOWER Oh, do not despond already! I feel sure there are good
ingredients in Rose's character. (*Clinging to him*) In time, William, 85
we shall shape her to be a fitting wife for our rash and unfortunate
Arthur—(*He shakes his head*) In time, William, in time!

SIR WILLIAM (*soothing her*) Well, well, well! There, there, there! At
least, my dear sister, I am perfectly aweer that I possess in you the
woman above all others whose example should compel such a 90
transformation.

MISS GOWER (*throwing her arms about his neck*) Oh, brother, what a
compliment—!

SIR WILLIAM Tut, tut, tut! And now, before Charles sets the
card-table, don't you think we had better—eh, Trafalgar? 95

MISS GOWER Yes, yes—our disagreeable duty; let us discharge it.
(*Sir William takes snuff*) Rose, dear, be seated. (*To everybody*) The
Vice-Chancellor has something to say to us. Let us all be seated.

> There is consternation among the young people. All sit

SIR WILLIAM (*peering about him*) Are ye seated?

ALL Yes. 100

SIR WILLIAM What I desire to say is this. When Miss Trelawny took
up her residence here, it was thought proper, in the peculiar

circumstances of the case, that you, Arthur—(*Pointing a finger at Arthur*) you—

ARTHUR Yes, sir.

SIR WILLIAM That you should remove yourself to the establishment of your sister Clara and her husband in Holles Street,° round the corner—

ARTHUR Yes, sir.

CLARA Yes, Grandpa.

DE FOENIX Certainly, Sir William.

SIR WILLIAM Taking your food in this house, and spending other certain hours here, under the surveillance of your Great-Aunt Trafalgar.

MISS GOWER Yes, William.

SIR WILLIAM This was considered to be a decorous, and, toward Miss Trelawny, a highly respectful, course to pursue.

ARTHUR Yes, sir.

MISS GOWER Any other course would have been out of place.

SIR WILLIAM And yet—(*Again extending a finger at Arthur*) What is this that is reported to me?

ARTHUR I don't know, sir.

SIR WILLIAM I hear that ye have on several occasions, at night, after having quitted this house with Captain and Mrs de Foenix, been seen on the other side of the way, your back against the railings, gazing up at Miss Trelawny's window; and that you have remained in that position for a considerable space of time. Is this true, sir?

ROSE (*boldly*) Yes, Sir William.

SIR WILLIAM I venture to put a question to my grandson, Miss Trelawny.

ARTHUR Yes, sir, it is quite true.

SIR WILLIAM Then, sir, let me acqueent you that these are not the manners, nor the practices, of a gentleman.

ARTHUR No, sir?

SIR WILLIAM No, sir, they are the manners, and the practices, of a troubadour.°

MISS GOWER A troubadour in Cavendish Square! Quite out of place!

ARTHUR I—I'm very sorry, sir; I—I never looked at it in that light.

SIR WILLIAM (*snuffing*) Ah—h—h—h! Ho! Pi—i—i—sh!

ARTHUR But at the same time, sir, I dare say—of course I don't speak from precise knowledge—but I dare say there were a good many—a good many—

SIR WILLIAM Good many—what, sir?

ARTHUR A good many very respectable troubadours, sir—

ROSE (*starting to her feet, heroically and defiantly*) And what I wish to   145
say, Sir William, is this. I wish to avow, to declare before the
world, that Arthur and I have had many lengthy interviews while
he has been stationed against those railings over there; I murmur-
ing to him softly from my bedroom window, he responding in
tremulous whispers—   150

SIR WILLIAM (*struggling to his feet*) You—you tell me such things—!
      All rise

MISS GOWER The Square, in which we have resided for years—! Our
neighbours—!

SIR WILLIAM (*shaking a trembling hand at Arthur*) The—the character of my house—!   155

ARTHUR Again I am extremely sorry, sir—but these are the only
confidential conversations Rose and I now enjoy.

SIR WILLIAM (*turning upon Clara and De Foenix*) And you, Captain
de Foenix—an officer and a gentleman! And you, Clara! This could
scarcely have been without your cognizance, without, perhaps,   160
your approval—!
      Charles, in plush and powder° and wearing luxuriant whiskers,
      enters, carrying two branch candlesticks with lighted candles

CHARLES The cawd-table,° Sir William?

MISS GOWER (*agitatedly*) Yes, yes, by all means, Charles; the card-
table, as usual. (*To Sir William*) A rubber will comfort you, soothe
you—   165
      Charles carries the candlesticks to the card-table, Sir William
      and Miss Gower seat themselves upon a couch, she with her
      arm through his affectionately. Clara and De Foenix get behind
      the screen; their scared faces are seen occasionally over the
      top of it. Charles brings the card-table, opens it and arranges
      it, placing four chairs, which he collects from different parts of
      the room, round the table. Rose and Arthur talk in rapid
      undertones

ROSE Infamous! Infamous!

ARTHUR Be calm, Rose, dear, be calm!

ROSE Tyrannical! Diabolical! I cannot endure it.
      She throws herself into a chair. He stands behind her, apprehens-
      ively, endeavouring to calm her

ARTHUR (*over her shoulder*) They mean well, dearest—

ROSE (*hysterically*) Well! Ha, ha, ha!   170

ARTHUR But they are rather old-fashioned people—

ROSE Old-fashioned! They belong to the time when men and women
were put to the torture. I am being tortured—mentally tortured—

ARTHUR They have not many more years in this world—

ROSE Nor I, at this rate, many more months. They are killing   175
me—like Agnes in *The Spectre of St Ives*.° She expires, in the
fourth act, as I shall die in Cavendish Square, painfully, of no
recognized disorder—

ARTHUR And anything we can do to make them happy—

ROSE To make the Vice-Chancellor happy! I won't try! I will not!   180
He's a fiend, a vampire—!

ARTHUR Oh, hush!

ROSE (*snatching up Sir William's snuffbox, which he has left upon the
table*) His snuffbox! I wish I could poison his snuff, as Lucrezia
Borgia would have done. *She* would have removed him within two   185
hours of my arrival—I mean, her arrival. (*Opening the snuffbox and
mimicking Sir William*) And here he sits and lectures me, and
dictates to me! To Miss Trelawny! 'I venture to put a question to
my grandson, Miss Trelawny'! Ha, ha! (*Taking a pinch of snuff,
thoughtlessly but vigorously*) 'Yah—h—h—h! Pish! Have we no   190
cheers? Do we lack cheers here, Trafalgar?' (*Suddenly*) Oh—!

ARTHUR What have you done?

ROSE (*in suspense, replacing the snuffbox*) The snuff—!

ARTHUR Rose, dear!

ROSE (*putting her handkerchief to her nose, and rising*) Ah—!   195
    *Charles, having prepared the card-table, and arranged the
candlesticks upon it, has withdrawn. Miss Gower and Sir
William now rise*

MISS GOWER The table is prepared, William. Arthur, I assume you
would prefer to sit and contemplate Rose—?

ARTHUR Thank you, aunt.
    Rose sneezes violently, and is led away, helplessly, by Arthur

MISS GOWER (*to Rose*) Oh, my dear child! (*Looking round*) Where are
Frederick and Clara?   200

CLARA and DE FOENIX (*appearing from behind the screen, shamefacedly*)
Here.
    *The intending players cut the pack and seat themselves. Sir
William sits [up the stage,] facing Captain De Foenix, Miss
Gower on the right of the table, and Clara on the left*

ARTHUR (*while this is going on, to Rose*) Are you in pain, dearest?
Rose!

ROSE Agony!   205

ARTHUR Pinch your upper lip—
    She sneezes twice, loudly, and sinks back upon the couch

SIR WILLIAM (*testily*) Sssh! Sssh! Sssh! This is to be whist, I
  hope.°

MISS GOWER Rose, Rose! Young ladies do not sneeze quite so
  continuously.   210
    De Foenix is dealing

SIR WILLIAM (*with gusto*) I will thank you, Captain de Foenix, to
  exercise your intelligence this evening to its furthest limit.

DE FOENIX I'll twy, sir.

SIR WILLIAM (*laughing unpleasantly*) He, he, he! Last night, sir—

CLARA Poor Frederick had toothache last night, Grandpa.   215

SIR WILLIAM (*tartly*) Whist is whist, Clara, and toothache is
  toothache. We will endeavour to keep the two things distinct, if
  you please. He, he!

MISS GOWER Your interruption was hardly in place, Clara, dear—
  ah!   220

DE FOENIX Hey! What—?

MISS GOWER A misdeal.

CLARA (*faintly*) Oh, Frederick!

SIR WILLIAM (*partly rising*) Captain de Foenix!

DE FOENIX I—I'm fwightfully gwieved, sir—   225
    The cards are redealt by Miss Gower. Rose now gives way to a
    violent paroxysm of sneezing. Sir William rises

MISS GOWER William—!
    The players rise

SIR WILLIAM (*to the players*) Is this whist, may I ask?
    They sit

SIR WILLIAM (*standing*) Miss Trelawny—

ROSE (*weakly*) I—I think I had better—what d'ye call it?—withdraw
  for a few moments.   230

SIR WILLIAM (*sitting again*) Do so.
    Rose disappears. Arthur is leaving the room with her

MISS GOWER (*sharply*) Arthur! Where are you going?

ARTHUR (*returning promptly*) I beg your pardon, aunt.

MISS GOWER Really, Arthur—!

SIR WILLIAM (*rapping upon the table*) Tsch, tsch, tsch!   235

MISS GOWER Forgive me, William.
    They play

SIR WILLIAM (*intent upon his cards*) My snuffbox, Arthur; be so
  obleeging as to search for it.

ARTHUR (*brightly*) I'll bring it to you, sir. It is on the—

SIR WILLIAM Keep your voice down, sir. We are playing—(*Emphatic-*   240
ally throwing down a card, as fourth player) Whist. Mine.

MISS GOWER (*picking up the trick*) No, William.

SIR WILLIAM (*glaring*) No!

MISS GOWER Clara played a trump.

DE FOENIX Yes, sir, Clara played a trump—the seven—   245

SIR WILLIAM I will not trouble you, Captain de Foenix, to echo Miss
Gower's information.

DE FOENIX Vevy sowwy, sir.

MISS GOWER (*gently*) It *was* a *little* out of place, Frederick.

SIR WILLIAM Sssh! Whist.   250

> *Arthur is now on Sir William's right, with the snuffbox.*

Eh? What? (*Taking the snuffbox from Arthur*) Oh, thank ye. Much
obleeged, much obleeged.

> *Arthur walks away and picks up a book. Sir William turns in*
> *his chair, watching Arthur*

MISS GOWER You to play, William. (*A pause*) William, dear—?

> *She also turns, following the direction of his gaze. Laying down*
> *his cards, Sir William leaves the card-table and goes over to*
> *Arthur slowly. Those at the card-table look on apprehensively*

SIR WILLIAM (*in a queer voice*) Arthur.

ARTHUR (*shutting his book*) Excuse me, grandfather.   255

SIR WILLIAM Ye—ye're a troublesome young man, Arthur.

ARTHUR I—I don't mean to be one, sir.

SIR WILLIAM As your poor father was, before ye. And if you are fool
enough to marry, and to beget children, doubtless your son will
follow the same course. (*Taking snuff*) Y—y—yes, but I shall be   260
dead 'n' gone by that time, it's likely. Ah—h—h—h! Pi—i—i—sh!
I shall be sitting in the Court Above by that time—

> *From the adjoining room comes the sound of Rose's voice singing*
> *'Ever of Thee' to the piano. There is great consternation at the*
> *card-table. Arthur is moving towards the folding doors, Sir*
> *William detains him*

No, no, let her go on, I beg. Let her continue. (*Returning to the*
card-table, with deadly calmness) We will suspend our game while
this young lady performs her operas.   265

MISS GOWER (*rising and taking his arm*) William—!

SIR WILLIAM (*in the same tone*) I fear this is no longer a comfortable
home for ye, Trafalgar; no longer the home for a gentlewoman. I
apprehend that in these days my house approaches somewhat

closely to a Pandemonium. (*Suddenly taking up the cards, in a fury,*   270
and flinging them across the room) And this is whist—whist—!

    Clara and De Foenix rise and stand together. Arthur pushes open
    the upper part of the folding doors

ARTHUR Rose! Stop! Rose!

    The song ceases and Rose appears

ROSE (*at the folding doors*) Did anyone call?

ARTHUR You have upset my grandfather.

MISS GOWER Miss Trelawny, how—how dare you do anything   275
so—so out of place?

ROSE There's a piano in there, Miss Gower.

MISS GOWER You are acquainted with the rule of this household—no
music when the Vice-Chancellor is within doors.

ROSE But there are so many rules. One of them is that you may not   280
sneeze.

MISS GOWER Ha! You must never answer—

ROSE No, that's another rule.

MISS GOWER Oh, for shame!

ARTHUR You see, aunt, Rose is young, and—and—you make no   285
allowance for her, give her no chance—

MISS GOWER Great Heaven! What is this you are charging me
with?

ARTHUR I don't think the 'rules' of this house are fair to Rose! Oh,
I must say it—they are horribly unfair!   290

MISS GOWER (*clinging to Sir William*) Brother!

SIR WILLIAM Trafalgar! (*Putting her aside and advancing to Arthur*)
Oh, indeed, sir! And so you deliberately accuse your great-aunt of
acting toward ye and Miss Trelawny *mala fide°*—

ARTHUR Grandfather, what I intended to—   295

SIR WILLIAM I will afford ye the opportunity of explaining what ye
intended to convey, downstairs, at once, in the library. (*A general
shudder*) Obleege me by following me, sir. (*To Clara and De
Foenix*) Captain de Foenix, I see no prospect of any further social
relaxation this evening. You and Clara will do me the favour of   300
attending in the hall, in readiness to take this young man back to
Holles Street. (*Giving his arm to Miss Gower*) My dear sister—(*To
arthur*) Now, sir.

    Sir William and Miss Gower go out. Arthur comes to Rose and
    kisses her

ARTHUR Good-night, dearest. Oh, good-night! Oh, Rose—!

SIR WILLIAM (*outside the door*) Mr Arthur Gower!   305

ARTHUR I am coming, sir—
    He goes out quickly
DE FOENIX (*approaching Rose and taking her hand sympathetically*)
    Haw—!I—weally—haw!—
ROSE Yes, I know what you would say. Thank you, Captain Fred.
CLARA (*embracing Rose*) Never mind! We will continue to let Arthur
    out at night as usual. I am a married woman! (*Joining De Foenix*)
    And a married woman will turn, if you tread upon her often
    enough—!
    De Foenix and Clara depart
ROSE (*pacing the room, shaking her hands in the air desperately*)
    Oh—h—h! Ah—h—h!
    The upper part of the folding doors opens, and Charles appears
CHARLES (*mysteriously*) Miss Rose—
ROSE What—?
CHARLES (*advancing*) I see Sir William h'and the rest descend the
    stairs. I 'ave been awaitin' the chawnce of 'andin' you this, Miss
    Rose.
    He produces a dirty scrap of paper, wet and limp, with writing
    upon it, and gives it to her
ROSE (*handling it daintily*) Oh, it's damp!—
CHARLES Yes, miss; a little gentle shower 'ave been takin' place
    h'outside—'eat spots, Cook says.°
ROSE (*reading*) Ah! From some of my friends.
CHARLES (*behind his hand*) Perfesshunnal, Miss Rose?
ROSE (*intent upon the note*) Yes—yes—
CHARLES I was reprimandin' the organ, miss, when I observed
    them lollin' against the Square railin's examinin' h'our
    premises, and they wentured for to beckon me. An egstremely
    h'affable party, miss. (*Hiding his face*) Ho! One of them caused me
    to laff!
ROSE (*excitedly*) They want to speak to me—(*Referring to the note*) To
    impart something to me of an important nature. Oh, Charles, I
    know not what to do!
CHARLES (*languishingly*) Whatever friends may loll against them
    railin's h'opposite, Miss Rose, you 'ave one true friend in this
    'ouse—Chawles Gibbons—
ROSE Thank you, Charles. Mr Briggs, the butler, is sleeping out
    tonight, isn't he?
CHARLES Yes, miss, he 'ave leave to sleep at his sister's. I 'appen to
    know he 'ave gone to Cremorne.°

ROSE Then, when Sir William and Miss Gower have retired, do you
     think you could let me go forth; and wait at the front door while
     I run across and grant my friends a hurried interview?

CHARLES Suttingly,° miss.   345

ROSE If it reached the ears of Sir William, or Miss Gower, you would
     lose your place, Charles!

CHARLES (*haughtily*) I'm aweer, miss; but Sir William was egstreme-
     ly rood to me dooring dinner, over that mis'ap to the ontray°—(*A
     bell rings violently*) S'william!   350

> *He goes out. The rain is heard pattering against the window-
> panes. Rose goes from one window to another, looking out. It is
> now almost black outside the windows*

ROSE (*discovering her friends*) Ah! yes, yes! Ah—h—h—h!

> *She snatches an antimacassar° from a chair and jumping on to
> the couch, waves it frantically to those outside*

The dears! The darlings! The faithful creatures—! (*Listening*)
Oh—!

> *She descends, in a hurry, and flings the antimacassar under the
> couch, as Miss Gower enters. At the same moment there is a
> vivid flash of lightning*

MISS GOWER (*startled*) Oh, how dreadful! (*To Rose, frigidly*) The
     Vice-Chancellor has *felt* the few words he has addressed to Arthur,   355
     and has retired for the night.

> *There is a roll of thunder. Rose is alarmed; Miss Gower clings
> to a chair*

Mercy on us! Go to bed, child, directly. We will all go to our beds,
hoping to awake tomorrow in a meeker and more submissive spirit.
(*Kissing Rose upon the brow*) Good-night. (*Another flash of lightning*)
Oh—! Don't omit to say your prayers, Rose—and in a simple   360
manner. I always fear that, from your peculiar training, you may
declaim them. That is so out of place—oh—!

> *Another roll of thunder. Rose goes across the room, meeting
> Charles, who enters carrying a lantern. They exchange signific-
> ant glances, and she disappears*

CHARLES (*coming to Miss Gower*) I am now at liberty to accompany
     you round the 'ouse, ma'am—

> *A flash of lightning*

MISS GOWER Ah—! (*Her hand to her heart*) Thank you, Charles—but   365
     tonight I must ask you to see that everything is secure, alone. This
     storm—so very seasonable; but, from girlhood, I could never—(*A
     roll of thunder*) Oh, good-night!

She flutters away. The rain beats still more violently upon the
window-panes

CHARLES (*glancing at the window*) Ph—e—e—w! Great 'evans!
He is dropping the curtains at the window when Rose appears at
the folding doors

ROSE (*in a whisper*) Charles!   370

CHARLES Miss?

ROSE (*coming into the room, distractedly*) Miss Gower has gone to bed.

CHARLES Yes, miss—oh—!
A flash of lightning

ROSE Oh! My friends! My poor friends!

CHARLES H'and Mr Briggs at Cremorne! Reelly, I should 'ardly   375
advise you to wenture h'out, miss—

ROSE Out! No! Oh, but get them in!

CHARLES *In*, Miss Rose! indoors!

ROSE Under cover—
A roll of thunder
Oh! (*Wringing her hands*) They are my friends! Is it a rule that I   380
am never to see a friend, that I mayn't even give a friend shelter
in a violent storm? (*To Charles*) Are you the only one up?

CHARLES I b'lieve so, miss. Any'ow the wimming servants is quite
h'under my control.

ROSE Then tell my friends to be deathly quiet, and to creep—to   385
tiptoe—
The rain strikes the window again. She picks up the lantern
which Charles has deposited upon the floor, and gives it to him
Make haste! I'll draw the curtains—
He hurries out. She goes from window to window, dropping the
curtains, talking to herself excitedly as she does so
My friends! My own friends! Ah! I'm not to sneeze in this house!
Nor to sing! Or breathe, next! Wretches! Oh, my! Wretches!
(*Blowing out the candles and removing the candlesticks to the table,*   390
singing, under her breath, wildly) 'Ever of thee I'm fondly dream-
ing—' (*Mimicking Sir William again*) 'What are ye upon the floor
for, my dear? Have we no cheers? Do we lack cheers here,
Trafalgar—?'
Charles returns

CHARLES (*to those who follow him*) Hush! (*To Rose*) I discovered 'em   395
clustered in the doorway—
There is a final peal of thunder as Avonia, Gadd, Colpoys, and
Tom Wrench enter, somewhat diffidently. They are apparently

> *soaked to their skins, and are altogether in a deplorable*
> *condition. Avonia alone has an umbrella, which she allows to*
> *drip upon the carpet, but her dress and petticoats are bedraggled,*
> *her finery limp, her hair lank and loose*

ROSE 'Vonia!

AVONIA (*coming to her, and embracing her fervently*) Oh, ducky,
ducky, ducky! Oh, but what a storm!

ROSE Hush! How wet you are! (*Shaking hands with Gadd*) Ferdi-   400
nand—(*Crossing to Colpoys and shaking hands with him*) Augustus—
(*Shaking hands with Tom*) Tom Wrench—

AVONIA (*to Charles*) Be so kind as to put my umbrella on the landing,
will you? Oh, thank you very much, I'm sure.

> *Charles withdraws with the umbrella. Gadd and Colpoys shake*
> *the rain from their hats on to the carpet and furniture*

TOM (*quietly, to Rose*) It's a shame to come down on you in this way.   405
But they would do it, and I thought I'd better stick to 'em.

GADD (*who is a little flushed and unsteady*) Ha! I shall remember this
accursed evening.

AVONIA Oh, Ferdy—!

ROSE Hush! You must be quiet. Everybody has gone to bed, and   410
I—I'm not sure I'm allowed to receive visitors—

AVONIA Oh!

GADD Then we are intruders?

ROSE I mean, such late visitors.

> *Colpoys has taken off his coat, and is shaking it vigorously*

AVONIA Stop it, Augustus! Ain't I wet enough? (*To Rose*) Yes, it is   415
latish, but I so wanted to inform you—here—(*Bringing Gadd*
forward) allow me to introduce—my husband.

ROSE Oh! No!

AVONIA (*laughing merrily*) Yes! Ha, ha, ha!

ROSE Sssh, sssh, sssh!   420

AVONIA I forgot. (*To Gadd*) Oh, darling Ferdy, you're positively
soaked! (*To Rose*) Do let him take his coat off, like Gussy—

GADD (*jealously*) 'Vonia, not so much of the Gussy!

AVONIA There you are, flying out again! As if Mr Colpoys wasn't an
old friend!   425

GADD Old friend or no old friend—

ROSE (*diplomatically*) Certainly, take your coat off, Ferdinand.

> *Gadd joins Colpoys; they spread out their coats upon the couch*

ROSE (*feeling Tom's coat sleeve*) And you?

TOM (*after glancing at the others, quietly*) No, thank you.

AVONIA (*sitting*) Yes, dearie, Ferdy and I were married yesterday.   430
ROSE (*sitting*) Yesterday!
AVONIA Yesterday morning. We're on our honeymoon now. You
   know, the 'Wells' shut a fortnight after you left us, and neither
   Ferdy nor me could fix anything, just for the present, elsewhere;
   and as we hadn't put by during the season—you know it never   435
   struck us to put by during the season—we thought we'd get
   married.
ROSE Oh, yes.
AVONIA You see, a man and his wife can live almost on what keeps
   one, rent *and* ceterer; and so, being deeply attached, as I tell you,   440
   we went off to church and did the deed. Oh, it will be such a save.
   (*Looking up at Gadd coyly*) Oh, Ferdy—!
GADD (*laying his hand upon her head, dreamily*) Yes, child, I confess
   I love you—
COLPOYS (*behind Rose, imitating Gadd*) Child, I confess I adore you.   445
TOM (*taking Colpoys by the arm and swinging him away from Rose*)
   Enough of that, Colpoys!
COLPOYS What!
ROSE (*rising*) Hush!
TOM (*under his breath*) If you've never learnt how to behave—   450
COLPOYS Don't you teach behaviour, sir, to a gentleman who plays
   a superior line of business to yourself! (*Muttering*) 'Pon my soul!
   Rum start—!°
AVONIA (*going to Rose*) Of course I ought to have written to you,
   dear, properly, but you remember the weeks it takes me to write   455
   a letter—
>   *Gadd sits in the chair Avonia has just quitted; she returns and*
>   *seats herself upon his knee*
And so I said to Ferdy, over tea, 'Ferdy, let's spend a bit of our
   honeymoon in doing the West End thoroughly, and going and
   seeing where Rose Trelawny lives.' And we thought it only nice
   and polite to invite Tom Wrench and Gussy—   460
GADD 'Vonia, much less of the Gussy!
AVONIA (*kissing Gadd*) Jealous boy! (*Beaming*) Oh, and we *have* done
   the West End thoroughly. There, I've never done the West End
   so thoroughly in my life! And when we got outside your house I
   couldn't resist—(*Her hand on Gadd's shirtsleeve*) Oh, gracious! I'm   465
   sure you'll catch your death, my darling—!
ROSE I think I can get him some wine. (*To Gadd*) Will you take some
   wine, Ferdinand?

Gadd rises, nearly upsetting Avonia

AVONIA Ferdy!

GADD I thank you. (*With a wave of the hand*) Anything, anything—   470

AVONIA (*to Rose*) Anything that goes with stout,° dear.

ROSE (*at the door, turning to them*) 'Vonia—boys—be very still.

AVONIA Trust *us!*

> *Rose tiptoes out. Colpoys is now at the card-table, cutting a pack
> of cards which remains there*

COLPOYS (*to Gadd*) Gadd, I'll see you for pennies.

GADD (*loftily*) Done, sir, with you!   475

> *They seat themselves at the table, and cut for coppers.° Tom is
> walking about, surveying the room.*

AVONIA (*taking off her hat and wiping it with her handkerchief*) Well,
Thomas, what do you think of it?

TOM *This* is the kind of chamber I want for the first act of my
comedy—

AVONIA Oh, lor', your head's continually running on your comedy.   480
Half this blessed evening—

TOM I tell you, I won't have doors stuck here, there, and everywhere;
no, nor windows in all sorts of impossible places!

AVONIA Oh, really! Well, when you do get your play accepted, mind
you see that Mr Manager gives you exactly what you ask for—   485
won't you?

TOM You needn't be satirical, if you *are* wet. Yes, I will! (*Pointing to
the left*) Windows on the one side—(*Pointing to the right*) doors on
the other—just where they should be, architecturally. And locks
on the doors, *real locks*, to work; and handles—to turn! (*Rubbing*   490
his hands together gleefully) Ha, ha! You wait! Wait—!

> *Rose re-enters, with a plate of biscuits in her hand, followed
> by Charles, who carries a decanter of sherry and some wine-
> glasses*

ROSE Here, Charles—

> *Charles places the decanter and the glasses on the table*

GADD (*whose luck has been against him, throwing himself, sulkily, on to
the couch*) Bah! I'll risk no further stake.

COLPOYS Just because you lose sevenpence in coppers you go on like   495
this!

> *Charles, turning from the table, faces Colpoys*
> (*Tearing his hair, and glaring at Charles wildly*) Ah—h—h, I am
ruined! I have lost my all! My children are beggars—!

CHARLES Ho, ho, ho! He, he, he!

ROSE Hush, hush!   500
   Charles goes out laughing
  (*To everybody*) Sherry?
GADD (*rising*) Sherry!
   Avonia, Colpoys, and Gadd gather round the table, and help
   themselves to sherry and biscuits
ROSE (*to Tom*) Tom, won't you—?
TOM (*watching Gadd anxiously*) No, thank you. The fact is, we—we   505
have already partaken of refreshments, once or twice during the
evening—
   Colpoys and Avonia, each carrying a glass of wine and
   munching a biscuit, go to the couch, where they sit
GADD (*pouring out sherry, singing*) 'And let me the canakin clink,
clink—'°
ROSE (*coming to him*) Be quiet, Gadd!
COLPOYS (*raising his glass*) The Bride!   510
ROSE (*turning, kissing her hand to Avonia*) Yes, yes—
   Gadd hands Rose his glass; she puts her lips to it
  The Bride!
   She returns the glass to Gadd
GADD (*sitting*) My bride!
   Tom, from behind the table, unperceived, takes the decanter and
   hides it under the table, then sits. Gadd, missing the decanter,
   contents himself with the biscuits
AVONIA Well, Rose, my darling, we've been talking about nothing
but ourselves. How are you getting along here?   515
ROSE Getting along? Oh, I—I don't fancy I'm getting along very
well, thank you!
COLPOYS and AVONIA Not—!
GADD (*his mouth full of biscuit*) Not—!
ROSE (*sitting by the card-table*) No, boys; no, 'Vonia. The truth is, it   520
isn't as nice as you'd think it. I suppose the Profession had its
drawbacks—mother used to say so—but—(*Raising her arms*) one
could fly. Yes, in Brydon Crescent one was a dirty little London
sparrow, perhaps; but here, in this grand square—! Oh, it's the
story of the caged bird, over again!   525
AVONIA A love-bird, though.
ROSE Poor Arthur? Yes, he's a dear. (*Rising*) But the Gowers—the
old Gowers! The Gowers! The Gowers!
AVONIA and COLPOYS The Gowers! what does she mean by 'the
Gowers'?   530

253

> *Rose paces the room, beating her hands together. In her*
> *excitement, she ceases to whisper, and gradually becomes loud*
> *and voluble. The others, following her lead, chatter noisily—ex-*
> *cepting Tom, who sits, thoughtfully, looking before him.*

ROSE The ancient Gowers! The venerable Gowers!

AVONIA You mean, the grandfather—?

ROSE And the aunt—the great-aunt—the great bore of a great-aunt!
The very mention of 'em makes something go 'tap, tap, tap, tap'
at the top of my head.   535

AVONIA Oh, I *am* sorry to hear this. Well, upon my word—!

ROSE Would you believe it? 'Vonia—boys—you'll never believe it! I
mayn't walk out with Arthur alone, nor see him here alone. I
mayn't sing; no, nor sneeze even—

AVONIA (*shrilly*) Not sing or sneeze!   540

COLPOYS (*indignantly*) Not sneeze!

ROSE No, nor sit on the floor—the *floor!*

AVONIA Why, when we shared rooms together, you were always on
the floor!

GADD (*producing a pipe, and knocking out the ashes on the heel of his* 545
boot) In Heaven's name, what kind of house can this be!

AVONIA I wouldn't stand it, would you, Ferdinand?

GADD (*loading his pipe*) Gad, no!

AVONIA (*to Colpoys*) Would you, Gus, dear?

GADD (*under his breath*) Here! Not so much of the Gus dear—   550

AVONIA (*to Colpoys*) Would you?

COLPOYS No, I'm blessed if I would, my darling.

GADD (*his pipe in his mouth*) Mr Colpoys! Less of the darling!

AVONIA (*rising*) Rose, don't you put up with it! (*Striking the top of*
the card-table vigorously) I say, don't you stand it! (*Embracing Rose*) 555
You're an independent girl, dear; they came to you, these people,
not you to them, remember.

ROSE (*sitting on the couch*) Oh, what can I do? I can't do anything.

AVONIA Can't you! (*Coming to Gadd*) Ferdinand, advise her. You tell
her how to—   560

GADD (*who has risen*) Miss Bunn—Mrs Gadd, you have been all over
Mr Colpoys this evening, ever since we—

AVONIA (*angrily, pushing him back into his chair*) Oh, don't be a
silly!

GADD Madam!   565

AVONIA (*returning to Colpoys*) Gus, Ferdinand's foolish. Come and
talk to Rose, and advise her, there's a dear boy—

> *Colpoys rises; she takes his arm, to lead him to Rose. At that*
> *moment Gadd advances to Colpoys and slaps his face*

COLPOYS Hey—!

GADD Miserable viper!

> *The two men close. Tom runs to separate them. Rose rises with*
> *a cry of terror. There is a struggle and general uproar. The*
> *card-table is overturned, with a crash, and Avonia utters a long*
> *and piercing shriek. Then the house-bells are heard ringing*
> *violently*

ROSE Oh—! 570

> *The combatants part; all look scared*

(*At the door, listening*) They are moving—coming! Turn out the—!
> *She turns out the light at the table. The room is in half-light*
> *as Sir William enters, cautiously, closely followed by Miss*
> *Gower. They are both in dressing-gowns and slippers; Sir*
> *William carries a thick stick and his bedroom candle. Rose is*
> *standing by a chair; Gadd, Avonia, Colpoys, and Tom are*
> *together*

SIR WILLIAM Miss Trelawny—!

MISS GOWER Rose—! (*Running behind the screen*) Men!

SIR WILLIAM Who are these people?

ROSE (*advancing a step or two*) Some friends of mine who used to 575
be at the 'Wells' have called upon me, to inquire how I am
getting on.

> *Arthur enters, quickly*

ARTHUR (*looking round*) Oh! Rose—!

SIR WILLIAM (*turning upon him*) Ah—h—h—h! How come you here?

ARTHUR I was outside the house. Charles let me in, knowing 580
something was wrong.

SIR WILLIAM (*peering into his face*) Troubadouring—?

ARTHUR Troubadouring; yes, sir. (*To Rose*) Rose, what is this?

SIR WILLIAM (*fiercely*) No, sir, this is my affair. (*Placing his candle-
stick on the table*) Stand aside! (*Raising his stick furiously*) Stand 585
aside!

> *Arthur moves to the right*

MISS GOWER (*over the screen*) William—

SIR WILLIAM Hey?

MISS GOWER Your ankles—

SIR WILLIAM (*adjusting his dressing-gown*) I beg your pardon. (*To* 590
Arthur) Yes, I can answer your question. (*Pointing his stick, first at*
Rose, then at the group) Some friends of that young woman's

connected with—the playhouse, have favoured us with a visit, for
the purpose of ascertaining how she is—getting on. (*Touching
Gadd's pipe, which is lying at his feet, with the end of his stick*) A   595
filthy tobacco-pipe. To whom does it belong? whose is it?
   Rose picks it up and passes it to Gadd, bravely

ROSE It belongs to one of my friends.

SIR WILLIAM (*taking Gadd's empty wineglass and holding it to his nose*)
Phu, yes! In brief, a drunken debauch. (*To the group*) So ye see,
gentlemen—(*To Avonia*) and you, madam—(*To Arthur*) and you,   600
sir; you see, all of ye—(*Sinking into a chair, and coughing from
exhaustion*) exactly how Miss Trelawny is getting on.

MISS GOWER (*over the screen*) William—

SIR WILLIAM What is it?

MISS GOWER Your ankles—   605

SIR WILLIAM (*leaping to his feet, in a frenzy*) Bah!

MISS GOWER Oh, they seem so out of place!

SIR WILLIAM (*flourishing his stick*) Begone! A set of garish, dissolute
gypsies! Begone!
   *Gadd, Avonia, Colpoys, and Wrench gather together, the men
   hastily putting on their coats, etc.*

AVONIA Where's my umbrella?   610

GADD A hand with my coat here!

COLPOYS 'Pon my soul! London artists—!

AVONIA We don't want to remain where we're not heartily welcome,
I can assure everybody.

SIR WILLIAM Open windows! Let in the air!   615

AVONIA (*to Rose, who is standing above the wreck of the card-table*)
Goodbye, my dear—

ROSE No, no, 'Vonia. Oh, don't leave me behind you!

ARTHUR Rose—!

ROSE Oh, I'm very sorry, Arthur. (*To Sir William*) Indeed, I am very   620
sorry, Sir William. But you are right—gypsies—gypsies! (*To
Arthur*) Yes, Arthur, if you were a gypsy, as I am, as these friends
o' mine are, we might be happy together. But I've seen enough of
your life, my dear boy, to know that I'm no wife for you. I should
only be wretched, and would make you wretched; and the end,   625
when it arrived, as it very soon would, would be much as it is
tonight—!

ARTHUR (*distractedly*) You'll let me see you, talk to you, tomorrow,
Rose?

ROSE No, never!   630

SIR WILLIAM (*sharply*) You mean that?

ROSE (*facing him*) Oh, don't be afraid. I give you my word.

SIR WILLIAM (*gripping her hand*) Thank ye. Thank ye.

TOM (*quietly to Arthur*) Mr Gower, come and see *me* tomorrow—
     He moves away to the door

ROSE (*turning to Avonia, Gadd, and Colpoys*) I'm ready—   635

MISS GOWER (*coming from behind the screen to the back of the couch*)
     Not tonight, child! Not tonight! Where will you go?

AVONIA (*holding Rose*) To her old quarters in Brydon Crescent. Send
     her things after her, if you please.

MISS GOWER And then—?   640

ROSE Then back to the 'Wells' again, Miss Gower! Back to the
     'Wells'—!

     CURTAIN

Act Three

Scene One

The scene represents an apartment on the second floor of Mrs Mossop's house in Brydon Crescent. The room is of a humbler character than that shown in the first act; but, though shabby, it is neat. On the right is a door, outside which is supposed to be the landing. In the wall at the back is another door, presumably admitting to a further chamber. On the left there is a fireplace, with a fire burning, and over the mantelpiece a mirror. In the left-hand corner of the room is a small bedstead with a tidily made bed, which can be hidden by a pair of curtains of some common and faded material, hanging from a cord slung from wall to wall. At the foot of the bedstead stands a large theatrical dress-basket. On the wall, by the head of the bed, are some pegs, upon which hang a skirt or two and other articles of attire. On the right, against the back wall, there is a chest of drawers, the top of which is used as a washstand. In front of this is a small screen, and close by there are some more pegs with things hanging upon them. On the right wall, above the sofa, is a hanging bookcase with a few books. A small circular table, with a somewhat shabby cover upon it, stands near the fireplace. The walls are papered, the doors painted in a stone-colour. An old felt carpet is on the floor. The light is that of morning; it is December. Mrs Mossop, now dressed in a workaday gown, has just finished making the bed. There is a knock at the centre door

AVONIA (*from the adjoining room*) Rose!

MRS MOSSOP (*giving a final touch to the quilt*) Eh?

AVONIA Is Miss Trelawny in her room?

MRS MOSSOP No, Mrs Gadd; she's at rehearsal.

AVONIA Oh— 5

Mrs Mossop draws the curtains, hiding the bed from view. Avonia enters by the door on the right in a morning wrapper which has seen its best days. She carries a pair of curling-tongs, and her hair is evidently in process of being dressed in ringlets

Of course she is; I forgot. There's a call for *The Pedlar of Marseilles*. Thank Gawd, *I'm* not in it. (*Singing*) 'I'm a great guerilla chief, I'm a robber and a thief, I can either kill a foe or prig a pocket handkerchief—'°

MRS MOSSOP (*dusting the ornaments on the mantelpiece*) Bless your   10
heart, you're very gay this morning!

AVONIA It's the pantomime.° I'm always stark mad as the pantomime approaches. I don't grudge letting the rest of the company have their fling at other times—but with the panto comes *my* turn. (*Throwing herself full length upon the sofa gleefully*) Ha, ha, ha! The   15
turn of Avonia Bunn! (*With a change of tone*) I hope Miss Trelawny won't take a walk up to Highbury, or anywhere, after rehearsal. I want to borrow her gilt belt. My dress has arrived.

MRS MOSSOP (*much interested*) No! Has it?

AVONIA Yes, Mrs Burroughs is coming down from the theatre at   20
twelve thirty to see me in it. (*Singing*) 'Any kind of villainy cometh natural to me, So it endeth with a combat and a one, two, three—!'

MRS MOSSOP (*surveying the room*) Well, that's as cheerful as I can make things look, poor dear!

AVONIA (*taking a look round, seriously*) It's pretty bright—if it wasn't   25
for the idea of Rose Trelawny having to economize!

MRS MOSSOP Ah—h!

AVONIA (*rising*) That's what I can't swallow. (*Sticking her irons° in the fire angrily*) One room! And on the second floor! (*Turning to Mrs Mossop*) Of course, Gadd and me are one-room people   30
too—and on the same floor; but then Gadd is so popular *out* of the theatre, Mrs Mossop—he's obliged to spend such a load of money at The Clown—

MRS MOSSOP (*who has been dusting the bookcase, coming to the table*) Mrs Gadd, dearie, I'm sure I'm not in the least inquisitive; no one   35
could accuse me of it—but I should like to know just one thing.

AVONIA (*testing her irons upon a sheet of paper which she takes from the table*) What's that?

MRS MOSSOP Why *have* they been and cut down Miss Trelawny's salary at the 'Wells'?   40

AVONIA (*hesitatingly*) H'm, everybody's chattering about it; you could get to hear easily enough—

MRS MOSSOP Oh, I dare say.

AVONIA So I don't mind. Poor Rose! They tell her she can't act now, Mrs Mossop.   45

MRS MOSSOP Can't act!

AVONIA No, dear old girl, she's lost it; it's gone from her—the trick of it—

259

Tom enters by the door on the right, carrying a table-cover° of a bright pattern

TOM (*coming upon Mrs Mossop, disconcerted*) Oh—!

MRS MOSSOP My first-floor table-cover!   50

TOM Y—y—yes. (*Exchanging the table-covers*) I thought, as the Telfers have departed, and as their late sitting-room is at present vacant, that Miss Trelawny might enjoy the benefit—hey?

MRS MOSSOP (*snatching up the old table-cover*) Well, I never—!
She goes out

AVONIA (*curling her hair, at the mirror over the mantelpiece*) I say,   55
Tom, I wonder if I've done wrong—

TOM It all depends upon whether you've had the chance.

AVONIA I've told Mrs Mossop the reason they've reduced Rose's salary.

TOM You needn't.   60

AVONIA She had only to ask any other member of the company—

TOM To have found one who could have kept silent!

AVONIA (*remorsefully*) Oh, I could burn myself!

TOM Besides, it isn't true.

AVONIA What—?   65

TOM That Rose Trelawny is no longer up to her work.

AVONIA (*sadly*) Oh, Tom!

TOM It isn't the fact, I say!

AVONIA Isn't it the fact that ever since Rose returned from Cavendish Square—?   70

TOM She has been reserved, subdued, ladylike—

AVONIA (*shrilly*) She was always ladylike!

TOM I'm aware of that!

AVONIA Well, then, what do you mean by—?

TOM (*in a rage, turning away*) Oh—!   75

AVONIA (*heating her irons again*) The idea!

TOM (*cooling down*) She was always a ladylike *actress*, on the stage and off it, but now she has developed into a—(*At a loss*) into a—

AVONIA (*scornfully*) Ha!

TOM Into a ladylike human being. These fools at the 'Wells'! Can't   80
act, can't she! No, she can no longer *spout*, she can no longer *ladle*,
the vapid trash, the—the—the turgid rodomontade°—

AVONIA (*doubtfully*) You'd better be careful of your language,
Wrench.

TOM (*with a twinkle in his eye, mopping his brow*) You're a married   85
woman, 'Vonia—

AVONIA (*holding her irons to her cheek, modestly*)   I know, but still—

TOM   Yes, deep down in the well of that girl's nature there has been lying a little, bright, clear pool of genuine refinement, girlish simplicity. And now the bucket has been lowered by love; experi-   90 ence has turned the handle; and up comes the crystal to the top, pure and sparkling. Why, her broken engagement to poor young Gower has really been the making of her! It has transformed her! Can't act, can't she! (*Drawing a long breath*) How she would play Dora in my comedy!   95

AVONIA   Ho, that comedy!

TOM   How she would murmur those love-scenes!

AVONIA   Murder—!

TOM (*testily*)   Murmur. (*Partly to himself*) Do you know, 'Vonia, I had Rose in my mind when I imagined Dora—?   100

AVONIA   Ha, ha! You astonish me.

TOM (*sitting*)   And Arthur Gower when I wrote the character of Gerald, Dora's lover. (*In a low voice*) Gerald and Dora—Rose and Arthur—Gerald and Dora. (*Suddenly*) 'Vonia—!

AVONIA (*singeing her hair*)   Ah—! Oh, lor'! What now?   105

TOM   I wish you could keep a secret.

AVONIA   Why, can't I?

TOM   Haven't you just been gossiping with Mother Mossop?

AVONIA (*behind his chair, breathlessly, her eyes bolting*)   A secret, Tom?   110

TOM (*nodding*)   I should like to share it with you, because—you are fond of her too—

AVONIA   Ah—!

TOM   And because the possession of it is worrying me. But there, I can't trust you.   115

AVONIA   Mr Wrench!

TOM   No, you're a warm-hearted woman, 'Vonia, but you're a sieve.

AVONIA (*going down upon her knees beside him*)   I swear! By all my hopes, Tom Wrench, of hitting 'em as Prince Charming° in the coming pantomime, I swear I will not divulge, leave alone tell a   120 living soul, any secret you may entrust to me, or let me know of, concerning Rose Trelawny of the 'Wells'. Amen!

TOM (*in her ear*)   'Vonia, *I know where Arthur Gower is.*

AVONIA   *Is!* Isn't he still in London?

TOM (*producing a letter mysteriously*)   No. When Rose stuck to her   125 refusal to see him—listen—mind, not a word—!

AVONIA   By all my hopes—!

TOM (*checking her*) All right, all right! (*Reading*) 'Theatre Royal, Bristol. Friday—'

AVONIA Theatre Royal, Br—! 130

TOM Be quiet! (*Reading*) 'My dear Mr Wrench, A whole week, and not a line from you to tell me how Miss Trelawny is. When you are silent I am sleepless at night and a haggard wretch during the day. Young Mr Kirby, our Walking Gentleman, has been unwell, and the management has given me temporarily some of his 135 business to play—'

AVONIA Arthur Gower—!

TOM Will you—? (*Reading*) 'Last night I was allowed to appear as Careless in *The School for Scandal*.° Miss Mason, the Lady Teazle, complimented me, but the men said I lacked vigour'—the old 140 cry!—'and so this morning I am greatly depressed. But I will still persevere, as long as you can assure me that no presuming fellow is paying attention to Miss Trelawny. Oh, how badly she treated me—!'

AVONIA (*following the reading of the letter*) 'How badly she treated 145 me—!'

TOM 'I will never forgive her—only love her—'

AVONIA 'Only love her—'

TOM 'Only love her, and hope I may some day become a great actor, and, like herself, a gypsy. Yours very gratefully, Arthur 150 Gordon.'

AVONIA In the Profession!

TOM Bolted from Cavendish Square—went down to Bristol—

AVONIA How did he manage it all? (*Tom taps his breast proudly*) But isn't Rose to be told? Why shouldn't she be told? 155

TOM She has hurt the boy, stung him to the quick, and he's proud.

AVONIA But she loves him now that she believes he has forgotten her. She only half loved him before. She loves him!

TOM Serve her right.

AVONIA Oh, Tom, is she never to know? 160

TOM (*folding the letter carefully*) Some day, when he begins to make strides.

AVONIA Strides! He's nothing but General Utility at present?

TOM (*putting the letter in his pocket*) No.

AVONIA And how long have you been that? 165

TOM Ten years.

AVONIA (*with a little screech*) Ah—h—h! She ought to be told!

TOM (*seizing her wrist*) Woman, you won't—!

AVONIA (*raising her disengaged hand*) By all my hopes of hitting 'em—!   170

TOM All right, I believe you. (*Listening*) Sssh!
> *They rise and separate, he moving to the fire, she to the right, as Rose enters. Rose is now a grave, dignified, somewhat dreamy young woman*

ROSE (*looking from Tom to Avonia*) Ah—?

TOM and AVONIA Good-morning.

ROSE (*kissing Avonia*) Visitors!

AVONIA My fire's so black—(*Showing her irons*) I thought you   175
wouldn't mind—

ROSE (*removing her gloves*) Of course not. (*Seeing the table-cover*)
Oh—!

TOM Mrs Mossop asked me to bring that upstairs. It was in the
Telfers' room, you know, and she fancied—   180

ROSE How good of her! Thanks, Tom. (*Taking off her hat and mantle*)
Poor Mr and Mrs Telfer! They still wander mournfully about the
'Wells'; they can get nothing to do.
> *Carrying her hat and umbrella, she disappears through the curtains*

TOM (*to Avonia, in a whisper, across the room*) The Telfers—!

AVONIA Eh?   185

TOM She's been giving 'em money.

AVONIA Yes.

TOM Damn!

ROSE (*reappearing*) What are you saying about me?

AVONIA I was wondering whether you'd lend me that belt you   190
bought for Ophelia; to wear during the first two or three weeks of
the pantomime—

ROSE Certainly, 'Vonia, to wear throughout—

AVONIA (*embracing her*) No, it's too good; I'd rather fake one for the
rest of the time. (*Looking into her face*) What's the matter?   195

ROSE I will make you a present of the belt, 'Vonia, if you will accept
it. I bought it when I came back to the 'Wells', thinking everything
would go on as before. But—it's of no use; they tell me I cannot
act effectively any longer—

TOM (*indignantly*) Effectively—!   200

ROSE First, as you know, they reduce my salary—

TOM and AVONIA (*with clenched hands*) Yes!

ROSE And now, this morning—(*Sitting*) You can guess—

AVONIA (*hoarsely*) Got your notice?

ROSE Yes.   205
TOM and AVONIA Oh—h—h!
ROSE (*after a little pause*) Poor mother! I hope she doesn't see.
    Overwhelmed, Avonia and Tom sit
    I was running through Blanche, my old part in *The Pedlar of
    Marseilles*, when Mr Burroughs spoke to me. It is true I was doing
    it tamely, but—it is such nonsense.   210
TOM Hear, hear!
ROSE And then, that poor little song I used to sing on the bridge—
AVONIA (*singing, softly*) 'Ever of thee I'm fondly dreaming—'
TOM and AVONIA (*singing*) 'Thy gentle voice my spirit can cheer.'
ROSE I told Mr Burroughs I should cut it out. So ridiculously   215
    inappropriate!
TOM And that—did it?
ROSE (*smiling at him*) That did it.
AVONIA (*kneeling beside her, and embracing her tearfully*) My ducky!
    Oh, but there are other theatres besides the 'Wells'—   220
ROSE For me? Only where the same trash is acted.
AVONIA (*with a sob*) But a few months ago you l—l—liked your work.
ROSE Yes—(*Dreamily*) And then I went to Cavendish Square, en-
    gaged to Arthur—
    Tom rises and leans upon the mantelpiece, looking into the fire
    How badly I behaved in Cavendish Square! How unlike a young   225
    lady! What if the old folks *were* overbearing and tyrannical, Arthur
    could be gentle with them. 'They have not many more years in
    this world', he said—dear boy!—'and anything we can do to make
    them happy—' And what *did* I do? *There* was a chance for me—to
    be patient, and womanly; and I proved to them that I was nothing   230
    but—an actress.
AVONIA (*rising, hurt but still tearful*) It doesn't follow, because one is
    a—
ROSE (*rising*) Yes, 'Vonia, it does! We are only dolls, partly human,
    with mechanical limbs that *will* fall into stagey postures, and heads 235
    stuffed with sayings out of rubbishy plays. It isn't *the* world we live
    in, merely *a* world—such a queer little one! I was less than a month
    in Cavendish Square, and very few people came there; but they
    were *real* people—*real*! For a month I lost the smell of gas and
    oranges, and the hurry and noise, and the dirt and the slang, and   240
    the clownish joking, at the 'Wells'. I didn't realize at the time the
    change that was going on in me; I didn't realize it till I came back.
    And then, by degrees, I discovered what had happened—

> *Tom is now near her. She takes his hand and drops her head*
> *upon Avonia's shoulder*

(*Wearily*) Oh, Tom! Oh, 'Vonia—!

> *From the next room comes the sound of the throwing about of*
> *heavy objects, and of Gadd's voice uttering loud imprecations*

(*Alarmed*) Oh—!   245

AVONIA (*listening attentively*) Sounds like Ferdy.—

> *She goes to the centre door*

(*At the keyhole*) Ferdy! Ain't you well, darling?

GADD (*on the other side of the door*) Avonia!

AVONIA I'm in Miss Trelawny's room.

GADD Ah—?   250

AVONIA (*to Rose and Tom*) Now, what's put Ferdy out?

> *Gadd enters with a wild look*

Ferdinand!

TOM Anything wrong, Gadd?

GADD Wrong! wrong! (*Sitting*) What d'ye think?

AVONIA Tell us!   255

GADD I have been asked to appear in the pantomime.

AVONIA (*shocked*) Oh, Ferdy! You!

GADD I, a serious actor, if ever there was one; a poetic actor—!

AVONIA What part, Ferdy?

GADD The insult, the bitter insult! The gross indignity!   260

AVONIA What part, Ferdy?

GADD I have not been seen in pantomime for years, not since I shook
the dust of the T.R. Stockton° from my feet.

AVONIA Ferdy, what part?

GADD I simply looked at Burroughs, when he preferred his request, 265
and swept from the theatre.

AVONIA What part, Ferdy?

GADD A part, too, which is seen for a moment at the opening of the
pantomime, and not again till its close.

AVONIA Ferdy.   270

GADD Eh?

AVONIA What part?

GADD A character called the Demon of Discontent.°

> *Rose turns away to the fireplace; Tom curls himself up on the*
> *sofa and is seen to shake with laughter*

AVONIA (*walking about indignantly*) Oh! (*Returning to Gadd*) Oh, it's
a rotten part! Rose, dear, I assure you, as artist to artist, that part 275
is absolutely rotten. (*To Gadd*) You won't play it, darling?

GADD (*rising*) Play it! I would see the 'Wells' in ashes first.

AVONIA We shall lose our engagements, Ferdy. I know Burroughs; we shall be out, both of us.

GADD Of course we shall. D'ye think I have not counted the cost?   280

AVONIA (*putting her hand in his*) I don't mind, dear—for the sake of your position—(*Struck by a sudden thought*) Oh—!

GADD What—?

AVONIA There now—we haven't put by!

> *There is a knock at the door*

ROSE Who is that?   285

COLPOYS (*outside the door*) Is Gadd here, Miss Trelawny?

ROSE Yes.

COLPOYS I want to see him.

GADD Wrench, I'll trouble you. Ask Mr Colpoys whether he approaches me as a friend, an acquaintance, or in his capacity of   290
stage-manager at the 'Wells'—the tool of Burroughs.

> *Tom opens the door slightly. Gadd and Avonia join Rose at the*
> *fireplace*

TOM (*at the door, solemnly*) Colpoys, are you here as Gadd's bosom
friend, or as a mere tool of Burroughs?

> *An inaudible colloquy follows between Tom and Colpoys. Toms's*
> *head is outside the door; his legs are seen to move convulsively,*
> *and the sound of suppressed laughter is heard*

GADD (*turning*) Well, well?

TOM (*closing the door sharply, and facing Gadd with great seriousness*)   295
He is here as the tool of Burroughs.

GADD I will receive him.

> *Tom admits Colpoys, who carries a mean-looking 'part',° and a*
> *letter*

COLPOYS (*after formally bowing to the ladies*) Oh, Gadd, Mr Burroughs instructs me to offer you this part in the pantomime.
(*Handing the part to Gadd*) Demon of Discontent.   300

> *Gadd takes the part and flings it to the ground; Avonia picks it*
> *up and reads it*

You refuse it?

GADD I do. (*With dignity*) Acquaint Mr Burroughs with my decision,
and add that I hope his pantomime will prove an utterly mirthless
one. May Boxing Night,° to those unfortunate enough to find
themselves in the theatre, long remain a dismal memory; and may   305
succeeding audiences, scanty and dissatisfied—!

> *Colpoys presents Gadd with the letter. Gadd opens it and reads*

I leave. (*Sitting*) The Romeo, the Orlando, the Clifford°—leaves!

AVONIA (*coming to* GADD, *indicating some lines in the part*) Ferdy, this ain't so bad. (*Reading*)

> *I'm Discontent! From Orkney's isle to Dover*
> *To make men's bile bile-over I endover—*°

GADD 'Vonia! (*Taking the part from Avonia; with mingled surprise and pleasure*) Ho, ho! No, that's not bad. (*Reading*)   310

> *Tempers, though sweet, I whip up to a lather,*
> *Make wives hate husbands, sons wish fathers farther.*

'Vonia, there's something to lay hold of here! I'll think this over. (*Rising, addressing Colpoys*) Gus, I have thought this over. I play it.
> *They all gather round him, and congratulate him. Avonia embraces and kisses him*

TOM and COLPOYS That's right!

ROSE I'm very pleased, Ferdinand.   315

AVONIA (*tearfully*) Oh, Ferdy!

GADD (*in high spirits*) Egad, I play it! Gus, I'll stroll back with you to the 'Wells'. (*Shaking hands with Rose*) Miss Trelawny—!
> *Avonia accompanies Colpoys and Gadd to the door, clinging to Gadd, who is flourishing the part*

'Vonia, I see myself in this! (*Kissing her*) Steak for dinner!
> *Gadd and Colpoys go out. Tom shrieks with laughter*

AVONIA (*turning upon him, angrily and volubly*) Yes, I heard you with   320
Colpoys outside that door, if Gadd didn't. It's a pity, Mr Wrench, you can't find something better to do—!

ROSE (*pacifically*) Hush, hush, 'Vonia! Tom, assist me with my basket; I'll give 'Vonia her belt—
> *Tom and Rose go behind the curtains and presently emerge, carrying the dress-basket, which they deposit near the sofa*

AVONIA (*flouncing across the room*) Making fun of Gadd! An artist to   325
the roots of his hair! There's more talent in Gadd's little finger—!

ROSE (*rummaging among the contents of the basket*) 'Vonia, 'Vonia!

AVONIA And if Gadd *is* to play a demon in the pantomime, what do *you* figure as, Tom Wrench, among half-a-dozen other things? Why, as part of a dragon! Yes, and *which end*—?°   330

ROSE (*quietly to Tom*) Apologize to 'Vonia at once, Tom.

TOM (*meekly*) Mrs Gadd, I beg your pardon.

AVONIA (*coming to him and kissing him*) Granted, Tom; but you should be a little more considerate—

ROSE (*holding up the belt*) Here—!   335

AVONIA (*taking the belt, ecstatically*) Oh, isn't it lovely! Rose, you
  dear! You sweet thing!
          *She sings a few bars of the Jewel song from 'Faust',° then rushes
          at Rose and embraces her*
  I'm going to try my dress on, to show Mrs Burroughs. Come and
  help me into it. I'll unlock my door on my side—
          Tom politely opens the door for her to pass out
  Thank you, Tom—(*Kissing him again*) Only you should be more   340
  considerate toward Gadd—
          She disappears

TOM (*calling after her*) I will be; I will—(*Shutting the door*) Ha, ha, ha!

ROSE (*smiling*) Hush! Poor 'Vonia! (*Mending the fire*) Excuse me,
  Tom—have you a fire upstairs, in your room, today?

TOM Er—n—not today—it's Saturday. I never have a fire on a   345
  Saturday.

ROSE (*coming to him*) Why not?

TOM (*looking away from her*) Don't know—creatures of habit—

ROSE (*gently touching his coat sleeve*) Because if you would like to
  smoke your pipe by my fire while I'm with 'Vonia—   350
          *The key is heard to turn in the lock of the door of the further
          room*

AVONIA (*from the further room*) It's unlocked.

ROSE I'm coming.
          *She unbolts the door on her side, and goes into Avonia's room,
          shutting the door behind her. The lid of the dress-basket is open,
          showing the contents; a pair of little satin shoes lie at the top.
          Tom takes up one of the shoes and presses it to his lips. There is
          a knock at the door on the right. He returns the shoe to the
          basket, closes the lid, and walks away*

TOM Yes?
          The door opens slightly and Imogen is heard

IMOGEN (*outside*) Is that you, Wrench?

TOM Hullo!   355
          Imogen, in outdoor costume, enters breathlessly

IMOGEN (*closing the door, speaking rapidly and excitedly*) Mossop said
  you were in Rose's room—

TOM (*shaking hands with her*) She'll be here in a few minutes.

IMOGEN It's you I want. Let me sit down.

TOM (*going to the armchair*) Here—   360

IMOGEN (*sitting on the right of the table, panting*) Not near the fire—

TOM What's up?

IMOGEN Oh, Wrench! P'r'aps my fortune's made!

TOM (*quite calmly*) Congratulate you, Jenny.

IMOGEN Do be quiet; don't make such a racket. You see, things   365
haven't been going at all satisfactorily at the Olympic lately.
There's Miss Puddifant—

TOM I know—no lady.

IMOGEN *How* do you know?

TOM Guessed.   370

IMOGEN Quite right; and a thousand other annoyances. And at last
I took it into my head to consult Mr Clandon, who married an
aunt of mine and lives at Streatham, and he'll lend me five
hundred pounds.

TOM What for?   375

IMOGEN Towards taking a theatre.

TOM (*dubiously*) Five hundred—

IMOGEN It's all he's good for, and he won't advance that unless I can
get a further five, or eight, hundred from some other quarter.

TOM What theatre!   380

IMOGEN The Pantheon° happens to be empty.

TOM Yes; it's been that for the last twenty years.

IMOGEN Don't throw wet blankets—I mean—(*Referring to her
tablets,° which she carries in her muff*) I've got it all worked out in
black and white. There's a deposit required on account of rent—   385
two hundred pounds. Cleaning the theatre—(*Looking at Tom*)
What do *you* say?

TOM Cleaning *that* theatre?

IMOGEN I say, another two hundred.

TOM That would remove the top layer—   390

IMOGEN Cost of producing the opening play, five hundred pounds.
Balance for emergencies, three hundred. You generally have a
balance for emergencies.

TOM You generally have the emergencies, if not the balance!

IMOGEN Now, the question is, will five hundred produce the play?   395

TOM What play?

IMOGEN Your play.

TOM (*quietly*) My—

IMOGEN Your comedy.

TOM (*turning to the fire, in a low voice*) Rubbish!   400

IMOGEN Well, Mr Clandon thinks it *isn't*. (*He faces her sharply*) I
gave it to him to read, and he—well, he's quite taken with it.

TOM (*walking about, his hands in his pockets, his head down, agitatedly*)
    Clandon—Landon—what's his name—?

IMOGEN Tony Clandon—Anthony Clandon—   405

TOM (*choking*) He's a—he's a—

IMOGEN He's a hop-merchant.

TOM No, he's not—(*Sitting on the sofa, leaning his head on his hands*)
    He's a stunner.°

IMOGEN (*rising*) So you grasp the position. Theatre—manageress—   410
    author—play, found; and eight hundred pounds *wanted!*

TOM (*rising*) Oh, lord!

IMOGEN Who's got it?

TOM (*wildly*) The Queen's got it! Miss Burdett-Coutts° has got it!

IMOGEN Don't be a fool, Wrench. Do you remember old Mr   415
    Morfew, of Duncan Terrace? He used to take great interest in us
    all at the 'Wells'. *He* has money.

TOM He has gout; we don't see him now.

IMOGEN Gout! How lucky! That means he's at home. Will you run
    round to Duncan Terrace—?   420

TOM (*looking down at his clothes*) I!

IMOGEN Nonsense, Wrench; we're not asking him to advance money
    on your clothes.

TOM The clothes are the man, Jenny.

IMOGEN And the woman—?   425

TOM The face is the woman; there's the real inequality of the sexes.

IMOGEN I'll go! Is my face good enough?

TOM (*enthusiastically*) I should say so!

IMOGEN (*taking his hands*) Ha, ha! It has been in my possession
    longer than you have had your oldest coat, Tom!   430

TOM Make haste, Jenny!

IMOGEN (*running up to the door*) Oh, it will last till I get to Duncan
    Terrace. (*Turning*) Tom, you may have to read your play to Mr
    Morfew. Have you another copy? Uncle Clandon has mine.

TOM (*holding his head*) I think I have—I don't know—   435

IMOGEN Look for it! Find it! If Morfew wants to hear it, we must
    strike while the iron's hot.

TOM While the gold's hot!

IMOGEN and TOM Ha, ha, ha!
       Mrs Mossop enters, showing some signs of excitement

IMOGEN (*pushing her aside*) Oh, get out of the way, Mrs Mossop—   440
       Imogen departs

MRS MOSSOP Upon my—! (*To Tom*) A visitor for Miss Trelawny!
    Where's Miss Trelawny?

TOM With Mrs Gadd. Mossop!

MRS MOSSOP Don't bother me now—

TOM Mossop! The apartments vacated by the Telfers! Dare to let   445
'em without giving me the preference.

MRS MOSSOP You!

TOM (*seizing her hands and swinging her round*) I may be wealthy,
sweet Rebecca! (*Embracing her*) I may be rich and honoured!

MRS MOSSOP Oh, have done! (*Releasing herself*) My lodgers do take   450
such liberties—

TOM (*at the door, grandly*) Beccy, half a scuttle of coal, to start
with.
        He goes out, leaving the door slightly open

MRS MOSSOP (*knocking at the door of the further room*) Miss Trelawny,
my dear! Miss Trelawny!   455
        The door opens, a few inches

ROSE (*looking out*) Why, what a clatter you and Mr Wrench have
been making—!

MRS MOSSOP (*beckoning her mysteriously*) Come here, dear.

ROSE (*closing the door and entering the room wonderingly*) Eh?

MRS MOSSOP (*in awe*) Sir William Gower!   460

ROSE Sir William!

MRS MOSSOP Don't be vexed with me. 'I'll see if she's at home,' I
said. 'Oh, yes, woman, Miss Trelawny's at home,' said he, and
hobbled straight in. I've shut him in the Telfers' room—
        *There are three distinct raps, with a stick, at the right-hand
        door*

ROSE and MRS MOSSOP Oh—h!   465

ROSE (*faintly*) Open it.
        *Mrs Mossop opens the door, and Sir William enters. He is
        feebler, more decrepit, than when last seen. He wears a plaid°
        about his shoulders and walks with the aid of a stick*

MRS MOSSOP (*at the door*) Ah, and a sweet thing Miss Trelawny is—!

SIR WILLIAM (*turning to her*) Are you a relative?

MRS MOSSOP No, I am *not* a relative—!

SIR WILLIAM Go.   470
        She departs; he closes the door with the end of his stick
(*Facing Rose*) My mind is not commonly a wavering one, Miss
Trelawny, but it has taken me some time—months—to decide
upon calling on ye.

ROSE Won't you sit down?

SIR WILLIAM (*after a pause of hesitation, sitting upon the dress-basket*)   475
Ugh!

ROSE (*with quiet dignity*) Have we no chairs? Do we lack chairs here, Sir William?

    He gives her a quick, keen look, then rises and walks to the fire

SIR WILLIAM (*suddenly, bringing his stick down upon the table with violence*) My grandson! My grandson! Where is he?   480

ROSE Arthur—!

SIR WILLIAM I had but one.

ROSE Isn't he—in Cavendish Square—?

SIR WILLIAM Isn't he in Cavendish Square! No, he is not in Cavendish Square, as you know well.   485

ROSE Oh, I don't know—

SIR WILLIAM Tsch!

ROSE When did he leave you?

SIR WILLIAM Tsch!

ROSE When?   490

SIR WILLIAM He made his escape during the night, twenty-second of August last—(*Pointing his finger at her*) As you know well.

ROSE Sir William, I assure you—

SIR WILLIAM Tsch! (*Taking off his gloves*) How often does he write to ye?   495

ROSE He does not write to me. He did write day after day, two or three times a day, for about a week. That was in June, when I came back here. (*With drooping head*) He never writes now.

SIR WILLIAM Visits ye—?

ROSE No.   500

SIR WILLIAM Comes troubadouring—?

ROSE No, no, no. I have not seen him since that night. I refused to see him—(*With a catch in her breath*) Why, he may be—!

SIR WILLIAM (*fumbling in his pocket*) Ah, but he's not. He's alive—(*Producing a small packet of letters*) Arthur's alive—(*Advancing to her*) and full of his tricks still. His Great-Aunt Trafalgar receives a letter from him once a fortnight, posted in London—   505

ROSE (*holding out her hand for the letters*) Oh!

SIR WILLIAM (*putting them behind his back*) Hey!

ROSE (*faintly*) I thought you wished me to read them. (*He yields them to her grudgingly, she taking his hand and bending over it*) Ah, thank you.   510

SIR WILLIAM (*withdrawing his hand with a look of disrelish*) What are ye doing, madam? What are ye doing?

    He sits, producing his snuffbox; she sits, upon the basket, facing him, and opens the packet of letters

ROSE (*reading a letter*) 'To reassure you as to my well-being, I cause   515
this to be posted in London by a friend—'

SIR WILLIAM (*pointing a finger at her again, accusingly*) A friend!

ROSE (*looking up, with simple pride*) He would never call me *that*.
(*Reading*) 'I am in good bodily health, and as contented as a man
can be who has lost the woman he loves, and will love till his dying   520
day—' Ah—!

SIR WILLIAM Read no more! Return them to me! Give them to me,
ma'am! (*Rising, she restores the letters, meekly. He peers up into her
face*) What's come to ye? You are not so much of a vixen as you
were.   525

ROSE (*shaking her head*) No.

SIR WILLIAM (*suspiciously*) Less of the devil—?

ROSE Sir William, I am sorry for having been a vixen, and for all my
unruly conduct, in Cavendish Square. I humbly beg your, and
Miss Gower's, forgiveness.   530

SIR WILLIAM (*taking snuff, uncomfortably*) Pi—i—i—sh! Extraordinary change.

ROSE Aren't *you* changed, Sir William, now that you have lost him?

SIR WILLIAM I!

ROSE Don't you love him now, the more? (*His head droops a little, and   535
his hands wander to the brooch which secures his plaid*) Let me take
your shawl from you. You would catch cold when you go out—

> He allows her to remove the plaid, protesting during the process

SIR WILLIAM I'll not trouble ye, ma'am. Much obleeged to ye, but
I'll not trouble ye. (*Rising*) I'll not trouble ye—

> He walks away to the fireplace. She folds the plaid and lays it
> upon the sofa. He looks round, speaking in an altered tone

My dear, gypsying doesn't seem to be such a good trade with ye,   540
as it used to be by all accounts—

> The door of the further room opens and Avonia enters boldly, in
> the dress of a burlesque prince°—cotton-velvet shirt, edged with
> bullion trimming, a cap, white tights, ankle boots, etc.

AVONIA (*unconsciously*) How's this, Rose—?

SIR WILLIAM Ah—h—h—h!

ROSE Oh, go away, 'Vonia!

AVONIA Sir Gower! (*To Sir William*) Good-morning.   545
> She withdraws

SIR WILLIAM (*pacing the room, again very violent*) Yes! And these are
the associates you would have tempted my boy—my grandson—to
herd with! (*Flourishing his stick*) Ah—h—h—h!

ROSE (*sitting upon the basket, weakly*) That young lady doesn't live in
    that attire. She is preparing for the pantomime—   550

SIR WILLIAM (*standing over her*) And now he's gone; lured away, I
    suspect, by one of ye—(*Pointing to the door of Avonia's room*) by
    one of these harridans!—

    Avonia reappears defiantly

AVONIA Look here, Sir Gower—

ROSE (*rising*) Go, 'Vonia!   555

AVONIA (*to Sir William*) We've met before, if you remember, in
    Cavendish Square—

ROSE (*sitting again, helplessly*) Oh, Mrs Gadd—!

SIR WILLIAM Mistress! A married lady!

AVONIA Yes, I spent some of my honeymoon at your house—   560

SIR WILLIAM What!

AVONIA Excuse my dress; it's all in the way of my business. Just one
    word about Rose.

ROSE Please, 'Vonia—!

AVONIA (*to Sir William, who is glaring at her in horror*) Now, there's   565
    nothing to stare at, Sir Gower. If you must look anywhere in
    particular, look at that poor thing. A nice predicament you've
    brought her to!

SIR WILLIAM Sir—! (*Correcting himself*) Madam!

AVONIA You've brought her to beggary, amongst you. You've broken   570
    her heart; and, what's worse, you've made her genteel. She can't
    act, since she left your mansion; she can only mope about the stage
    with her eyes fixed like a person in a dream—dreaming of him, I
    suppose, and of what it is to be a lady. And first she's put upon
    half-salary; and then, today, she gets the sack—the entire sack, Sir   575
    Gower! So there's nothing left for her but to starve, or to make
    artificial flowers.° Miss Trelawny I'm speaking of! (*Going to Rose,*
    and embracing her) Our Rose! Our Trelawny! (*To Rose, breaking*
    down) Excuse me for interfering, ducky. (*Retiring, in tears*) Good-
    day, Sir Gower.   580

    She goes out

SIR WILLIAM (*After a pause, to Rose*) Is this—the case?

ROSE (*standing, and speaking in a low voice*) Yes. As you have noticed,
    fortune has turned against me, rather.

SIR WILLIAM (*penitently*) I—I'm sorry, ma'am. I—I believe ye've
    kept your word to us concerning Arthur. I—I—   585

ROSE (*not heeding him, looking before her, dreamily*) My mother knew
    how fickle fortune could be to us gypsies. One of the greatest
    actors that ever lived warned her of that—

SIR WILLIAM Miss Gower will also feel extremely—extremely—
ROSE Kean° once warned mother of that.   590
SIR WILLIAM (*in an altered tone*) Kean? Which Kean?°
ROSE Edmund Kean. My mother acted with Edmund Kean when
she was a girl.
SIR WILLIAM (*approaching her slowly, speaking in a queer voice*) With
Kean? With Kean!   595
ROSE Yes.
SIR WILLIAM (*at her side, in a whisper*) My dear, I—I've seen
Edmund Kean.
ROSE Yes?
SIR WILLIAM A young man then, I was; quite different from the man   600
I am now—impulsive, excitable. Kean! (*Drawing a deep breath*) Ah,
he was a *splendid* gypsy!
ROSE (*looking down at the dress-basket*) I've a little fillet° in there that
my mother wore as Cordelia to Kean's Lear°—
SIR WILLIAM I may have seen your mother also. I was somewhat   605
different in those days—
ROSE (*kneeling at the basket and opening it*) And the Order and chain,
and the sword, he wore in Richard.° He gave them to my father;
I've always prized them.
> *She drags to the surface a chain with an Order attached to it,*
> *and a sword-belt and sword—all very theatrical and tawdry—*
> *and a little gold fillet. She hands him the chain*

That's the Order.   610
SIR WILLIAM (*handling it tenderly*) Kean! God bless me!
ROSE (*holding up the fillet*) My poor mother's fillet.
SIR WILLIAM (*looking at it*) I may have seen her. (*Thoughtfully*) I was
a young man then. (*Looking at Rose steadily*) Put it on, my dear.
> *She goes to the mirror and puts on the fillet*

(*Examining the Order*) Lord bless us! How he stirred me! How   615
he—!
> *He puts the chain over his shoulders. Rose turns to him*

ROSE (*advancing to him*) There!
SIR WILLIAM (*looking at her*) Cordelia! Cordelia—with Kean!
ROSE (*adjusting the chain upon him*) This should hang so. (*Returning
to the basket and taking up the sword-belt and sword*) Look!   620
SIR WILLIAM (*handling them*) Kean! (*To her, in a whisper*) I'll tell ye!
I'll tell ye! When I saw him as Richard—I was young and a
fool—I'll tell ye—he almost fired me with an ambition to—to—
(*Fumbling with the belt*) How did he carry this?
ROSE (*fastening the belt, with the sword, round him*) In this way—   625

SIR WILLIAM Ah!

>*He paces the stage, growling and muttering, and walking with a*
>*limp and one shoulder hunched. She watches him, seriously*

Ah! He was a little man too! I remember him as if it were last
night! I remember—(*Pausing and looking at her fixedly*) My dear,
your prospects in life have been injured by your unhappy acquaintanceship with my grandson.   630

ROSE (*gazing into the fire*) Poor Arthur's prospects in life—what of
them?

SIR WILLIAM (*testily*) Tsch, tsch, tsch!

ROSE If I knew where he is—!

SIR WILLIAM Miss Trelawny, if you cannot act, you cannot earn   635
your living.

ROSE How is he earning *his* living?

SIR WILLIAM And if you cannot earn your living, you must be
provided for.

ROSE (*turning to him*) Provided for?   640

SIR WILLIAM Miss Gower was kind enough to bring me here in a
cab. She and I will discuss plans for making provision for ye while
driving home.

ROSE (*advancing to him*) Oh, I beg you will do no such thing, Sir
William.   645

SIR WILLIAM Hey!

ROSE I could not accept any help from you or Miss Gower.

SIR WILLIAM You must! You shall!

ROSE I will not.

SIR WILLIAM (*touching the Order and the sword*) Ah!—Yes, I—I'll   650
buy these of ye, my dear—

ROSE Oh, no, no! Not for hundreds of pounds! Please take them off!

>*There is a hurried knocking at the door*

SIR WILLIAM (*startled*) Who's that? (*Struggling with the chain and
belt*) Remove these—!

>*The handle is heard to rattle. Sir William disappears behind the*
>*curtains. Imogen opens the door and looks in*

IMOGEN (*seeing only Rose, and coming to her and embracing her*) Rose 655
darling, where is Tom Wrench?

ROSE He was here not long since—

IMOGEN (*going to the door and calling, desperately*) Tom! Tom
Wrench! Mr Wrench!

ROSE Is anything amiss?   660

IMOGEN (*shrilly*) Tom!

ROSE Imogen!

IMOGEN (*returning to Rose*) Oh, my dear, forgive my agitation—!

    Tom enters, buoyantly, flourishing the manuscript of his play

TOM I've found it! At the bottom of a box—'deeper than did ever
    plummet sound—'!° (*To Imogen*) Eh? What's the matter?   665

IMOGEN Oh, Tom, old Mr Morfew—!

TOM (*blankly*) Isn't he willing—?

IMOGEN (*with a gesture of despair*) I don't know. He's dead.

TOM No!

IMOGEN Three weeks ago. Oh, what a chance he has missed!   670

    Tom bangs his manuscript down upon the table savagely

ROSE What is it, Tom? Imogen, what is it?

IMOGEN (*pacing the room*) I can think of no one else—

TOM Done again!

IMOGEN We shall lose it, of course—

ROSE Lose what?   675

TOM The opportunity—her opportunity, *my* opportunity, *your*
    opportunity, Rose.

ROSE (*coming to him*) *My* opportunity, Tom?

TOM (*pointing to the manuscript*) My play—my comedy—my young-
    est born! Jenny has a theatre—could have one—has five hundred   680
    towards it, put down by a man who believes in my comedy, God
    bless him! The only fellow who has ever believed—?

ROSE Oh, Tom! (*Turning to Imogen*) Oh, Imogen!

IMOGEN My dear, five hundred! We want another five, at least.

ROSE Another five!   685

IMOGEN Or eight.

TOM And you are to play the part of Dora. Isn't she, Jenny—I mean,
    wasn't she?

IMOGEN Certainly. Just the sort of simple little Miss you *could* play
    now, Rose. And we thought that old Mr Morfew would help us in   690
    the speculation. Speculation! It's a dead certainty!

TOM *Dead* certainty? Poor Morfew!

IMOGEN And here we are, stuck fast—!

TOM (*sitting upon the dress-basket dejectedly*) And they'll expect me to
    rehearse that dragon tomorrow with enthusiasm.   695

ROSE (*putting her arm around his shoulder*) Never mind, Tom.

TOM No, I won't—(*Taking her hand*) Oh, Rose—! (*Looking up at her*)
    Oh, Dora—!

    *Sir William, divested of his theatrical trappings, comes from
    behind the curtain*

IMOGEN Oh—!

TOM (*rising*) Eh?   700

ROSE (*retreating*) Sir William Gower, Tom—

SIR WILLIAM (*to Tom*) I had no wish to be disturbed, sir, and I
withdrew—(*Bowing to Imogen*) when that lady entered the room. I
have been a party, it appears, to a consultation upon a matter of
business. (*To Tom*) Do I understand, sir, that you have been   705
defeated in some project which would have served the interests of
Miss Trelawny?

TOM Y—y—yes, sir.

SIR WILLIAM Mr Wicks—

TOM Wrench—   710

SIR WILLIAM Tsch! Sir, it would give me pleasure—it would give
my grandson, Mr Arthur Gower, pleasure—to be able to aid Miss
Trelawny at the present moment.

TOM S—s—sir William, w—w—would you like to hear my play—?

SIR WILLIAM (*sharply*) Hey! (*Looking round*) Ho, ho!   715

TOM My comedy?

SIR WILLIAM (*cunningly*) So ye think I might be induced to fill the
office ye designed for the late Mr—Mr—

IMOGEN Morfew.

SIR WILLIAM Morfew, eh?   720

TOM N—n—no, sir.

SIR WILLIAM No! No!

IMOGEN (*shrilly*) Yes!

SIR WILLIAM (*after a short pause, quietly*) Read your play, sir. (*Pointing
to a chair at the table*) Sit down. (*To Rose and Imogen*) Sit down.   725

> Tom goes to the chair indicated. Miss Gower's voice is heard
> outside the door

MISS GOWER (*outside*) William!

> Rose opens the door; Miss Gower enters

Oh, William, what has become of you? Has anything dreadful
happened?

SIR WILLIAM Sit down, Trafalgar. This gentleman is about to read
a comedy. A cheer! (*Testily*) Are there no cheers here!   730

> Rose brings a chair and places it for Miss Gower beside Sir
> William's chair

Sit down.

MISS GOWER (*sitting, bewildered*) William, is all this—quite—?

SIR WILLIAM (*sitting*) Yes, Trafalgar, quite in place—quite in
place—

> *Imogen sits as Colpoys and Gadd swagger in at the door,*
> *Colpoys smoking a pipe, Gadd a large cigar*

(*To Tom, referring to Gadd and Colpoys*) Friends of yours?   735

TOM Yes, Sir William.

SIR WILLIAM (*to Gadd and Colpoys*) Sit down. (*Imperatively*) Sit down and be silent.

> *Gadd and Colpoys seat themselves upon the sofa, like men in a*
> *dream. Rose sits on the dress-basket*

AVONIA (*opening her door slightly, in an anxious voice*) Rose—!

SIR WILLIAM Come in, ma'am, come in!   740

> *Avonia, still in her pantomime dress, enters, coming to Rose*

Sit down, ma'am, and be silent!

> *Avonia sits beside Rose, next to Miss Gower*

MISS GOWER (*in horror*) Oh—h—h—h!

SIR WILLIAM (*restraining her*) Quite in place, Trafalgar; quite in place. (*To Tom*) Now, sir!

TOM (*opening his manuscript and reading*) 'Life,° a comedy, by   745 Thomas Wrench—'

CURTAIN

Act Four

Scene One

The scene represents the stage of a theatre (the Pantheon),° a few days later, with the proscenium arch and the dark and empty auditorium in the distance. The stage extends a few feet beyond the line of the proscenium, and is terminated by a row of old-fashioned footlights with metal reflectors. In the wall on the left is an open doorway supposed to admit to the green-room. Right and left of the stage are the 'P' and 'OP'° and the first and second entrances,° with wings running in grooves, according to the old fashion. Against the walls are some 'flats'.° Just below the footlights is a T-light,° burning gas, and below this the prompt-table. On the right of the prompt-table is a chair, and on the left another. Against the edge of the proscenium arch is another chair; and nearer, on the right, stands a large throne-chair, with a gilt frame and red velvet seat, now much dilapidated. On the left, in the 'second entrance', there are a 'property' stool, a table, and a chair, all of a similar style to the throne-chair and in like condition; and in the centre, as if placed there for the purpose of rehearsal, are a small circular table and a chair. On this table is a work-basket containing a ball of wool and a pair of knitting-needles; and on the prompt-table there is a book. A faded and ragged green baize covers the floor of the stage. The wings, and the flats and borders, suggest by their appearance a theatre fallen somewhat into decay. The light is a dismal one, but it is relieved by a shaft of sunlight entering through a window in the flies on the right. Mrs Telfer is seated upon the throne-chair, in an attitude of dejection. Telfer enters from the green-room

TELFER (*coming to her*) Is that you, Violet?

MRS TELFER Is the reading over?°

TELFER Almost. My part is confined to the latter 'alf of the second act; so being close to the green-room door—(*With a sigh*) I stole away.

MRS TELFER It affords you no opportunity, James?

TELFER (*shaking his head*) A mere fragment.

MRS TELFER (*rising*) Well, but a few good speeches to a man of your stamp—

TELFER Yes, but this is so line-y, Violet; so very line-y.° And what   10
d'ye think the character is described as?

MRS TELFER What?

TELFER 'An old, stagey, out-of-date actor'.

They stand looking at each other for a moment, silently

MRS TELFER (*falteringly*) Will you—be able—to get near it, James?

TELFER (*looking away from her*) I dare say—   15

MRS TELFER (*laying a hand upon his shoulder*) That's all right, then.

TELFER And you—what have they called you for, if you're not in the
play? They 'ave not dared to suggest understudy?

MRS TELFER (*playing with her fingers*) They don't ask me to act at
all, James.   20

TELFER Don't ask you—!

MRS TELFER Miss Parrott offers me the position of wardrobe
mistress.

TELFER Violet—!

MRS TELFER Hush!   25

TELFER Let us both go home.

MRS TELFER (*restraining him*) No, let us remain. We've been idle six
months, and I can't bear to see you without your watch and all
your comforts about you.°

TELFER (*pointing toward the green-room*) And so this newfangled   30
stuff, and these dandified people, are to push us, and such as us,
from our stools!

MRS TELFER Yes, James, just as some other new fashion will, in
course of time, push *them* from their stools.

From the green-room comes the sound of a slight clapping of
hands, followed by a murmur of voices. The Telfers move away.
Imogen, elaborately dressed, enters from the green-room and goes
leisurely to the prompt-table. She is followed by Tom, manu-
script in hand, smarter than usual in appearance; and he by
O'dwyer—an excitable Irishman of about forty, with an ex-
travagant head of hair—who carries a small bundle of 'parts' in
brown-paper covers. Tom and O'dwyer join Imogen

O'DWYER (*to Tom*) Mr Wrench, I congratulate ye; I have that   35
honour, sir. Your piece will do, sir; it will take the town, mark
me.

TOM Thank you, O'Dwyer.

IMOGEN Look at the sunshine! There's a good omen, at any rate.

O'DWYER Oh, sunshine's nothing. (*To Tom*) But did ye observe the   40
gloom on their faces whilst ye were readin'?

IMOGEN (*anxiously*) Yes, they did look glum.

O'DWYER Glum! It might have been a funeral! There's a healthy
prognostication for ye, if ye loike! it's infallible.

> *A keen-faced gentleman and a lady enter, from the green-room,
> and stroll across the stage to the right, where they lean against
> the wings and talk. Then two young gentlemen enter, and Rose
> follows. (Note: The actors and the actress appearing for the first
> time in this act, as members of the Pantheon Company, are
> outwardly greatly superior to the Gadds, the telfers, and
> Colpoys)*

ROSE (*shaking hands with Telfer*) Why didn't you sit near me, Mr   45
Telfer? (*Going to Mrs Telfer*) Fancy our being together again, and
at the West End! (*To Telfer*) Do you like the play?

TELFER Like it! There's not a speech in it, my dear—not a real
speech; nothing to dig your teeth into—

O'DWYER (*allotting the parts, under the direction of Tom and Imogen*)   50
Mr Mortimer!

> *One of the young gentlemen advances and receives his part from
> O'Dwyer, and retires, reading it*

Mr Denzil!

> *The keen-faced gentleman takes his part, then joins Imogen on
> her left and talks to her. The lady now has something to say to
> the solitary young gentleman*

TOM (*to O'Dwyer, quietly, handing him a part*) Miss Brewster.

O'DWYER (*beckoning to the lady, who does not observe him, her back
being towards him*) Come here, my love.   55

TOM (*to O'Dwyer*) No, no, O'Dwyer—not your 'love'.

O'DWYER (*perplexed*) Not?

TOM No.

O'DWYER No?

TOM Why, you are meeting her this morning for the first time.   60

O'DWYER That's true enough. (*Approaching the lady and handing her
the part*) Miss Brewster.

LADY Much obliged.

O'DWYER (*quietly to her*) It 'll fit ye like a glove, darlin'.

> *The lady sits, conning her part. O'Dwyer returns to the table*

TELFER (*to Rose*) Your lover in the play? Which of these young   65
sparks plays your lover—Harold or Gerald—?

ROSE Gerald. I don't know. There are some people not here today,
I believe.

O'DWYER Mr Hunston!

> *The second young gentleman advances, receives his part, and
> joins the other young gentleman in the wings*

ROSE Not that young man, I hope. Isn't he a little bandy?   70
TELFER One of the finest Macduffs I ever fought with° was bow-
legged.
O'DWYER Mr Kelfer.
TOM (*to O'Dwyer*) No, no—Telfer.
O'DWYER Telfer.   75
     *Telfer draws himself erect, puts his hand in his breast, but
     otherwise remains stationary*
MRS TELFER (*anxiously*) That's you, James.
O'DWYER Come on, Mr Telfer! Look alive, sir!
TOM (*to O'Dwyer*) Sssh, sssh, sssh! Don't, don't—!
     *Telfer advances to the prompt-table, slowly. He receives his part
     from O'Dwyer*
(*To Telfer, awkwardly*) I—I hope the little part of Poggs appeals to
you, Mr Telfer. Only a sketch, of course; but there was nothing   80
else—quite—in your—
TELFER Nothing? To whose share does the Earl fall?
TOM Oh, Mr Denzil plays Lord Parracourt.
TELFER Denzil? I've never 'eard of 'im. Will you get to me° today?
TOM We—we expect to do so.   85
TELFER Very well. (*Stiffly*) Let me be called in the street.
     He stalks away
MRS TELFER (*relieved*) Thank Heaven! I was afraid James would
break out.
ROSE (*to Mrs Telfer*) But you, dear Mrs Telfer—you weren't at the
reading—what are *you* cast for?   90
MRS TELFER I? (*Wiping away a tear*) I am the wardrobe mistress of
this theatre.
ROSE You! (*Embracing her*) Oh! Oh!
MRS TELFER (*composing herself*) Miss Trelawny—Rose—my child, if
we are set to scrub a floor—and we may come to that yet—let us   95
make up our minds to scrub it legitimately—with dignity°—
     She disappears and is seen no more
O'DWYER Miss Trelawny! Come here, my de—
TOM (*to O'Dwyer*) Hush!
O'DWYER Miss Trelawny!
     *Rose receives her part from O'Dwyer and, after a word or two
     with Tom and Imogen, joins the two young gentlemen who are
     in the 'second entrance' on the left. The lady, who has been
     seated, now rises and crosses to the left, where she meets the
     keen-faced gentleman, who has finished his conversation with
     Imogen*

LADY (*to the keen-faced gentleman*) I say, Mr Denzil, who plays   100
Gerald?

GENTLEMAN Gerald?

LADY The man I have my scene with in the third act—the hero—

GENTLEMAN Oh, yes. Oh, a young gentleman from the country, I
understand.   105

LADY From the country!

GENTLEMAN He is coming up by train this morning, Miss Parrott
tells me; from Bath or somewhere—

LADY Well, whoever he is, if he can't play that scene with me
decently, my part's not worth rags.   110

TOM (*to Imogen, who is sitting at the prompt-table*) Er—h'm—shall we
begin, Miss Parrott?

IMOGEN Certainly, Mr Wrench.

TOM We'll begin, O'Dwyer.

> *The lady titters at some remark from the keen-faced gentleman*

O'DWYER (*coming down the stage, violently*) Clear the stage there! I'll   115
not have it! Upon my honour, this is the noisiest theatre I've ever
set foot in!

> *The wings are cleared, the characters disappearing into the
> green-room*

I can't hear myself speak° for all the riot and confusion!

TOM (*to O'Dwyer*) My dear O'Dwyer, there is *no* riot, there is *no*
confusion—   120

IMOGEN (*to O'Dwyer*) Except the riot and confusion *you* are making.

TOM You know, you're admirably earnest, O'Dwyer, but a little
excitable.

O'DWYER (*calming himself*) Oh, I beg your pardon, I'm sure. (*Emphatically*) My system is, begin as you mean to go on.   125

IMOGEN But we *don't* mean to go on like that.

TOM Of course not; of course not. Now, let me see—(*Pointing to the
right centre*) We shall want another chair here.

O'DWYER Another chair?

TOM A garden chair.   130

O'DWYER (*excitably*) Another chair! Now, then, another chair!
Properties! Where are ye? Do ye hear me callin'? Must I raise my
voice to ye—?

> *He rushes away*

IMOGEN (*to Tom*) Phew! Where did you get *him* from?

TOM (*wiping his brow*) Known Michael for years—most capable,   135
invaluable fellow—

IMOGEN (*simply*) I wish he was dead.

TOM So do I.

> *O'Dwyer returns, carrying a light chair*

Well, where's the property man?

O'DWYER (*pleasantly*) It's all right, now. He's gone to dinner.   140

TOM (*placing the chair in position*) Ah, then he'll be back some time during the afternoon. (*Looking about him*) That will do. (*Taking up his manuscript*) Call—haven't you engaged a call-boy yet, O'Dwyer?

O'DWYER I have, sir, and the best in London.

IMOGEN Where is he?   145

O'DWYER He has sint an apology for his non-attindance.

IMOGEN Oh—!

O'DWYER A sad case, ma'am; he's buryin' his wife.

TOM Wife!

IMOGEN The call-boy?

TOM What's his age?   150

O'DWYER Ye see, he happens to be an elder brother of my own—

IMOGEN and TOM Oh, lord!

TOM Never mind! Let's get on! Call Miss—(*Looking toward the right*) Is that the hall-keeper?   155

> *A man, suggesting by his appearance that he is the hall-keeper, presents himself, with a card in his hand*

O'DWYER (*furiously*) Now then! Are we to be continually interrupted in this fashion? Have I, or have I not, given strict orders that nobody whatever—?

TOM Hush, hush! See whose card it is; give me the card—

O'DWYER (*handing the card to Tom*) Ah, I'll make rules here. In a   160
week's time you'll not know this for the same theatre—

> *Tom has passed the card to Imogen without looking at it*

IMOGEN (*staring at it blankly*) Oh—!

TOM (*to her*) Eh?

IMOGEN Sir William!

TOM Sir William!   165

IMOGEN What can he want? What shall we do?

TOM (*after referring to his watch, to the hall-keeper*) Bring this gentleman on to the stage.

> *The hall-keeper withdraws*

(*To O'Dwyer*) Make yourself scarce for a few moments, O'Dwyer. Some private business—   170

O'DWYER All right. I've plenty to occupy me. I'll begin to frame those rules—

He disappears

IMOGEN (*to Tom*) Not here—

TOM (*to Imogen*) The boy can't arrive for another twenty minutes.
  Besides, we must, sooner or later, accept responsibility for our act.   175

IMOGEN (*leaning upon his arm*) Heavens! I foretold this!

TOM (*grimly*) I know—'said so all along'.

IMOGEN If he should withdraw his capital!

TOM (*with clenched hands*) At least, that would enable me to write a
  melodrama.   180

IMOGEN Why?

TOM I should then understand the motives and the springs of crime!

> *The hall-keeper reappears, showing the way to Sir William
> Gower. Sir William's hat is drawn down over his eyes, and the
> rest of his face is almost entirely concealed by his plaid. The
> hall-keeper withdraws*

(*Receiving Sir William*) How d'ye do, Sir William?

SIR WILLIAM (*giving him two fingers,° with a grunt*) Ugh!

TOM These are odd surroundings for you to find yourself in. (*Imogen*   185
  comes forward) Miss Parrott—

SIR WILLIAM (*advancing to her, giving her two fingers*) Good-morning, ma'am.

IMOGEN This is perfectly delightful.

SIR WILLIAM What is?   190

IMOGEN (*faintly*) Your visit.

SIR WILLIAM Ugh! (*Weakly*) Give me a cheer. (*Looking about him*)
  Have ye no cheers here?

TOM Yes.

> *Tom places the throne-chair behind Sir William, who sinks
> into it*

SIR WILLIAM Thank ye; much obleeged. (*To Imogen*) Sit.   195

> *Imogen hurriedly fetches the stool and seats herself beside the
> throne-chair. Sir William produces his snuffbox*

You are astonished at seeing me here, I dare say?

TOM Not at all.

SIR WILLIAM (*glancing at Tom*) Addressing the lady. (*To Imogen*)
  You are surprised to see me?

IMOGEN Very.   200

SIR WILLIAM (*to Tom*) Ah!

> *Tom retreats, getting behind Sir William's chair and looking
> down upon him*

The truth is, I am beginning to regret my association with ye.

IMOGEN (*her hand to her heart*) Oh—h—h—h!

TOM (*under his breath*) Oh! (*Holding his fist over Sir William's head*)
Oh—h—h—h!

IMOGEN (*piteously*) You—you don't propose to withdraw your capital, Sir William?

SIR WILLIAM That would be a breach of faith, ma'am—

IMOGEN Ah!

TOM (*walking about, jauntily*) Ha!

IMOGEN (*seizing Sir William's hand*) Friend!

SIR WILLIAM (*withdrawing his hand sharply*) I'll thank ye not to
repeat that action, ma'am. But I—I have been slightly indisposed
since I made your acqueentance in Clerkenwell; I find myself
unable to sleep at night. (*To Tom*) That comedy of yours—it
buzzes continually in my head, sir.

TOM It was written with such an intention, Sir William—to buzz in
people's heads.

SIR WILLIAM Ah, I'll take care ye don't read me another, Mr Wicks;
at any rate, another which contains a character resembling a
member of my family—a *late* member of my family. I don't relish
being reminded of late members of my family in this way, and
being kept awake at night, thinking—turning over in my mind—

IMOGEN (*soothingly*) Of course not.

SIR WILLIAM (*taking snuff*) Pa—a—a—h! Pi—i—i—sh! When I saw
Kean, as Richard, he reminded me of no member of my family.
Shakespeare knew better than that, Mr Wicks. (*To Imogen*) And
therefore, ma'am, upon receiving your letter last night, acqueent-
ing me with your intention to commence rehearsing your comedy—
(*Glancing at Tom*) *his* comedy—

IMOGEN (*softly*) *Our* comedy—

SIR WILLIAM Ugh—today at noon, I determined to present myself
here and request to be allowed to—to—

TOM To watch the rehearsal?

SIR WILLIAM The rehearsal of those episodes in your comedy which
remind me of a member of my family—a *late* member.

IMOGEN (*constrainedly*) Oh, certainly—

TOM (*firmly*) By all means.

SIR WILLIAM (*rising, assisted by Tom*) I don't wish to be steered at
by any of your—what d'ye call 'em?—your gypsy crew—

TOM Ladies and Gentlemen of the Company, we call 'em.

SIR WILLIAM (*tartly*) I don't care what ye call 'em.

    Tom restores the throne-chair to its former position

Put me into a curtained box, where I can hear, and see, and not
be seen; and when I have heard and seen enough, I'll return
home—and—and—obtain a little sleep; and tomorrow I shall be   245
well enough to sit in Court again.

TOM (*calling*) Mr O'Dwyer—
> *O'Dwyer appears; Tom speaks a word or two to him, and hands*
> *him the manuscript of the play*

IMOGEN (*to Sir William, falteringly*)   And if you are pleased with
what you see this morning, perhaps you will attend another—?

SIR WILLIAM (*angrily*) Not I. After today I wash my hands of ye.   250
What do plays and players do, coming into my head, disturbing
my repose! (*More composedly, to Tom, who has returned to his side*)
Your comedy has merit, sir. You call it *Life*. There is a character
in it—a young man—not unlike life, not unlike a late member of
my family. Obleege me with your arm. (*To Imogen*) Madam, I have   255
arrived at the conclusion that Miss Trelawny belongs to a set of
curious people who in other paths might have been useful members of society. But after today I've done with ye—done with
ye—(*To Tom*) My box, sir—my box—
> *Tom leads Sir William up the stage*

TOM (*to O'Dwyer*) Begin rehearsal. Begin rehearsal! Call Miss Tre-   260
lawny!
> *Tom and Sir William disappear*

O'DWYER Miss Trelawny! Miss Trelawny! (*Rushing to the left*) Miss
Trelawny! How long am I to stand here shoutin' myself hoarse—?
> *Rose appears*

ROSE (*gently*) Am I called?

O'DWYER (*instantly calm*) You are, darlin'.   265
> *O'Dwyer takes his place at the prompt-table, book in hand.*
> *Imogen and Rose stand together in the centre. The other*
> *members of the company come from the green-room and stand in*
> *the wings, watching the rehearsal*

Now then! (*Reading from the manuscript*) 'At the opening of the
play Peggy and Dora are discovered—' Who's Peggy? (*Excitedly*)
Where's Peggy? Am I to—?

IMOGEN Here I am! Here I am! I am Peggy.

O'DWYER (*calm*) Of course ye are, lovey—ma'am, I should say—   270

IMOGEN Yes, you should.

O'DWYER 'Peggy is seated upon the Right, Dora on the Left—'
> *Rose and Imogen seat themselves accordingly. There is a difficulty*
No—Peggy on the Left, Dora on the Right. (*Violently*) This is the
worst written scrip I've ever held in my hand—

Rose and Imogen change places

So horribly scrawled over, and interlined, and—no—I was quite   275
correct. Peggy is on the Right, and Dora is on the Left.

Imogen and Rose again change seats. O'Dwyer reads from the manuscript.

'Peggy is engaged in—in—' I can't decipher it. A scrip like this is
a disgrace to any well-conducted theatre. (*To Imogen*) I don't know
what you're doin'. 'Dora is—is—' (*To Rose*) You are also doin'
something or another. Now then! When the curtain rises, you are   280
discovered, both of ye, employed in the way described—

Tom returns

Ah, here ye are! (*Resigning the manuscript to Tom, and pointing out
a passage*) I've got it smooth as far as there.

TOM Thank you.

O'DWYER (*seating himself*) You're welcome.   285

TOM (*to Rose and Imogen*) Ah, you're not in your right positions.
Change places, please.

Imogen and Rose change seats once more.

O'Dwyer rises and goes away

O'DWYER (*out of sight, violently*) A scrip like that's a scandal! If
there's a livin' soul that can read bad handwriting, I am that man!
But of all the—!   290

TOM Hush, hush! Mr O'Dwyer!

O'DWYER (*returning to his chair*) Here.

TOM (*taking the book from the prompt-table and handing it to Imogen*)
You are reading.

O'DWYER (*sotto voce*) I thought so.   295

TOM (*to Rose*) You are working.

O'DWYER Working.

TOM (*pointing to the basket on the table*) There are your needles and
wool.

*Rose takes the wool and the needles out of the basket. Tom
takes the ball of wool from her and places it in the centre of the
stage*

You have allowed the ball of wool to roll from your lap on to the   300
grass. You will see the reason for that presently.

ROSE I remember it, Mr Wrench.

TOM The curtain rises. (*To Imogen*) Miss Parrott—

IMOGEN (*referring to her part*) What do I say?

TOM Nothing—you yawn.   305

IMOGEN (*yawning, in a perfunctory way*) Oh—h!

TOM As if you meant it, of course.

IMOGEN Well, of course.

TOM Your yawn must tell the audience that you are a young lady
who may be driven by boredom to almost any extreme.   310

O'DWYER (*jumping up*) This sort of thing. (*Yawning extravagantly*)
He—oh!

TOM (*irritably*) Thank you, O'Dwyer; thank you.

O'DWYER (*sitting again*) You're welcome.

TOM (*to Rose*) You speak.   315

ROSE (*reading from her part, retaining the needles and the end of the
wool*) 'What are you reading, Miss Chaffinch?'

IMOGEN (*reading from her part*) 'A novel.'

ROSE 'And what is the name of it?'

IMOGEN '*The Seasons.*'   320

ROSE 'Why is it called that?'

IMOGEN 'Because all the people in it do seasonable things.'

ROSE 'For instance—?'

IMOGEN 'In the spring, fall in love.'

ROSE 'In the summer?'   325

IMOGEN 'Become engaged. Delightful!'

ROSE 'Autumn?'

IMOGEN 'Marry. Heavenly!'

ROSE 'Winter?'

IMOGEN 'Quarrel. Ha, ha, ha!'   330

TOM (*to Imogen*) Close the book—with a bang—

O'DWYER (*bringing his hands together sharply by way of suggestion*) Bang!

TOM (*irritably*) Yes, yes, O'Dwyer. (*To Imogen*) Now rise—

O'DWYER Up ye get!

TOM And cross to Dora.°   335

IMOGEN (*going to Rose*) 'Miss Harrington, don't you wish occasionally that you were engaged to be married?'

ROSE 'No.'

IMOGEN 'Not on wet afternoons?'

ROSE 'I am perfectly satisfied with this busy little life of mine, as   340
your aunt's companion.'

TOM (*to Imogen*) Walk about, discontentedly.

IMOGEN (*walking about*) 'I've nothing to do; let's tell each other our
ages.'

ROSE 'I am nineteen.'   345

TOM (*to Imogen*) In a loud whisper—

IMOGEN 'I am twenty-two.'

O'DWYER (*rising and going to Tom*) Now, hadn't ye better make that *six*-and-twenty?

IMOGEN (*joining them, with asperity*) Why? Why?   350

TOM No, no, certainly not. Go on.

IMOGEN (*angrily*) Not till Mr O'Dwyer retires into his corner.

TOM O'Dwyer—

> *O'Dwyer takes his chair, and retires to the 'prompt-corner', out of sight, with the air of martyrdom. Tom addresses Rose*

You speak.

ROSE 'I shall think, and feel, the same when I am twenty-two, I am   355
sure. I shall never wish to marry.'

TOM (*to Imogen*) Sit on the stump° of the tree.

IMOGEN Where's that?

TOM (*pointing to the stool down the stage*) Where that   stool is.

IMOGEN (*sitting on the stool*) 'Miss Harrington, who is the Mr Gerald   360
Leigh who is expected down today?'

ROSE 'Lord Parracourt's secretary.'

IMOGEN 'Old and poor!'

ROSE 'Neither, I believe. He is the son of a college chum of Lord
Parracourt's—so I heard his lordship tell Lady McArchie—and is   365
destined for public life.'

IMOGEN 'Then he's young!'

ROSE 'Extremely, I understand.'

IMOGEN (*jumping up, in obedience to a sign from Tom*) 'Oh, how can
you be so spiteful!'   370

ROSE 'I!'

IMOGEN 'You mean he's too young!'

ROSE 'Too young for what?'

IMOGEN 'Too young for—oh, bother!'

TOM (*looking towards the keen-faced gentleman*) Mr Denzil.   375

O'DWYER (*putting his head round the corner*) Mr Denzil!

> *The keen-faced gentleman comes forward, reading his part, and meets Imogen*

GENTLEMAN (*speaking in the tones of an old man*) 'Ah, Miss Peggy!'

TOM (*to Rose*) Rise, Miss Trelawny.

O'DWYER (*his head again appearing*) Rise, darlin'!

> *Rose rises*

GENTLEMAN (*to Imogen*) 'Your bravura° has just arrived from Lon-   380
don. Lady McArchie wishes you to try it over; and if I may add
my entreaties—'

IMOGEN (*taking his arm*) 'Delighted, Lord Parracourt. (*To Rose*) Miss Harrington, bring your work indoors and hear me squall. (*To the gentleman*) Why, you must have telegraphed to town!'   385

GENTLEMAN (*as they cross the stage*) 'Yes, but even telegraphy is too sluggish in executing your smallest command.'

> *Imogen and the keen-faced gentleman go off on the left. He remains in the wings, she returns to the prompt-table*

ROSE 'Why do Miss Chaffinch and her girl-friends talk of nothing, think of nothing apparently, but marriage? Ought a woman to make marriage the great object of life? Can there be no other? I   390 wonder—'

> *She goes off, the wool trailing after her, and disappears into the green-room. The ball of wool remains in the centre of the stage*

TOM (*reading from his manuscript*) 'The piano is heard; and Peggy's voice singing. Gerald enters—'

IMOGEN (*clutching Tom's arm*) There—!

TOM Ah, yes, here is Mr Gordon.   395

> *Arthur appears, in a travelling-coat. Tom and Imogen hasten to him and shake hands with him vigorously*

(*On Arthur's right*) How are you?

IMOGEN (*on his left, nervously*) How are you?

ARTHUR (*breathlessly*) Miss Parrott! Mr Wrench! Forgive me if I am late; my cab-horse galloped from the station—

TOM We have just reached your entrance. Have you read your part   400 over?

ARTHUR Read it! (*Taking it from his pocket*) I know every word of it! It has made my journey from Bristol like a flight through the air! Why, Mr Wrench—(*Turning over the leaves of his part*) Some of this is almost *me!*   405

TOM AND IMOGEN (*nervously*) Ha, ha, ha!

TOM Come! You enter—(*Pointing to the right*) there! (*Returning to the prompt-table with Imogen*) You stroll on, looking about you! Now, Mr Gordon!

ARTHUR (*advancing to the centre of the stage, occasionally glancing at*   410 *his part*) 'A pretty place. I am glad I left the carriage at the lodge and walked through the grounds.'

> *There is an exclamation, proceeding from the auditorium, and the sound of the overturning of a chair*

IMOGEN Oh!

O'DWYER (*appearing, looking into the auditorium*) What's that? This is the noisiest theatre I've ever set foot in—!   415

TOM Don't heed it! (*To Arthur*) Go on, Mr Gordon.

ARTHUR 'Somebody singing. A girl's voice. Lord Parracourt made
no mention of anybody but his hostess—the dry, Scotch widow.
(*Picking up the ball of wool*) This is Lady McArchie's, I'll be
bound. The very colour suggests spectacles and iron-grey   420
curls—'

TOM Dora returns. (*Calling*) Dora!

O'DWYER Dora! Where are ye?

GENTLEMAN (*going to the green-room door*) Dora! Dora!
     Rose appears in the wings

ROSE (*to Tom*) I'm sorry.   425

TOM Go on, please!
     *There is another sound, nearer the stage, of the overturning of
     some object*

O'DWYER What—?

TOM Don't heed it!

ROSE (*coming face to face with Arthur*) Oh—!

ARTHUR Rose!   430

TOM Go on, Mr Gordon!

ARTHUR (*to Rose, holding out the ball of wool*) 'I beg your pardon—are
you looking for this?'

ROSE 'Yes, I—I—I—' Oh, Mr Gower, why are you here?

ARTHUR Don't you know?   435

ROSE No.

ARTHUR Why, Miss Trelawny, I am trying to be what *you* are—

ROSE What I am!

ARTHUR Yes—a gypsy.

ROSE A gypsy—a gyp—(*Dropping her head upon his breast*) Oh, Arthur!   440
     Sir William enters, and comes forward on Arthur's right

SIR WILLIAM Arthur!

ARTHUR (*turning to him*) Grandfather!

O'DWYER (*indignantly*) Upon my soul—!

TOM Leave the stage, O'Dwyer!
     *O'Dwyer vanishes. Imogen goes to those who are in the wings
     and talks to them; gradually they withdraw into the green-room.
     Rose sinks on to the stool; Tom comes to her and stands
     beside her*

SIR WILLIAM What's this? what is it—?   445

ARTHUR (*bewildered*) Sir, I—I—you—and—and Rose—are the last
persons I expected to meet here—

SIR WILLIAM Ah—h—h—h!

ARTHUR Have you not learnt, sir, from Mr Wrench or Miss Parrott, that I have—become—an actor, sir?   450

SIR WILLIAM Not *I*. (*Pointing to Tom and Imogen*) These—these people have thought it decent to allow me to make the discovery for myself.

> *He sinks into the throne-chair. Tom goes to Sir William. Arthur joins Imogen; they talk together rapidly and earnestly*

TOM (*to Sir William*) Sir William, the secret of your grandson's choice of a profession—   455

SIR WILLIAM (*scornfully*) Profession!

TOM Was one that I was pledged to keep as long as it was possible to do so. And pray remember that your attendance here this morning is entirely your own act. It was our intention—

SIR WILLIAM (*struggling to his feet*) Where is the door? The way to   460
the door?

TOM And let me beg you to understand this, Sir William—that Miss Trelawny was, till a moment ago, as ignorant as yourself of Mr Arthur Gower's doings, of his movements, of his whereabouts. She would never have thrown herself in his way, in this manner.   465
Whatever conspiracy—

SIR WILLIAM Conspiracy! The right word—conspiracy!

TOM Whatever conspiracy there has been is my own—to bring these two young people together again, to make them happy.

> *Rose holds out her hand to Tom; he takes it. They are joined by Imogen*

SIR WILLIAM (*looking about him*) The door! The door!   470

ARTHUR (*coming to Sir William*) Grandfather, may I, when rehearsal is over, venture to call in Cavendish Square—?

SIR WILLIAM Call—!

ARTHUR Just to see Aunt Trafalgar, sir? I hope Aunt Trafalgar is well, sir.   475

SIR WILLIAM (*with a slight change of tone*) Your Great-aunt Trafalgar? Ugh, yes, I suppose she will consent to see ye—

ARTHUR Ah, sir—!

SIR WILLIAM But *I* shall be out; *I* shall not be within doors.

ARTHUR Then, if Aunt Trafalgar will receive me, sir, do you think   480
I may be allowed to—to bring Miss Trelawny with me—?

SIR WILLIAM What! Ha, I perceive you have already acquired the impudence of your vagabond class, sir; the brazen effrontery of a set of—!

ROSE (*rising and facing him*) Forgive him! Forgive him! Oh, Sir   485
William, why may not Arthur become, some day, a *splendid* gypsy?

SIR WILLIAM Eh?

ROSE Like—

SIR WILLIAM (*peering into her face*) Like——?

ROSE Like—

TOM Yes, sir, a gypsy, though of a different order from the old order which is departing—a gypsy of the new school!

SIR WILLIAM (*to Rose*) Well, Miss Gower is a weak, foolish lady; for aught I know she may allow this young man to—to—take ye—

IMOGEN I would accompany Rose, of course, Sir William.

SIR WILLIAM (*tartly*) Thank ye, ma'am. (*Turning*) I'll go to my carriage.

ARTHUR Sir, if you have the carriage here, and if you would have the patience to sit out the rest of the rehearsal, we might return with you to Cavendish Square.

SIR WILLIAM (*choking*) Oh—h—h—h!

ARTHUR Grandfather, we are not rich people, and a cab to us—

SIR WILLIAM (*exhausted*) Arthur—!

TOM Sir William will return to his box! (*Going up the stage*) O'Dwyer!

SIR WILLIAM (*protesting weakly*) No, sir! No!

    O'Dwyer appears

TOM Mr O'Dwyer, escort Sir William Gower to his box.

    Arthur goes up the stage with Sir William, Sir William still uttering protests. Rose and Imogen embrace

O'DWYER (*giving an arm to Sir William*) Lean on me, sir! Heavily, sir—!

TOM Shall we proceed with the rehearsal, Sir William, or wait till you are seated?

SIR WILLIAM (*violently*) Wait! Confound ye, d'ye think I want to remain here all day!

    Sir William and O'Dwyer disappear

TOM (*coming forward, with Arthur on his right, wildly*) Go on with the rehearsal! Mr Gordon and Miss Rose Trelawny! Miss Trelawny!

    Rose goes to him

Trelawny—late of the 'Wells'! Let us—let— (*Gripping Arthur's hand tightly, he bows his head upon Rose's shoulder*) Oh, my dears—! Let us—get on with the rehearsal—!

CURTAIN

EXPLANATORY NOTES

The Magistrate

1.1 S.D. *Bloomsbury*: a middle-class residential district of Victorian London, around the British Museum.

S.D. *manly . . . jacket*: the Eton jacket was boy's wear up to the age of 15 or so, and was short, single-breasted, with wide lapels; it was worn with a wide, starched turn-down shirt collar. Cis's 'manly' appearance in this child's dress instantly marks the ambiguity of his age and position, as does his name, which had overtones of femininity to the contemporary ear as it does now. The first American manager to stage the play, Daly, suggested that the role should be played by a woman, Ada Rehan. This was a common casting practice at the time, when women often played boys and youths in straight plays as well as in pantomime, but Pinero insisted on a masculine player: Cis is an embodiment of the power of young manhood, veiled but in no way impaired by his false position of dependence.

10 *grub with us*: Beatrice is, as she says, only a servant, though in the ambiguous category of the hired teacher; she would not expect to eat with the family. Cis's gift of food, his use of slang, his smoking, his familiar use of body language (leaning against Beatie) during this passage of exposition are all devices to generate and exploit ambiguity by offering conflicting signs about his age, boy or man, while establishing him as likeable to the audience. Beatie is similarly shown to be endearingly youthful when she speaks with her mouth full of apple, and by her childish sense of honour about getting Cis into a scrape.

12 *four guineas*: four pounds four shillings, £4.20.

20 *guv'nor*: schoolboy slang for 'father', with casually affectionate overtones indicating that Cis is less than overawed by Posket's authority, especially when, in the abbreviated form of 'Guv', he uses it later to address his stepfather. It has now migrated from inter-generational to inter-class use, where the overtones of familiarity and some affection still cling to it.

31 *the Derby . . . the Oaks*: classic horse-races, founded in 1780 and 1779 respectively, run as part of the Epsom meeting, taking place in May, in the week following Trinity Sunday; Derby Day was the Londoner's great day out. It is very unlikely, as we are to discover, that Posket would want to do anything of the sort; Cis draws his illustration from his own concerns.

55 *mind . . . 's*: take care in speech and behaviour.

79 *to himself*: the stage direction is phrased for the benefit of the reader, but in theatrical terms Wyke's musing remark is obviously an aside, not only containing information for the audience, but asking to be delivered in the comedy tradition of a direct, frame-breaking address to them, taking them into his confidence about another character. Pinero, while creating a reputation for adhering strictly to the rules of the theatre of fourth-wall illusion, in fact made quite extensive use of this older tradition in his farces. For further discussion, see the Introduction, p. xii.

106 *Bow Bells*: a cheap periodical containing stories of love, mystery, and adventure (as the title given here suggests) which was founded in 1862, part of the nineteenth-century explosion of printing for the people, and which had a huge circulation. It continued to appear until 1896.

152 *jujube*: a soothing lozenge, supposedly flavoured with the jujube (jojoba) fruit; his bronchitis is Bullamy's excuse for a childish taste for sweets.

181 *Czerny's exercises*: Karl Czerny, 1791–1857, was a prolific Viennese composer and noted teacher whose many exercises were popular training material for young pianists all over Europe.

194 *baby-farmer*: baby-farming was the practice of taking in unwanted infants for nursing and bringing up, at a small fee; cruelty and neglect were often the result. To nineteenth-century dramatists, it was a useful, often comically treated means of confusing identities; see, for example, Gilbert's *HMS Pinafore*. Posket's philanthropic hobby-horse, collecting people from his professional legal encounters, has a literary inspiration in Jaggers, the much more sinister lawyer in Dickens's *Great Expectations*.

196 *milkman . . . inspector*: in 1860 public health acts empowered local authorities to appoint analysts to inspect milk and other foods for quality and purity, and to oblige retailers to supply samples.

215 *committed*: both Bullamy and Posket are inclined to employ the jargon of their profession, sometimes inappropriately: the comparison of Agatha to a convict is inadvertent, but prophetic.

232 *Tours des Fontaines*: the building housing the spring from which visitors came to drink, at Spa, where Agatha and Posket met. Spa is a Belgian town twenty miles south-east of Liège whose name became the generic designation for resorts with supposedly health-giving mineral springs.

303 *the Lincolnshire Handicap*: founded in 1853, this was a less prestigious race than the Darby and the Oaks, revealing that Cis's interest in racing is fairly extensive.

304 *one, two, three*: he is backing the horse to take one of the first three places.

307 *tips*: a pun, the word meaning money given to a child, or racing information.

312 *a sov*: sovereign, i.e. one pound.

340 *two-year-old . . . hansom*: Agatha has adopted Charlotte's horsy parlance, and compares herself to a horse in its first vigour and to an old and broken-down creature used to pull a cab. Charlotte's next speech elaborates the metaphor, inventing a horse-race in which Agatha is entered, describing her breeding and giving her a handicap, 'ten pounds extra'. It is not made explicit whether Charlotte means this as a compliment to her strong form, or as a personal remark about her waistline.

409 *Aeneas . . . uneven*: this second sentence is an addition from the copy of the play submitted to the Lord Chamberlain's office for licensing.

464 *Baroda*: some 257 miles from Bombay, the capital of the principal Maharatta state under the British Raj, Baroda had a notable cantonment and large garrison; the church where the christening would have taken place was consecrated by Bishop Heber in 1824.

505 *closed cab*: a four-wheeled cab or 'growler', as opposed to the hansom, in which the passengers were more exposed to the elements.

522 *Greenwich mean*: short for Greenwich Mean Time. Cis is being jocular— to Posket's bewilderment. The following scene between them consists of a series of role reversals which boost Cis's stature to mythic levels of all-knowing, all-powerful young manhood, devaluing the 'natural' superiority of Posket as an authority figure; this gesture, of grabbing his watch and flipping it back at him, encapsulates Cis's effortless ascendency in physical terms, and sets Posket up for defeat. He cannot stave off the challenge to his masculine authority, because he cannot recognize Cis as being a man; he constantly attempts to relate to him as a child.

534 *Hôtel des Princes, Meek Street*: the precise implications of this establishment are important. Its name is significant—Cis is one of the princes, the lords of creation; the fact that its address is Meek Street adds to the joke. Such a hotel, letting rooms for all sorts of social activities in the West End of London, was not overtly beyond the pale of respectability— it was a humbler, commercial equivalent of a gentleman's club in many of its functions—but it had overtones of raffishness, suggestions of gambling and other night-time activities more covert than mere eating and drinking. This innuendo suffuses the whole episode set in Cis's private room with tension, and imparts the suggestion of imminent disgrace, without ever making anything of the sort explicit.

552 *crammer*: schoolboy slang for a lie. Cis's use of the childish term provokes Posket's automatic approval for his schoolboy honour, which only serves to sink the magistrate further into the moral quagmire which Cis is creating around him.

561 *W.*: stands for West, one of the postal divisions of London when these were first introduced, before numbered subdivisions became necessary.

641 *Indian clubs*: a pun, on weighted clubs for exercise and on officers' and gentlemen's clubs in British India.

665 *togs*: clothes.

2.1 S.D. *a supper-room*. This stage setting, a place of public amusement with several doors, suggestive of private retreats hired by the hour, would trigger in Pinero's audience a precise set of associations with the improper Palais Royal farces imported from Paris; see the Introduction, p. xiii. In the National Theatre production in 1986 the director Michael Rudman provoked some critical hostility by attempting to re-create that *frisson* by having an extra, wearing the dishevelled finery of a chorus girl or prostitute, wake up on the sofa and stagger off before the scene began.

21 *Posket*. In the copy submitted for licensing, this speech is as follows: 'POSKET (*reading*) June 3rd the Lord Chancellor. (*Turning*) Dear me, the Lord Chancellor patronises this house, he has scratched his name on the mirror. How very interesting!' This is not blue-pencilled, but it would seem that it was too indiscreet to use.

38 *a half-crown*: half a crown, two shillings and six old pence, i.e. $12\frac{1}{2}$p; the change discussed is out of nine pounds—eight pounds four shillings, £8.20p, plus sixteen shillings, 80p.

75 *for Auld Lang Syne*: for old times' sake.

99 *canapé*: not an appetizer which Cis and Posket have eaten, but a French word for the sofa which Isidore wheeled away to reveal the communicating door.

105 *Kensal Green*: a large London cemetery.

135 *Parascho's*: a real brand of cigarettes. Vale's care for his creature comforts, or perhaps for his image, despite his supposed grief, is part of Pinero's fun at the expense of the 'heavy swell', the self-indulgent man about town, a joke which was greatly appreciated by the critics of the first production.

269 *mug*: face, and also christening-cup.

363 *bona fide traveller*: the traveller was, according to the crucial licensing laws, entitled to buy refreshment during hours when a public house or hotel would not normally be allowed to sell alcohol; this was a loophole allowing Sunday drinking.

547 *stamped tomorrow at Somerset House*: Somerset House in the Strand housed various government offices, including the probate and divorce registries of the High Court. She means that she will enter the letter as evidence, in case, presumably, of an action for breach of promise of marriage.

553 *a debt of honour*: Pinero is making play with the various codes of correct behaviour in having Charlotte feel—or at least claim—that she must pay a horse-racing debt despite the impropriety of giving a personal item to a man other than her fiancé. Propriety was the overriding consideration for a lady, but Vale is too dense to see that she is manipulating him by claiming the right to live by the masculine code. By acknowledging the

primacy of her debt of honour over her loyalty to him, he puts himself in her power, as she demonstrates in the following exchange.

731 *Very nice part, Colonel*: Cork Street is in Mayfair, opposite the fashionable shopping centre of the Burlington Arcade.

3.1 S.D. *the magistrate's room.* The back room of the Court is a simple setting, occupying only the down-stage area, so that the drawing-room set from the first act can be in place behind it, ready for the final scene of the play.

S.D. *proceeds to cut it*: newspapers, and many books, were sold with the leaves still attached at the edges, where they had been folded after printing, and the reader cut them apart. The licensing copy included a longish soliloquy here, full of contemporary references, which would have been a conventional way of building up a low comedy part which was being introduced like this, late in the play.

17 *Why he's . . . sir.* 'A City magistrate, censuring a constable for the indistinctness of his utterances in the witness-box, suggested that the police should be instructed in a method of delivering evidence articulately' (Pinero's note).

57 *In Argyll Street*: Posket's soliloquy is another instance of Pinero's willingness to offer the performer an opportunity to break the frame of illusion and speak directly to the audience. The epic chase described took them north from Oxford Street (the hotel seems to have been imagined as neighbouring the site now occupied by the London Palladium) for a distance of at least four miles into the suburbs, before Posket lost Cis in Kilburn. The familiar references to current London life—to Madame Tussaud's waxwork show, which moved from Baker Street to its present site in Marylebone Road in 1884, a few months before the play opened, to Lord's, the headquarters of English cricket, established in St John's Wood Road near Regent's Park since 1814 and about to buy more ground there in 1887—is calculated to evoke responsive recognition from the audience, reflecting as it does their own life and experiences. Posket can easily endear himself to an audience with such material; in the 1986 revival at the National Theatre Nigel Hawthorne, a much-loved British actor, made this the highlight of the performance.

299 *court plaster*: sticking-plaster, the dressing for a wound, was made from silk coated with isinglass and was often black in colour, hence the name 'court plaster' from its use for small black patches as facial decoration by court beauties in the eighteenth century.

418 *Attend . . . Fastenings.* Posket is wildly reeling off the headings of official memos, and throws in one which is not a list of people, but a notice about home security.

3.2.30 S.D. *they catch hold of Cis.* The stage picture formed of Cis, surrounded in his exhaustion by concerned females hanging on his every request, contrasts with his father's beleaguered state of isolation in the previous scene; when he casually mentions that he ran on to Hendon, as far again as Posket managed to go, his elevation to mythic hero is comically complete.

72 S.D. *Popham hurries off*: a correction, from a later edition, of an obviously misprinted direction which had Posket exit here.

98 *Evil communication*: a reference to a text from St Paul, 'Evil communications corrupt good manners' (1 Cor. 15: 33), which was often used as a child's copy for handwriting practice, especially as a punishment task: Posket still associates Cis with childish misdeeds.

147 *non compos mentis*: another of Bullamy's fragments of legal jargon, a Latin phrase meaning 'not in his right mind', insane, and therefore not legally responsible or capable of making decisions.

240 *Sillikin and Butterscotch for the St Leger*: he is getting confused; these were runners in the Lincolnshire Handicap, mentioned in the first act. The St Leger is another classic horse-race, founded in 1776, and run at Doncaster on 24 September each year.

267 *1866*: 1866 is the correct date in relation to the first production, in 1885; it has been variously given in editions of the play, either reflecting alterations for stage revivals, or simply because of errors in printing: the copy text has 'eighteen sixty-six' when Agatha announces it, and 1886 when it is repeated by Posket and Cis.

339 *He's an infant*: legal terminology, meaning he is under 21, therefore legally unable to marry without his guardian's consent—which Posket immediately gives.

The Schoolmistress

Cast. Rankling, CB: Companion of the Most Honourable Order of the Bath, the lowest grade of that honour, conferred on officers of or above the rank of Commander in the Navy who had been mentioned in despatches in time of war.

Volumnia: the stern Roman matron, mother of Coriolanus.

articled pupil: the nineteenth-century system of teacher training, set up in 1848, provided for the apprenticeship of pupil teachers for five years, from the age of 13, to be followed by a period of one to three years at a residential training-college. Peggy would be given board and lodging, and a very small salary, while she worked and learnt to teach.

1.1 S.D. *Portland Place*: a fashionable London location, between Oxford Street and Regent's Park.

25 *Collin'wood 'Ouse*: it is comic that Admiral Rankling, who is, as we shall see, a ferociously unjust and overbearing tyrant whose only claim to distinction in his career is not to have collided with other people's ships

(see p. 77), should live in a house named after Admiral Collingwood (1748–1810), who was beloved by his men for the humanity of his discipline, as well as famous for his courageous achievements during the heroic epoch in British naval history.

52 *meller*: pseudo-cockney for 'mellow': that is, to ripen and mature them.

105 *the Cromwell Road*: a less fashionable but still eminently respectable address in West London, in a residential area developed in the mid-century.

115 *'At Home' day*. The social custom was for a lady to let her acquaintances know a regular day of the week or month on which she would be 'at home' to all visitors; she might issue cards of invitation for special occasions, but she would expect her friends to come on her day whenever they chose, and to bring others they wished to introduce.

137 *Pandora*: the allusion is to the ancient Greek equivalent of the myth of Adam and Eve. The popular version of the story is that Pandora released all the ills of the world from a box given to her by Zeus, which she had been forbidden to open. It is an appropriate name for the ship ruled by the heavily patriarchal Rankling, whose domineering manner fails entirely to keep the women in his life under control.

142 *Flying Dutchman*: a legendary phantom sailor, accursed because of a murder, doomed to sail the seas until a woman consented to die in his place; the subject of several nineteenth-century stories and plays, including a famous Gothic melodrama by Fitzball, as well as Wagner's music drama.

146 *Whiteley's*: William Whiteley opened one of the first department stores in Westbourne Grove, West London, in 1863. By this date it was a huge concern, employing more than a thousand people.

161 *not in my articles*: that is, her articles of apprenticeship—her contract as a pupil teacher; see note to the cast list.

185 *Junior Amalgamated Club, St James's Street*: the gentlemen's clubs of Victorian London provided masculine company and comforts for men alone in town, whether permanently, as bachelors, when away from their country estates or military or colonial duties, or simply when they wished to escape from the demands of their domestic circles. Queckett's club is fictional, but its name suggests the United Service Club, founded for officers in 1815, and the Junior Carlton, founded in 1868. The most prestigious clubs were located in St James's Street or Pall Mall.

186 *The Honourable*: a courtesy title given to the children of peers of the realm of the rank of baron or above.

190 *entertaining a swell unawares*: a swell means a fashionable gentleman, with some mocking or pejorative overtones of self-regard and self-importance; the phrase as a whole is a jocular echo of 'entertaining angels unawares',

which is used later (Act 3, l. 182) and alludes to St Paul's words: Heb. 13: 2.

192 *siles*: cockney for 'soils'.

193 *per diem daily*: the Latin means the same as the English—Tyler uses the tag to make his complaint sound weighty, but ignorantly repeats himself in so doing.

222 *'the three years' system*: hire purchase.

229 *respirator*: a device of gauze or even wire mesh worn over the mouth and nose to filter the air breathed; no doubt very useful against the London smog, but hardly a romantic recognition token.

239 *not girls but Gorgons*: the Gorgons were three female monsters in Greek myth whose look turned people to stone. The phrase as a whole is a comic echo of 'non Angli sed Angeli'—'not Angles (English) but angels'—which is supposed to have been Pope Gregory I's response to seeing beautiful English captives at Rome.

254 S.D. *Bernstein, a little, elderly German*: for the Victorians, there was an association between Germans and popular music, and the street band of German or pseudo-German musicians was the butt of many jokes; the versatility of popular composers, from Sir Arthur Sullivan downwards, was also a frequent topic for slightly scandalized amusement. This role was played in the first production by Albert Chevalier, who was to become a famous music-hall performer in the character of the cockney costermonger. According to reviewers, he made up for this part to look like Julius Benedict, whose compositions included an oratorio as well as successful light operas (*The Lily of Killarney* (1862) in particular), and who both presented classical concerts and worked as musical director at Covent Garden.

285 *gentleman in a mere parliamentary sense*: in a merely polite, complimentary sense—parliamentary language being emptily formal and correct.

333 *coryphées*: ballet or chorus girls; their attraction and availability to 'swells' were notorious.

351 *Grand Old Man*: William Ewart Gladstone, 1809–98. Four times Liberal prime minister, his third term began in the month of the play's première, March 1886, after a year of great political excitements. Controversy centred upon Gladstone's Home Rule Bill for Ireland, which in the course of the summer, while the play was running, split the Liberal party and resulted in his resignation in July.

354 *my stern political convictions*: it would appear that we are to take her for a supporter of Home Rule; this is obliquely confirmed in the final act, l. 583, when she mentions the song again. Direct political allusion was inadmissible on the Victorian stage, hence the ironic implication used here and the innuendo in the topical songs of the kind she is discussing. There might have been a further layer of comedy for the actress to

exploit in the idea of Home Rule, since in the course of the play Miss Dyott secures it for herself.

370 S.D. *Vere Queckett enters*. Note the setting-up of a visual joke in the discrepancy of size between him and his wife—an undignified, seaside-postcard comicality which counterpoints the 'rigid demeanour' and 'dignified presence' of Miss Dyott when she first appeared as the schoolmistress.

461 *diggings*: lodgings.

463 *Counting the words*: telegrams were charged for by the word, including the address.

469 *Guy Fawkes*: she means that he is a conspirator, like those who plotted to blow up the Houses of Parliament in 1605.

473 *'Rovers' Club'* . . . *'Stragglers'*: these names are intended to suggest less formally grand, more bohemian London clubs founded to bring together men with non-political interests in common. Examples of such clubs were the Travellers, founded in 1819, whose members were supposed to have travelled 500 miles from London in a straight line, and the Savage Club, whose meeting-rooms were in the artistic world of Covent Garden rather than the West End.

503 *Lord Mayor's Show*: a procession through the streets on 9 November each year, to celebrate the installation of the new Lord Mayor of London. The crowds and the crush were notorious in the narrow streets of the Victorian city.

519 *British origin*: the best cigars were made in the countries where the tobacco was grown, not in Britain, where cigar manufacturers tended to concentrate on smaller, cheaper kinds; Caroline's shopping policy is prudent as well as patriotic.

525 S.D. *Admiral and Mrs Rankling*. Though Mrs Rankling is described as 'weak-looking' and Admiral Rankling as 'fine', their subordinate/dominant roles are not nearly so clear-cut in the scene that ensues; Mrs Rankling is making quite a successful attempt at managing a completely irrational egoist, a man who behaves like a 2-year-old child put into a position of authority: both women handle him as if he were a dangerous animal. The passage makes an interesting sequel to Caroline's management of the equally childish but physically harmless Queckett.

544 *King Lear's curse*: that is, his denunciation of Goneril in Shakespeare's play (I. iv. 254–69), provoked by the ingratitude of his daughters; it was the most famous speech in the role, greatly looked forward to when it was performed by eighteenth- and nineteenth-century actors. (The Shakespearian line references here and in subsequent notes are to the *Complete Works* edited by Stanley Wells and Gary Taylor (Oxford, 1986).

573 *herring*: errand.

605 *respond for the Navy*: make a speech, in response to the toast 'the Navy'.

624 *'Por Carolina'*: the completion of the joke about the British cigars: Queckett has actually bought very expensive Havanas, the best cigars available. Caroline's response can be read in two ways: either her 'Poor Caroline' acknowledges that this is another expense that she has foolishly let herself in for, or she assumes that the name means that his choice is a compliment to her rather than a defiance of her instructions, and invites the knowing members of the audience to enjoy a sense of superior worldliness.

681 *upon how long it runs to it*: however long it will last, or will take, usually implying 'as long as there is money available'.

685 *Je vous embrasse . . . sages*: an elaborate farewell in French, literally 'I embrace (or kiss) you with all my heart—Be good!', which comically combines the practice of the schoolroom, where French conversation was cultivated as an accomplishment for young ladies, with suggestions of the *demi-mondaine* world of the theatre. The girls respond with conventional phrases of farewell, wishing her a good journey.

690 *Eagle office*: a large insurance company, still in business.

2.1.43 *uncle*: slang for pawnbroker.

110 *Illustrations of Deportment . . . Queckett*: the correct greeting that he has just offered Geraldine makes him imagine himself figuring in a handbook on etiquette. The turn of thought continues with 'Instructions in Polite Conversation': see l. 118.

164 *'whistling woman'*: either a reference to the adage that there are two things of no use to any man, a whistling woman and a crowing hen, or perhaps a contemporary music-hall turn who named her act after the saying.

207 *a cub*: a common Victorian aspersion upon an ill-mannered youngster, probably shorthand for 'an unlicked cub', alluding to the belief that baby bears were born formless and had to be licked into shape.

215 *My card, sir*: to hand one's card to another man during an argument was a way of challenging him to a duel.

232 *The hanging committee have skied you*: this refers to the annual exhibition of the Royal Academy, featuring hundreds of pictures; when the Victorian practice of filling the length and breadth of walls with pictures prevailed, paintings that did not find favour with the committee deciding upon the arrangement of the rooms would be placed out of easy sight, in an upper row.

256 *'Britannia rules the waves'*: the original line, in a song first heard in 1740 as part of a *Masque of Alfred* with music by Thomas Arne, was 'Rule, Britannia, rule the waves', but the injunction to take power was rapidly converted into an assertion of its possession, and became the anthem of

armchair supporters of the Navy. The professional officer Mallory deprecates such tired theatrical displays of patriotism.

269 *'the old gentleman'*: a euphemism for the devil.

295 *the Albany*: a fashionable apartment block between Burlington Gardens and the Royal Academy, much favoured by wealthy young bachelors; Pinero has Tanqueray living there before his marriage, in the first act of *The Second Mrs Tanqueray*.

341 *Berkshire Royals*: an (imaginary) regiment of the British Army.

422 *The pudding is in the arey*: the first delivery from the caterer whom Queckett has employed to provide the supper has arrived at the kitchen door, which was often in an 'area', a paved enclosure below the level of the road, excavated to provide access and some light to semi-basement servants' quarters in London houses.

510 *Gunter's*: his bachelor suppers came from a far superior caterer, the fashionable confectioner in Berkeley Square. The running gag about food is a feature of the middle act in this play as it was in *The Magistrate*, and shows Pinero's mastery of his craft. He repeats a highly successful ingredient of the first play, but invents a wholly new way for hungry people to be deprived of sustenance and for a would-be sophisticated social occasion gradually to be reduced to rubble.

540 *Keep it warm*: Tyler intends to enjoy the pie himself: the leavings of the table were the servants' perquisites, but lark pies were a delicacy which cannot often have found their way to the servants' table at the school.

645 *merely a quadrille*: a country dance in sets, which Dinah feels cannot be romantic enough to provoke Reginald's jealousy, as might a dance in couples involving more bodily contact.

708 *tell off*: separate, detach (for a particular duty—here, 'to help the ladies').

712 S.D. *Jaffray, a fireman*: the episode with the firemen suggests a memory of Gilbert and Sullivan's *Iolanthe* (Savoy Theatre, 1882), in which the Fairy Queen, a role very like Miss Dyott's 'queen of the opera buffa', appeals in song to Captain Shaw, the commander of the London Fire Brigade, to quench her dangerous physical attraction to a soldier.

764 S.D. *short covert coat*: a short overcoat, fly-fronted and with strapped seams, vents in the side seams. It was popular with 'horsy young gentlemen' (*Tailor and Cutter*, 1881).

3.1.125 *finishing*: the final polishing of a girl's education; but Mallory takes it more literally.

182 *entertaining an angel unawares*: see note to *The Schoolmistress*, 1.1.190.

203 *Hallo*. Rankling's soliloquy and further soliloquies by Queckett and Miss Dyott (pp. 128–9 below), can be compared with Posket's similarly placed speech in *The Magistrate* (pp. 49–50) as more examples of Pinero's

repeated use of devices drawn from older farce; for further discussion, see the Introduction, p. xii.

287 *Uneasy lies the head . . . crown*: Shakespeare, *2 Henry IV*, III. i. 31.

291 *Scylla and Charybdis*: he is caught between two dangers. In classical mythology sailors attempting to pass between Sicily and the Italian mainland were beset on one side by the monster Scylla and on the other by the whirlpool Charybdis.

292 S.D. *peignoir*: a loose dressing-gown.

300 *Oh, Mrs Queckett*. This scene between Miss Dyott and Mrs Rankling, in which mutual accusation is unexpectedly turned into an understanding which will fuel the dénouement of the action, is a further instance of Pinero's skill in making over dramatic conventions: it can be seen as a parody of the 'explanation' scene, which leads up to the climactic moment of many serious plays of the period.

526 *Any collection . . . described*. Miss Dyott refers to 'diggings' in the sense of 'lodgings', which was Queckett's original meaning, and Queckett attempts to make a joke of it by punning on 'diggings' as the site of prospecting and mining operations.

533 *What Tyler*: a pun on the name of the revolutionary leader Wat Tyler, who led a rebellion in 1381.

565 *after all, gone and married a Connie*: Connie is a typical name for a lower-class girl, more especially a chorus girl, at this period; he means that, thinking he was doing something very unusual for a dissipated aristocrat in marrying a highly respectable middle-class woman, he finds that he has conformed to the popular stereotype and married a chorus girl.

571 *free list*: complimentary seats.

586 *The Rock*: 'an organ of the united church of England and Ireland', published 1868–1905; an evangelical, often anti-Catholic religious periodical, appropriate to the schoolroom rather than to Queckett.

606 *Poole . . . Kino*: pool is the billiard-table game still played, and therefore appropriate to the gentlemanly side of Caroline's list of pleasures; Kino was an early form of the humbler amusement of lotto or bingo.

616 *Than . . . La*: Caroline's song is a clever pastiche of W. S. Gilbert's verbal games in its double-rhymed stanzas, vulgarized by the addition of a chorus that could be from the music hall, suggesting, for example, 'What Cheer, 'Ria?' sung by Bessy Bellwood.

624 S.D. *'spooning'*: slang for embracing and kissing.

684 *vexing girl*. George Rowell (*Plays by A. W. Pinero* (Cambridge, 1986), 73–4) prints an alternative ending, from Pinero's manuscript, which begins at this point. In it Miss Dyott sacks Peggy, and Mallory proposes to her on stage; she responds with lines very reminiscent of

W. S. Gilbert's artful *ingénue* heroines, especially those in his *Engaged!* (Haymarket, 1877), and goes on to beg for flowers for her bridal wreath from her friends and applause from the audience, in a very old-fashioned rhyming curtain-speech. Rowell suggests that since she has been prominent in the action, especially in the second act, the play and its conclusion are rightfully hers, and were only denied her because Mrs John Wood, the leading lady, 'evidently objected' (p. 3). This is undoubtedly a possibility, but Miss Dyott's unrepentant triumph, and her demand for endorsement as an entertainer, are far stronger and less conventional as a conclusion than falling back upon an appealing pretty girl and the ritual invocation of wedding bells.

The Second Mrs Tanqueray

1.1 S.D. *the Albany*: a luxurious apartment building in Mayfair, London, favoured by rich single gentlemen; see the note to *The Schoolmistress*, 2.1.295.

96 S.D. *at the other end of the room*: Shaw, in his carping comments on the play (see *Our Theatre in the Nineties*, 3 vols. (1932), 1. 41–8), picked on this piece of business—and indeed the whole of this scene—as evidence of the clumsiness of the play's construction: see the Introduction, p. xviii. He claimed that Jayne and Misquith were 'sham parts' introduced merely for the exposition and then dropped; and that Aubrey's retreat into letter-writing to allow them to be heard was an 'ignominiously' clumsy device. No other critics found it particularly awkward, however; and it could be argued that the appearance of a group of close friends, who then disappear when Aubrey goes into self-imposed exile, is an integral part of the meaning of the play.

147 *like Queen Bess among her pillows*: Queen Elizabeth I refused to lie down and die in her bed, and spent her last hours propped amongst pillows and surrounded by her court.

167 *actress . . . dressmaker*: Drummle is repeating the commonplace perception of his class and time that prostitutes were, or described themselves as, occupied in these trades when taken to court or cited in divorce proceedings. Tracy Davis's statistical investigation of this claim (*Actresses as Working Women* (1991), 78–80) demonstrates that, at least in the case of actresses, the equation was a fabrication by middle-class observers for their own ideological purposes in rendering all women's paid work questionable.

282 *stays*: corsets.

297 *Armagh*: in what is now Northern Ireland. Tanqueray would need to go beyond Great Britain to find a choice of Catholic convent schools, and in Ireland the medium of instruction would be English.

319 S.D. *Aubrey enters*. At this point the prompt copy marks an increase of lighting intensity on the side of the stage where Aubrey appears. This may even have been a spotlight, since limelight spots had been available for some time. The direction is repeated at several important points in the play (identified in this edition in notes accompanying the relevant passages). The effect would contribute markedly to a glorification of Aubrey as hero.

350 *Aix in August*: Aix-les-Bains in southern France is a spa town where visitors bathe in hot, sulphurous natural springs as a cure for rheumatic ailments; it was also, at this date, a very fashionable resort.

378 *Society*: with a capital 'S', Society means not the social body as a whole, but the privileged and wealthy fraction of the English upper and upper-middle class sometimes calling itself 'the Upper Ten Thousand', which maintained a strictly regulated and ritualized social intercourse as well as exercising political and executive power. Society preferred to practise exclusivity and endogamy, though the frequency with which it was penetrated by outsiders of wealth or beauty was one of its anxieties at this date—and also, paradoxically, one of its self-justifications, since it could be claimed that worth and talent were welcome to join the élite.

403 *Homburg*: another fashionable spa frequented by English and continental Society.

418 *cursed hospitality*: Aubrey is finding this dialogue painful, and transfers his anger at Ethurst's keeping of Paula as his mistress to his inviting Drummle to supper, and so exposing her position to him.

438 *Drummle is silent*. The original printed copies of the text from which Pinero worked with the company have a direction here for Aubrey to 'turn hotly' towards Drummle; this is intensified in the prompt copy to him 'advancing hotly' towards his friend.

445 *little parish of St James's*: Victorian Society was often referred to under this name, which properly designates the most exclusive quarter of London, surrounding the palace of St James and St James's Church, Piccadilly. The play's première took place there, at the St James's Theatre, King Street; it also included Pall Mall, which Aubrey mentions in his next speech and which was the location of many of the exclusive gentlemen's clubs and a favourite promenading place for the rich and idle.

480 *at the lodge*: the rooms of the porter, at the entrance to the block of flats, where messages could be received and transmitted and visitors would be checked.

481 *No, sir—here*: Morse's hesitation is in response to the extreme impropriety of Paula's arrival late at night, unaccompanied, at Aubrey's apartment. She is behaving with the freedom of a woman with no reputation to lose; the contemporary audience would perceive this as the

first demonstration of the truth of Aubrey's prognostication of their social ostracism.

488 *dooced serious*: 'dooced' for 'deuced', a mild euphemism for 'damned'. Drummle falls into the jocular slang and slipshod pronunciation of the empty-headed good companion in an attempt to lighten the atmosphere between them as old friends.

491 *neck-handkerchief*: a warm scarf worn in the neck of his overcoat; Drummle and Aubrey are not in their first youth.

498 *a stall*: 'A man at a play' on his own would sit in the stalls, the individually bookable seats at the front of the ground floor of the theatre, rather than with the family parties in the dress circle or boxes.

506 *Gunter's cook and waiter*: the supper that Aubrey has just served his guests came from the fashionable confectioner's Gunter's, in Berkeley Square, who sent their servants as well as the provisions for the meal. Cf. the note to *The Schoolmistress*, 2.1.510.

508 *Certainly not*: Aubrey wants to stress to Morse that Paula's visit is not, as his query suggests, anything private. His concern that Morse should not think that they are behaving improperly is then one of the first things that he mentions to Paula as she arrives, only to be met by her flippant and ominous indifference to servants' opinions.

585 *Pont Street*: Paula lives in Brompton, just south of Knightsbridge, another central and exclusive locality.

2.1.86 *bezique*: a two-handed game played with a modified pack of cards. Its French terminology, and the fact that it required skill rather than simply luck in the fall of the cards, gave it a certain social cachet.

237 *balance the cart for three*: she drives to the village in a dog-cart, as Drummle mentions later (l. 363), which was the usual horse-drawn vehicle for short trips in the country. It had two transverse seats back to back, needing some adjustment to balance the uneven weight of the two passengers and the groom.

342 *the Jeweller's Son in the 'Arabian Nights'*: the story is of a youth whose father strove to protect him from a prophecy of early death by incarcerating him in a secret chamber, where the foretold murderer innocently came upon him and quite accidentally killed him; the moral is that, despite the best of intentions, fate is inescapable.

376 *for the season*: The London season was the period from May to July during which the fashionable world assembled in town to organize and enjoy social events and to initiate new entrants, like Ellean, into Society.

395 *two cherries on one stalk*: a reminiscence of Shakespeare's Hermia and Helena, in *A Midsummer Night's Dream*, III. iii. 210–12 ('Two lovely berries moulded on one stem').

470 *Chester Square*: Mrs Cortelyon's London house is in Belgravia, not far from Paula's Pont Street home.

525 *Bayliss's*: contemporary guides and directories make no mention of a Bayliss's Hotel, but there was a first-class establishment called Bailey's in the Gloucester Road. Given Pinero's careful verisimilitude in all his references in this play, it may be that Bayliss's is a misprint for the real name.

535 S.D. *He goes out with Aubrey*. The directions for these final moves are given here as they stand in the authorized published text, but they betray a confusion: Ellean is directed to come in from the hall, without ever having been told to go out. This would seem to be the consequence of revision in rehearsal. The printed pre-performance texts had a simpler sequence of moves, with Ellean going out to join Aubrey, and Mrs Cortelyon and Drummle moving up stage and then going to join them; the prompt copy overrides this with instructions for Drummle and Aubrey to go out, leaving Mrs Cortelyon. This change was reproduced in the final text, and has resulted in an entrance for Ellean with no indication of an exit before it. The main objective is obvious enough: to withdraw the other players slowly, marking Ellean's allegiance to Mrs Cortelyon and Paula's isolation, and then to leave a clear stage for Paula's display of helpless anger. The prompt copy directs her to tear her hat and coat off furiously, and adds that, 'upon removing her hat, she stabs it viciously' with a hat-pin.

537 S.D. *Aubrey returns*. Another point where a lighting cue in the prompt copy, illuminating Aubrey, emphasizes the original production's valorization of him as hero. One would have thought that the spotlight here would be on Paula's anguish.

3.1 S.D. *ottoman*: a padded couch; the 'drum' against which she rests her head is a cylindrical cushion.

11 *whisky and potass*: potass or potash water was a variant upon soda water, and was made by adding potassium bicarbonate to water aerated with carbonic acid.

79 *wrecky*: clearly means 'like a wreck', demolished or badly damaged; the recorded slang use of the term, not noted until 1925 by the *Oxford English Dictionary*, is 'broken-down' or 'debilitated', referring to people rather than rooms. In Lady Orreyed's use, the overtones of dissipation are perhaps significant.

193 *mustard plaster*: mustard mixed with oil and applied externally was used as a remedy against various ailments; if the mixture was too strong, there was danger of burning or irritating the skin.

232 S.D. *Aubrey enters quickly*: another lit-up entrance for the hero in the original production.

305 *club . . . smoking-room*: that is, to all-male gatherings. Paula has been contaminated by becoming party, as a kept woman, to the verbal freedom which gentlemen do not allow themselves in front of their wives and daughters.

369 *entresol*: an intermediate floor immediately above the ground level; presumably a smaller and less expensive apartment than Mrs Cortelyon's.

380 *his company and a VC*: he was promoted to command of a company, as a captain, and awarded the Victoria Cross, the highest British honour for individual bravery, instituted by Queen Victoria in 1856.

613 *What am I maundering about*. A note in the prompt copy reads: 'The three lines preceding she has said quite quietly and retrospectively. Suddenly she realizes the horror and helplessness of it all, and starting to her feet utters an hysterical cry of rage' and strides across the stage. This sounds like powerful melodrama to a modern ear, but the whole exchange struck the contemporary critics as near-miraculous in its realism: the *Observer* called it 'appalling in its touches of the truth', creating 'a scene the shock of which can hardly be described'. The shock was perhaps a response to the realization that the stereotype category of a 'fallen woman', normally presented as a social danger, in fact contained ordinary individuals with commonplace interests in real estate and the capacity to be nostalgic about pretty furniture. See the Introduction, p. xvii, for further discussion.

664 *rackety*: Ardale's slang term for leading a social life beyond the bounds of respectability is boyish and, in the context, is self-excusing as well as self-pitying. Its root meaning is to be fond of making a noise, of the excitements of drink and good fellowship, and it therefore suggests juvenile irresponsibility rather than graver misdemeanours of a sexual kind.

4.1.20 *gaping*: yawning; a very unladylike thing to do so openly.

27 *mark*: to keep score; the billiard-marker was a Victorian moralist's shorthand for the type of shiftless, scrounging hanger-on who survived by preying upon young gentlemen who allowed themselves to be led astray into playing billiards for money in public houses, and thence to the card-table and the racecourse, gambling, and ruin.

45 *Bruton Street*: a Mayfair address, off Berkeley Square; Sir George's mother's town house is in the very best locality.

163 *Meurice's*: the Hôtel Meurice, in the rue de Rivoli opposite the Tuileries; a very expensive first-class hotel.

261 *what a man's life is!*: the original printed text followed this with the more explicit condemnation: 'You accepted it without a murmur, with a smile perhaps!', but this is cut in the prompt copy.

375 *Aubrey!* . . . *I'm very sorry*: the original text directed Paula to look at Aubrey 'pityingly' as she spoke his name, and Aubrey to respond with a slight movement, provoking her to preface her apology with the very strong phrase 'God help you!' This is cut in the prompt copy. In its original form, the exchange concentrates sympathy on Aubrey rather

than on Paula, which seems to have been Pinero's conception of the balance of the play.

442 *raddled and ruddled*: both words mean painted with coarse red, originally that used for marking sheep. Paula may be using an intensifying repetition, or she may be thinking of the transferred meaning of 'raddled', the deterioration of the complexion with age, reddened by being criss-crossed with broken blood vessels, which the 'ruddle' or rouge would be intended to cover up.

507 S.D. *She beats her breast*: direction taken from the prompt copy.

508 S.D. *stands looking out*. The first printed texts of the play had an additional line, for Drummle, as he stood at the door: 'And I—I've been hard on this woman! Good God, we are all hard on all women!' It is cut in the prompt copy.

Trelawny of the 'Wells'

Comedietta: the term means a short or slight comedy; Pinero is deprecatory about the play, and most newspaper critics of the day unwarily took him at his word and did not look for its more profound meanings.

Bagnigge Wells: Pinero's note here, obliquely and perhaps playfully reminding the reader that Sadler's Wells should be kept in mind, ran as follows: 'Bagnigge (locally pronounced, Bagnidge) Wells—formerly a popular mineral spring in Islington, London, situated not far from the better remembered Sadler's-wells. The gardens of Bagnigge-Wells were at one time much resorted to; but, as a matter of fact, Bagnigge-Wells, unlike Sadler's-Wells, has never possessed a playhouse. Sadler's-Wells Theatre, however—always familiarly known as the "Wells",—still exists. It was rebuilt in 1876–77.' When he revived the play in 1925, he dropped all concealment of its real reference to that theatre, the playhouse of his boyhood. See note 1.1.35, below. He was not quite correct in asserting that Bagnigge Wells never had a playhouse, but its theatrical aspirations were confined to the boom years of the 1830s.

A direction to the stage-manager. Pinero is insistent upon the period of the play, for reasons to do with his sense of his own history and heritage in the theatre: see the Introduction, p. xix. He needed to forestall the impulse to soften and modernize the costume of the 1860s because, as his note suggests, it was absurdly grotesque to the eyes of the 1890s. The first-night critics of the play expended incredulous paragraphs upon the hideousness of the crinoline in particular, expressing their amazement that anyone could have chosen to make themselves so ugly; they commiserated with the disfigured actresses. An obvious parallel is the scorn directed towards flared trousers, fashionable in the 1960s, by young people in the 1980s. Peg-top trousers tapered in from the thighs and the knees to a narrow ankle; a modified version was fashionable again in the 1890s, and gave rise to the slang 'bags' for trousers, which persisted into the twentieth century. The furniture described is the intricate but heavy carving in dark varnished woods and overstuffed and uncomfortably hard upholstery of the mid-Victorian period, which struck the 'artistic' 1890s as an abomination in interior design equivalent to the crinoline in dress—artificially elaborate and disfiguring of natural shapes and lines.

1.1 S.D. *cottage piano*: a small, upright piano of the cheapest kind, a sign of aspiration to the gentility conferred by one of the most pervasive of Victorian class symbols.

8 *pertaters*: pseudo-cockney for potatoes. Pinero's jocularity at Ablett's expense is a commonplace of Victorian comedy, which is acutely aware of the class distinction of accents; Ablett is more interesting and complex than many such figures (cf. for example the very distasteful portrayal of the plumber Sam Gerridge in Robertson's *Caste* (1867)) in that his language is not simply ridiculed for its mispronunciation, but also enjoyed in a more imaginative and positive way for its enrichment by his enthusiasm for the theatre. He is nostalgically seen as representing the vulgar audience for whom the Wells used to cater. Hence, below, his phrase 'caught disaster', meaning courted disaster: he has picked up a melodramatic phrase from the stage, by ear, and misconstrued its form. 'Setting-room' for 'sitting-room', however, is simply a cockney vowel sound.

35 *'Wells'... Mr Phillips's management*: when the play was first staged, Pinero chose to veil its relationship to a real theatre, Sadler's Wells, and its famous manager Samuel Phelps in a thin disguise, which he dropped completely when he revised the play for production at the Old Vic in 1925. After Phelps's management, which ended in 1862, the house reverted to an undistinguished level, staging melodramas and spectacles of the simple kind suggested here. The Wells was Pinero's local theatre in his boyhood: hence his affection for it, despite its shortcomings.

41 *Draught for Miss Trelawny, invariably*: as bottled beer became more reliable in quality as a result of the introduction of carbonation and mechanical bottling in place of natural maturing in hand-sealed bottles, its extra clarity, brightness, and sparkle became an advertised attraction. Bass, the pioneers in the field, aimed their publicity especially at ladies, and emphasized their product's refinement. In establishing her preference for the cheaper, older, more 'natural', and more working-class draught beer, Pinero is investing Rose with pastoral virtues of simplicity and straightforwardness, an aversion to the false refinement of drinking with the eye instead of the palate; it is a sign of her innate good breeding.

48 *Vice-Chancellor*: a high legal office in the Court of Chancery, which ceased to have a separate existence in 1876. The implication to a late Victorian audience would be of an extremely old-fashioned position of ceremony and aristocratic privilege, now abolished.

52 *Cavendish Square*: a prestigious address in London's West End, to the north of Oxford Street.

56 *fallals*: frills, small decorative items of dress and toilette.

59 *benefit*: a performer could negotiate the (sometimes rather doubtful) advantage of a benefit night at the end of a season or an engagement, receiving a fixed sum or some proportion of the takings, by arrangement with the management, and being expected to sell tickets to personal friends and supporters; the rest of the company were expected to perform without payment. The device was part of the old patronage and friendship system of theatrical management, not entirely defunct by Pinero's time, but largely discredited.

92 *Inverness*: a loose overcoat or sleeved cloak, with a wrist-length cape added; common masculine wear in the 1860s.

100 *Rosoman Street*: very close to Sadler's Wells Theatre. Thomas Rosoman was proprietor of the Wells from 1742 to 1772, and he built a row of houses along the path leading to the pleasure garden, creating a road which was later given his name.

105 *Epping*: Epping Forest is a remnant of ancient woodland east of London which has been the destination of metropolitan excursions for many years; indeed, parts of it are the property of the City of London.

113 *Sheridan Knowles's immortal work*: James Sheridan Knowles, 1784–1862, an Irish dramatist who wrote eighteen plays, several of which were immensely successful and earned him inflated praise at the time as the nineteenth-century Shakespeare; his work was popular for its qualities of domestic feeling, of 'heart'. Wrench, representing a new generation of writers in the 1860s, implies that he suspects that Knowles's work is less than immortal; by 1898 this perception required no great foresight. It may not be coincidental that in the 1832 première of *The Hunchback*, which is probably the play referred to here (see below, l. 311), an actor called Wrench appeared.

137 *Olympic Theatre*: in the early 1860s the Olympic, first built as a West End base by the circus entrepreneur Philip Astley in 1805, was a highly regarded theatre under the management of the famous tragi-comic actor Frederick Robson. Apart from the burlesques of tragedy and the specially written comic plays that provided vehicles for his own extraordinary talent, Robson staged some serious drama, such as the première of Tom Taylor's *The Ticket-of-Leave Man* and other successful plays of his that were the prototypes of the realistic 'problem' play of the 1890s.

174 *Undine, the Spirit of the Waters*: the reference is to a very popular romantic story by Friedrich de la Motte Fouqué, first published in 1807. It tells of a water-sprite who acquired a soul by marriage to a knight, was cast off by him, went back to her sister sylphs in the river, then returned and fetched him away on the day that he was to marry another woman.

It underwent various stage adaptations, including Lortzing's opera, first heard in London in 1845. By his selection of references to particular pieces and characters throughout this act, Pinero creates a kind of subtext, indicating the themes and emotional patterns of his own play out of what appears on the surface to be simply a decorative layer of period theatrical chit-chat. Here the reference is clearly to Rose's imminent venture into society, its failure, and her eventual drawing of Arthur into her own world. Mrs Mossop renders the romantic reference comic by her mispronunciation of the name 'Undyne' for 'Undeen', perhaps representing Pinero's sense of the debasement of delicate and refined ideas by the popular stage.

178 *Prince Cammyralzyman in the pantomime*: Joel Kaplan (*Theatre Notebook*, 45 (1991), 40–1) has traced three appearances of the name 'Cammyralzyman' for the pantomime prince between 1848 and 1884, when it was the role of the star actress Nellie Farren in a 'burlesque fairy drama' at the Gaiety. Pinero's audience might well remember the iconic Farren; the Gaiety burlesques had only been superseded by musical comedy within the last few years. While Mrs Mossop's memory of Imogen in the romantic role of Undine invokes a vision of the bell-shaped, calf-length dancing skirt of tantalizingly diaphanous fabrics which sprites and fairies wore, Ablett's memory is more pointed. He recalls her as the pantomime 'principal boy', whose costume revealed thighs clad in flesh-pink tights and draped only with a spangled fringe. Imogen's shudder at his enthusiasm for her 'limbs' indicates the great difficulty that Rose is bound to have in moving from the position of a woman who displays her legs to a paying public to that of a lady, not generally admitted to have legs at all. By 1898 the transition from chorus girl to titled lady was being made with scandalous frequency, and was to become the subject of Pinero's favourite play, *The 'Mind the Paint' Girl*.

184 *General Utility*: the nineteenth-century stock company of actors was commonly divided according to 'lines of business': a formalized arrangement of what would now be called type-casting confined each individual to a particular range of roles, and therefore a fixed place in the hierarchy of the company. General Utility was the bottom rung, outranking only the supernumeraries who were taken on casually for particular pieces.

204 *gallery-boys*: the gallery of a theatre would be crowded with a youthful audience, paying the lowest prices but attending often and enjoying an ongoing relationship with the regular performers, whose peculiarities they recognized and greeted, and whose popularity they largely determined, by ritualized vocal responses.

205 *half-past seven*: the bill at the Wells would probably begin at 7.00. Tom plays a minor, expository part in the first of the three plays which would be performed in the course of an evening.

248 *a heavy woman*: a higher-ranking 'line', the prerogative of the senior lady in the company, if she were too old for leads.

252 *'Take back thy glove, thou faithless fair!'*: a line from a drawing-room ballad, perhaps a translation of Schiller's 'Der Handschuh', a chivalric tale of a lady who idly tests the devotion of her lover by casting her glove into a pit of lions for him to retrieve; he does so, but casts it in her face, since her selfish demand showed that she did not truly love him. Wrench apparently succumbs to theatricality, the reflex spouting of inappropriate tags and snatches of song, under the pressure of his sense of failure and rejection, but if the line is from a version of Schiller's story, it is part of the subtext of the play, in that it reflects his anger and desire to assert his independence of Rose, who has ignored his love and expects him to behave politely, according to the code, on this painful occasion.

254 *Walking Gentleman*: the line immediately above General Utility.

271 *club windows in St James's Street*: Pinero's placing of 'everyday men' at the windows of the exclusive gentlemen's clubs of London is indicative of the elevated social circle in which he chose to regard his audience as moving.

301 S.D. *clubbed*: 'clubbed' hair is all cut to the same length, sliced off squarely rather than shaped or shaved up the back of the neck; the effect would suggest the costume drama in private life. In the 1890s, as in the 1860s, short hair was usual for men: indeed, by the 1890s the connotation of 'artistic' and possibly unmanly affectation was already attached to the wearing of a longer style. Sir Henry Irving wore his hair clubbed.

311 *Sir Thomas Clifford . . . Julia*: characters in Sheridan Knowles's play *The Hunchback*. Fanny Kemble, who created the role of Julia, testified to the appeal of the piece on stage, adding: 'but let nobody who has seen it well acted attempt to read it in cold blood' (*Records of a Girlhood* (1879)).

316 *Rosalind*: in Shakespeare's *As You Like It*.

319 *Orlando*: also in *As You Like It*; not the role in the play for which most spectators would be 'waiting'. The implication is that, although he will not admit it, Gadd chose the play for his benefit in the expectation that Rose's Rosalind would draw a good house, and is now braving out his misfortune.

346 *old guys*: 'guy' here means someone of ludicrous appearance, an object of mockery, particularly used of overdressed and ageing women.

347 S.D. *suburban soubrette*: Pinero is rather harsh in his portrayal of Avonia, presumably because she represents the young women on the stage who have *not* Rose's 'instinctive' aspiration towards gentility and who drag down the general tone. This designation places her as the soubrette—i.e. female supporting role in comedy, musical plays, and so on, requiring good looks and audience appeal rather than any great talent—and damns her by the addition of 'suburban', implying third-rate theatres catering

for unfashionable lower-class audiences. Sadler's Wells, in Islington, was such a 'suburban' house when Phelps took it over, and it reverted to type when he left.

358 S.D. *washed muslin*: during the nineteenth century many light and easily soiled fabrics were impossible to wash or clean without adverse effects; to wear washed muslin or washed kid gloves was a sign of shabby gentility, or one might say of good taste outstripping income. Rose aspires to the simple elegance of those who could afford to wear and then discard impractical delicate clothing, displaying both her innate good taste and her equally important virginal innocence.

362 *Brydon Crescent*: a Brydon Walk still exists in London, in the Islington / St Pancras area; but the reference here is probably to Rydon Crescent, which faced Sadler's Wells, on the opposite bank of the New River, and where Pinero lived as a boy in the 1860s.

366 *Miss Parrott as Jupiter*: the Olympic had a long tradition of staging classical/mythological extravaganzas, beginning with those created by Planché as vehicles for Madame Vestris during her management of the theatre from 1831 to 1839, with *Olympic Revels* as her opening piece. Vestris was famous for her legs, shown off in a series of roles of the sort suggested by a woman playing 'Jupiter'; she was also, however, a manager whom Pinero would have respected for her staging of comedy with realistic modern interiors and costumes, foreshadowing the transformation of comedy accomplished by Robertson.

367 S.D. *below the table*: down stage.

376 *Ruffian*: Pinero makes a comic stand-by of old-fashioned melodramatic mannerisms—see the servants Tyler and Emma Popham in *The Schoolmistress* and *The Magistrate*; this role gives him an opportunity to indulge in the joke at greater length.

404 *The Pedlar of Marseilles*: an invented play, a typical romantic melodrama, which Pinero obviously enjoys creating in the subtext of this one. The snatches of song are appropriate to the formal stereotype he is sketching. 'Ever of thee I'm fondly dreaming' is a real drawing-room ballad by George Linley and Foley Hall. It may be found in George Rowell (ed.), *Plays of A. W. Pinero* (Cambridge, 1986), appendix B, 200–1.

437 *Trafalgar year*: the sea battle of Trafalgar, 21 October 1805, where Nelson received his death wound; his victory was celebrated for having preserved Britain from invasion by Napoleon.

441 S.D. *left*. Avonia's preceding speech and the stage directions for putting the food on the table and for Gus's clowning with the pie are taken from the revised edition of 1936. The passage is not printed in the preperformance texts or the copy text, but there is evidence that it should have been: Gus's activities with the pie were certainly part of the original production, since a photograph of him, with a later line of Ablett's as

the caption, 'Ho, ho, ho . . . don't sir!' (l. 502), appears in the 1898 souvenir programme.

474 S.D. *Amid much chatter*. The invitation to ad lib is more apparent than real, the result of Pinero's careful presentation of the play for the reader. He would no doubt have orchestrated the staging of the meal very precisely when he directed the play, as the specification of the seating-plan suggests. He often uses food and its consumption, or rather the characters' failure to consume it, for broad comic effect—compare the suppers in *The Magistrate* and *The Schoolmistress*; although there is broad humour here, especially in the climax of the running gag about Ablett's glove, he is more concerned with the formal occasion as the opportunity for displaying cross-currents of emotion on one level, and, corresponding to that, on another level, the precise pinpointing of character and social standing through the action, the manners that he specifies. Social being and social consciousness, demonstrated by fooling about with hats and jostling for seats, are about to be transformed by economics.

475 *Mr Gower*: another line supplied from the 1936 edition.

489 '*good man's feast*': an allusion to Shakespeare, *As You Like It*, III. vi. 123; the tags that inflate the vocabulary of the 'theatricals', combined with vulgarities like the dropped 'h', serve to underline the inferiority of their speech and manners to the reticence and simplicity of 'the gentleman'.

507 *More tongue here!*: while Telfer's vulgar eccentricities of speech are presented affectionately, Gadd is boorish; Pinero's distaste for the pseudo-gentility of the stage deals as waspishly with him as with Avonia.

547 *The malt is with you*: he means 'pass the beer', but employs a ludicrous adaptation of a phrase from more exalted circles, where it was applied to the port circling after dinner; part of Pinero's joke about real and mock gentility. The old actor knows the proper gentlemanly phrase, but does not know enough to realize that it is merely comic to apply it to his own circumstances.

592 *gyirl*: not a cockneyism, but a stagey pronunciation.

600 '*expectancy and Rose of the fair state*': another Shakespearian tag, *Hamlet*, III. i. 155. Gadd jealously damns the allusion as forced, but one might take it as having more relevance to Rose's situation than Telfer realizes, since she, like Hamlet, is about to find that her promising future has collapsed and to be driven to desperate measures by the false position in which she finds herself.

2.1 S.D. *heavily whiskered 'swell' of the period*: in the 1860s the heavy swell took over from the dandy or exquisite as the model of the fashionable male; the difference lay in an increased weight and physical presence under the assumed languor, reflecting perhaps the growing interest in sports and games for the gentry. The copious whiskers were popularized by the archetypal swell Lord Dundreary, a character in *Our American*

Cousin by Tom Taylor, played by E. A. Sothern in 1861, who became an instant and influential leader of fashion. The term 'swell' was also used less precisely to indicate any wealthy gentleman of leisure; for example, Rose refers to Arthur in this way in her farewell speech on p. 236.

57 *cheers*: Sir William is given an accent supposedly old-fashioned in 1860, and ridiculous to the ears of the 1890s.

107 *Holles Street*: opens out of Cavendish Square, running southwards to Oxford Street.

136 *a troubadour*: Sir William's laughable conception of the narrow bounds of correct behaviour throws up the notion of a 'troubadour' (properly a fifteenth-century lyric poet who recited or sang his or her own works, moving from court to court in pursuit of aristocratic patronage) to express the impropriety which tinges the artistic lifestyle; he later employs the term 'gypsy' with the same overtones. Pinero means to mock him, of course, but also to invoke the associations of vagabondage and lack of stability that he himself sees as so deleterious to the theatrical profession—hence Arthur's tentative (and comic) invocation of the possibility of 'respectable' troubadours.

161 s.d. *Charles, in plush and powder*: another touch that would seem ludicrous in the 1890s—the footman wears the velvet-pile knee-breeches and powdered hair or wig of the liveried servant, the butt of ridicule even in its own day, figuring in *Punch* cartoons and the comic sketches of William Thackeray. It was old-fashioned by the 1860s.

162 *cawd-table*: Charles speaks with the tortured accent of the servant classes as portrayed by Thackeray.

176 *Agnes in 'The Spectre of St Ives'*: this would appear to be another invented play, this time the archetypal Gothic melodrama, with ghosts, mysteries, and murders.

208 *This is to be whist, I hope*: the name of the game, which can be an injunction to be quiet, was taken, by old-fashioned players, to confirm that it should be played in silence, as Sir William insists.

294 *mala fide*: legal Latin for bad faith.

323 *'eat spots, Cook says*: presumably the Cook's jocular term for a summer rainstorm: it is June.

341 *Cremorne*: the last of the great pleasure-gardens of London, on the bank of the Thames at Chelsea. Visitors could see balloon ascents, acrobatics, and firework displays, listen to a concert, or dance in the open air. The gardens closed in 1877.

345 *Suttingly*: certainly.

349 *ontray*: entrée, the course after the fish. Charles's servants' French is as tortured as his English.

351 S.D. *antimacassar*: a strip of cloth laid over the back of a chair to protect the upholstery from hair-oil, of which macassar is a variety. It would be a universal item of drawing-room furniture, one of the products of the Victorian lady's endless hours of embroidery, and its presence in Sir William's house is not particularly fussy or old-fashioned; it is, however, quite unmannerly to pick up such a thing and wave it about.

453 *Rum start*: low slang, meaning roughly 'a strange event': Colpoys is startled by a show of anger from the normally self-contained Tom Wrench.

471 *Anything that goes with stout*: Avonia tries to ensure that Gadd does not get too embarrassingly drunk, or sick, by preventing him from mixing his drinks. In the first act the unaffected Rose sensibly preferred draught beer; in this high-class setting, Avonia's reference to stout, the Londoner's dark, sweetish beer with its uncompromisingly inelegant name, marks her and her husband down as irredeemably vulgar.

474 S.D. *see you for pennies . . . cut for coppers*: they bet in old pence—the penny was a large copper coin—on who will turn up the higher card by cutting the pack.

507 *'And let me the canakin clink, clink'*: the alert audience might find it amusing that the jealous Gadd chooses Iago's drinking song, from *Othello*, II. iii.

3.1.9 *'I'm a great guerilla chief. . .'*: this time Pinero quotes from a real 1860s piece, and therefore credits the original in a footnote: 'These snatches of song are from *The Miller and his Men*, a burlesque mealy-drama, by Francis Talfourd and Henry J. Byron, produced at the Strand Theatre, April 9, 1860.' The appalling pun in the title is a fair sample of burlesque writing of the period; it may be presumed that Avonia knows this song, sung by 'the great guerilla chief', because she has played the role—cross-gender casting was a leading feature of burlesque.

12 *It's the pantomime*: Avonia is a burlesque actress, a comic singer and dancer, performing in the musical spectacular pieces which made up one strand of Victorian theatre. The annual pantomime, therefore, which opened on Boxing Day and often ran until Easter, was her taste of stardom. By the 1860s the development of the pantomime had reached a climax, and the form was about to change once more. The original dumb-show harlequinade imported from Italy in the early eighteenth century, in which a traditional group of characters enacted the old story of the young lovers' flight, pursuit, and ultimate triumph, had soon been augmented by an opening spectacle in which a different story was told. By 1860 these 'openings' had become the more important part of the entertainment, on which a great deal of ingenuity was expended by composers, writers of rhyming and punning dialogue, and the inventors of tricks and spectacular devices. Their stories were drawn from a wide range of sources, and their wit depended on verbal humour and

abundant reference to contemporary events and politics. Their performers, more women than men, played a variety of fantastic roles in splendid and figure-revealing costumes. Gradually, after 1870, the Christmas pantomime narrowed its appeal to children, concentrating on a small selection of fairy-tales for its stories and dulling the satirical and burlesque edge of its contemporary reference. The 'principal boy', whose adult appeal in Avonia's time included satire and witty songs as well as a pretty voice and a display of legs, remained as a fossilized survival, an amusement for the escorting fathers of the predominantly juvenile audience.

28 *irons*: the curling-tongs which she brought on with her and which were heated directly in the fire, and so need to be tested on a sheet of paper (a few lines further on) in case they are too hot.

48 S.D. *table-cover*: the permanent cover which was replaced by a table-cloth for meals.

82 *rodomontade*: bragging, verbal display, but Avonia does not recognize the word and suspects that, like all big words, it might be somehow indecent; her mistake recalls Tom to his usual good-humoured tolerance of his colleagues, as opposed to the kind of plays in which they appear, and he switches to teasing her by pretending it is a rude word, as she suspected.

119 *Prince Charming in the coming pantomime*: the pantomime is perhaps *Cinderella*, but 'Charming' was not the invariable name for the Prince until after 1898; in H. J. Byron's version, performed (like the Byron burlesque that Avonia was singing earlier) at the Strand in 1860, he was called Poppetti. Avonia's high spirits and great expectations about the pantomime are obviously being used in this act to underline the change in Rose, who was once equally able to 'hit 'em' in burlesque and comedy. Avonia still values, as her greatest chance of the year, the role which above all others marks off the actress from the lady. The clinching enactment of Pinero's point occurs at the end of the act: see below, p. 277.

139 *The School for Scandal*: by R. B. Sheridan; one of the few important roles that Pinero played in his career as an actor was Sir Anthony Absolute in a Bancroft production of Sheridan's *The Rivals*, and the critical verdict that he 'lacked vigour' in the part was probably influential in his decision to give up acting. The part of Careless requires considerable vigour, but it is not a leading role: he is one of the drinking companions of the feckless hero Charles Surface, and he appears in only two scenes, abetting and urging Charles on in his wild career.

263 *T.R. Stockton*: Theatre Royal, Stockton-on-Tees.

273 *Demon of Discontent*: when the harlequinade began to fade away as the *raison d'être* of the pantomime, the fairy or folk-tale story was often framed by some sort of allegory. This pitted a good force—Industry, say,

or Education—against its opposite, Idleness or Ignorance; they debated their dominion over Humanity, and eventually agreed on some test or other device which would lead into the main story. Thus, such a character as the Demon of Discontent would only have a short opening scene, and perhaps a few lines in the finale.

297 S.D. *'part'*: the nineteenth-century actor did not receive a whole script, only his or her own lines written out with what fragments of others were necessary to act as cues. The American equivalents were called 'sides'. A 'part' therefore revealed instantly how good a role it represented, by its length.

304 *Boxing Night*: the first night of the pantomime season.

307 *The Romeo . . . the Clifford*: Romeo in *Romeo and Juliet*, Orlando in *As You Like It*, Clifford in *The Hunchback*.

309 *'I'm Discontent . . . I endover'*: This punning doggerel is by no means a travesty of the pantomime scripts which Pinero is mimicking. Gerald du Maurier played Gadd in the first production; this little scene was singled out by several of the reviewers (who were lukewarm about the play as a whole) as a great comic success.

330 *which end*: that is, which end of the dragon; the larger pantomime animals, such as horses and Jack's mother's cow in *Jack and the Beanstalk*, required two performers inside an elaborate costume; playing the back end is traditionally cited as the lowest possible position on the theatrical ladder. Skin-work, as it was called, was in fact a highly skilled speciality, and poor Wrench would probably make no great success of it.

337 S.D. *the Jewel song from 'Faust'*: from Gounod's opera based on Goethe's version of the Faust legend. It was one of the songs that was frequently borrowed and recycled on the Victorian stage and by drawing-room singers. Its subtextual relevance here is the temptation of the simple peasant girl who sings it by the glitter of jewellery; Avonia is easily pleased by theatrical tinsel.

381 *The Pantheon*: there were several theatres in London at various times which had this name, none of them very successful; but the intention here, picked up by the reviewers of the first production, was to evoke the transformation by Marie Wilton of the Queen's Theatre in Charlotte Street, which had the nickname of 'The Dusthole', into a beautiful and hugely successful little theatre. She opened it in 1865, under the name of the Prince of Wales's, and it was there that Robertson's comedies were staged in the way that Wrench dreams of.

384 *tablets*: notebook.

409 *stunner*: this may be an error in period language; it is slang of the 1860s, but it normally meant a beautiful woman, rather than conveying general approbation.

414 *Miss Burdett-Coutts*: Angela Georgina (1814–1906), created Baroness Burdett-Coutts in 1871. She was the richest heiress in England, child of an alliance between the politically powerful Burdett family and Coutts the bankers. Her fortune came to her from her step-grandmother, the actress Harriot Mellon, who had inherited the Coutts millions. Although she—like Queen Victoria in the days before Albert's death—was a keen theatre-goer, and used her social influence on behalf of her friend Henry Irving, she regarded her fortune as dedicated to serious philanthropic purposes, and did not finance plays.

466 s.d. *plaid*: shawl. Gentlemen wore shawls over greatcoats for travelling by coach in the first half of the century; Sir William is old-fashioned in retaining his into the era of railways. Scottish garments were made fashionable by Victoria's love of the Highlands and her adoption of tartan.

541 s.d. *Avonia enters boldly, in the dress of a burlesque prince*: the dramatic point about Rose's alienation from the theatrical world culminates, appropriately theatrically, in this entrance. Avonia, the working woman, is seen suddenly at her least ladylike and, paradoxically, her most dignified. It is Sir William who is abashed; she is enabled to transcend her personal preoccupations, and tells him not only where he should look, but what he should see; what the respectable world that he represents has done to the hapless object of its guilty admiration and hypocritical scorn. The 'cotton-velvet shirt' was her main garment, its bullion trimming—a golden fringe—hanging over her thighs, with points reaching almost to her knees. The real thing, in the 1860s, would have been less modest.

576 *to . . . make artificial flowers*: one of the notorious sweated trades, picked on in many contemporary social commentaries for the sentimental ironies that it offered.

590 *Edmund Kean*: the great romantic actor, *c.*1787–1833.

591 *which Kean*: Edmund's son Charles was also an actor, but not a 'splendid gypsy'—rather, an ambitious manager.

603 *fillet*: a headband, worn on the stage by royal personages like Cordelia as an indication of their rank, like a coronet.

604 *Cordelia to Kean's Lear*: Pinero must have intended this performance to have been around 1820, before Kean's descent into alcoholic incapacity. With only a few exceptions, Kean played Lear in the Nahum Tate version, which has a love affair between Cordelia and Edgar and a happy ending. It gives Cordelia a much larger part than Shakespeare's text, especially in the last act, which takes place in the dungeon where Lear and Cordelia are confined, and culminates in their rescue and restoration.

608 *he wore in Richard*: Shakespeare's Richard III was the role above all others with which Kean was identified by his admirers and also by his

critics; the many satirical and scurrilous popular cartoons always showed him in that character, with hunched shoulder and a limp, wearing the Order and sword-belt described here.

664 *'deeper than did ever plummet sound'*: Shakespeare's *The Tempest*, v. i. 56; the next line is 'I'll drown my book', and it belongs to Prospero's abjuration of his art at the end of the play—the tag is again a counterpoint to the text, prophesying, as Tom utters it in triumph, the imminent descent into despair.

745 *'Life'*: a Robertsonian title; his famous plays are all monosyllabically titled.

4.1 s.d. *the stage of a theatre*. Pinero made his biggest changes to the text for the Old Vic revival in 1925 in this act, and began by altering the perspective on the setting, showing the stage from the audience's point of view instead of presenting this mirrored scene from the stage. The change, with the cuts in the presentation of the rehearsal of Wrench's play (see below, p. 326), greatly alter the sense of a decisive movement into the working world of the theatre which seems, in this version, to be the dramatist's resolution of the conflict that he presents.

s.d. *the 'P' and 'OP'*: prompt side and opposite prompt, which would normally be stage left and right, the opposite of what the text suggests.

s.d. *the first and second entrances*: the first entrance is between the proscenium wing and the first stage wing, the second is between the first two stage wings; these ran in the first and second sets of grooves, on the stage floor and suspended above.

s.d. *'flats'*: sections of painted scenery, canvas stretched on a wooden frame.

s.d. *a T-light*: a T-shaped section of metal tubing supplied with burners, part of the movable lighting available with theatrical gas-lighting systems.

2 *Is the reading over*: the author reads the play to the company, since they have only their individual parts written down.

10 *line-y*: there are no 'good speeches', only individual lines of more 'realistic' dialogue.

29 *without your watch . . . about you*: poverty has forced them to sell, or more probably pawn, their 'comforts'.

71 *One of the finest Macduffs I ever fought with*: Telfer the old actor judges the minor players according to their usefulness to the star: Macduff is Macbeth's last-act fighting partner.

84 *Will you get to me*: will you reach my entrance in the rehearsal.

96 *legitimately—with dignity*: she means according to the tradition of the 'legitimate' stage, to which the Telfers have not really ever belonged, despite their lifelong pretensions; it is an appropriately tragi-comic exit

line, by which Pinero disposes of his sentimental attachment to the old stagers. It is noticeable that the more awkward vulgarians Gadd and Avonia are simply not accommodated in this act, despite Avonia's inclusion, as 'quite in place', in the reconciliation of the Gowers with the stage, via Wrench's play, at the end of the third act.

118 *I can't hear myself speak*: O'Dwyer's blustering interruptions of Wrench's rehearsal represent Pinero's perception of the state of affairs in the theatre when the stage-manager was in charge of rehearsals, an unsatisfactory arrangement which he sees Robertson as beginning to alter towards direction by the author, as Pinero practised it himself. The critics in 1898 did not find it amusing or understand the point being made.

184 *giving him two fingers*: to shake, a common nineteenth-century form of disdainful greeting.

335 *And cross to Dora*: the 1925 Old Vic version cut from here to 'I've nothing to do.'

357 *Sit on the stump*: the 1925 Old Vic version cut from here to Tom's 'Mr Denzil'; there were also other small cuts, lessening the time devoted to establishing the tone of Wrench's comedy. It differs as markedly from the play into which it is set as do the snapshots from ancient melodramas evoked in the first act: it is lyrical, sentimental, attempting to bring natural innocence into the tawdry theatre world—notice that it is the only scene of the play to be set out of doors, and much of the difficulty that Wrench has in directing it is in establishing the characters of the innocent girls and in envisaging the country garden on the shabby London stage.

380 *bravura*: the sheet music, ordered from a London music publisher; the technical term 'bravura', meaning a musical passage requiring exceptional ability, is presumably used as period slang for a difficult and showy song.